GREAT-AUNT LAVINIA

By JOSEPH C. LINCOLN

GREAT-AUNT LAVINIA

By

JOSEPH C. LINCOLN

D. APPLETON-CENTURY COMPANY
INCORPORATED
NEW YORK   **1936**   **LONDON**

GREAT-AUNT LAVINIA

CHAPTER I

THE long hand of the clock on the dining-room mantel pointed to within a nail's breadth of the figures at the top of the dial and the short hand to the figure at the bottom. It was a veteran, that clock. Joshua Holt—Lavinia's father—bought it in 1820 when he married and set up housekeeping. That was two years before Amaziah, Lavinia's older brother, father of the present Amaziah, was born and twelve years before Lavinia herself "came to town," as she would have expressed it. Ever since Lavinia could remember anything she remembered that clock. It was ticking on the shelf in the sitting-room of the old home in Denboro while Parson Hodgkins preached Joshua's funeral sermon—that was in 1846. She had looked at it over her shoulder when she and her husband, Judah Badger, left that home after their wedding—that was in 1849. When she and Judah came back from their honeymoon, they had found it awaiting them on the mantel of their new home in South Denboro. Amaziah had brought it over, placed it there, wound and set it. "Thought likely you'd like to have it 'round to look at, Laviny," said Amaziah. "Kind of homey and old-timey, that clock is to you and me."

Lavinia was only seventeen when she married. She was thirty-seven when Judah Badger, her husband, left her to go "out West where a smart man had a real chance—" that was in 1869. When Hulda, Amaziah's wife died, Lavinia sold the South Denboro house and moved to Wellmouth to keep house for her brother. Then, when he died—in 1885, that was—she had moved again, this time to the little brick house at Wapatomac Neck, where Amaziah's oldest son—also named

Amaziah—had, within the year, been appointed keeper of the lighthouse. In all her movings the clock had moved with her.

Now that clock was at least eighty-seven years old and still going strong; but so, too, was Lavinia. She was seventy-five, but she did not look it, nor act it, nor care to be reminded of it. "I've got enough to do without settin' down and countin' up birthdays," she announced. "I ain't so old yet but what I can keep busy, thank the Lord, if it's only huntin' for somethin' to keep busy at."

She was busy now. She had set the table in the little dining-room of the keeper's cottage, and was skurrying back and forth from the kitchen, where the family supper of fried flatfish and rye muffins was being kept hot in the oven of the cook-stove. Lavinia Badger was a little woman, thin and wiry and with snapping black eyes behind her spectacles. Her hair was gray, but not white, and her gingham dress and white apron were spotless. Everything about her and about the rooms in that tiny house was spick and span.

Amaziah Holt, her nephew, was seated in the rocker by the window, smoking and disinterestedly gazing at the waters of the harbor, rippling in the light June breeze. Amaziah was thirty when Lavinia first came to keep house for him; he was fifty-three now, still a bachelor, and still keeper of Long Cove Point light, at the entrance of Wapatomac harbor. Long Cove Point light was not one of the important beacons in that section of the Atlantic coast, nor was the office of keeper an important or highly paid one requiring the exercise of much brain-power or responsibility. There were no disastrous wrecks at the upper end of Long Bay, very little maritime traffic except small fishing-craft, dories, catboats and an occasional two-masted schooner. The town of Wapatomac was only a mile away by water and three and a half along the Neck by road.

To keep the light burning from sunset to sunrise, the glass

and brass of the lantern polished, the brick tower and house whitewashed and the little yard reasonably neat were the only essential duties he was called upon to perform. It was an easy job, with a good deal of spare time in which to loaf and gossip and smoke, and it suited Amaziah Holt perfectly. If Aunt Lavinia had been content to confine her attention to the housework and to Ethel, Amaziah would have found life a bit more enjoyable—but then, one can't have everything.

Ethel Holt was Amaziah's niece and Lavinia Badger's grand-niece. She had joined the pair at the lighthouse when she was but two years old. Her father was Edgar Holt, Amaziah's younger brother, and her mother was, before marriage, Ethel Corey, school-teacher in Denboro, which is the town about ten miles from Wapatomac on the Sound side. Ethel Corey Holt had died when her baby was born, and Edgar, her husband, was drowned two years later off Gay Head, when his schooner, the *Anna R.*, was lost with all hands. There were no near relatives on the Corey side and Lavinia—Edgar had been her favorite nephew—adopted the little orphan, took her from the Denboro cottage and the care of Edgar's hired house-keeper, brought her to Wapatomac and had reared her as carefully and strictly—yes, and as tenderly—as if she were her own. Now she—Ethel Holt—was seventeen and complet-ing her final year in the Wapatomac high school.

The old clock on the mantelpiece hiccoughed sharply. Then it grumbled, wheezed, whined and struck—six tinny clangs. Amaziah turned his head to look at it. Lavinia glanced up at it, muttered something under her breath, and trotted to the kitchen once more. She moved quickly. Amaziah, who never did anything quickly, watched her through the smoke from his pipe, as she trotted back with two warm plates which she placed, one at each end of the table. He was languidly sur-prised.

"What you settin' only two places for?" he asked. "Ain't Ethel goin' to be home to supper?"

Lavinia sniffed. "I presume likely she is," she replied. "She didn't say she wasn't when she started for school this mornin'."

"Humph! Late, ain't she. School's out around half past one or so. Say she was goin' to do anything special up town afore she started back?"

"No."

"Huh! Rowed acrost same as usual, didn't she?"

"Yes."

"What do you cal'late's keepin' her?"

"Don't know, but I suppose she'll tell us when she gets here.... There, there! Pull up your chair. We'll have our supper and she can have hers when she comes. I'm keepin' it hot for her."

"Humph! Well—"

"Well what?"

"Nothin'—only—there ain't any tearin' *hurry* for supper, is there?"

"It's ready, that's all. Come, come! Sit down. Do!"

Amaziah put his pipe in his pocket and moved over to the table. He sat down, took his napkin from the silver ring with his initials on it, tucked the napkin under his chin, and waited to be served. His aunt whisked to the kitchen and whisked back again bearing a platter of fish and the teapot. The rye muffins, hot and steaming, were already on the table.

Amaziah, watching her, slowly shook his head. She looked up and saw him.

"What are you shakin' your head about?" she asked.

"Eh? Why—why, nothin'."

"Folks don't shake their heads at nothin' unless they've got the shakin' palsy. You ain't old enough for that, I shouldn't say."

"Course I ain't. I—I was thinkin', that's all."

"Well, thinkin's a good thing to do once in a while. What was you thinkin' about this time?"

"I was just thinkin' about you, Aunt Lavvy. Supper's got to be right on the minute, no matter whether there's anybody here to eat it or not. You're always in a hurry; been so ever since I can remember. Way you fly 'round a body'd think you didn't have another minute to live."

"Maybe I haven't. Got a whole lot less minutes than I used to have, that's certain."

"So have we all, far's that goes. Well, I guess likely you can't help it, but it makes me nervous to look at you."

Lavinia Badger glanced up at him. There was a twinkle in her eye.

"How do you tell when you get nervous, Am?" she asked, drily.

"Eh? Tell? What do you mean?"

"What do you do when you get that way?"

"Do! Why, nothin' special."

"That's no symptom; you do that most of the time. Did you finish polishin' that lantern this afternoon?"

Amaziah rubbed his chin. "Why—why, no," he admitted. "I didn't. I was goin' to do it this noon, right after dinner, but I wanted to have my smoke first. Can't smoke up in the lantern-room. That's against Gov'ment regulations," virtuously; "I'd lose my job if I smoked up there. You know that, Aunt Lavvy."

"Yes, I know that. And keepin' that lantern shiny is another part of those same regulations, as I recollect. What did you do when you'd had your smoke? Anything except light up for another one?"

"Eh? Course I did! You see, Ben Crowell stopped by for a little spell. Comin' ashore from settin' his lobster pots, he was. He hauled his dory up abreast here and him and me got to talkin'—about town affairs and one thing or 'nother. Stayed

till after four o'clock, he did.... But that's all right; I'm
cal'latin' to get at that lantern first thing after breakfast
to-morrow."

"That's the trouble with you, Am, you're always cal'latin' to
do and not doin'. But there, I've told you that at least once
before, haven't I?"

"Huh! You've told it to me about twice a day for twenty-
odd years. I was keepin' this lighthouse afore you came here
to live. How do you suppose I got along then?"

"Land knows."

"Well, I did get along somehow."

" 'Somehow' is the right word for it, I shouldn't wonder.
There's your cup of tea. Take it quick; I want to put the pot
back on the stove for Ethel. Dear me! where *do* you suppose
that girl is?"

"That's what I asked you a minute ago and you pretty nigh
snapped my head off. Ethel's all right. She's old enough to
look out for herself. Been foolin' around with some of the other
girls, probably; or," with a chuckle, "some of the boys."

"Boys!" sharply. "What do you mean by that? She isn't
bothered about boys—not yet awhile, I *hope*."

"Maybe not, but some of the boys are bothered about her,
I shouldn't wonder. She's a mighty pretty girl, Ethel is. Ben
Crowell says his John's always talkin' about how popular she
is with the young fellows up at school. One or two of 'em
hangin' 'round her elbow most of the time, 'cordin' to John.
There, there, needn't look so savage, Aunt Lavvy. Nature's
nature, you know. Ethel's seventeen, we mustn't forget that."

His aunt did not answer. She stirred her tea a little more
rapidly than usual, that was all. Amaziah grinned.

"Seventeen is seventeen," he added. "Some girls get married
when they're seventeen, or so I've heard," slyly.... "Eh?
What's that noise? Some kind of an engyne, ain't it? Listen!"

Lavinia, the sugar-bowl in one hand and a teaspoon in the

other, turned toward the window behind her. At first she heard nothing out of the ordinary. The terns—"Mackerel gulls" or "ki-acks," the fishermen called them—wheeling and dipping above the shallows at the end of the Point, were screaming as usual, and the morning-glory vine on the lattice by the side door rattled occasionally as a light puff of air moved it, but that was all.

"I don't hear anything," said Aunt Lavinia.

"Neither do I—now; but I did. Listen! . . . There! Now you can hear it, can't you?"

Sure enough. From somewhere up the long narrow stretch of sand separating the harbor from the bay came a faint sound, an unusual sound, a sort of asthmatic cough. "Chuff, chuff, chuff, chuff." Regular in recurrence and evidently drawing nearer.

Now, when practically every craft leaving and entering Wapatomac harbor is equipped with a gasoline motor, a sound like that is so ordinary as to be unnoticed, but in those early years of the twentieth century, motors of any kind were still a rarity, almost a novelty. There were but three motor-cars in Wapatomac township and people turned to look at them when they passed and gathered about to stare and comment when they stopped. Amaziah, the napkin still tucked between his chin and shirt collar, rose and hurried to the window.

"I declare, it sounds like—" he muttered. "Yes, that's what 'tis. One of them automobile things. And it's comin' along the Neck Road."

Lavinia sniffed. "Rubbish!" she exclaimed. "Who on earth would be crazy enough to try and pilot one of those contrivances down the Neck Road? It's nothin' but sand the whole way."

"It might be Dr. Hardy. He's just bought an automobile. I ain't seen it yet, but Ben Crowell told me he had. The doctor only got it last week. You see—"

"Oh, don't talk so silly! What would the doctor be comin' this way for? There's nowhere to go but this lighthouse and there's nobody sick here."

"Can't help it. If that ain't an automobile then I don't know what she is... I'm goin' out door."

He went out through the kitchen. His aunt called after him that his supper would be stone cold, but he paid no attention. Lavinia, sputtering, rose from the table and carried his plate and teacup back to the kitchen range. Then, after a moment, she carried her own there also. The "chuff-chuffing" was nearer now and her curiosity was, if not as keen as his, keen enough.

When she joined him he was standing on the low dune beyond the fence peering back along the parallel stretch of rutted sand and beach grass which, by courtesy, was called the Neck Road. Bad as it was it was the only road between Wapatomac and the Point light. In summer—yes, and in good winter weather, Amaziah rowed to and from the village in his dory. Ethel had a skiff of her own and used it, in fair weather, when she went to and from school. There was an ancient horse and still more ancient buggy in the shed at the rear of the cottage, but the horse and buggy were Aunt Lavinia's property, bought with her own money, and she was very particular as to their use. She had bought them six years before at the sale of the effects of an old couple in the village.

"I'm gettin' too old to climb in and out of a boat," declared Lavinia. It was one of the rare occasions when she referred to her age and Ethel and Amaziah were surprised. She may have realized something of their surprise for she added, hastily: "Not that I couldn't climb in and out if I wanted to, but I've done it ever since I was a girl and I'm tired of it. Folks'll say I'm extravagant, I presume likely, buyin' this horse 'n' team, but I don't care. Only you two have got to understand this— you can't use 'em unless I say so. Ethel, you can row to school and back in good weather, same as you always have.

When it's too bad Amaziah can ride you over in the buggy, and come for you after school, but that won't be often. You're young and rowin's good exercise. As for you, Am—well, any kind of change from settin' 'round ought to do you good. You'll row, or walk—most of the time, anyhow."

Amaziah had grumbled at first, but he obeyed orders. His aunt's word was law in that household.

As Lavinia reached the crest of the dune he turned. "Aha!" he crowed triumphantly. "It is an automobile. I told you 'twas. See! there 'tis up yonder and headin' this way."

Lavinia could both see it and hear it. A small car, its crimson paint and polished brass glittering in the late afternoon sunlight. It was rocking and bumping along the rutted road and coughing steadily as it approached. Its buggy top was folded back and there were two people on its single seat. Amaziah peered under his hand.

"It's one of them two-cylinder Maxwells," he announced, after a moment. "Yes sir, that's what 'tis, same kind the doctor's got, so Ben Crowell says. But that ain't the doctor runnin' it. It's a younger man than him. And who's that woman with him? Why, she's wavin', ain't she? . . . My soul and body, it's Ethel! Look, Aunt Laviny! It's Ethel. Can't you see her?"

Lavinia, who had removed her spectacles, wiped them on her apron and replaced them on her nose, did not trouble to answer.

"Can't you see her?" repeated Amaziah excitedly. "See her wavin' to us. Look!"

"Oh, be still. If I was so blind I couldn't see a grown-up girl no further off than that I'd go to the doctor's. Who's that young fellow with her?"

"I can't quite make out. It ain't nobody I know, don't seem so. And yet—why, yes, it's that Thornlow boy. Bert, they call him. He and his mother have rented that summer place used to belong to the Thayers, on the Shore Road, up to the west end of the town. Seems to me I heard they had an automobile. They would have, of course; got barrels of money.... Hello, there, Ethel! Comin' home in style, ain't you?"

The little car rocked and chuffed and bumped to a point opposite the knoll. There it stopped. Steam was rising from the edges of its radiator-cap. The young fellow sprang from the seat to the road and assisted his passenger to alight. Ethel Holt was a pretty girl—a very pretty girl indeed—and now, with her cheeks flushed and her eyes sparkling with excitement, her good looks were accentuated. Young Bert Thornlow was very solicitous as he lifted her to the sand. Aunt Lavinia noticed the solicitude; she had a habit of noticing things.

Ethel came hurrying toward them. "I'm so sorry I'm late, Auntie," she said. "We expected to get here ever so long ago. We would have, too, only the road is so dreadfully rough— for a car, you know. And twice something happened to the engine and Bert had to stop and fix it. And once we had a puncture and taking off the tire and everything—that took hours, or seems as if it did. I knew you would wonder what had become of me. I'm so sorry. But," with a sudden gasp of enthusiasm, "it was just *wonderful!* I had never ridden in an automobile before. And Bert wasn't quite sure whether we could make it or not—so much sand and everything—but we did and—oh, it was *splendid!*"

She finished with another rapturous gasp. Lavinia smiled.

"Yes, yes," she agreed, rather absently; "must have been."

She was looking, not at her grand-niece, but at the owner of the car. He was a good-looking young fellow, his age about twenty or twenty-one, she guessed. His clothes, just now a good deal soiled with grease from the motor and dirt from the tire, were of the city summer-vacation style of the period. They were not at all showy—many of Wapatomac's young bloods were far more gorgeously apparelled on Sundays or holidays—but, unless Lavinia's shrewd estimate was wrong, they were expensive and, unlike some of the young bloods just mentioned, he wore them as if he were used to them.

Ethel caught the direction of her relative's glance.

"Oh!" she exclaimed. "I forgot. You don't know Bert, do you, Auntie. . . . Oh, Bert!"

Amaziah had not waited for an introduction. He had already scrambled down the slope of the sandhill and was now bending over the car, exclaiming and questioning. Its owner was proudly exhibiting its finer points. Now, as his name was called, he turned, looked, and leaving Mr. Holt to go on with his inspection without expert supervision, climbed the bank and approached the pair on its summit.

"Bert"—in spite of her evident desire not to appear the least embarrassed Ethel's color was a trifle deeper and she stammered a bit—"Bert, I want you to meet Mrs. Badger. She is my—my great-aunt, you know; you have heard me speak of her. Auntie, this is Bert Thornlow. He is—he and his mother, I mean—living in the Thayer house on the Shore Road this summer. You know where that is."

"I ought to; I've been around here for a good many years. How do you do, Mr. Thornlow?"

The young man smiled. His was a pleasant smile and a distinct help to his good looks. He extended his hand, then, after a hasty glance at it, wiped it on the leg of his trousers before offering it again.

"I should say I had heard about you, Mrs. Badger," he declared. "Ethel is always talking about her Aunt Lavinia. I'm afraid she and I have upset your supper arrangements, Mrs. Badger. You mustn't blame her, though. It is all my fault. I just wanted to see if this go-cart of mine could do what the makers claimed for it. They said it would run anywhere on any sort of road. Well," with a grin, "it did, but it didn't run all the time, eh, Ethel?"

Ethel, after a quick glance at her great-aunt's face, hastened to explain.

"Aunt Lavinia is wondering, I suppose, how I happened to be in the car at all," she said. "Well, you see, Auntie, I—we—the graduating class, I mean—stayed after school to rehearse for the exercises—they are only a fortnight off now—and, when the rehearsal was over I—I met Bert—just happened to meet him, you know—and he asked me if I wouldn't like a ride. Well, I had never ridden in an automobile and I have wanted to awfully, and—so I did. Then—"

"Then," Thornlow put in, "I suggested that we try the trip down here. I was pretty sure no car had ever tackled the Neck Road and I thought it would be fun to be the first. Of course I didn't count on two kinds of engine trouble and having to change a tire besides. But it *was* fun, wasn't it, Ethel?"

"Oh, wonderful! But, Auntie, I'm very sorry to be late, truly I am. And I suppose your supper is all spoiled."

Lavinia shook her head. "Supper is on the back of the stove," she said. "It may not be as good as it would have been a half-hour ago, but I guess likely it isn't spoiled. Humph! How about your supper, Mr. Thornlow? If it takes you as long to go back in that thing as it did to come down your supper will be pretty close to breakfast, won't it?"

"Oh, I guess not. She," with a jerk of the head toward the car, "may behave herself on the return trip. If she does I'll get home by half past seven—or eight, anyway."

"And that would be late enough, in all conscience. You better stay and have supper with us. It's all ready, there's enough of it, and we'll be real glad to have you. At least," gravely, "Amaziah and I will. Of course, I don't know about Ethel."

"Auntie! Why—why, how silly! Bert, you know— Oh, Auntie!"

Lavinia cut in on her embarrassed protestations. "Then

that's all right," she announced. "Come right in, Mr. Thornlow. Am, take Mr. Thornlow into your bedroom. He'll want to wash his hands, I guess likely: they look as if a little soap and water wouldn't hurt 'em. You come with me, Ethel; we've got to set another place."

Young Thornlow, still protesting but not too strenuously, was led away by the obsequious Amaziah, who was evidently deeply impressed by their guest's social position and the fact that he actually owned an automobile. Amaziah filled the hand-basin on the commode with water from the pitcher and took a clean towel from the rack.

"Now, if you don't mind," he said, apologetically, "I'll have to leave you for a minute or so. It's lightin' up time. Get along all right by yourself, can you? You go right out to the dinin'-room soon's you're clean—I mean soon's you're ready. I'll be back time you get there. Godfreys, that's a fine car you've got, Mr. Thornlow. Don't know's I ever see one of 'em afore—close to, I mean. Beats all what they're gettin' up nowadays, don't it."

When he reëntered the house, after attending to his duties in the lantern-room of the lighthouse, the others were already gathered about the supper table. Lavinia occupied her accustomed seat, Amaziah sat opposite her, and the two young people faced each other across the board. Bert Thornlow did most of the talking. He was quite at his ease, praised the muffins, ate heartily of the fried flatfish and declared the beachplum preserves to be the "best stuff of its kind" he had ever tasted.

"Did you make this, Ethel?" he asked, as he was offered, and accepted, a second saucerful.

"No. Aunt Lavinia made it. I picked some of the beachplum, though."

" 'Twas me that picked the heft of 'em," proclaimed Amaziah. "Last fall was a good season for beachplums. Over on

Simmons's land there at the upper end of the Neck there was millions of 'em. I bet you I could have picked a barrel if I'd set out to."

Lavinia passed the butter to their guest.

"You did set out to," she observed. "You was loaded with pails like a tin peddler's cart when you started. I expected to have beachplums enough to freight a schooner."

"Eh?" indignantly. "Well, you had a plenty, anyhow. I'd have picked more only for the *mis*keeters. Honest, Mr. Thornlow, I never see so many *mis*keeters in my born days. And ary one of 'em could bite through a side of sole leather. I wisht you could have seen the back of my neck when I got home. Every time I looked at it I vow to man it scared me. *That* was a job, don't say a word."

"Lookin' at the back of his own neck would be liable to be a job for anybody, seems to me." This from Lavinia, of course. "There, there, Am! Mr. Thornlow ain't interested in your work, 'tain't likely. How do you and your mother like the Thayer place, Mr. Thornlow? It's a pretty big house for two folks, isn't it?"

"Is it?" Bert Thornlow evidently had not considered that phase. "Why—yes, perhaps it is, but it is comfortable enough. There was some trouble with the servants at first, or so Mother tells me. Their rooms were old-fashioned and they weren't used to pumps and things like that, but Mother says they are more contented now; she raised their wages or something."

"You live out West somewhere—in the winter, I mean—don't you?"

"Yes. Just outside of Chicago. Father was in the banking business in the city. He died two years ago."

"How did your mother and you happen to come to Wapatomac?"

"Oh, I don't know. I was responsible as much as any one, I suppose. Mother wanted to go abroad again, but I was rather sick of that. I said, 'Let's go to the seashore somewhere, for a change.' Then I saw the ad of the Thayer house in a Boston paper—I am in college up there, you know—and I came down and looked the place over. It suited me pretty well and Mother was suited if I was. She generally is, I suppose," with a good-natured grin. "I've about decided I was a good picker. I like Wapatomac."

"Fine town as there is alongshore," commented Amaziah, proudly.

"Does your mother like it as well as you do?" asked Lavinia.

"Oh, she grumbles sometimes. Says there isn't any society and things like that, but I tell her there will be more when the season really starts."

"There's lots of societies, when you get to know about 'em," Amaziah protested. "There's the Masons and Odd Fellows and Red Men—course they're for men-folks; but there's the Eastern Star, that's women, and the Town Improvement Club and—"

"Sshh!" cut in his aunt. "You say you're in college up to Boston, Mr. Thornlow—"

"Oh, call me Bert. Everybody does."

"Well—all right; Bert then. Sounds as if I'd known you ten years instead of half an hour, but maybe it doesn't sound so fussy as Mister. When do you get through college—er—Bert?"

"In another year, if I keep at it. I'm a junior now."

"And what are you plannin' to do when you graduate?"

"Give it up," carelessly. "Go in with father's old firm, I suppose. That's what they want me to do. You are the light-keeper here, aren't you, Mr. Holt? That ought to be an interesting job, I should think."

"Oh, 'tis—'tis." Amaziah was emphatic. "Kind of keeps a fellow up nights, but you get used to that. Course we don't have as many wrecks up here as they do off Setucket or them places, but once in a while there's somethin' happens. Now last February—no, a year ago February 'twas—we had a devil of a no'theaster and George Hammond's catboat— What was her name, Lavvy? The *Wide Awake,* was it? . . . No, that was Sam Small's. Let me see— Oh, yes, the *Divin' Duck,* that was it."

" 'Twas the *Slipalong,* as a matter of fact," corrected Mrs. Badger. "And she belonged to Seth Farmer."

"Eh! That's so. You're right. How'd I ever come to think 'twas George Hammond's? Well, anyhow, she fetched from her moorin's up in the harbor and the next anybody knew there she was hard and fast on West Long Flat, right over yonder, about abreast Jonathan Greenleaf's fish shanty. Well, sir, they had a time gettin' her off. I sighted her first thing in the mornin' from the light tower and says I—"

He went on to tell what he said and what others said and thought and did. It was a long, involved yarn and he was the only one who seemed to be greatly interested in it. Bert Thornlow apparently did his best to appear the attentive listener but his attention wandered. Several times Lavinia, the ever watchful, caught his gaze wandering across the table toward Ethel's straying in his direction. Once their glances met and, when they did, the girl colored, smiled slightly and looked away. Mrs. Badger decided then, as she had decided before during that evening, that Amaziah's hints concerning the naturalness of nature might not be as unworthy of notice as they had seemed to her when he offered them. Girls *had* fallen in love when they were only seventeen—yes, and had married at that early age. And paid for the mistake afterwards. Well, this one should not do anything so foolish if she—Lavinia— could prevent it. Probably—oh, yes, almost certainly—there was nothing serious in the present situation, but she must keep her eyes open.

Young Thornlow left for home about eight. He seemed to be

in no hurry to go; it was Lavinia's hints concerning his mother's worry as to his whereabouts which finally sent him on his way. Without appearing to do so she made it a point not to afford the young couple an opportunity to be together and she accompanied them when Bert went out to board the car. Amaziah went along, too, of course; in fact he was beside the car before its owner arrived. He was tremendously interested in everything, providing and scratching matches for the lighting of the lamps, bending down to watch the cranking and breathing a sigh of admiration and relief when, after a half-dozen times, the motor began to cough regularly and the auto to tremble from stem to stern.

"Godfreys, ain't that slick!" he exclaimed, excitedly. "Just grind her up and off she goes. No harnessin' nor nothin'. Whew!"

"I'll give you a ride sometime, Mr. Holt."

"Will you—honest? Gee, I'd like to have one. Any time you say. Just let me know and I'll be ready."

Aunt Lavinia's voice called him back to reality. "While you're waitin'," she observed, "you might go out to the lighthouse and see how things are there. Good-by, Mr. Thornlow—Bert, I mean. Hope you don't have any trouble on the way up."

"If I do it won't amount to much. Thank you, Mrs. Badger. Had a wonderful supper and a fine time.... Oh, Ethel, just a second."

Ethel went over to the side of the car. He whispered. They both laughed. Then the car moved away. They watched it as it rocked and chuffed out of sight in the early darkness of the summer night.

"Godfreys, look at her go!" breathed Amaziah, ecstatically. "Slick? Don't say a word!"

Ethel spoke, apparently without realizing that she did so. "Oh, I hope he gets back home all right," she murmured.

Her great-aunt sniffed. "He will," she declared. "Can't anything very bad happen to him between here and the village. Hum! I wonder what his mother will say when he does get there."

"Oh, she won't scold him, I'm sure. He says she hardly ever does."

"Is that so? Wonder if he'll tell her where he's been."

"Why—why, I suppose he will. Why shouldn't he?"

"No reason that I know of. Well, come along; you and I've got dishes to do."

During the dishwashing Lavinia asked a few questions. She asked them judiciously and, or so she hoped, without arousing suspicion in the girl's mind. Ethel had met Bert Thornlow quite casually at the post-office a week—no, perhaps it was two weeks—before. She was trying to open the Holt letter-box and the lock had stuck or something and he happened to be close by and offered to help. Ye-es, she had seen him—oh, three or four times since. No, she had never met his mother. She had seen her, though, when she was driving down the Wapatomac main road in the Thornlow carriage. She didn't like automobiles, at least Bert said she didn't. The car was quite new; it was Mrs. Thornlow's present to her son on his birthday. Oh, no, he wasn't in Wapatomac all the time, only Saturdays or Sundays. He was at college studying.

"But this is Monday. How did he happen to be here to-day?"

"Oh, he just stayed over. Had a headache or something. He is going back to-morrow morning; he told me so."

It just happened, his bringing her down to the Point in the automobile. She was on her way to the wharf where she had left her skiff and he came along in the car. They were talking and she told him she was going to row across the harbor and he said why not get in. He could drive her home in half the time it took to row. Of course, there was the skiff, but perhaps

Amaziah would row her across in his dory to-morrow morning
and, after school, she could bring the skiff back as she always
did.

"You don't really mind, do you, Auntie? It was such a
chance. I've always wanted to ride in an auto, and—"

"There, there! Course I don't mind. Am can row you over
to-morrow well as not."

They sat in the tiny sitting-room until half past nine when
Lavinia announced that she was going to bed. Ethel said she
guessed she would go, too; she had her part in the school
play to study, anyhow. Amaziah cal'lated he'd go out and take
another look at things. His room was on the lower floor of
the cottage, near the lighthouse and in pleasant summer
weather he slept there. During storms, or in mid-winter, he
was supposed—it was principally supposing—to keep awake
and on watch all night. The light was, as has been said, only
of minor importance to navigators and its supervision by the
authorities was not too strict.

His final remark, as he left the sitting-room, was in ·glorifi-
cation of their supper guest.

"I like that young Thornlow fellow," he declared. "Don't
put on no airs. You'd think he was just common folks like
us, wouldn't you now?"

He was addressing his Aunt Lavinia, but, as she made no
reply, he tried again.

"Why to hear him talk—" he began. This time the reply
was an interruption.

"We didn't have much chance to hear him," she snapped.
"You was doin' two-thirds of the talkin' yourself."

"Eh? Why, now, Aunt Laviny—"

"Oh, clear out, for mercy sakes!"

He looked at her, then at Ethel, shook his head significantly
at the latter, and departed. Ethel took a hand-lamp from the
shelf, lighted it and moved toward the stairs. Then she hesi-

tated, put down the lamp and came over to where her great-aunt was standing.

"Auntie," she said, anxiously, "you—you aren't cross at me, are you?"

Lavinia turned. "Eh?" she queried. "Cross? No, no, child. What should I be cross at you about?"

"I mean you didn't mind his—his coming here? Or my riding down with him in the car?"

"No, no. Don't fret about that. As for his comin' here, I'm glad he did. I'd a whole lot rather have him come here than—"

"Than what, Auntie?"

"Oh, nothin'. Good night, child. Don't set up too long fussin' over that play part of yours."

"I won't. Good night."

They kissed and the girl went up the narrow stairs. Lavinia lighted her own hand-lamp, blew out the lamp on the center table, made her regular inspection of doors and windows—not that there was any necessity for locking up at the Point, but because it was a lifelong habit of hers—and then she, too, went up to her room on the floor above.

There, she placed the lamp on the painted pine dresser and, crossing to the "Salem rocker" by the window, sat down to think.

Not that there was anything totally unexpected in the events of the evening just past. Of course it was high time to expect something of the sort. No doubt there had been more of which she knew nothing. It did not seem possible, but it was true; Ethel was a grown-up girl now. Yes—and a very pretty girl; it was odd how little attention she—Lavinia—had paid to that fact, too. Amaziah had, apparently, noticed it, he and his provoking hints about nature being nature. The idea of Amaziah's noticing anything, anything that she had not noticed first and called to his attention, was provoking of itself. She must be getting old—really old. Of course she was seventy-five, but she had never felt seventy-five. She was an old woman and getting careless and stupid. Dear, dear!

Well, she would not be stupid any longer, she could not afford to be, on Ethel's account. That girl was—was—why, she and her happiness and future were life itself to Lavinia Badger. She had never had a child of her own. Judah, her husband, had never wanted a child. "Wait till I get rich and we can afford it," had always been his counsel. Well, his various rash ventures in search of easy riches had kept them poor. If she had not secretly put aside a little from time to time, she would have had nothing when he went away except the house, and the house had been mortgaged. Poor foolish, selfish Judah. She wondered where he had gone, whatever became of him, where he might be now.

Dead, probably. He was a year or two older than she. She had been so happy on her wedding day. And so sure her choice of a husband had been the right one. Her brother Amaziah had cautioned her—odd that his oldest son should be so different. "Lavvy," her brother said, "don't be in a hurry. Judah may be all right, everybody says he's smart enough, but he hasn't got very far yet. You're only seventeen; pretty young, that is. Why not wait a year or two and see how you feel then?" But she would not wait.

And now Ethel was "having fellows." Perhaps she, too, would be as certain and independent and headstrong. Perhaps she would insist on having her own way. She—Lavinia—must be more careful, careful not only of Ethel but of herself, she must take care of her health. She might be growing old—she supposed she was—but she must not permit herself to *think* old. Ethel needed her now more than she ever did.

There was a knock at the door. Ethel's voice came from the narrow hall outside.

"Auntie, are you awake?"

"Eh? Yes, yes, course I am. Haven't even got undressed yet. Come in."

Ethel, in her nightgown, entered. "Auntie," she said. "I almost forgot. There was a letter for you at the post-office. I put it in my waist and when—when Bert came along in the automobile I didn't think of it again. Here it is. I hope it is nothing important."

Lavinia took the letter and, after adjusting her spectacles, looked at the envelop.

"Hum," she observed. "Addressed care of the South Denboro postmaster and forwarded over here. And what's that postmark up in the corner? See if you can make it out, I can't."

Ethel took the letter to the dresser and held it under the lamplight. "It isn't very plain," she said. "Silver—Silver something. And—and—what is that—COL beneath it? Why that's Colorado, isn't it? Who do you know in Colorado, Auntie?"

"Nobody. It doesn't amount to much, I guess. Some sort of circular advertisement, I shouldn't wonder. There's an awful lot of them nowadays. Patent medicine, cure everything on earth, I suppose. Wouldn't be much harm if you'd lost it altogether. Now run back to bed or you'll catch cold. . . . Oh, wait a jiffy. Kiss me again. I—I feel kind of blue to-night; too much fried flatfish, I presume likely."

It was some moments after the girl left before Lavinia absently tore open the envelop. The enclosure was not a circular, it was a letter. There was a printed heading. "U. G. Hawtry, Attorney at Law, Silver Rock, Colorado." The letter began: "Mrs. Judah Badger, South Denboro, Mass. Dear Madam:"

Lavinia read the letter through. Then she leaned back in the rocker. The color had left her face and her hands were trembling.

CHAPTER II

WHEN Ethel came down the next morning she found the breakfast table laid and her great-aunt busy in the kitchen. There was nothing unusual in this, but, or so it seemed to the girl, there were something unusual in Lavinia's appearance and manner. She looked tired and her acknowledgment of Ethel's cheery "Good morning" was perfunctory. She was very quiet during the final preparations for the meal and, when Amaziah made his appearance from the light, whither he had gone to extinguish the lantern and do a little of what he called "lookin' around" before breakfast, his comments concerning the prospects of weather for the day seemed to interest her not at all.

Amaziah, also noticing the peculiarity of his aunt's manner and prodded by a guilty conscience, attempted to head off the reminder which he felt sure was coming.

"Know what I'm goin' to do first thing this forenoon, Aunt Lavvy?" he queried, as they sat down at the table.

Lavinia's reply was prompt enough and short enough, but it was not the reply he expected.

"Yes," she said.

"Eh? You do? Well, you're right. I'm goin' to pitch in and shine up that lantern. If Ben Crowell hadn't stopped here yesterday, same as I told you, I'd have had her all shined by now. But Ben, he's the greatest fellow to set around and talk that ever was and I couldn't get rid of him, seemed so. But now, soon's ever I get back from rowin' Ethel over to town, I'm a-goin' up them stairs and pitch right in."

"You won't have to row Ethel over to-day. I'll take her up

23

to school myself. I'm going to drive to town soon as breakfast is done with and the first thing for you to do is harness up Major. When that job's finished you can tackle the lantern. If you ask me I should say you'd better."

This was a real surprise to both her hearers. Lavinia's trips to Wapatomac were few and far between. Amaziah expressed his feelings.

"Eh?" he stammered. "You goin' to town to-day? What for?"

"I've got an errand to do."

"But, Laviny, I can do your errands for you when I take Ethel. I'd like to."

"Don't doubt it, but you won't. There, there! hurry up and eat. I want to get started."

"But, Lavvy, ain't this kind of—of sudden? You never said anything yesterday about cal'latin' to go."

"I'm sayin it now."

She offered no explanation. Amaziah glanced across the table at his niece, lifting his eyebrows in mute interrogation. Ethel shook her head; she was as puzzled as he.

She noticed that her great-aunt ate almost nothing. This too was astonishing, for Lavinia's appetite was, as a usual thing, very good indeed. Amaziah, hastily finishing his second cup of coffee, went out to the barn.

"Put the dishes in the sink, Ethel," ordered Mrs. Badger. "They can stay there till I come back."

The drive to the village was a pleasant one. It was a beautiful morning. The harbor to their right was calm and placid. Over the low hills at its farther side the spires and roofs of Wapatomac rose amid the green of elm trees and silver-leaf poplar. From the northern end of the inlet, where it narrowed and the salt marshes began, drifted the salty-sweet marsh odors. At their left was the expanse of the bay, dancing in the northwest breeze, occasional whitecaps dotting the blue.

Major, the old horse, pounded doggedly along, the ancient buggy rattling and squeaking behind him. The stretch of road between the dunes ended and wound upward over Simmons's Hill between the pitch-pines. June wild flowers were sprinkled along its edges.

Lavinia had said almost nothing during the journey. She held the reins, but old Major, who knew that road quite as well as either of his passengers, needed no guidance. Ethel, who had tried to make conversation, gave it up after a little. Plainly Aunt Lavinia did not wish to talk. Just as plainly, she was preoccupied and, the girl was almost sure, troubled.

At last Ethel could stand it no longer.

"Auntie," she ventured, "what is the matter?"

"Eh? Matter? Oh, nothin', nothin'. What made you think there was?"

"Because I know there is. You look so—so worried. Has anything happened? Tell me, was there anything in that letter I brought you last night—anything wrong, I mean?"

Lavinia slowly shook her head. "No," she said. "There was nothin' wrong in it. Nothin' that a body might not have expected—if they hadn't given up expectin' long ago. When you haven't heard from a person, or of that person, for thirty-odd year you never do expect to hear. If you do, why—why, then it comes as kind of a shock."

"But, Auntie, I don't understand. Who—what person do you mean?"

"Your Great-uncle Judah."

Ethel gasped. "Great-uncle Judah." she repeated. "Why—why, he—"

"He was my husband—yes."

"But he is dead, isn't he?"

"He is now, dead and buried. That was what the letter was about. Seems he has been livin' out there in Colorado and two weeks ago he died. A lawyer in some little one-horse town out there wrote to tell me so."

Ethel did not know what to say. That there had been a Judah Badger she, of course, had known ever since she was old enough to reason and ask questions. Great-aunt Lavinia had been married and her husband's name was Judah Badger. That was the extent of her knowledge for a long time, for Lavinia never mentioned his name and Uncle Amaziah, when questioned, merely shook his head and warned her that there were some things not to be talked about in that household. As a child that was sufficient, but, as she grew older, the mystery became more intriguing, and—she was nearly fourteen at that time—she seized the opportunity when she and Amaziah were alone one day to cross-question him. He dodged and evaded— "Your Aunt Laviny wouldn't like it a mite if she knew I told you." But in the end he did tell her.

Judah Badger was, when Lavinia Holt married him, skipper of a fishing schooner. He was a native of Denboro.

"That was afore my day," said Amaziah. "They was married in '49 and I wa'n't born till '54. Edgar, your pa, and Father—Laviny's brother he was—used to visit Uncle Judah and Aunt Laviny regular and I can remember Uncle Judah plain. He'd give up goin' fishin' by that time—said there wasn't enough what he called 'prospects' in it for a smart man. He was runnin' a kind of general store in Denboro then, but he sold that out afterwards and went on the road. Drummer for a Boston notion-house, he was—takin' orders for spool cotton and needles and knick-knacks up and down the county. He always had some sort of a job—I'll say that for him—but he wa'n't never satisfied with ary one of 'em, always wishin' he was doin' somethin' different. He was a good-natured fellow, as I recollect him, but a great one for spendin' every dollar he had soon's he got it. If it hadn't been for Laviny I don't know how they'd got along.

"Well, to make the yarn shorter, and tellin' it the way me and Edgar heard it from Father, for Aunt Laviny never said a word about her affairs then any more'n she does now, there come a time when Uncle Judah lost his drummin' job—just 'cause he wasn't paid enough, so he said; but whether that was true or not I don't know. Anyhow, he got the notion that he wanted to go out West. West was the place for a hustlin' man, so he vowed. Laviny she didn't want to go—not until there was somethin' besides 'prospects' to go to, anyhow. So he said he'd go himself, do what he called look the ground over, and send for her soon's he got settled at good wages. She didn't like the looks of that much either, but he gen'rally did what he wanted to, I judge.

"Anyhow, go he did. I was fifteen then and Edgar—your pa, Ethel—was thirteen. That was the last we ever saw of Uncle Judah, and the last his wife ever saw of him, either. She heard from him from Chicago, then from Omaha, then from somewheres else. The letters got farther and farther between and finally stopped comin' altogether. Your Great-aunt Laviny she struggled along, run a little shop in Denboro village, and managed to make both ends meet some way. Father—that's your grandpa, Ethel—wanted her to get the police after her husband, make him contribute to her support or the like of that, but she was proud and independent. Then when Father give up goin' to sea she sold out her shop and house and went to live with Father at our old place. When he died—me and Edgar sold that house and Aunt Laviny came here to the light to housekeep for me. When Edgar was drowned and you was only a two-year-old baby Laviny had you fetched here to live with us and you've been here ever since. There! that's the whole story; and if you ever let Aunt Laviny know I told it to you she'll never forgive me and I won't forgive you."

"But Great-uncle Judah, whatever became of him?"

"Nobody knows. Chances are he's dead long ago. And not

much loss neither, the way I look at it. He ain't talked about around here, you mustn't forget that."

So Ethel had never talked about him, had, in fact, practically forgotten there had ever been such a person. She, like Amaziah, had taken it for granted that he had been dead for years. And yet, all this time; until but a fortnight ago, he had been living. And his widow had not been a widow at all.

She was silent, gazing wide-eyed at the road ahead, and seeing nothing. Lavinia turned to look at her.

"You are surprised, I guess likely. Well, so was I."

"But—but, Auntie—I can't believe it. I supposed—"

"How much do you know about him—about him and me, I mean?"

"Not so very much ... I used to wonder—you see, of course I knew you had been married—and, after I got older, I wondered more. You never spoke about him, and he wasn't with the rest of our family in our lot in the Denboro cemetery, and so—well, then I found out a few things."

"How did you find out? Amaziah, of course. He'd be bound to tell you; he tells everything."

"Oh," hastily, "you mustn't blame him, I made him tell me. He didn't want to."

"I know. He never does want to, but he generally does. Oh, don't worry about it. If you know it saves my tellin' you and I had made up my mind to tell you this mornin'. I'd rather you found it out from one of us than from an outsider and a girl that is old enough to have beaux is old enough to know things—and keep 'em to herself afterwards. At least she ought to be."

The reference to beaux was not emphasized, nor did she again repeat it. Instead she went on to impress the need of secrecy.

"I don't want you to tell anybody about this letter, or what's in it, not even Amaziah. You must promise me you won't."

"Why, of course I won't, Auntie, if you don't want me to."

"I don't. No need to start a lot of talk about things that most people around here don't know and the rest have forgotten. I never saw any good come of turnin' private affairs into public ones and I have seen a lot of harm. Keep your eyes and ears open and your mouth closed, so your grandpa used to say, and it's just as good a rule nowadays as 'twas in his time. What folks don't know can't hurt 'em. . . . Git dap, Major! What are you goin' to sleep for?"

She did not speak again for some minutes. Ethel, although her mind was seething with questions which she would have liked to ask, said not a word. It was Mrs. Badger herself who broke the silence.

"Maybe you'd like to read that lawyer's letter," she suggested. "You can if you want to. Here it is."

She opened the black silk reticule which lay in her lap, took out the letter and handed it to the girl. Ethel unfolded the sheets of cheap commercial paper with their printed headings and read as follows.

MRS. JUDAH BADGER,
  SOUTH DENBORO, MASSACHUSETTS.

DEAR MADAM:
As the friend and legal adviser of the late Judah P. Badger of this town I am addressing this letter to you. Mr. Badger passed away, after a lingering illness, on the twenty-first of May. During his last sickness he requested me to draw his will in which he left his property, real and personal, to Lavinia Holt Badger, his wife, her heirs or assigns. Mr. Badger informed me, I am quoting his exact words, that he did not know whether or not you were still living, but that, if you were, he felt pretty sure that a communication to the above address would reach you. If you receive this letter will you, or your legal representative, kindly notify

me at once. I will then forward particulars concerning the inheritance, also itemized bills for expenses, etc.

Respectfully yours,

ULYSSES G. HAWTRY

Attorney at Law

Ethel finished the letter. Her great-aunt took it from her
hand and replaced it in the reticule.

"So that was what 'twas," she observed. "After hearin'
nothin' for twenty-seven years I get that."

The girl looked at her. She had never seen Aunt Lavinia
cry, but, unless she was greatly mistaken, the keen black eyes
behind the spectacles were wet now. Impulsively she laid a
hand upon the black-mitted one holding the reins.

"Oh, Auntie," she said, "I'm—I'm so sorry."

"Eh? There, there, there's nothin' to be sorry about. I've
counted him as dead for more than half of my life. I've got
over thinkin' of him or bein' sorry for myself long ago. It's
only that—that this sort of brings back old times, that's
all. Ah hum—well, those times are as dead as he is; and as I
shall be before very long, of course. I mustn't be a fool. Now
we'll talk about somethin' else."

She dropped the reins in her lap, took off her spectacles and
wiped them. "There!" she said, briskly, after replacing them
on her nose, "now we'll try and be sensible. I'm goin' to
drop you up at the meetin'-house corner. You can walk to
school from there. And row home this afternoon in the skiff,
same as you always do."

"But, Auntie, where are you going?"

"I'm goin' to see Judge Payne. He's attended to my business
affairs, such as they are, since before Father died. He'll have
to attend to this, I suppose. This man," tapping the reticule,
"talks about bills for expenses. Those bills'll have to be paid
and I judge there's nobody but me to pay 'em."

"But, Auntie," there was excitement in Ethel's voice, "why should you have to pay anything? He—this lawyer in Colorado, I mean—says there is a will and—and that—" she hesitated, reluctant to mention her great-uncle's name; "that he left everything to you," she concluded. "He speaks about property; he does, there in his letter."

Lavinia shook her head. "You can't fish without bait," was her dry comment. "And if you're a jack-leg lawyer, same as I imagine this Hawtry one is, you can't hope to get answers to letters by just sayin' you'd like to have your bill paid. Not when you write to strangers you can't. The doctor and the undertaker are hopin' to be paid, I presume likely, and folks don't draw wills for nothin'. No, what I've inherited are those bills and nothin' else, or I miss my guess."

"But, Auntie, there might be more. There might be a lot more. You don't know."

"I knew Judah, poor soul. If he made money one week he spent it the next and ran in debt the third. He couldn't help it, he was made that way."

"But he did make a will. If he had nothing to leave why would he do that?"

"Because he was Judah Badger. No matter how far down he was or how much he owed he'd never own up to it, even to himself. If the poor-house was right ahead of him his mind would put a mansard roof and a gold weather-vane on it and call it the mansion he was goin' to move into day after to-morrow. If he thought he was dyin' he'd make a will, because it was the genteel thing to do. He was the greatest make-believe that ever was, I guess, and he'd make-believe to his last breath.... Oh, dear! well, he's gone, poor thing, and I hadn't ought to be bitter about him, I suppose. He was kind enough to me when he was around with me, but he never let me or my concerns or feelin's interfere with his. When he wanted to go

West he went and I was left at home with the debts I didn't know about."

She paused, sighed, and then added, with the brisk nod of decision which was so characteristic of her, "I paid those debts, every last one of 'em, and I'll pay these. He left me his name, anyhow, and nobody of that name shall be buried at the town's expense if I can help it."

She said no more, nor did Ethel, until they reached the corner by the Methodist church. There, as the high school was but a little way down the main road, the girl clambered out of the buggy.

"Auntie," she faltered, as she paused by the edge of the walk, "I do hope you believe I am sorry. I truly am."

"There, there, child. I told you there was nothin' for you to be sorry about. Only remember, not a word to anybody, not even to your Uncle Am. Might as well paint it on the fence as tell it to him."

"I won't tell, Auntie, I promise you; honest and truly I won't."

"All right. You've never lied to me yet, far's I know. Good-by. See you this afternoon. Look out for the tide when you row across. Keep around by the inside shore, that's the easiest way."

Judge Philander Payne—he was a judge by courtesy only, lived in the large white house on the main road a quarter of a mile beyond the church. At the front, right-hand corner of his property was a small, white-clapboarded building with the sign in faded gold lettering over its door "P. G. PAYNE, Attorney at Law. Office Hours 10 to 12 A.M. 2 to 5 P.M."

It was not yet nine, but Lavinia was not the least troubled on that account. She hitched old Major to the granite post by the Judge's front gate and, entering the yard and ignoring the law office altogether, pulled the glass knob of the bell beside the side door, the "family entrance" of the dwelling itself.

A plump, middle-aged woman—Judge Payne's housekeeper, she was—answered the ring.

"Why, good mornin', Mrs. Badger," she said. "My! You're out early, ain't you?"

"Either that or the town clock's wrong. Judge in, is he?"

"Why, yes, he's in; but he's hardly got down stairs. Just started eatin' his breakfast a minute ago."

"All right, he can finish it. Tell him I'm here, that's all. I'll go into the sittin'-room and wait till he's through. Run along, Martha, don't bother about me, you've got your work to attend to."

The Payne sitting-room was as old-fashioned as its owner. Its haircloth furniture, Brussels carpet and steel engravings were as they had been when Mrs. Payne died, fourteen years before. Lavinia seated herself in the black walnut rocker with the crocheted "tidy" on its back and gazed absently out of the window at the little yard with the lilac and syringa bushes bordering the drive to the barn. The housekeeper hastened out to tell her employer of his caller.

He came in ten minutes later. A white-haired man, several years younger than Lavinia, but looking much older.

"Well, well, Lavinia!" he exclaimed. "You must have turned out before breakfast and that's a fact."

"I generally do, Philander; if I didn't there wouldn't be any breakfast. Sorry if I've made you hurry yours, though."

"That's all right. I was late. Getting lazy in my old age, I guess. Now what can I do for you?"

Lavinia's reply was in the form of an unexpected question.

"That Martha Cahoon of yours isn't hard of hearin', is she?" she asked.

"What? Martha? No, of course she isn't."

"Then the first thing you can do for me is shut the door. I don't want her or anybody else to hear what I've got to say."

Judge Payne was surprised, that was evident, but he carefully closed and latched the door leading to the dining-room. His visitor motioned toward a chair near the one she occupied.

"Sit down, Philander," she ordered. "There! Now read that."

She took from her reticule the letter she had shown Ethel and handed it to the lawyer. He adjusted his gold-rimmed spectacles and read the first few lines. Then he looked up and at her.

"Why—why; Lavinia!" he gasped.

"Um-hm, I know. Go on, read the whole of it."

He read it to the end. Then he drew a long breath.

"Dear me!" he sighed. "Dear, dear me! Why, this is— this is—"

"Yes, so 'tis. *But* it is, or so that letter says."

"Dear me! After all these years. Why, I supposed—"

"Sshh, sshh! So did I, but it was the wrong supposin'."

"Lavinia, I—I hardly know what to say to you. This must have been a—a shock. It is, even to me. After all these years. Tut, tut! Dear me, dear me!"

"Philander, you said all that before. Now I want you to do some things. I might have done 'em myself, I presume likely, but I thought a lawyer could do 'em better and with consider'ble less fuss. That—what's-his-name—that Hawtry man— says there are bills for expenses. I want you to find out what those bills are and, if they are what they should be and no more than they should be, I want 'em paid. I want you to find out, too, where"—she hesitated an instant—"where he is buried and, maybe, see that some sort of a—a plain stone is put up to him. I'll pay for that, too, of course."

"But, Lavinia, there is no reason why you—"

"I know, I know; but I want to do it, just the same. I'll feel a little better when it's done. After all, there was a time when—when he and I were— But we won't rake that up.

You look out for everything, Philander, won't you, same as you always have?"

"Of course, of course, Lavinia. . . . But, look here, you may not have to pay anything. There may be—yes, there may be, something coming to you. This letter says he—your—"

"My husband. You needn't be afraid to say it. I've been sayin' it to myself all night long. And tryin' to make myself believe it was true. Philander, if you could realize all that that letter has—has started me thinkin' about. Not only all the bad things, but the good things. Do you wonder I got up before breakfast, as you tell about? Got up! I stayed up; haven't slept a wink since I read the thing."

He leaned over and patted her hand.

"You're a good woman, Lavinia," he said, "and you always have been. A lot too good for that— Hum! Mustn't speak ill of the dead, I suppose; but," grimly, "if I had known, if I had even imagined, he was alive all this time I should have spoken *to* him. I should, if I had to travel to Colorado to do it."

"Oh no, you wouldn't. If you and I had known he was alive it wouldn't have changed anything. I long, long ago made up my mind on that. Things were a good deal better as they were; better for me certain, and for him, too, maybe. . . . Well, there, I must run along. Got an errand or two to do afore I start back home."

"Wait a minute. As I was going to say when you interrupted me, there is a lot in this letter we haven't talked about at all. He made a will—the letter says so—and you are his only heir. Surely that is worth looking into, isn't it?"

She smiled. "Philander," she said, "you knew Judah Badger in the old days, knew him well. Do you think it likely that he's left anything—except those bills the Hawtry man tells about? If you do, I don't. Do you think he ever had anything worth while—and held on to it? Course you don't and neither do I."

"All the same I'm going to find out before I let you spend

one nickel of your own money.... All right, Lavinia, leave it to me. I'll write this Hawtry now, this minute, before I open the office. Is there anything else I can do?"

"Nothin', except keep it all to yourself. You know Wapatomac. I won't have it talked about."

"It sha'n't be. You can depend on me for that."

"I always have, Philander. And, yes, there is one more thing you can do for me. You can take care of yourself. You look tired out. You work too hard, everybody says so."

"Nonsense. Nothing troubles me but my age and that I can't help. Wish I had your receipt for keeping young. Some of these days I am going to take it a little easier, though. If I could find the right sort of young fellow to come in to my office with me I could shift a little of the practice, the less important part, to his shoulders. Maybe I shall find him some day. I'm keeping my eyes open. Good-by. As soon as I hear from my answer to this," tapping the letter, "I shall drive down and see you. Keep up your courage, Lavinia. Don't brood."

"I sha'n't. The only critter that seems to make anything by broodin' is a settin' hen. Don't worry about me. Now I must do my errands."

The doing of the errands necessitated her stopping at the grocery store, at the establishment of Seth Townsend, Boots and Shoes, Dry Goods and Notions, at that of E. P. Hamlin, Hardware, Kitchen Fittings, Tinsmith and Wooden Ware, and, finally at the Wapatomac Bank. It was nearly eleven when she left the last-named institution and turned Major's head toward home. The bank was located in the center of the town, not far from the post-office, and there were several other horses attached to carts and carriages standing by the edges of the sidewalks on either side of the road. It was, for Wapatomac, a busy place at that time of day.

Lavinia piloted the old horse into the narrow lane between the vehicles, urged him into a jog-trot and settled back on the buggy seat. Just then she heard, from somewhere ahead, a sound which she had heard not so many hours before, the "chuff-chuff" of a motor engine. The horses by the roadsides heard it also and pricked up their ears. Major heard it and lifted his ancient head.

"Whoa, there, Major! Steady, steady!" cautioned Lavinia.

Then, from around the corner beyond the hardware store, came a red automobile, coughing and humming. Its rate of speed was not, just then, more than ten miles an hour, but ten miles an hour in Wapatomac at that period was a reckless rush. The horses by the sidewalk edges danced and snorted and tugged at their hitching-straps. Their owners came running from shop doors shouting orders as they came.

Old Major was directly in the path of the oncoming crimson terror. An automobile at that time was, even to a town horse, a distinctly novel and frightening apparition, and Major was not a town horse; he came to the village only infrequently and had never before seen a bogey like this one. Stark panic possessed his equine soul. For the first time in at least fifteen years he stood upon his hind legs and pawed the air.

The buggy was whirled sidewise and began to rise upon its starboard wheels. Lavinia, clinging grimly to the reins, shouted and commanded. More people rushed from the shops. There were cries and confusion. Mrs. Azuba Bradley, who had paused on her way to the Notion Store to chat with the young Baptist minister, threw her arms about the clergyman's neck and declared she should die. She did not die then, she lived for a dozen more years, but at each sewing-circle meeting during the dozen she never failed to refer to her narrow escape. "I give right up. Thinks I: 'Here I go!'" It was the thrill of Aunt 'Zuba's mortal span.

The crisis was but momentary. The motor-car, checked in its mad dash by its driver's foot on the brake pedal, turned to the left, bumped against Dr. Hardy's iron hitching-post and stopped. The horses, their bridles held by the hands of their owners or those of bystanders, snorted, trembled and were still. Old Major, becoming conscious of the bit sawing his mouth, ceased trying to emulate Pegasus and descended to earth.

"Whew!" gasped Lavinia Badger.

CHAPTER III

SEVERAL of the onlookers came hurrying out into the road. Gustavus Doane, the postmaster, his hand on the buggy dash, looked anxiously up at her.

"You all right, Mrs. Badger?" he queried, his voice shaking.

"Don't know why I shouldn't be."

"But, good Lord above, that was a nigh thing, if ever I saw one. For a second there I thought—"

Old Deacon Townsend, his bald head glistening in the sun— he had run out of his store when the excitement began—broke in with a prophecy.

"This is just about the end," he declared, with shrill indignation. "Last selectmen's meeting I told the rest of 'em, says I: 'Those things are a danger to life and liberty,' I says. 'They hadn't ought to be allowed to run loose on the main roads. Somebody's going to be run away with and killed first thing you know. It's our business to make a town law forbidding 'em altogether.' That's what I said, only last week 'twas, and now see what's happened."

Dr. Hardy, who had also joined the group about the buggy, put in a word.

"Don't you want to come into my office and rest a few minutes, Mrs. Badger?" he suggested. "Your nerves must be pretty well shaken. If you will come in and sit down—"

But Lavinia had heard enough. "There's nothin' the matter with my nerves," she declared, tartly. "The only thing that's liable to trouble 'em is havin' all this crowd pushin' around and starin' at me. Get 'em out of the way, Gustavus, for mercy sakes. Git dap, Major!"

But Major was still eyeing the old motor-car with apprehension and, before the order could be repeated, another individual pushed his way to the front. He was a young fellow, smartly dressed, and he had just vacated the seat of that same motor-car.

"I say," he stammered, "I'm awfully sorry. Glad there was no damage done. I haven't had this car but a little while and I keep forgetting that horses down this way aren't used to them yet. I hope I didn't frighten you too badly.... Eh? Why—why, it's Aunt Lavinia—Mrs. Badger, I mean! Great Scott, now I *am* sorry! I had no idea it was you."

Lavinia recognized him, of course. He was young Thornlow, her supper guest of the previous evening.

"Oh," she observed. "It's you, is it? No, you needn't worry; I'm all right."

"Gee, I'm glad of that! And Major—he isn't hurt, I hope?"

"He's scared, but that's all. How did you know his name was Major?"

Bert Thornlow colored just a trifle. "Oh, Ethel told me, I guess. She tells me a lot about you people down at the light."

"Um-hm, I shouldn't wonder. Well, young man—Gustavus, for goodness' sake, can't you and all these folks clear out and leave us alone? This horse of mine will have another fit if you keep dancin' under his nose this way. Mr. Thornlow, suppose you take hold of his bridle and lead him to that clear place over yonder beyond the doctor's."

The crowd, some chuckling and others—Deacon Townsend, in particular—indignantly arguing, melted away. Young Thornlow led old Major past the red car and parked him and the buggy by the sidewalk just beyond. Lavinia noticed that there was a woman in the car, a plump, matronly woman, wearing nose-glasses, and dressed as no matron of Wapatomac ever dressed, even on Sunday.

"Well, young man," said Lavinia, picking up her sentence

where she had dropped it to give orders to the postmaster, "I judge you got home all right last night. What did your mother think had become of you? Gettin' nervous, was she?"

"Oh no, she knew I would turn up all right. She—"

"Is that her in the car with you now?"

"Why—why, yes ... Yes, Mother, I'm coming; be there in a sec. ... Well, *au revoir*, Mrs. Badger. Don't hold this against me, will you?"

He was turning away, but Lavinia detained him. The stout matron on the seat of the automobile was looking toward them. She, obviously, was growing impatient.

"I don't believe I ever met your mother," said Lavinia.

It was a hint, of course, and a pretty broad one. Bert Thornlow recognized it as such, but his acceptance was not enthusiastic. "She would like to meet you, I'm sure," he said, with a little hesitancy. It was this trace of hesitation which caused Lavinia to make up her mind.

"And I'd like to meet her," she agreed, promptly. "I believe —yes, I will; I'll just get out and say howdy-do to her now. I presume likely she's wonderin' what we're talkin' about. Thinks I'm goin' to sue you for damages or somethin', I shouldn't wonder. Here, Willie," calling to a boy on the sidewalk, "just stand by this horse of mine a minute, will you? No, no, he won't run away; if you see him goin' to sleep just wake him up, that's all.... No, no," waving aside the Thornlow offer of assistance, "I can get out by myself; ain't too old for that, I hope."

She alighted from the buggy and, with the young man beside her, walked down to where the red car was standing.

"How do you do, Mrs. Thornlow," she said. "Well, between the three of us we've stirred up quite a little excitement, haven't we?"

Mrs. Charles Thornlow regarded her through the noseglasses. She looked at the old-fashioned gown, the old-fashioned hat, obviously home-made and several times made over, at the shrewd, smiling old face beneath it. Obviously she was rather taken aback by the familiarity of the address and scarcely knew how to reply.

"How do you do?" she said, after a moment, and added: "Why—why, yes, I suppose we have. There was no damage done, so far as I can see."

"No, no, not a mite. I was afraid you might think there was, though, and I just wanted to ease your mind, that's all."

Bert put in a word.

"Mother," he said, "this is Mrs. Badger. Mrs. Badger, my mother."

Lavinia declared she was real glad to meet Mrs. Thornlow and Mrs. Thornlow bowed.

"I've been telling Mrs. Badger how sorry I am that this thing happened," Bert went on. "It was my fault, I suppose. But, as I said to her, I keep forgetting that Wapatomac horses aren't used to autos."

"Mine isn't, anyhow," announced Lavinia. "He and the rest of our family live down to the Point light and we don't see automobiles there—that is, not often."

Mrs. Thornlow said she supposed not. Her son changed the subject.

"It's a beautiful day, isn't it," he observed. "Mother and I came down town for a little shopping. She hasn't ridden in my car more than twice before; have you, Mother? I've only had it a little while."

Mrs. Thornlow shuddered. "And I don't intend to ride in it again, if this sort of thing is a part of the experience. My nerves are not strong enough for excitement." She emphasized the statement with another shudder.

Lavinia waited for her to continue, but she did not, and, as Bert too, seemed to find conversation a trifle difficult, she made the next remark herself.

"Well," she said, "you want to do your shoppin', I know, and I must be gettin' along home. I'm real glad to know you, Mrs. Thornlow. When you're out ridin' some time, either in this thing," referring to the car, "or with a horse, I wish you'd come down to the Point and stop in and see us. It's kind of pretty down there in summer."

Mrs. Thornlow said, "Thank you," and then, as if faintly aware that she was not being too gracious, added that she was sure it must be.

"We think so. You know where it is, of course? How to get there and all like that?" She paused an instant, and then added, "I guess likely your son does, anyhow."

The final sentence was not emphasized, but it was not as casual as it sounded. Lavinia was in search of information upon a certain point. She obtained it, or was almost certain that she did. Bert seemed, so she thought, embarrassed, even a trifle apprehensive. His mother, however, politely concealed a yawn with her gloved hand, consulted her watch, which was pinned with a diamond-studded clasp to the bosom of her gown, and murmured, "Oh, yes, probably." Then she seemed to lose the little interest she had had in the conversation and looked toward the other side of the road.

Lavinia said good-by and hastened back to the boy and Major. Bert would have accompanied her but his mother called him impatiently and he hesitated. Lavinia gave the boy a five-cent piece, boarded the buggy, picked up the reins and drove away.

The happenings of the hour just passed, the coming of the automobile, Major's fright, her own narrow escape from what might have been a serious accident, and the interview with the Thornlows—these had occupied her attention and had kept her busy. They had given her enough to think about and had caused her to forget, for the time, the subjects upon which she had been brooding ever since Ethel brought the letter to her room the evening before. All night, and all the morning until after she left Judge Payne's home, she had been thinking of the man she married, who had deserted her so long ago, who had had no part in her life for nearly forty years and who, now that he was dead, had been so strangely brought back into it again.

She had been thinking of him, reviving old memories, reliving old scenes, seeing faces once so familiar and hearing voices long silent. She had been back in the little house in Denboro, the home which had meant so much to her in those days, where she had dreamed and planned, only to see those dreams and plans go down to utter ruin. She had been thinking of him as he was when she first knew him, and of her father and of Amaziah, her brother, and of Edgar, her favorite nephew, and of Susan, Edgar's young wife. All dead and gone. Of the family only she and the present Amaziah and Ethel remained. Ethel was like Edgar; looked like him and reminded Lavinia of him in so many ways.

Being, above all else, practical, Lavinia had determined, when she left Judge Payne's home, to put the past out of her mind and dwell no more upon it. Her own wrecked life and the man who had wrecked it were gone forever. Memories and vain regrets were useless. She would brood over them no more. Having made up her mind what to do, she had entrusted the doing to Judge Payne and therefore, until or if new developments came, it was his business. That was that.

Nevertheless, in spite of her resolution, she had not succeeded in dismissing or forgetting and it was of the past she was still thinking when the exciting adventure with the red car broke upon her. Then came the meeting with the Thornlows and now, as she rocked along the sandy Neck Road behind old Major, Lavinia was thinking, not of herself or her own affairs, but of Ethel. It was of Ethel she had been thinking when the Colorado letter came and of Ethel she was thinking now. Ethel, and Ethel's future and hapiness were, as she saw it, distinctly the business of Lavinia Badger; she could not shift that responsibility to a lawyer or any one else.

In spite of her philosophic conclusion that the friendship between her grand-niece and young Thornlow was, in all human probability, just another one of those boy and girl "puppy love" affairs which would last but a little while and die out before the summer was over, Lavinia was a little troubled. There had been several little incidents during the previous evening, during supper and afterward, which her keen eyes had noticed. The exchange of glances, the whispered parting, Ethel's embarrassment when her great-aunt questioned her about previous meetings with Bert Thornlow.

Ethel was a good girl and a straightforward, sensible one. Lavinia trusted her implicitly and had no fear that she would ever do anything bad or, deliberately, reckless or silly. But Bert Thornlow was a handsome young fellow and a likable one; Lavinia herself had liked him on first acquaintance. That Ethel liked him and that he liked her were obvious. But what did Lavinia or the girl really know about him? Nothing essential, of course.

And, this very morning, Mrs. Badger had learned—or was confident she had learned—one thing which she did not like. It was evident to her that Bert had told his mother nothing of his visit to the lightkeeper's cottage. Nothing of his supper there, of meeting her, Lavinia, or Amaziah, probably nothing of his friendship with Ethel Holt. Why not?

Was he ashamed of the company he had been in? He had no reason to be and he had better not be. Lavinia nourished no inferiority complex, as it is called in these modern days. True, the Thornlows, with all their money and social position, might be what Amaziah would term "a different breed of cats" from the Holts, but the breed was not a better one. The Holts were, and had been since Captain Joshua's day, honest, respected citizens, who paid their bills when they were due and bent the knee to nobody. As for Ethel—well, the man who married her would be a lucky man, no matter who or what he was.

And no one but the right kind of man should get her—if Lavinia could prevent it. But suppose she could not prevent it? Suppose those two young idiots should make up their minds to marry in spite of everything and everybody? That had happened before in similar cases. Lavinia remembered well enough how earnestly her own brother had advised against her marrying Judah Badger. And how much heed had she given to that advice?

Major stumbled just then and jerking him to his feet and speaking to him as he deserved to be spoken to, broke the continuity of Mrs. Badger's thoughts. Also the interruption served to awaken her to the realization that she had been borrowing trouble when, in all probability, no real trouble existed. This was a boy and girl affair, that was all, and she had, so far, no justification in believing it to be anything else.

"Well, we'll just wait and see," she soliloquized aloud. "There, there, Major! Do pick up your hoofs. Mercy on us! I declare I 'most wish there was another automobile around to put more life into you. Git *dap!*"

When Ethel came home that afternoon—she rowed across the harbor in the skiff—she was very much excited. She had heard of her great-aunt's narrow escape from being run away with. At the post-office, when she called for the mail, they were still talking about it. Mr. Doane had told her that he expected any minute to see the buggy upset and old Deacon Townsend was still making proclamations concerning what he would have to say at the next Selectmen's meeting.

"Mr. Doane said you were as cool as a cucumber, Auntie," she went on. "That is what he called it, cool as a cucumber.

He told me that you weren't half as frightened as he was. A wonderful old woman, that's what he called you in front of everybody."

This eulogistic appraisal was not as enthusiastically received as the girl no doubt expected it to be. Lavinia's eyes snapped.

"Humph!" she sniffed. "Old woman, eh? I want to know! Well, Gus Doane isn't so young himself that he has growin' pains. He's got one grandchild already and another one expected, and they tell me he talks about nothin' else from mornin' till night. Fussin' and fumin' and runnin' back and forth to his daughter's house when he ought to be attendin' to his job. Humph! If I'm one old woman he's another."

Amaziah was as excited as his niece. He wanted to hear all the particulars.

"And you never told me one word, Aunt Lavvy," he complained. "When I asked you what was goin' on up town you said, 'Nothin'.' And you all but killed dead! Godfreys mighty! I presume likely if you *had* been killed you'd have called that nothin', too. I never see such a woman. And 'twas that young Thornlow's auto that was responsible, the very car that was down here last night. My, my, that's strange, ain't it? What they call a coin*ci*dent. Tell me more about it, Ethel."

Ethel retold the tale as she had heard it. Her uncle shook his head.

"I'll bet that Thornlow boy felt sick when he saw who 'twas in the buggy," he observed. "Nobody's fault but his, either."

Ethel turned upon him. "It wasn't anybody's fault, really," she declared. "It just happened. He wasn't going faster than ten miles an hour and ten miles an hour isn't anything for an automobile. Why, up around the city the cars often go twice as fast as that, and the horses are getting so they hardly mind them at all. Down here, of course, it is different. And our Major—why, I don't suppose he ever saw one before."

Amaziah's mouth was open but it was Lavinia who spoke first.

"How do you know how fast he was goin?" she asked.

"Why, he told me so himself. He said—"

She stopped short, faltered, and then added hurriedly, "You see, I—I happened to meet him after school and—and—"

"Happened to? Yus, yus!" crowed Amaziah, and laughed loudly.

"Well, I did. At least—well, you see, Auntie, he felt dreadfully about it and—and he waited till school was out to tell me before any one else did. He said it was just his luck that it happened to be you. If it had been any one else he wouldn't have felt so bad. He made me promise to tell you how sorry he was and he is coming down here soon to tell you himself."

Lavinia nodded. "That's nice of him," she said, pleasantly. "Well, if he comes in that red go-cart we'll cover up the barn windows so Major won't have another conniption. . . . There, there, Am, be still; she's told you the whole yarn twice over and that ought to be enough. I must go up and see that lantern pretty soon. It must shine like a cat's eye in the dark now that you spent the whole forenoon polishin' it."

The eager glow of excitement faded from Amaziah's face. He swallowed before replying.

"Well, I shined half of it, anyhow," he sputtered. "And I'm figgrin' to do the rest soon's I can find time."

His aunt glanced at the clock. "Maybe you could find some now," she observed, "if you looked for it in the right place."

Bert Thornlow visited the Point again the following afternoon. He came in the red car and once more Ethel was his passenger.

"Thought I might as well bring her along, Mrs. Badger," he explained breezily. "She had to come and I was coming, so why not come together?"

He was profuse in his apologies to Lavinia for the fright he had given her and was as agreeable and sociable—"folksy," Amaziah termed it—as one could be. He declined the invitation to stay for supper but, just before leaving, he asked Mrs. Badger's permission to take Ethel for a drive on Sunday afternoon.

"Over along the north shore somewhere," he explained. "We sha'n't go far, not more than thirty miles altogether."

"Thirty miles—in one afternoon! My soul!" gasped Amaziah, in awed admiration.

"You won't mind, will you, Mrs. Badger? I'll take good care of her and she shall be home long before dark, I promise you."

Lavinia looked at him and then at the girl.

"I don't mind," she said. "She can go, I guess—if she wants to."

"Oh, she wants to all right. Eh, Ethel?"

Ethel nodded. "I'd love to, if Auntie doesn't mind. And I will be home by supper time, I promise you, Auntie."

"Um-hm. Provided that machine doesn't break down or something. All right, you can go this time and we'll see. If you're not home though—"

"Oh, but I will be! Honest and truly I will."

And she was. The automobile had behaved wonderfully well. There had been a puncture and something had happened to the engine which had necessitated its owner's lying flat on his back in the middle of a dusty road for half an hour, but those were but the minor incidents which owners of motor-cars expected in these days.

"Does your mother like the thing any better than she did?" inquired Lavinia. "When I talked with her she vowed she'd never ride in one again."

"Why, I didn't know you and Mrs. Thornlow had met," broke in Ethel. "You didn't tell me that, Auntie. And you didn't either, Bert."

"Oh, I met her for a minute or so that forenoon when Major took to doin' circus tricks. I guess I must have forgotten to mention it. And you forgot too—er—Bert, eh?"

"Why—why, yes, I did. So many things happened that morning."

"That's true enough. You haven't met her yet, Ethel, I suppose likely."

"No."

"Well, you will some day, of course. She'd like to meet you, I'm sure. Don't you think she would, Bert?"

"Oh yes, of course. Certainly, Mrs. Badger. Mother doesn't go out a great deal, not here in Wapatomac."

On Friday of that week another visitor came to the light-keeper's cottage. Judge Philander Payne drove down in his own buggy behind his own horse; the latter, by no means youthful, was a colt compared to Major. The Judge had, the very morning of Mrs. Badger's call upon him, written to Lawyer U. G. Hawtry, of Silver Rock, Colorado, and Hawtry's reply had just been received.

Ethel was at school, of course, and Amaziah had gone out in his dory to the buoy marking the course of the Big Flat and the edge of the channel to try for flounders. Fishing was one variety of work which he never shirked or postponed. Judge Payne and Lavinia therefore had the little sitting-room to themselves.

"You've got somethin' to tell me, Philander, I suppose likely," was Lavinia's first remark, after the greetings and the observations concerning the weather were through with and Judge Payne was seated in the hickory "Windsor" arm-chair by the window.

The old gentleman nodded. "I have," he said. "A number of things; some of them pretty interesting and—well, yes, surprising."

"All right, go ahead and tell 'em. You and I ain't likely

to have a better chance to talk by ourselves than we have this minute, not down here, anyhow."

The Judge took a letter—it was obviously a long one for it covered both sides of at least a half a dozen large-sized sheets of paper—from his pocket, set his spectacles firmly on his nose and began to read.

The first part of the letter dealt with matters concerned with Judah Badger's last illness, his death and burial. Also with the little of his recent history with which the Colorado attorney was acquainted. Badger had come to Silver Rock in 1898, or thereabouts, an elderly man even then. He had at first hired and then bought, a tiny house—not much more than a shanty, Hawtry explained—on the outskirts of the town of Silver Rock.

"Which isn't much of a town, I should imagine," commented the Judge, in passing.

No one in the community had ever seen him before or, for the matter of that, ever did come to know him very well. "From the few things he said about himself—not many, for he was pretty close-mouthed—"

"Must have changed since I knew him," muttered Lavinia. "Never mind, Philander, heave ahead."

"Um. Let's see . . . Um, yes. 'From the few things he said about himself,' etc., etc., 'people gathered that he had been a prospector, a mine-looker, hunting for silver deposits and that sort of thing. He never told any one where he came from in the beginning and, until he called me in, just before he died, to draw his will none of us knew that he had ever been married.' "

"I won't read all that, Lavinia. I'll leave the letter with you to read for yourself; only take care of it, for goodness' sake. Let me say here, though, that you won't have to pay his funeral expenses and doctor's bills; apparently he had enough cash on hand to take care of all that, and arranged for it, too."

"But this Hawtry talked about expenses in that first letter of his. Are you sure, Philander? Somehow I can't think of—of Judah's lookin' far enough ahead to worry about payin' what was owin' after he'd gone."

"I know, but it looks as if he did. And Hawtry's reference to expenses meant just sending you, the heir, the itemized bill for what had been spent from the estate, plus his own fee for services rendered. He seems to be a pretty honest sort of fellow, I must say. . . . What are you smiling about?"

Lavinia turned hastily and looked out of the window. Payne saw her draw her hand across her eyes. She cleared her throat before she answered.

"Was I smilin', Philander?" she asked, with a shrug. "I don't know's I feel very funny. Poor thing! All alone out there, dyin' all alone— Ah hum! . . . As for the smile—well, I guess that must have come when you said somethin' about his 'estate.' The notion of Judah Badger's leavin' an estate *is* funny."

"Yes. And yet, Lavinia, there is one, such as it is and it's yours now. The house—or shanty—he lived in may be worth fifty dollars; Hawtry says not more than that. And there may be a few dollars left after all the bills are paid. But he's left you some stock, quite a lot of stock, in the Lost Prospect Silver Mining Company."

He made this announcement gravely, even impressively, and leaned back in his chair to wait for the reaction. That reaction, when it came, was not of the kind he expected.

Lavinia nodded. "He would," she said.

The Judge stared. "Why, what on earth do you mean?" he demanded.

"I mean if he left anything, except debts, it was bound to be some sort of stock. Even in the old days he was always talkin' big about buyin' this stock and that, always goin' to make his fortune out of 'em and never makin' it. Lucky for

him, and for me too, it was mostly talk—he never had enough
ready cash to really buy much—but he loved to make-believe.
He'd come home with a piece of paper all printed up fancy and
with his name written on it and tell me it was ten shares in the
Sure Catch Patent Fishhook Company or somethin' and that
So-and-So had given him what he called 'inside information'
about it and that 'twas bound to make him rich. It never did,
of course, he 'most generally lost what he put into it, but he
kept right on. And, accordin' to this Hawtry man, he must have
kept on till the day of his death. Well, as I said, that's just
what he would do, poor foolish critter."

"But, now—wait a minute, Lavinia. This stock he owned
when he died and which he has willed to you, is worth a little
something."

" 'Little' is the right word, I should cal'late. If he lived for
nine years in a shanty that might, on a pinch, be worth fifty
dollars, and then had just about money enough to get himself
buried with, this stock he's left me must be wonderful. Come,
come, Philander Payne, I'm not a young-one and neither are
you; we can't afford to start stock-dreamin' at our age. What
did you say its name was?"

"The Lost Prospect Silver Mining Company. I shall look it
up, of course. There hasn't been a sale, so far as I can find out,
for over two years. The last quotation was ten cents a share,
I believe."

He could not help smiling as he made this statement and
Lavinia smiled with him.

"Ten cents a share," she repeated, drily. "And he had ten
shares, I presume likely? Well, that's a dollar anyhow, if we
can collect it."

"He had fifteen thousand shares, so Hawtry writes. And
that's fifteen hundred dollars—if, as you say, it can be col-
lected."

And now it was Lavinia who leaned back to stare.

"Fifteen hundred *dollars!*" she gasped. "My soul and body! Why—why, Philander!"

"Yes, but that was more than two years ago. It was ten cents then; it may be less now."

"Never mind if it's three, you sell it quick."

Judge Payne shook his head. "Lavinia," he said, "you trust me, don't you?"

"I've trusted you for two-thirds of my life. If I don't trust you now I don't trust anybody. Don't be silly."

"All right. Then you trust me with this a little longer. Let me look into it. Let me have my brokers in Boston look into it. Leave it to me for a while, will you, Lavinia?"

"Certain sure I will, if you say so. Though if, when you've looked in, you see anything but nothin' I'll be a good deal more than surprised."

"I know, I know. But I don't like to do things in a hurry. I want, as I say, to have my brokers look up this Lost Prospect business. If it sold for something at some time the people who bought it must have thought it was worth at least as much as they paid for it. Possibly they think it may, some day, be worth more. I want to write Hawtry about it. I want to find out where the mine, if there is one, is located. I want to—oh, I want to be satisfied in my own mind before I do anything. If it is bad business to buy a pig in a poke it may be just as bad to sell one that way. Leave it to me, Lavinia, for a while, that's all."

So the matter was left in his hands. Lavinia was still firmly of the opinion that the stock should be sold—if it was salable at all, which she doubted—but she deferred to her old friend's judgment. She was not seriously interested in that phase of the affair; as a matter of fact she did not believe that her "inheritance" was really worth anything or ever likely to be. Remembering her husband and his visions and disastrous petty speculations she was quite sure that any mine in which he might have been concerned was indeed a "lost prospect."

"You'll attend to everything there is to do out there, won't you, Philander?" she begged, as they parted at the door. "The settlin' up and havin' the gravestone put up and all like that. I'd tell that Hawtry man to get rid of the house—shanty, whatever it is—for what it would fetch. Don't you think so? . . . Yes, and one other thing. Don't for the good land sakes, ever mention to anybody a word about Judah's comin' to life and dyin' out there, or about this Lost Prospect silliness or any of it. I showed Ethel that first letter, but I sha'n't show even her this one. Why, if Wapatomac knew I'd come into fifteen thousand shares of stock they'd have it fifteen million before night and would be askin' me to build over the Baptist meetin'-house in memory of the man who ran off and left me. Don't tell, Philander."

She heard nothing from him for another fortnight. Then, having driven to town on other errands, she again called at his law office. He assured her that he was still looking into the Lost Prospect matter, that there was nothing new to report and, in all probability, would not be for some time to come. The little he had to tell her was not encouraging. The brokers reported that there was no market for Lost Prospect shares and they doubted if they could be sold at any price.

"There is one little hint of promise for the future," he said, "but it may not come to anything. Probably it won't. I don't want to tell you about it, for you might be expecting—"

"Don't talk such rubbish, Philander. I expect just what I'll get, and that's nothin'. I've forgotten it already and my advice to you is to do the same thing. What I came to ask about is that gravestone and payin' Judah's bills and that Hawtry lawyer for his work. You're attendin' to that?"

"Certainly. When I get a full report from him I'll bring it to you."

"You needn't. I shall be satisfied, if you are. Then you add your own bill to what the rest of it is and I'll pay the whole lot. That is, I will if it isn't too heavy. If it is I'll pay it off as fast as I can."

"You won't have to do that; it won't be a great deal."

"That's a comfort. Well, don't work too hard, Philander. You aren't as young as you used to be."

"And you are, I suppose? You're a wonder, Lavinia."

"I've got to be. I have other folks besides myself to look after. I can't afford to wear out."

CHAPTER IV

THE Graduation Exercises—they had not yet begun to call a graduation a Commencement in Wapatomac—were held in the town-hall on a Thursday evening. The class play was given the evening before. Amaziah and Lavinia would have been present on both occasions had it been possible, but some one had to remain at home to 'tend light, so Amaziah went to the play and his aunt to the exercises. Amaziah, with Ethel on the buggy seat beside him, drove over to the village early in the evening in order that Ethel might have time to dress and make up for her part before the curtain rose. When he came home, however, he came alone.

Lavinia was in the sitting-room when he arrived. It was after eleven but she was dressed and wide-awake.

"Where's Ethel?" was her first question.

Amaziah grinned. "Ethel's all right," he announced. "She's took care of, don't worry."

"What do you mean?"

"What I say," with a smile. "Ethel's comin' home in style. Horse-'n'-team ain't good enough for her nowadays. She's gettin' past that."

"What on earth are you talkin' about? Stop screwin' your face out of shape and answer me. Where is she?"

"Bert Thornlow's fetchin' her home in the automobile. He was waitin' for her to come out of the hall. He saw me waitin', too, and he hove alongside. He's a nice, sociable fellow, that boy; talks to you just same as if you was his own kind. That's what I like about him, not stuck-up a mite."

"Oh, be still! Did you expect him to pat you on the head and call you a good dog? ... There, there, go on, go on!"

"Well, he hove alongside, same as I said, and asked me if I was waitin' for somebody and I said yes, I was, and then he said I'd have quite a spell of waitin', he guessed, on account of her havin' to get off all her actin' clothes and into her reg'lar things again, and I said yes, I shouldn't wonder. And then he—"

"Oh, for mercy sakes! Then he said why didn't you start along home and he'd bring her down in his automobile. That was it, wasn't it?"

"Why, yes, 'twas. How'd you know?"

"How do I know enough to go in when it rains? And you thought his notion was a good one, I presume likely. You would, of course."

"Why, yes," defiantly, "I did and I do. It's a fine night, sky all starred up and everything, and he could fetch her home in that machine enough sight quicker'n I could with that old horse of ours."

"Of mine, you mean. Well, all I can say is that you're here and she isn't, not yet. Dear, dear! Why didn't I tell you to keep an eye out for that boy? I thought of it after you'd gone."

"But, Aunt Lavvy, what you frettin' about? She's all right. Most likely he had to wait ever and ever so long. They'll be here any minute now. He's used to the road down to the Neck nowadays, told me he was."

"He ought to be, he's traveled it enough lately."

She walked to the window, raised the shade and peered out. Her nephew, evidently still feeling the need of self-satisfaction, talked on.

"We ought to be proud," he declared, "to think that a young fellow like him is keepin' comp'ny with Ethel. I want to tell you that there's plenty of girls in Wapatomac would give their back teeth to have him chasin' after 'em. And that auto of his—why, there was as much as a dozen folks hangin' 'round it when I left, pawin' it over and talkin' about it and—"

"Sshh! He was at the play, I suppose?"

"You bet he was! Right in the front row. I saw him there myself."

"Was his mother with him?"

"Eh? Why, no, I guess she wasn't. I didn't see her, anyhow."

The chuffing of the Thornlow car became audible at that moment and the dialogue ended. Amaziah bolted out of the house to welcome its driver and passenger and Lavinia followed him. Ethel was radiant. She was sorry she was so late, but it had taken her a long time to get out of her costume and into her street clothes and then she had to get her things together and pack them. She did hope her auntie hadn't worried about her. She and Bert had had such a wonderful ride. The night was simply marvelous.

"I guess likely 'twas," observed Lavinia. "Looks that way now. Did you come straight home?"

Why, yes, they had. Of course—well, they went just a little out of their way, up to the end of the other road at the top of Simmon's hill to look at the water and the lights and all. But that only took a few minutes. And the car behaved beautifully.

"Sorry you couldn't be at the play, Mrs. Badger," put in Bert. "You would have been proud of Ethel. She was the star of the performance."

"Bert, don't be silly. The idea!"

"But you were, you know. No one else could touch her; could they, Mr. Holt?"

Amaziah's agreement was prompt and emphatic. "Never got within hailin' distance of her," he vowed. "Proud! Why,

say, Ethel, that time when you stood up to that rich fellow—
'twas Oscar Paisley's boy played that part, as I recollect
—when you faced him right down and told him what you
thought of him I all but riz up off my seat and yelled."

"Pity you didn't, then *everybody* would have been proud,"
was Lavinia's tart comment. "Well, Ethel, you must come
right in now, it is 'most twelve o'clock. Good night, Bert.
Thank you for fetchin' her home."

Young Thornlow took the hint. He cranked the car, climbed
to its seat and moved off.

"Good night, Ethel," he called.

"Good night, Bert. I'm ever so much obliged. Hope you
get home without any trouble."

"Oh, I shall. See you at the great doings to-morrow night,
of course."

He did see her then, but he did not see her home, for
her great-aunt was her escort on this occasion and they returned, as they had gone, in the buggy. Ethel delivered the
"Class Chronicles" and they made a great hit. As she walked
down the aisle after the affair was over diploma in one hand
and a big bouquet in the other, people crowded to offer congratulations. They congratulated Lavinia, too, on her grand-
niece's cleverness.

Ethel leaned from the buggy seat to look back as they
drove out of the hall yard. She sighed. Her great-aunt asked
her what was the matter.

"Oh nothing," she said. "I was just thinking this was the
end of it, the very end. . . . And now what?"

Lavinia had been thinking the same thing. And now what?
She wished she knew. Just then she saw Bert Thornlow
hurrying down the steps, looking about him as he pushed
through the crowd, and she jerked the reins and urged Major
into a trot.

As they moved along the dark road toward the corner she asked a question.

"Where did the flowers come from?" she asked. "Not the little bunch, those are from Amaziah and me, of course; but the big one with the roses. Who gave you that?"

Ethel's hesitation was but momentary. "Why—why, Bert sent those," she said. "They're lovely, aren't they?"

"Um-hm. Lovely and expensive, I shouldn't wonder. He was there, in the front row again. You saw him, of course?"

"Yes."

"All alone, wasn't he? Wonder he didn't bring his mother; she wasn't with him last night either, accordin' to Amaziah's tell."

"Mrs. Thornlow doesn't go out much. Bert says the night air down here doesn't agree with her. It is too damp."

"Too bad. I wouldn't have called her delicate, judgin' by her looks, would you?"

"I—I've only seen her at a distance. I've never met her—to speak with, I mean."

"Yes, yes. I remember you said you hadn't."

CHAPTER V

DURING the next fortnight Ethel remained at home for the most part, helping with the housework, and going over to the village twice a week on the family errands. Bert came down to the Point but once during those two weeks. It was Commencement time at his college also and he was supposed to be very busy there. That the young couple corresponded during his absence Lavinia was quite sure. Ethel's "errand" days were usually Wednesdays and Mondays and she always called for the mail.

Once her great-aunt asked a question. "How is Bert gettin' along with his studyin'?" she inquired, casually.

Ethel shook her head. "He is a little worried, I'm afraid. He thinks his chance of going on to the senior class next year isn't so good. It isn't his fault, really. You see he has to be here in Wapatomac with his mother so often that he got behind, missed lectures and things like that. They put him on probation and that doesn't help, of course. But he can go to a tutoring school this summer and catch up. He will, too, I know; he says he is going to."

Lavinia judged that this must have been said in a letter; Ethel had just rowed back from town that noon. This was a Monday and from her trip on Wednesday she returned in what, to her great-aunt's watchful eye, seemed to be a state of repressed excitement. She said nothing during dinner concerning the reasons for that excitement, but, afterward, when she and Lavinia were alone together, she said much.

At the post-office she had met Mrs. Temperance Mayo, the middle-aged matron who owned and operated the Welcome Inn on the Sea Front Road in the village. The Inn was little more than a moderate-sized boarding-house catering to summer vacationists, but it was a Wapatomac institution of long standing and its clientele was a select one. Mrs. Mayo's boarders were, for the most part, families who came regularly in June, after the city schools had closed, and remained until fall. The Inn was a distinctly respectable establishment— Mrs. Mayo spoke of it as "genteel"—and the view of sea and shore from its piazza and windows was unsurpassed. When Gustavus Doane, the postmaster, received letters from Boston or New York or Hartford or Providence asking him to recommend a quiet hotel or boarding-house in which the writers, their wives and children, might spend the summer months, the Welcome Inn was always first on his list.

"No style," wrote Mr. Doane, "but good cooking and nice beds and fine folks. You can't do better than the Welcome, provided they can find room for you there."

During their meeting at the post-office Mrs. Mayo—most of her regular guests addressed her as "Aunt Tempy"—had told Ethel that she was in "a peck of trouble." Maizie Elmore, who had kept the books and attended to the accounts at the Inn for almost nine years, had suddenly decided to marry the "drummer" for the Boston men's outfitting house who visited Wapatomac every month, taking orders for hats, caps, shoes, ties, shirts, bathing suits, etc., in the spring and summer and for fishermen's oilskins, sou'westers, rubber boots, sweaters, and the like in the autumn and winter. According to Mrs. Mayo the drummer had been "chasing after" Maizie for a long while, but she couldn't seem to make up her mind. Now she had made it up and they were to marry within the week. "And the house is half-full of boarders already and *what* in the wide world am I goin' to do?" demanded Aunt Tempy.

Ethel had waited not an instant. She told her what to do. Hire her, Ethel Holt, to fill Miss Elmore's place.

"I know I can do it, Aunt Lavinia," she declared, earnestly. "I like figures and managing and things like that and I studied bookkeeping in school. I was the best in the class, too; you know Miss Baker said I was. I told Aunt Tempy —Mrs. Mayo, I mean—all that and I'm sure she would give me the chance if she didn't feel afraid I was too young. Young! And I'll be eighteen in a few more months. You tell her I'm not too young, Auntie. You talk to her; she'll listen to you. Please! Please!"

Lavinia scarcely knew what to say. She was surprised, of course, although the surprise was not overwhelming. Even before her graduation Ethel had announced that she was going to work as soon as she found a position of the kind she wanted. She was not going to stay around the house down there at Long Cove Point and do nothing but wash dishes and listen to Uncle Am and the gulls. She did not propose to be a burden on her great-aunt either. The latter had worked for her ever since she, Ethel, was a baby and now it was her turn to do something to help.

Lavinia had paid little attention to all this. Her speculations concerning her grand-niece's future had been along other lines, especially of late. But now it was evident that the girl was really in earnest, had gone so far as to apply for the position on her own responsibility. And, as she apparently really meant to enter a business career there was no one Lavinia would have preferred her to work for than Temperance Mayo. The latter was a kindly, shrewd, God-fearing woman; with old-fashioned ideas concerning responsibility for the morals and conduct of those in her employ. But—oh dear!

"If you worked at the Inn," she said, after a moment's reflection, "you'd have to stay there all the time, wouldn't you? I shouldn't like that."

"Oh no, I wouldn't. I would have to be there every morning at half-past eight, but I could come home at five every night. And on Sundays I wouldn't have to work at all. Mrs. Mayo's cousin, Emma Low, is night-clerk and Mrs. Mayo attends to things Sunday forenoon, she told me so. I should be with you almost as much as I used to be in school time. Don't you see, Aunt Lavinia? It couldn't be better, could it?"

Lavinia wasn't sure. She wanted to think it over and said that she did. She did, however, promise to see and talk with Mrs. Mayo the very next day and with that promise Ethel had to be contented for the time.

The next day, however, it was settled. Lavinia once more drove to the village and she and the proprietor of the Welcome Inn spent two hours together in earnest and strictly private conversation. Most of what Mrs. Mayo said was enlightening and some of it was reassuring. Ethel had, in her enthusiasm, exaggerated just a trifle. She would not, at first certainly, be expected to handle all the accounts and bookkeeping for the Inn, as Miss Elmore had done.

"I intend to look out for most of that myself," said the landlady, "at first anyhow. Of course I could hire an experienced bookkeeper and cashier up to Boston but I don't want to do that, if I can help it. The Welcome has always been a Wapatomac place run by Wapatomac folks. What I thought of doing was to get some nice, smart, sensible girl from somewhere right here in town and break her in. She'd have to be somebody I knew first-rate and whose folks I knew. Well, your Ethel is that kind. Matter of fact, she's one of the ones I had had in mind. You needn't worry about her, Lavinia; I'll look after her same as if she was my own."

Mrs. Badger nodded. "I know you will, Tempy," she said. "That part doesn't worry me any. But—well, she's just a girl and, if I do say so, a nice-lookin' girl and, in a boardin'-house full of other young folks, some of 'em with plenty of money to spend and some of 'em young fellows, I—well, I wouldn't want her to get wrong notions and too high-falutin' ideas. She—"

Mrs. Mayo broke in here. "If you're afraid she'll get to runnin' around with my boarders," she declared, "you needn't be. This job of hers will be only a summer job—that is, it will be unless I change my plans—and I'll see that she's kept busy day times. Of course, after she leaves here at five o'clock I won't have anything to say. Her time'll be her own then. But, so far as that concerns, I take it for granted that you would see she came home right away."

"I certainly should," promptly.

"Yes, knowing you, I don't doubt it. And, after all, she'll have less time to be cruising 'round with the young fellows than she had when she was in high school."

"Meanin' that she used to cruise with 'em?"

"Oh, no, no! Not more than any healthy, lively girl her age does. She could have beaux enough if she wanted 'em, but I judge she's pretty choosy. Of course, just now I understand that that young Thornlow is tagging after her a good deal, but he's got an automobile and I guess likely that is full as much of an attraction as he is, himself. All the girls are crazy to ride in that thing. They call Ethel lucky."

Lavinia did not comment on the luck.

"But she's so young to go to work," she observed, with a shake of the head.

"So much the better for me. She won't be skipping off to get married—not for a few years, anyhow."

"I hope not," with involuntary fervor. "Well, Tempy, I believe I'll let her try it. She wants to awfully and—you'll look out for her, won't you?"

"I give you my word I'll watch her and take care of her same as I was her mother. If she comes along with the work all right there'll be a real good chance for her in time. I'm getting older and I'll need somebody to take the care off my shoulders."

"There, there! For the land sakes don't talk about gettin' old, or I'll begin to feel that way myself."

The salary was not large, but it was quite as much as Lavinia expected. When she reached home that afternoon she informed her grand-niece that she might accept Mrs. Mayo's offer and one member of the family at the lighthouse was happy and excited. Lavinia pretended to be, but Amaziah made little or no pretensions in that direction. Amaziah was disgruntled.

"I don't see no sense in it," he grumbled, when he and his aunt were alone. "I cal'lated when Ethel finished up school, that she'd be down here along with us, keepin' us comp'ny and—well, helpin' out with the work."

"What work?" demanded Mrs. Badger, sharply.

"Oh, the work 'round the house; she could help you with that. Yes, and she could help 'tend light for me sometimes, when I have to go up to town on business or somethin'."

"'Or somethin'.' I'm glad you put that in. Well, I don't need any help around the house and as for you—I'm afraid you'll have to slave along same as you've been doin'. It's tough on you, I know; you've got so you can't eat more than three meals a day with somethin' to stay your stomach in between. Oh well, you'll last a spell on that if you're careful."

"Don't make no difference. The whole thing is foolish anyhow. Ethel's the prettiest girl there is in this town and now you're cal'latin' to shut her up astern of a desk in a boardin'-house. How do you figure Bert Thornlow is goin' to take her out ridin' in his automobile if she's jailed there in that Welcome Inn place?"

"I don't know as I have figured it. Maybe it isn't so dreadful important if he doesn't."

"Eh? What kind of talk's that? Why, that young fellow

is dead gone on Ethel—anybody can see he is. And look at the money he's got—or his mother's got; it's the same thing. Suppose he should marry her? Eh? Did you ever think of that?"

"No, and I'm not likely to. For a boy to marry his mother isn't—"

"His mother! Don't be so ridiculous! I mean suppose him and Ethel should marry? *That* would be somethin' to think about, I guess likely."

Lavinia turned on him. "Oh, get out!" she snapped. "If you say another word I don't know what I'll do to you. Go, this minute."

Amaziah went, but he said his final word on the threshold of the kitchen door.

"You might think of me, once in a while," he protested. "I've been hopin' to get a ride in that car myself some of these days. Now I bet you I never get the chance."

Ethel's business career began the first of the following week. At the end of that week she declared that she liked the work very much. Every one was nice to her, Mrs. Mayo had told her that she was doing very well and she, herself, believed she was learning rapidly. Of course she was going to keep on! Why not?

On pleasant days she rowed to and from the village. In inclement weather Amaziah or her great-aunt took her over in the buggy and called for her at five in the afternoon. Occasionally Bert Thornlow begged permission to bring her down in his car and sometimes that permission was granted by Lavinia.

The latter had pursued her policy of watchful waiting in regard to the friendship between the girl and Thornlow. She had decided—drawing upon her fund of experience and her common sense—that to offer any strenuous objections to the intimacy between the young people would be a great mistake.

In the first place there was no good reason why the two should not be friends, at least no reason which Ethel would grasp or appreciate. In the second place, to play the stern guardian and order Bert from the premises would be to make him, in the girl's eyes, a martyr; and martyrdom is romantic. Far better that they should meet openly than to meet secretly, better and much safer. And the summer season would end early in September, the Thornlow cottage would be closed and its inmates leave Wapatomac.

So Lavinia, although as certain as ever that the idea of a serious love affair between her grand-niece and the only son of wealthy Mrs. Thornlow would be a calamity destined to end in heartbreak and sorrow, made no objections to Bert's calling at the Point cottage, nor to the rides in the automobile. She made it a point to be gracious to the young fellow whenever he came, to invite him to supper or to a Sunday dinner, and to lead him on to speak frankly about himself and his personal concerns.

She could not help liking him. His manners were charming, he was full of fun and he enjoyed, or appeared to enjoy what, to him, must have seemed crude and rough in the life at the lightkeeper's cottage. She gathered that the Thornlows had a number of servants, including a butler, and that Mrs. Thornlow paid almost no attention to the management of her household affairs. Nevertheless, Bert ate heartily of Lavinia's cooking, and apparently enjoyed, rather than resented, the hit-or-miss way in which the meals were served. Sometimes he even wiped the supper dishes while Lavinia and Ethel washed them. Amaziah—who in spite of his dismal prophecy concerning his ruined chances, had had two rides in the red automobile—idolized him.

If there was any fault to find, Mrs. Badger found it in Bert's carelessness concerning his own future. He did not seem to have any definite plans as to what he should do when he left college. In fact, the very likely prospect of his having to remain in that college at least a year longer than his classmates appeared to trouble him little. Ethel had spoken of his employing a tutor during the summer; but, so far as Lavinia could learn, none had been employed. As to his career, his life work, he was very casual about that. Oh, he probably would enter the firm of which his father had been the head. Might as well do that as anything else, he supposed.

July had passed and August was half over. One afternoon Lavinia drove to Wapatomac and her errands there delayed her a little longer than she expected. It was five exactly when she pulled Major to a standstill before the door of the Welcome Inn. She had not known before Ethel left that morning that she should make a trip to town that day and so the girl would not be expecting her.

Mrs. Mayo was not behind the desk when she entered the lobby, nor was Ethel. Emma Low, who was there, informed her that Aunt Tempy was lying down in her room "with one of her headaches." As for Ethel—why, Ethel had gone a half-hour earlier than usual that afternoon.

"You see, that young Bert Thornlow dropped in about quarter past four or so and he wanted to know if Ethel couldn't go for a ride with him, 'twas such a lovely day and all like that. Well, I got here early on account of Aunt Tempy's being laid up, and I could attend to things, so I said, 'Of course, go right ahead.' She'll probably be home time you get there, Mrs. Badger, or before."

Lavinia was not altogether pleased. One of the stipulations governing her consent to Ethel's accepting employment at the Inn had been the plain understanding that the girl was to remain there until five every working day.

"Don't do this sort of thing often, does she?" she asked.

"Mercy me, no! She's always on time in the morning and right on the minute for leaving at night. Aunt Tempy sees to that and, most of the time when Ethel's going to row over in the skiff, Tempy has Sim—he's our trunk man, you know—drive her down to the wharf with the horse-'n'-team. But to-day—well, it was all my fault, Mrs. Badger. There wasn't any real reason why she couldn't get away and—oh, I don't know, I've been young myself. What a nice boy that Bert Thornlow is, isn't he? And so polite and attentive. Don't wonder the other girls are jealous of your grand-niece, Mrs. Badger. Don't know's I'm not myself."

Miss Low simpered behind her hand. Lavinia said good-by and walked out.

Ethel was not at home when her great-aunt reached there, nor had she arrived when supper was ready. Lavinia and Amaziah waited nearly an hour and then ate alone. Amaziah talked a great deal. He "cal'lated" that something had happened to the automobile, spoke casually of punctures and "engyne trouble." "But, Bert'll fix it up all right, though," he declared, confidently. "He's a smart one, that young fellow. They'll be here pretty quick, and safe and sound too. Don't fret, Aunt Lavvy; *I* ain't worried a mite."

It was after nine when the missing pair made their appearance. Both were very apologetic, but Bert insisted upon shouldering all the blame. After leaving the Inn they had not headed directly for the Point; it was such a beautiful afternoon that they had gone for a little ride through the woods and then, in a spot several miles from the nearest settlement, the "engine trouble" had really developed.

"It took me until after dark to find out what was the matter and by that time we both realized that you must have given up expecting Ethel at supper. So—"

"So Bert took me to the Sea Side House in Denboro," put in Ethel, hurriedly. "I didn't want him to do it, but he just would. We had supper there, Auntie. We didn't eat much and we hurried home just as fast as we could afterwards.

I hope we haven't worried you. I'm awfully sorry, but—but,"
very earnestly, "you mustn't think it was his fault any more
than it was mine.... No, Bert, I won't let you say it was,
because it really wasn't."

Lavinia replied that it didn't make any difference whose
fault it was, adding that she did not care so long as they
had got home safely at last. Her answer was rather absently
given. It seemed to her that Ethel was more excited and
embarrassed than the mere fact of her late arrival warranted.
She seemed nervous, the color came and went in her cheeks,
and more than once, when her great-aunt turned to look at
her, she did not meet the look, but avoided it. Lavinia did not
cross-question, this was not the time for that, but she was
uneasy in her mind. This thing had gone far enough; she and
the girl must have an understanding before another morning
came.

At any rate she was in no mood to entertain a caller and
she had no idea of permitting him to be entertained under
that roof that evening unless she were present. She brought
matters to a crisis.

"Now, Ethel," she said, "you must go right to bed. You've
got to get up and go to work to-morrow and you need your
sleep. Besides, I'm sure Bert's mother must be wondering
what in the world has become of him. So you two young
folks must say good night. Amaziah, you haven't been nigh
the light since you lit it and that was afore supper. Go and
take a look around this minute."

Amaziah would have demurred, but there was a gleam in
his aunt's eye which discouraged delay, so he said good night
to Thornlow and departed via the kitchen. Bert shook hands
with Mrs. Badger and went out by the side door, into the yard.
Lavinia and Ethel stood in the doorway watching him as he
cranked the car. Just then there came a hail from the rear
of the house.

"Lavvy," called Amaziah, "where's the key? The light's locked up and I can't find the key nowheres. Where'd you put it?"

His aunt turned impatiently. "You had it last," she snapped. "If anybody locked that light 'twas you, yourself. Look on the nail where it belongs."

"I've been lookin' and 'tain't there. Are you sure—"

"Oh, for the dear land sakes! . . . I'm comin'."

She hurried out to the kitchen. The key to the lighthouse had fallen from the nail by the back door where it was supposed to hang and a lamp had to be lighted in order to find it on the floor. When Lavinia came back to the sitting-room Ethel was no longer there. The outer door was ajar and Lavinia looked out through the crack. The engine of the Thornlow automobile was running but the car had not moved. The sitting-room lamp cast a dimmed yellow glow through the drawn window-shade and, standing by the car, Mrs. Badger saw Bert Thornlow and Ethel. Their arms were about each other and his head was bent to hers.

Lavinia watched the tableau only for an instant. Then she cautiously stepped backward, groped for the back of the Salem rocker and sank down upon its cushioned seat. She was sitting there when she heard the car puff out of the yard. Another instant and Ethel came in.

They looked at each other. Slowly the color faded from the girl's face. For a moment it was as white as the clean, fresh apron which her great-aunt had donned before supper that evening. Then the red came pouring back again. Ethel's shoulders squared and her eyes flashed.

"Well?" she said, defiantly. "You saw us, I suppose?"

"Yes, I saw. I wasn't peekin' at you, you mustn't think that. I came in and you wasn't here, so I went to the door and —I saw what was goin' on."

"I don't care. I'm glad. I'm not ashamed of it. I—I'm glad—yes, and proud. I am! I am!"

"Proud of what?"

"Proud of myself. And proud of him. Proud of it all. We—we love each other. I don't care who knows it. I—I'm going to marry him, Aunt Lavinia."

CHAPTER VI

AMAZIAH entered the back door just then; they heard him stumbling about the kitchen. Lavinia rose hastily from her chair. There must not be a scene.

"You'd better go right to your room, Ethel," she said, not unkindly. "Am mustn't know about this, not yet anyhow. Go to your room. I'll come there, after he's gone to bed, and we can have our talk. He mustn't see you; even thick-headed as he is he'd guess somethin' was up. Go, quick."

Ethel turned and hastened to the door leading to the stairs. Her great-aunt heard her sob as the door closed. When Amaziah came into the sitting-room Lavinia was reading the Denboro weekly paper; she had forgotten to put on her "nigh to" spectacles, but Amaziah did not notice that. He announced that he was going to turn in early and his aunt agreed that that was a good idea.

It was nearly an hour later when she knocked lightly on the door of Ethel's bedroom. In response to the whispered "Come in" she entered. The girl was sitting by the little table. She was still dressed and her eyes and cheeks looked as if she had been crying. She was quite calm now, however, and, rising, motioned to the chair from which she had just risen.

"Sit here, Auntie," she said, "I'll sit on the bed."

Lavinia paused long enough to make certain that the door was tightly shut. Then she sat down.

"Now tell me about it," she said.

Her tone was still kind and her manner gentle. Ethel, who had evidently braced herself for a distressing interview, glanced at her in evident surprise; then she looked away.

"There isn't so very much to tell," she said, slowly. "Bert and I are engaged, that's all."

"Yes, but that's somethin'. How long have you been engaged?"

"Just now—to-night. He asked me to marry him and—and I am going to. No one is going to stop us. *No* one."

"Maybe nobody will want to. When are you plannin' to marry?"

"Why—why, I don't know. We haven't talked about that scarcely at all. You see, we—we didn't either of us realize; it was only to-night that we—that we— Oh, please, Auntie, don't you see? How can I tell you about—how could I tell anybody? It just happened."

"Yes, yes, I know. Hum! So he has asked you to marry him?"

"Yes, he did. And—and I said I would. And I shall. I *shall*. No matter what any one says, we—we care for each other and —and that's all. It's settled."

"There, there, dear; I understand. Suppose I hadn't seen —what I did see, you wasn't goin' to keep it a secret from me, was you?"

"Of course I wasn't!" indignantly. "I should have told you right away. To-morrow, probably. I'm not ashamed of it, I'm proud."

"And he's proud, too, I presume likely."

"Of course he is. What do you mean?"

"Why, nothin' special. He ought to be proud, that's sure and sartin. He hasn't told his mother yet, I suppose. No, no; course he hasn't had time."

"He is going to tell her, though. He is going to tell her right away."

"She'll be surprised, won't she?"

"Well? I—I suppose she will; but we can't help that. She must expect he will marry somebody some time."

"Don't doubt she does. I was only thinkin', that's all."

"Thinking—what?"

"Why, that, considerin' that you and she have never met and that, judgin' from what you've told me, she doesn't know about you at all, this news is goin' to be somethin' of a shock to her. He's her only child."

"But she will want him to be happy, won't she? Oh, I know what you are thinking. You think that they have money and —and everything and we have hardly anything—and his father was a banker and mine was captain of a fishing-schooner— you think that will make her ashamed of me and—and hate me. I've thought of it, too, and I told him so, but he says that makes no difference at all. He doesn't care who or what my father was—"

"Here, here!" sharply. "Your father was as fine a man as ever walked. You, nor all the Thornlows in creation needn't be ashamed of him."

"I'm not ashamed of him; neither is Bert. I'm only saying this to show you how he feels. He doesn't care about families and money and all that. It is about me he cares and for me. And I care for him. It's just us two; no one else matters at all."

Lavinia sighed. "I guess likely you both think that's true," she said, with a shake of the head.

"It *is* true. Of course it is." Then, with a sudden flash of contrition, "Oh, Auntie, please don't think I'm selfish. Don't think I don't care about you. I do, you know I do. Next to— to him, I love you better than any one in the world. I just wanted you to understand—"

"Sshh, sshh, child! I do understand."

"But I want you to be happy about it."

"I shall be happy if you are. Now we won't talk much more to-night. It's awful late and you must get your sleep."

"Sleep! Why, you don't think I can sleep now? To-night? Why, I'm so—so excited and happy that I—"

"Yes, yes, course you are. But you must try to sleep, anyhow. Just let me ask you one or two questions and then we'll put the rest off until to-morrow. You haven't planned anything about gettin' married, you say?"

"No, not a thing. It won't be for a good while, of course. Bert must finish college—he says he supposes he'll have to—and then—then he will go into business, I suppose; though that we didn't even mention."

"No," drily, "you had other things to talk about, I don't doubt. When will he tell his mother?"

"Why, to-night, perhaps. To-morrow, anyhow. He promised me he would."

"Did he make that promise on his own hook or did you ask him to make it?"

"Why—why, I think I asked him; but what difference does that make?"

"Not any, I hope. Well, dearie, now you take off your things and go to bed. Oh, one more thing. You're not goin' to tell all hands about your engagement right off, are you? Seems to me I wouldn't, 'specially as you don't cal'late to marry for quite a while. You know Wapatomac. There'd be a lot of talk and questions to answer and all that, don't you think?"

"Yes. Bert said that himself. He thinks we had better keep it a secret, tell no one but you and his mother for the present. I don't believe I'd better tell even Uncle Am, do you?"

"I should say not!" with decisive emphasis. "Might as well paint it on the broadside of the lighthouse. No, no, don't tell Amaziah. We'll have another talk before you go to work in the mornin'. Now, good night."

She crossed, stooped, and kissed the girl tenderly. Ethel sprang up, threw her arms about the withered neck and hugged her.

"Oh, Auntie," she cried, her voice breaking, "you're such a dear. You've been so wonderful. I—I was afraid you—you might not like it, might think I was selfish and—and—"

"Sshh—sshh!"

"And I sha'n't have to leave you yet, shall I? Not for—for a long while."

"I hope not."

"And you don't mind because I'm happy, do you?"

Lavinia patted her head. "So long as you are happy and I know you're goin' to be for the rest of your life, I shall be satisfied," she declared, and hurried from the room.

The morning talk was very brief. Amaziah was on hand and, of course, nothing concerning the all-important subject could be said in his hearing. It was evident that Ethel, in spite of her great-aunt's counsel to try for sleep, had been awake most of the night and Lavinia, herself, although she said nothing about it, had scarcely closed her eyes. It bade fair to be a beautiful day and the girl crossed the harbor in the skiff. Lavinia watched her as she rowed away, her lithe young body swinging back and forth with the oars and her hair blowing in the light breeze. She was radiantly happy; even Amaziah noticed the sparkle in her eyes and the color in her cheeks and told her that she looked as she had had money willed to her.

"If that Thornlow boy sees you this mornin'," he chuckled, "he'll be for takin' you automobile ridin' again and spendin' his cash for another hotel dinner. Better keep out of his sight unless you both want to get dyspepsy from over-eatin'."

If he had seen the expression in his aunt's eyes when she heard this brilliant effort he might have been less satisfied with his own wit. He did not see it, however, and meandered out to the lighthouse, pipe in mouth.

All that forenoon Lavinia worked hard. She swept and dusted and baked, in the hope that hard work might keep her from thinking. She had thought much since the previous evening and her thinking had brought her to no decision whatever. What she had considered a remote possibility was now a present reality and what her next move should be she had no practical idea. An explosion was coming, she was sure of that, but whether it was her duty to hasten its coming or to wait until the powder was ignited by some one else she could not make up her mind.

If Bert, faithful to his promise, had already told his mother of the "engagement" the explosion had already occurred and she, Lavinia, might expect to hear the echoes at any moment. If, on the other hand, he had lacked the courage to face the crisis, then matters would drift on as they were. They could not—and, she determined should not—be permitted to drift long, for Wapatomac gossip, although good-humored so far, was already linking Ethel's name with that of young Thornlow. That gossip, if it continued, might become malicious. For Ethel's sake some sort of understanding, either for peace or war, must be reached without delay.

At about three o'clock that afternoon she was in the sitting-room, trying hard to keep her mind upon the jersey she was knitting for Ethel when she heard the rattle of wheels and a masculine voice commanding "Whoa!" She dropped her knitting and ran to the window. A spirited black horse attached to a smart surrey was standing by the gate in the white picket-fence bordering the Government property upon which the lighthouse and keeper's cottage stood and a driver, neatly capped and gloved, was assisting a lady to alight. Lavinia recognized the lady as Mrs. Thornlow.

Lavinia's first thought was one of thankfulness. Amaziah had gone to dig clams on a flat a mile or so distant and he would not be on hand to interfere and ask questions, which was a mercy. She glanced about the room to make sure that everything was neat and in its place and then walked to the door. As she reached it a knock sounded upon the panel.

Lavinia opened the door.

"Good afternoon, Mrs.—er—Badger, isn't it?" said Mrs. Thornlow. "Yes, of course it is. How do you do?"

Her smile was gracious. Lavinia, who had expected to be greeted by almost anything but a smile, was momentarily taken aback.

"Why, how d'ye do, Mrs. Thornlow?" she stammered. "Won't you come in?"

"Thank you." She followed Lavinia into the sitting-room. In obedience to the request that she take off her things and sit down she threw open the light wrap she was wearing and sat in the Salem rocker. Lavinia took one of the straight-backed chairs with the haircloth seat. They looked at each other. Of the two the caller was much the more at ease.

"Well, you see," she said, still smiling, "I have accepted your invitation. You asked me to drop in on you some day when I was out driving, you remember? And here I am."

Lavinia murmured that she was real glad to see her, adding that it was a nice day.

There was a moment of silence, each apparently waiting for the other to speak. Mrs. Thornlow glanced about the room, at the flowered wall-paper, at the ingrain carpet, at the pictures— colored prints and cheaply framed engravings for the most part—on the walls, at the ship model on the mantelpiece.

"What a cozy little place you have here," she observed. "And so very neat and trim. Your—er—niece helps you with the house-keeping, I suppose? Let me see, what is her name?"

"Her name is Ethel. Ethel Holt. She's my grand-niece. Her father was my nephew."

"I see, I see. Bert told me that, I believe. Yes, he did, of course. . . . Yes."

Another brief pause. Lavinia said nothing. Again it was Mrs. Thornlow who broke the silence. She laughed lightly.

"This is perfectly ridiculous, Mrs. Badger, isn't it?" she said.

"Here we are, each of us waiting for the other to mention the all-important subject. You know my real reason for calling on you to-day. Of course you do."

Lavinia smiled for the first time. "Why, maybe I might make a good guess at it," she admitted.

"I'm sure you could. I suppose your—er—grand-niece has told you, just as my son has told me. And he was *so* serious about it, poor child. It was all I could do to keep a straight face and yet if I had laughed his heart would have been broken. Boys and girls have *no* sense of humor, positively none."

She shook her head whimsically.

"Probably they don't see the funny side of it," suggested Lavinia. "Maybe they think there isn't any."

"I know, I know. Bert was as tragical as—as King Lear. He declares that he and this girl are head over heels in love with each other, that they are engaged, and that they are going to marry in spite of gods and men—and women, too, I suppose, including you and me, Mrs. Badger. Oh, dear, it is all *so* absurd."

Another rueful headshake. Lavinia's tenseness was relaxing. In a way her caller's attitude was a relief. She had expected a storm and this was, so far at least, only a light breeze. And one doubt which had troubled her mind was a doubt no longer. Bert had kept his promise and had told his mother; he had not shirked the issue. She gave him a good mark for that.

Mrs. Thornlow was watching her and now she spoke again.

"I take it for granted that you see the absurdity as I do, Mrs. Badger," she said, quickly.

"Why, yes, ma'am, in a way I suppose I do. They're young, both of 'em, Ethel especially. She's only just past seventeen."

"So I managed to drag from Bert during our happy little interview this morning."

"Oh, it was this morning he told you, not last night?"

"Yes. I could see that he was nervous and when I suggested that he and I take a short trip to the mountains together in the near future he became so rebellious that I suspected something was behind it all and I kept at him until I learned the truth. At first I was amused, then I was on the verge of losing my temper and then—well, then I realized that that wouldn't do at all. I must temporize, be tactful and diplomatic. You understand what I mean?"

"Shouldn't wonder if I did."

"Of course you must. And that is why I came here—to you. I took it for granted that you would see the impossibility of the situation as I did and would agree that we must have a plain, sensible discussion together. I infer from what Bert tells me, that this girl is your—ward, I suppose it is called, that she is an orphan and had been in your charge since her parents died. You are responsible for her welfare as I am for that of my son's."

"That's so, all of it. You came to me first, then? You haven't talked with Ethel?"

"No. Certainly not. Good heavens, Mrs. Badger, she is a child. They are both mere children. You and I are, at least, old enough to have some practical common sense. We don't want this nonsense to be known and talked about outside our families. For my part, I don't wish to be the laughing stock of my friends."

"But why should you be?"

"Why should I be! Surely it is ridiculous enough to make any one laugh."

"Well now, is it? Ethel is a good girl and a smart girl, if I do say so. There is nothin' comical about her that I know of. As for your boy—why, he's no funnier than other young fellows his age, is he? Doesn't seem so to me. And, as I said a minute ago, they don't, either of 'em, think it's a joke, not by any means."

Mrs. Thornlow stiffened slightly and leaned back in her chair.

"Well, really, Mrs. Badger!" she exclaimed.

Lavinia continued: "Mrs. Thornlow," she said, "you've never seen Ethel, to know her, I mean?"

"No."

"You've never met her to talk with?"

"I have never had that pleasure," sweetly.

"It might not be a pleasure to you just now, but a good many folks seem to find it one. You don't even know what she looks like. Let me show you?"

She left the sitting-room and returned almost immediately with a photograph which she handed to her caller.

"That's her graduation picture," she said. "All the class had theirs taken when they got through high school. I shouldn't be surprised if your son had one of his own, even though he hasn't shown it to you yet."

Mrs. Thornlow was looking at the photograph. She frowned slightly.

"She's really quite pretty," she admitted. "Yes. . . . Yes, quite pretty. I can see why Bert might be attracted—at his age."

"He is attracted, you can be sure of that."

"Oh, I am, he made that perfectly plain. But, Mrs. Badger, good looks and—er—all the rest of it aren't all that make for a suitable marriage, now are they? I have no doubt your niece is a good girl and I can see that she is a very pretty girl, but— oh, well, we are not children, you and I. Now, of course, I can understand that from—er—Ethel's viewpoint marriage to my son must seem a very wonderful thing. She—"

"Wait. Just what would be so 'specially wonderful about it?"

"What!" Mrs. Thornlow was losing her suave urbanity. The tone of her next remark was different from that of those preceding it. "Mrs. Badger," she said coldly, "I may have been under a misapprehension so far in this talk of ours. I sincerely hope not, but it is possible. I came to you with the idea that you, as a sane common-sense person would not sanction this ridiculous engagement and that you would consider the very idea of a marriage between those two—er—infants as utterly preposterous. Of course, if you do not feel that way, if you approve it—why, then I may as well go at once."

She was rising from the rocker but Lavinia motioned her to remain seated.

"Don't hurry, Mrs. Thornlow," she urged. "Seems to me we ought to talk a spell longer. I don't like this engagement much, if any, more than you do."

"Oh, good! I was beginning to— Well, I'm delighted to hear it."

"I don't like it. I feel pretty certain that for Ethel to marry your boy would turn out to be a big mistake on her part."

"On *her* part!"

"Now, please. I say on her part because, naturally, it is her and her happiness I'm most interested in. I don't know as I see anything so ridiculous about the notion of two young people fallin' in love with each other—it's happened a few billion times before and will keep on happenin', I guess; but I do believe there is more to a happy, lastin' marriage than fallin' in love in a hurry and runnin' to the minister in the same hurry. I know our Ethel, what she is, what she's been used to and what she would expect of a husband. I haven't had the chance to know your son the way you have, but I can imagine what he's been used to. Unless I'm more mistaken than I think I am he's always had what he wanted and got tired of it pretty soon afterwards. Then he started in wantin' somethin' else, somethin' new. I shouldn't want him to get tired of his wife, not if Ethel was that wife, I shouldn't. To speak out real plain—and I don't see much sense in you and me speakin' any other way about this business—your Bert isn't the kind of man I want my girl to marry."

Mrs. Thornlow, whatever she might have expected, had obviously not expected this. She listened to this long speech, at first with astonishment, then with growing indignation. The last trace of her suave condescension vanished. She sprang to her feet, her ample bosom heaving.

"Why!" she gasped. "Why, I never in my life heard such outrageous statements from any one. Do you realize who we are? Do you realize that my husband was—"

"Now, now, please. I didn't mean to say anything to hurt your feelin's. Probably I didn't smooth it down enough; I never was much for soft-soap. But I do want you to understand that you and I are agreed on the main point, even if we come to the agreement from opposite sides. You don't want your boy to marry Ethel and I don't want her to marry him. You said yourself that you and I were practical, common-sense women. All right, then why not talk common sense? You don't like this engagement and neither do I. The next question, seems to me, is what are we goin' to do about it?"

Her caller was still standing, her plump face crimson. She was apparently struggling with her emotions.

"That is the question, isn't it?" Lavinia repeated. "What are we goin' to do? Have you got any idea?"

"I—I—well, really, I— Oh, well," with a shrug, "I presume I should realize—and make allowances . . . Mrs. Badger, it is at least gratifying to know that you are not in favor of this piece of idiocy. As to your question: have you anything to suggest?"

"Nothin' much, I'm afraid. Have you?"

"No. Except that I shall stop it, break it off at once."

"But how? If you put your foot down and say no, do you think that Bert won't put his down and keep on sayin' yes? I think that's just what he'll do, if there's any man in him at all. If I tell Ethel she mustn't see Bert again do you cal'late she won't see him? She'll see him more than ever. I was young once and I know how young folks behave when they are in love, or think they are. The surest way to make those two run off and get married is to tell 'em to keep away from each other. Unless you and I want to wake up some mornin' and find you've got a daughter-in-law and I've got a grand-nephew by marriage we've got to step light and go easy. You see that, Mrs. Thornlow, now don't you?"

"Oh—yes," with angry impatience. "I suppose I do. Bert is just like his father, as selfish and headstrong as a—as a pig. But I won't let him throw his life away. I *won't!*"

"And Ethel shan't spoil hers, if I can help it. . . . Now don't get mad; we're together so far and we both want to get to the same place in the end, so let's talk it out a little more. I've been tryin' to think what to do; all night I've been thinkin' and I woke up with the same answer I took to bed with me. And that is, do nothin' for a while."

"Nothing! Well, *I* shall do something, be sure of that."

"Shouldn't, if I was you. Whatever either of us did now would be pretty sure to upset the fryin'-pan. I say wait. The young folks are willin' to keep this engagement of theirs quiet for a while, anyhow. We can tell 'em it is a good idea to do that and I think they'll agree. Let 'em keep comp'ny together, in reason, for the rest of the summer. Then you'll go away from Wapatomac and Bert'll go back to college."

"I don't know that he will—to that college, at any rate. It is too near to—what I mean for him to keep away from."

"Never mind, he'll go somewhere. They'll be separated for a good long spell. That may make 'em only more anxious to get together again or it may work the other way. They may, either or both of 'em, see somebody else they like better. In that case this snarl of ours will untangle itself. If it doesn't—why then—"

"Then what?"

"Why, then they will go through with it, I presume likely.

Get married and live happy forever afterwards—perhaps. Get married, anyway."

Mrs. Thornlow's lips tightened. "That's the best you have to offer, is it?" she observed.

"About all there is to offer, seems to me. Can you think of anything better? Anything less likely to bring on what we're tryin' to head off?"

It was a direct question, but the lady to whom it was addressed seemed to find it difficult to answer. She turned toward the door, but paused and turned again to look fixedly at the questioner.

"I wish I could be sure," she said, slowly. "It is too impossible, I can't believe it."

"What is it you can't believe? That I really am as set against my girl marryin' your boy as I say I am? You think I'm makin' believe."

"Well—well, of course—"

"That's it, isn't it?"

"Why, yes," with a toss of the head, "to be perfectly frank, it is. I can't believe you are in earnest."

"Then you had better try to believe it. I know what you expected when you came here. You expected to find us dancin' fandangos and hoistin' flags. Well, we're not; I'm not, anyhow. If I hoisted anything it would be a distress signal. . . . There, there, Mrs. Thornlow, I guess maybe we've both of us said enough. I've managed to keep my temper so far in this talk of ours and it would be a pity to lose it at the end. I am much obliged to you for callin' but I must tell you that, if you hadn't come to me, I should have come to you, and what I've said here in this house I should have said there in yours. And I hope, for all our sakes, you'll think things over and come to the same conclusion I have and that is, wait and be careful. Good afternoon, ma'am."

Mrs. Thornlow made no further remark, but the curtness of

her "Good afternoon" was expressive of her feelings. Lavinia followed her to the door. The uniformed driver was standing by the carriage and beside him and in conversation with him was Amaziah, a barefooted, bare-armed Amaziah, with a clam hoe in one hand and a bucket of clams in the other.

Mrs. Thornlow cast one glance at him and passed by, drawing her skirts carefully away from contact with the clam bucket. Amaziah dropped the bucket and removed his ancient straw hat.

"How d'ye do, Mrs. Thornlow?" he said, smiling cheerfully. "I've just been talkin' with your man here and he says you've been callin' on my aunt. Sorry I wasn't to home; I'd like to have showed you over the lighthouse. A good many summer folks come down here to see it; they seem to think it's kind of interestin'. Your son now, I've showed it to him half a dozen times."

Mrs. Thornlow did not deign to notice him. The driver opened the carriage door and assisted her to the rear seat. The driver climbed to his own seat, and the equipage moved away. Amaziah gazed after it.

"My, she's a fine-lookin' woman, ain't she," was his tribute. "Must be hard of hearin' though; never heard me when I spoke to her. That hired man of hers and me had quite a talk. He's a real sociable fellow. I told him who I was; said I felt pretty well acquainted with his folks 'count of seein' so much of Bert when he came down here every other day or so to see my niece.... Eh? What did you say, Aunt Lavvy?"

Lavinia drew a long breath. "If I said what I feel like sayin' to you just now," she declared, "I should be ashamed to hear it, myself."

She went into the house and closed the door behind her.

CHAPTER VII

FOR another week nothing of importance happened. Bert Thornlow visited the Point twice and, on the following Sunday, he and Ethel went for an automobile ride, returning— Lavinia had insisted upon the time of return before giving her consent to the excursion—in time for supper. Bert was, as always, agreeable and companionable with the older people, Amaziah was deferentially polite to the young man, Ethel was blissfully happy and Lavinia was, outwardly, cheerful.

Inwardly, however, she was anything but that. The explosion she had dreaded had not taken place, but she felt certain that it had been only postponed. The interview with Mrs. Thornlow had not been as stormy as she expected it would be, but it had ended at about the place where it began. She congratulated herself upon having, at least, made her own feelings and attitude perfectly plain to the lady, but she was certain that the latter's attitude had not changed one iota. Mrs. Charles Thornlow was determined that her son should not marry Ethel Holt and Lavinia was far from confident that she would follow the advice to wait and be careful. Mrs. Thornlow, she was sure, was not accustomed to waiting. She wanted what she wanted when she wanted it. She wanted this "ridiculous engagement" broken off at once and, unless Lavinia's judgment of character was entirely at fault, she would attempt some drastic means of terminating it at any moment.

But Bert Thornlow, who was like his mother in other respects than facial resemblance, was accustomed to having what he wanted when *he* wanted it. An open quarrel between mother and son might drive the young people to an elopement, a runaway marriage. Bert could, in Ethel's opinion, do nothing wrong. Ethel worshiped him. She was very fond of her great-aunt, but young love was young love. As day after day passed and nothing untoward happened, Lavinia's apprehension increased rather than lessened.

She had again tactfully approached the girl on the subject of keeping the engagement a secret for the present and was relieved to find that both she and Bert were still of the opinion that this was the best thing to do.

"It will only make a lot of talk, Auntie, just as you said, and, after all, it is no one's business but ours—and yours and Mrs. Thornlow's, of course. Tell me again, Auntie: was she really all right about it? She wasn't dreadfully cross or—or hurt—or anything like that?"

She knew of Mrs. Thornlow's call, of course. Amaziah had talked of nothing else during supper that evening. As soon as she and her great-aunt were alone together she had demanded to be told all about it, just what was said, how it was said and who said it. Lavinia had given her a diplomatically edited account of the interview. Mrs. Thornlow was not happy, but naturally she would not be; Bert was her only child, and she idolized him.

"Wait till you have a boy or girl of your own, young woman, and then have some one come along and plan to take him or her away from you. You won't feel like givin' three cheers, I can promise you that."

"I know, I know. It makes me feel almost wicked. But we're not going to marry for a good while, not for a whole year, at least."

"A year! I should think not. Why, he won't be out of college by that time."

"I know. Well, perhaps it will be two years, I suppose it will. Auntie, don't you think it is odd that his mother hasn't called to see me, or asked me to come and see her? I do. Of course if she hated me, as I was afraid she would when she heard, I could understand her never wanting to see me; but Bert says she doesn't hate me at all. He says she is what he calls very nice about our engagement."

"Did he tell you that?"

"Why, yes. He says," she hesitated momentarily, "he says he is afraid she doesn't take the engagement very seriously, acts sometimes almost as if it were a joke, but he says that is just her way. It is a queer way though and I don't like it. It isn't a joke for Bert and me; it is the most—most— Oh well, I can't talk even to you about that."

She caught her breath and looked away. Lavinia eyed her pityingly.

"Why doesn't Bert take you to see her?" she suggested. "I should think he would—if he's got any spunk." The last half of the sentence slipped out involuntarily. Ethel turned on her like a flash.

"Spunk!" she repeated, fiercely. "The idea! What do you mean by that, Aunt Lavinia? Do you mean that he is ashamed of me? Well, he isn't."

"Course he isn't. I never meant any such thing."

"He isn't, you can be sure of that. And he is going to take me to their house to meet her very soon. He has said so over and over again. He is just waiting until—well, until she is—is a little used to the idea of our being engaged, that's all. He may take me there to-morrow afternoon, after I am through work; he said perhaps he might."

He did not, however, and, before another week ended, the explosion came. It was not the sort of explosion Lavinia had expected and its results were absolutely contrary to those she had dreamed. Instead of driving the lovers into an elopement it separated them for a time, at least.

Ethel came home from the Inn one afternoon looking very

downcast and troubled. Her great-aunt, who was watching her more closely than ever these days, asked the reason.

"Somethin's wrong with you, child," she declared. "I can see it and so could anybody with eyes in their head. Ain't workin' yourself sick over Tempy Mayo's accounts, are you?"

"No, no," impatiently. "Of course I'm not."

"But somethin's the trouble. Oh!" as the thought came to her. "You and Bert haven't had a squabble, have you?"

"No," indignantly. "We don't squabble. His mother is sick, that's all, and it worries him. It worries both of us."

"Sick? You don't say! She didn't look sick—no, nor act sick when she was here to see me. Taken sudden, was she?"

"No-o. That is, I don't think she was. Bert says the climate here at Wapatomac hasn't agreed with her since she came. It is the sea dampness, or something. And now she is ever so much worse. She is in bed most of the time and—and the doctor says she ought to go away, to the mountains, or out West where the air is drier."

"I see. Too bad. Is she going?"

"I—I'm afraid so."

"And Bert is going with her, I suppose. . . . I see. . . . Yes, yes."

There was something in the tone which caused Ethel to glance at her suspiciously, but the shrewd old face was merely kindly sympathetic and solicitous, so the girl's momentary suspicion vanished.

"He'll have to go, if she does," she blurted, chokingly. "She is sick and—and she is his mother. He couldn't let her go away off there alone."

"Sartin sure he couldn't."

"But he doesn't want to go," miserably. "He feels terribly about it."

"I can understand that. It's really settled that they're going?"

"No-o, not quite, but I'm afraid it will be.... Oh, Auntie, I—"

She rose from the chair in which she had been sitting and hastened up the stairs to her own room. She was sobbing as she went. Her great-aunt rose to follow her but then, after a moment's hesitation, reseated herself in the Salem rocker. So this was Mrs. Thornlow's little scheme, was it? An effective one, too. She was more of a diplomat than Lavinia had credited her with being.

Well, at least here was a temporary easing of the tension. Only temporary possibly, even probably, for if Bert Thornlow was as seriously in love as he professed to be and as Ethel undoubtedly was he would be back before long. If his infatuation was but a light attack then the longer he remained away the better. At any rate this separation would be a test and, therefore, a very good thing for all concerned.

Ethel's wretchedness continued and deepened during the next few days. She came down to breakfast without a smile, ate almost nothing, spoke scarcely at all, and departed to work as if the bookkeeper's chair at the Welcome Inn were the seat of the condemned in the death cell. Amaziah noticed the change in her.

"For Almighty sakes what's the matter with you, girl?" he demanded. "A little spell ago you was flyin' 'round here chipper as a mackerel gull in sand-eel season. Now you look as solemn as if you was waitin' to have a tooth out. You've been workin' too hard up there to the Inn, I shouldn't wonder. If you listen to me you'll ease off. Health's more important than money, that's been my motto all my life and now look at me."

This was at the breakfast table and Lavinia, who was pouring the coffee, put in a word.

"What for?" she asked, tartly.

"Eh? What do you mean? What for what?"

"Why do you want her to look at you?"

"Eh? Why, 'cause I'm healthy, that's why. Past fifty year old and sound as a bell. I don't know's I can remember when I've had to have a doctor."

"I can. 'Twas the night of the Fourth of July two years ago. I can remember what he said, too. When I told him you'd been up town celebratin' all day he said you might have expected fireworks in the evenin'. . . . Now, Ethel, it's time for you to go. You can finish lookin' at your uncle when you come home; he and his health will be on exhibition then same as now."

Mrs. Thornlow and her son, accompanied by the lady's personal maid and a nurse, left Wapatomac on the following Monday. The red motor-car made its final trips to and from Long Cove Point on Sunday afternoon. Bert was solemn and downcast. He and Ethel went for a ride and then returned to the cottage for supper.

Lavinia left the young couple to themselves in the evening, taking pains to keep Amaziah with her in the kitchen until ten o'clock. When that hour struck she rapped on the sitting-room door and, a moment later, opened it and entered, followed by her nephew.

The lovers were sitting at opposite ends of the sofa. Ethel had obviously been crying and Bert looked anything but happy. He shook hands with Mrs. Badger and Amaziah and said good-by to them.

"Only for a little while, though," he declared. "I shall be back just as soon as Mother is settled in a climate that agrees with her and I feel it is safe to leave her. It won't be long, you can bet on that. Take care of—of her," with a motion of his head in Ethel's direction, "won't you, Mrs. Badger?"

Lavinia nodded. "I'll do my best," she assured him. "I've took care of her since she was two years old so I'm more or less used to it. Say good-by to your mother for me, Bert. Tell her," with a suspicion of a smile, "that I don't doubt she'll be lots better away from the salt air and what goes with it."

When he went out to the automobile Ethel accompanied him. Amaziah would have gone with them, but his aunt's quick motion of the hand detained him.

"You stay here," she whispered sharply. "I want to talk to you."

"Aw now, Lavvy! Can't you talk a spell later? This may be the last chance I'll have to look at that car. He's going to have it drove up to Boston to-morrow; told me so himself. I'll be right back."

"No, you won't."

"Yes, I will, too. I love to watch him get it under way. Don't seem to never tire of that, I don't. See you again in a jiffy."

"You'll see me now. Oh, for the land sakes, Am, didn't anybody ever tell you that there are times when two is comp'ny and three is a crowd?"

Amaziah thought it over. "Oh!" he observed, "I see what you mean. You cal'late maybe they'd rather be alone by themselves."

"I did have that notion—yes. Sit down and behave yourself."

Amaziah sat, reluctantly. During the minutes which followed his gaze strayed wistfully toward the drawn shade of the window. Lavinia was knitting steadily.

"Thought you wanted to talk to me," he observed, after a long interval. "You said you did."

"I did. And I have, haven't I?"

"All you said was for me to sit down."

"That was all I wanted to say."

It was at least another quarter of an hour before they heard the roar of the starting motor. Ethel came in a moment later. She did not look at either of the pair in the sitting-room but, her face averted, hurried to the door leading to the stairs.

"Good night," she said, and that was all.

Amaziah gazed after her. "Why, what on earth?" he demanded. "Gone to bed, ain't she? And—and she never took her lamp with her, neither. Sho! I'll take it up to her, myself."

He had risen but his aunt stepped between him and the table with the hand-lamps upon it.

"No, no, you won't," she ordered.

"Why not? That child can't go to bed in the dark, can she?"

"She can, I guess, if she wants to. And if she doesn't want to she'll come after the lamp herself. Now *I'm* goin' to bed and, if you'll take my advice, you'll go too. The fun's over for this evenin'."

"Fun? I ain't seen much fun around here to-night, I tell you that. Of all the glum crowd ever I saw! Why, if Ethel wasn't cryin' when she went past me just now, then I miss my guess. And, fur as that goes, you look as if you was next door to snivelin', yourself."

Lavinia did not answer.

Early the next morning she rapped on the door of Ethel's room. The girl was awake and dressed when she entered.

"Did you sleep any?" asked Lavinia.

"No," miserably, "not much."

"I was afraid you wouldn't. You mustn't make yourself sick, you know. He wouldn't want you to do that."

"I know. But, oh, Auntie—!"

"There, there! It might be worse. He isn't dead and he hasn't run away for good—that is, we'll take it for granted he hasn't."

"What do you mean—take it for granted? He's coming back just as soon as he possibly can. If you think—"

"I don't think anything I shouldn't. I only . . . Why, what's that on your finger?"

Ethel flushed. Then she extended her left hand. On the third finger was a ring; the stone in it was small but it was a diamond.

"He gave it to me last night," said Ethel, proudly. "It—it is lovely, isn't it?"

Lavinia examined the ring. "Indeed it is," she agreed. "Humph! Are you goin' to wear it all the time?"

The girl sighed. "No-o," she admitted, reluctantly. "I wanted to, but—but he thought perhaps I'd better not. So long as we are keeping our engagement a secret he thought my wearing it would only make a lot of talk. So I shall wear it only when I'm by myself—at night, when I'm here in my room. I can look at it then and think about—about what it means."

"Course you can. It means a lot. I had one of my own once and it meant about everything to me—then."

Ethel had paid no attention. She was turning the ring on her finger.

"It means 'always,'" she murmured. "Always, always, always."

Lavinia stopped and kissed her.

"And now I've got to get breakfast," she announced, briskly, her moment of sentimentality over. "You needn't hurry down; 'twon't be ready for quite a while yet."

CHAPTER VIII

BERT'S first letter came the next day. It was written from Boston, where he and his mother were staying overnight. There was another two days later, from Chicago this time. They were at their home in the suburb, but only for a short rest; then they were going further west, possibly to Colorado Springs. Lavinia was told this by Ethel, of course; she was not asked to read the letters, which were very bulky. Others came regularly and were answered with the same regularity. Ethel was still downcast and sad, but she found distraction in her work at the Inn, for which fact Lavinia was thankful. Ethel liked that work and Mrs. Mayo liked her and trusted her with more and more responsibility. She told Lavinia that the girl seemed to have a "regular knack" for managing. "She gets along with the boarders wonderfully. I declare I believe she was cut out for the hotel business."

One morning Lavinia, alone in the cottage, was surprised by a call from Judge Payne. She had seen him several times since the occasion when he had given her the information concerning her inheritance of the shares in the Lost Prospect Mine but he had had nothing further to report concerning them. The estate of Judah Badger, such as it was, had been settled, the tombstone ordered and erected, Lawyer Hawtry's bill of expenses approved and paid. Even the shanty in which Badger had spent the last years of his life had been sold. Hawtry had managed to get seventy-five dollars for it.

Lavinia had had time to recover from the shock and surprise of learning, first that her husband had been living so many years and, second, that he was now dead. The memories of the past which the Colorado letter had revived and which had temporarily disturbed and distressed her she resolutely refused to dwell upon. What had been had been, nothing could change that. His life had ended, his earthly problems, whatever they may have been, were settled. Hers were not—or Ethel's were not, which was the same thing. The girl needed her and so she must keep well, mentally and physically, just as long as she could. As she had told Judge Payne, she could not afford to wear out.

She was in the kitchen, busy with her baking, when the Judge entered the cottage. She had not heard the buggy stop by the gate and so she was surprised when he called to her from the sitting-room.

"Lavinia," he called, "where are you?"

She hastened through the dining-room, wiping her floury hands on her apron.

"Well, for the good land sakes, Philander," she demanded, "where'd you drop from?"

"Drove down to see you," he told her. "Got some news for you."

"News?" she repeated the word sharply. "What do you mean? Nothin' more has happened out West there, has there? No more bills turned up we've got to pay?"

He shook his head.

"Nothing of that sort, Lavinia. This is good news, for a change."

She took off her glasses, wiped them on the corner of her apron, put them on again and eyed him keenly.

"I want to know!" she exclaimed. "Humph! What kind of good news? Nobody else willed me a silver mine with no silver in it and bills with no money to pay 'em, I hope. Much more good news of that kind and I'd land in the poor-house."

Payne laughed. "I wouldn't make fun of that mine, if I

were you, Lavinia," he said. "It may be that the Lost Prospect isn't all lost."

"Why—why, my soul and body, Philander Payne, you don't mean you've been able to sell those shares for somethin', after all?"

"No. I haven't sold them."

"That doesn't astonish me to death. But what—"

"Look here, Lavinia, aren't you going to ask me to sit down? Or don't people take time to sit down here at Long Cove Point?"

"Some of 'em do. Amaziah's sittin' down out back of the light this minute. And sound asleep, too, or he'd have heard you drive up.... There, there, I'm ashamed of my bad manners. Course you'll sit down. Only you'll have to do it out in the kitchen, for I've got gingerbread in the oven and I can't leave it a minute longer. Come right along—that is, unless you're too high-toned to sit in a wooden chair."

She led the way to the kitchen and he followed. She pulled forward a chair and then rushed to the rescue of the gingerbread.

"Don't mind my flyin' around," she ordered. "Go ahead with your good news. I can stand the shock just as well when I'm workin'."

Judge Payne took a packet of papers from his pocket.

"Lavinia," he began, "you have fifteen thousand shares of this Lost Prospect Mining Company. You wanted me to find out if it could be sold for some price or other. Well, as you know, it couldn't."

"You haven't cruised way down here to tell me that, I don't believe. Have you found out that you can give it away? Is that your good news?"

"No, not exactly. I couldn't sell it for you then, but I think I could now, if you still want to sell it."

"*If* I do! Philander **Payne, don't talk** so ridiculous!"

"To my mind the ridiculous thing would be to sell. My advice, and my Boston broker's advice, is to hang on and hang on tight. Something has happened to the Lost Prospect Mine."

"Happened?" She was taking the pan of gingerbread from the oven. "What do you mean—happened to it? Hasn't caved in, has it?"

"Lavinia, put down that pan and pay attention. This is serious, this means something to you now and may mean a lot more. Sit down!"

She placed the pan of gingerbread carefully on the table and sat, reluctantly.

"Well," she observed, "I suppose likely this is the easiest way to get rid of you. You would come on bakin' mornin'. You lawyers just love to make trouble for folks, that's how you get your livin'.... Oh, all right, all right, I'm through. Now *you* talk."

He went on to explain. The Lost Prospect Company had holdings which covered considerable territory and which might or might not be valuable provided it had sufficient capital to work them. It did not possess that capital. A shaft had been sunk and some machinery installed, but little mining had been done. Adjoining the holdings of the Lost Prospect, however, were those of the Occidental Mines, a good-sized, fairly prosperous corporation, actually at work, and the stock of which paid occasional small dividends.

"Now here is the good news," he went on. "Perhaps you may remember that, in one of our first talks about this business, I told you that there was one hint of promise for the future which might amount to something or might not. My Boston brokers have been keeping in touch with the matter and now they report that it looks as if the promise was in the way of becoming a good deal more than a hint. The Occidental wants to take over the Lost Prospect holdings. Probably their engineers are convinced that the veins their company is working extend through their neighbor's property and that that property should be acquired. So they have made this proposition: For each share of Lost Prospect stock they offer one-third of a share of Occidental Mines. That is, for your fifteen thousand Lost Prospect you will be given five thousand Occidental. Considering everything, a very liberal offer and one which, it seems to me, goes a long way toward proving that the Occidental crowd consider the Lost Prospect holdings valuable. Of course the deal isn't made yet, the Lost Prospect stockholders—including you—will have to vote on it, but I don't doubt the majority will be glad to accept. That's the situation as it stands now and that's what I came to tell you, Lavinia."

Lavinia had been listening intently and now she was ready with a question.

"You say this Accidental stock—or whatever it is—is paying dividends. Then it must be worth something in real money —to sell, I mean. Is it?"

"Yes, it is. The last sale, so my brokers write me, was ninety-five."

"Ninety-five! Not ninety-five *dollars?*"

"Hardly. Ninety-five cents, of course. That is the price now; but if—"

"Stop right where you are, Philander Payne. Do you mean to tell me that, if those Accidental folks do take over this— this No Prospect stuff of mine I'd get new stock that I could sell—really sell—for—for close to five thousand dollars?"

"Yes. Perhaps a little more than that. But if I were you—"

"No buts about it. If I get it you sell it and sell it right off. Five thousand dollars! And Judah Badger actually speculated in somethin' that was worth all that money! Oh, I don't believe it, Philander! It can't be true. When I was little they learned me to believe in the miracles in the Bible, but this ain't in the Bible. This is one of those sleight-of-hand tricks you see at a town-hall show. You watch the fellow make flowers grow out of a hat, but you know all the time he don't."

Nevertheless, this particular miracle came to pass. Judge Payne made other calls at the cottage and Lavinia was summoned to his office, where she signed various papers. And, at last, the lawyer handed her a brand-new and beautifully engraved certificate certifying that Lavinia Badger was the owner of five thousand shares of stock in Occidental Mines.

"Now we'll sell it," she announced triumphantly. Judge Payne shook his head.

"Not if I can help it, you won't," he declared. "From what I am able to learn this may be worth a great deal more than it is now. My brokers feel sure that it will and I agree with them. In fact, I feel so certain of it that I am going to buy some shares for myself. Don't sell now, Lavinia. Wait. Waiting won't do you any harm and it may do you a lot of good. Wait—and watch."

Lavinia sniffed. "Especially the 'watch' part," she observed, drily. "Philander, if you wasn't about the oldest friend I've got and a whole lot the most sensible, I wouldn't pay any attention to you. When my father was livin' I've heard him say: 'If you got any money to save put it into somethin' that'll stay put. A sky-rocket looks pretty while it's goin' up but after it pops all you have left is a stick and you're lucky if you can find that.' I mistrust that a mine works the same, only it goes the opposite way. I'll wait a spell and see what happens, but I warn you that I may not wait long. If livin' with poor Judah ever learned me anything it was that a dollar I could see and handle was worth a dozen I could dream about."

She swore the Judge to secrecy; he was to tell no one of her good luck. And only to Ethel did she reveal the new and amazing development. Ethel was writing a letter to Bert when her great-aunt told the story and she laid down her pen and clasped her hands.

"Five thousand dollars!" she cried. "Why, that's ever and ever so much money! And Judge Payne thinks your stock may be worth a lot more! Why, Auntie, it is wonderful! I can hardly believe it. Perhaps you will be rich, really rich and—and have an automobile of your own some day."

"Humph! Cal'late I'll worry along with Major and the buggy for a spell, anyhow. They're more my gait than automobiles; may not go twenty mile an hour but they get me where I'm goin'—and all in one piece."

"Auntie, may I write Bert about your good luck? I'll tell him not to tell any one else."

"Eh? . . . Why, yes, you can tell him if you want to; he's a long ways from Wapatomac. When is he figurin' to come back?"

Ethel's expression changed. "He can't tell just yet," she admitted, sadly. "He doesn't feel that he should leave his mother right away. But he will come," confidently, "and before very long. He says so in this letter I'm answering now."

"Um-hm. Well, give him our regards—mine and Amaziah's. I see you're wearin' your ring."

"Yes, I always wear it when I'm alone. I know he would like to have me. This ring," she regarded it lovingly, "means so much to me; just as that little locket of mine means everything to him."

"Oh, so you gave him your baby locket, did you? I didn't know that."

Ethel blushed. "I meant to tell you," she said. "I—I forgot, I guess. Yes, I gave him the locket. He wanted something of mine to keep, something I had been used to wearing regularly, and you know I almost always wore that. He put it on his watch-chain before he left me. . . . I suppose this sounds awfully silly to you, Aunt Lavinia."

Lavinia shook her head. "Not so dreadful silly," she said. "I gave—er—somebody a locket of mine once, it had my picture in it. He put it on his watch-chain. He was goin' to wear it forever and ever, amen.... Good night."

"Oh, but Auntie, wait a minute. Did he always wear it?"

"We-ell, now that's kind of hard to swear to. You see, for-ever is a long time. Good night."

CHAPTER IX

BY the middle of September the last of Mrs. Mayo's city boarders had departed and, if the usual procedure had been followed, the Welcome Inn would have closed for the season. But "Aunt Tempy" had been doing much thinking and, one morning, she revealed to Ethel Holt the conclusion to which that thinking had brought her. She and Ethel had been drawn closer and closer together as the girl's capabilities and her very real business ability became more evident and the landlady had formed the habit of taking her into her confidence. She did so now. They were alone together.

"Ethel," said Aunt Tempy, "what have you planned to do after we shut up here? Goin' to live with Lavinia Badger and your Uncle Am down at the light, or have you got some other position in mind?"

Ethel shook her head, rather ruefully. "I suppose I shall have to go back to the Point," she replied. "There doesn't seem to be any other work for me in Wapatomac just now."

"Goin' to seem pretty lonesome down there for you, I'm afraid, especially after the cold weather really sets in and the no'theasters get blowin'. You've liked it here along with me, haven't you?"

"I've loved it. You and Emma and the boarders have been so nice to me. And I enjoy the work, all of it. I've grown to be so interested in this place, I feel almost as if it were my own."

"You act that way, too. I told your Aunt Lavvy a while ago that I did believe you were cut out for hotel business and I meant it. You've been a great help to me and you're goin' to be more, I can see that. Well, I've got a proposal to make to you. See how you like it."

The proposal was, to Ethel, surprising enough. Mrs. Mayo had practically decided to keep the Welcome Inn open throughout the year. Not the whole of it, of course—a number of the rooms and the dining-room would be shut up—but the rest of the establishment would remain as it was.

"We can use the small sitting-room for a winter dining-room," she went on, "and I'd keep one table-girl and the cook. I've been used to goin' up to Brockton to my sister-in-law's home winters—boardin' with her, you understand. But I'm gettin' old and, when you get old, your own home comes to mean more and more to you. I'm pretty sure that we would have regular boarders enough to keep us goin' in a small way. Cap'n John Small and his wife are shuttin' up their house for the winter and they'd like to come here. And Becky Hyer, the dressmaker, she don't like where she's been stayin' and she'd jump at the chance to come. And Harry Simpson, at the bank, his wife's dead now and he asked me if I knew of a good place for him to live. And there's a half-dozen more good prospects, besides the transients, drummers from out of town and such. I've made up my mind to try it. Now will you try it with me? That's what I'm askin' you."

Her idea was that she and Ethel together would carry on the business details and the management. Miss Low had planned to go South for the winter, had been saving money for the trip and was "dead set" on it, so she would be taken care of.

"It'll be just a sort of family affair, you and me, that's all. You could be home one day a week, and sometimes two, with your aunt and uncle and I'd pay you what you're gettin' now. Think it over and tell me how it sounds to you."

It needed no thinking over, so far as Ethel was concerned.

She welcomed the proposition with enthusiasm. The vision of long, empty, idle days at the lightkeeper's cottage had been hanging over her and she dreaded them. There was no immediate prospect of Bert's return to Wapatomac. In his most recent letter he had intimated that it was extremely doubtful if he went back to college at all. His mother depended upon him more and more; if he left her only for a little time she worried and was unhappy until he returned. She was talking of their going abroad for the winter. He would do his best to sidetrack that project, of course, but just where they might go he could not tell, as yet.

This portion of the letter Ethel read aloud to her great-aunt; there were many more pages which she did not read, of course. The girl was grievously disappointed, that was evident; but she was brave and hotly resented the slightest criticism of her lover's conduct. When Lavinia ventured to say that it was a pity the boy was not to finish his college course she flew to his defense.

"That doesn't make the least bit of difference," she declared. "It is just as he says in his letters; he is going into business, anyhow, and that last year of college doesn't count for much in banking. There are thousands and thousands of successful business men who never even saw the inside of a college."

Lavinia nodded. "He wrote you that, I suppose, eh? Oh, well, I guess it's true enough. When does he cal'late to start in on this banking job of his?"

"Why, just as soon as his mother is well and strong enough for him to leave her, I suppose. Good gracious, Auntie, you wouldn't expect him to desert her in the condition she is now, would you?"

Lavinia, although she did not say so, was inclined to believe that Mrs. Thornlow's convalescence would begin about the time when her son showed symptoms of recovering from his desire to return to Wapatomac and a certain person who lived there. As for the young man himself—well, according to her old-fashioned ideas, at least a portion of his obligation was due to the girl to whom he was engaged. If he had the self-reliance and grit he should have he would stand up in his shoes.

The Welcome Inn's first winter season was a success—that is to say, there was patronage sufficient to pay expenses of operation and yield a small profit, which was as much, and a little more, than Mrs. Mayo had expected. Ethel spent five days and nights of each week there and came home every Saturday to remain until Monday morning. She liked her work as well as ever and "Aunt Tempy" told Lavinia that she was beginning to wonder how she had ever got along all these years without some one like her.

"Give her another year or so," she declared, "and she could run this place by herself—yes, and run it better than I ever did, I do believe. She keeps thinkin' up new notions to make the boarders happier and make things go smoother and every single one of 'em works out, too."

It was, Lavinia felt, a mercy that this was so. The busy days and evenings at the Inn kept Ethel's mind occupied. It was lonely indeed at the Point, with no one except Amaziah for Lavinia to talk to or with, but when the girl came home for the week-ends her great-aunt was truly thankful, for her niece's sake, that those visits were not of longer duration. Except helping with the housework there was little for Ethel to do there and, before Monday morning came, she was moody and silent, saying little and smiling scarcely at all.

The Thornlows were in Honolulu. Mrs. Thornlow had felt certain that that soft, even, summery climate would be just what she needed.

"But just think, Auntie," moaned Ethel, in a moment of confidence, "I was unhappy because I was afraid they might go abroad. Why, Honolulu is farther—ever so much farther from here than Europe."

"But it belongs to the United States," said Lavinia, doing her best to comfort. "Makes it seem nigher home, anyhow. How does Bert like it out there?"

"Oh, he says he likes it very much. Of course—"

"Of course—what?"

"Well, I haven't had but one letter from him since they arrived.... That isn't his fault," promptly. "It is such a long way and the mail has to catch a steamer or wait, sometimes a whole week."

Occasionally, when Lavinia made a trip to the village, she called upon Judge Payne. His reports concerning Occidental Mines were encouraging. The company had taken over the Lost Prospect holdings and were installing new machinery. The stock had risen slightly in the Curb market. It was now one and a quarter bid and one and a half asked.

"Pretty good time to sell, isn't it, Philander?" Lavinia suggested, but the Judge pooh-poohed the idea.

"A better time to buy, in my opinion," he declared. "Hang on, Lavinia. I hope to see you a wealthy woman before I die."

She sniffed. "You must be figurin' to live longer than Methuselah and then die of surprise," was her comment. "When a stock that Judah Badger speculated in makes anybody rich the average constitution wouldn't be able to stand the shock, I know that."

"Tut, tut! Your holdings of that same stock are worth over six thousand at this very minute; you mustn't forget that, Lavinia."

"I don't—but I don't believe it and shouldn't until I see the real money in my hand. Philander, does this ever strike you funny, the whole of it?"

"Funny? How?"

"Why, you and me puttin' any dependence in minin' stocks, at our age. Accordin' to Scripture the only treasures we ought to be layin' up are those in heaven."

"You are a great one to be talking about ages. I don't remember ever having heard you admit before that you were old."

"I don't admit it now, but that doesn't alter the dates in the almanac.... Oh well, all right, Philander; I'll hang on, as you call it, for a while longer, but one of these days I may grab the wheel out of your hands and sail my own race. I can be stubborn when I set out to be."

Only to Ethel did she ever talk of her amazing windfall, its present status and its—according to Payne and his brokers —even more amazing possibilities. Ethel was always thrilled and youthfully optimistic.

"I said perhaps you would be rich some day, Auntie, and now it looks as if you really might be. I wrote to Bert about it all and he thinks it is wonderful. Of course five thousand dollars doesn't seem as much to him as it does to us, but," stoutly, "he says it is a fine beginning."

"Humph! If it wasn't for Philander Payne I'd be happy to call it a fine endin'! Haven't breathed a word to your Uncle Am, have you?"

"Of course not. I promised you I wouldn't."

"That's right. And don't. Five or six thousand dollars! Why, if Amaziah knew I had come in for that much money, even the prospect of it, he'd be for movin' us all up to Boston to live on Beacon Street and buyin' the Common for a front yard."

CHAPTER X

ANOTHER summer came and Ethel was in far better spirits for a time. The Thornlows were coming back to their Chicago home and Bert had written that he hoped and expected to come East for a flying visit to Wapatomac and to her. The visit was postponed and again postponed but, early in July, he came.

His stay was a short one, only three days. He was, so he informed them, about to enter the employ of the firm in which his father had been a partner. In fact he was really in that employ now, the firm having sent him to Boston to obtain some important documents and papers from its representatives in that city.

"It gave me the excuse I have been looking for," he added, with a laugh. "Boston isn't far from Wapatomac, so here I am."

He had a room at the Welcome Inn, but, as it was Friday evening, he had come down to the Point with Ethel and the quartette, he, Ethel, Amaziah and Lavinia, were having supper there. Bert was going back to the Inn that night and Ethel was to join him there the next day.

"You see, Auntie," she explained, with a sidelong glance at her uncle, "we thought it might be better for him not to visit us here—to stay, I mean. If he did that people would think—they might guess— Oh, you understand, don't you?"

Lavinia nodded. "Certain sure I understand," she said. "Good idea."

But Amaziah did not understand. He had never been in the

secret of the engagement, and his sense of hospitality was shocked.

"Good idea!" he snorted. "Why, what kind of talk's that! Of course he ain't goin' to stop at no hotel, Lavvy. He's come down here purpose to see us—us and Ethel, I mean— and it's a pretty notion if we can't board and lodge him while he is here. There's the front room with nobody in it, bed made up and everything. You'll stay right in this house 'long with us, Bert. We won't hark to nothin' else. Come now, Aunt Lavvy, you know he's goin' to. What's the matter with you?"

Ethel would have answered, but her great-aunt spoke before she did.

"There's nothin' the matter with me as I know of," she replied, crisply. "If Bert wants to stay here he's welcome and I guess he knows it. As I understand it he'd rather stay at the Inn. I don't blame him; there are things goin' on up around there. Down here there's nothin' alive that's inter- estin' but the gulls—and they get tiresome after a while."

"Eh? You and me are here, aren't we?"

"Yes, but I said interestin'."

"Ethel's goin' to be here till Monday mornin'. She al- ways is."

"I doubt if she will be this time. Isn't that so, Ethel?"

Ethel colored. "Why—why, if you are sure it is all right, Auntie," she hesitated. "I did think I might spend this week- end at the Inn. You see—"

"Course I see. And I haven't any objection at all. Fact is, I don't know but I'll go up there myself for a couple of days. Tempy's been invitin' me for ever so long and I've never said yes. Amaziah, you've been for having' Ben Crowell spend a day or two with you. Now would be a good time to get him, seems to me."

The young people looked at each other, but neither offered any objection to the plan. Amaziah pretended to object, on principle, but the prospect of having his closest friend, another easy-going, talkative loafer like himself, as his guest was too alluring to resist strenuously.

"I'll cook up a whole lot of things for you and Ben to eat," said Lavinia, "and then to-morrow afternoon I'll drive up to the Inn. A little mite of stirrin' around will do Major good and my couple of days off will be a real vacation for me."

In a way, it was. Mrs. Mayo was delighted to have her as a guest and they had long sessions of talk and gossip together. "Aunt Tempy" chanted Ethel's praises. She was a smart girl, if ever there was one. "She takes a big load of care off my shoulders, Lavinia, and that's a mercy, for I haven't been feelin' so awfully spry this summer. Dear, dear, it is a dreadful thing to know you're gettin' old, isn't it?"

"I presume likely 'tis—if you have time to sit down and realize it."

Lavinia saw little of Ethel and Bert during her stay. They were away on picnics or drives or at the beach in the daytime, but she saw to it that the girl was back at the Inn by eleven each night. And she took pains, whenever the opportunity offered, to talk with young Thornlow and to watch his behavior with the guests and Mrs. Mayo and also, when the chance came, with Ethel.

It seemed to her that that behavior and manner were not quite the same as they had been. He was a little older, of course, a little more of a man and less a boy, but it was not that change which she noted. He seemed, she thought, a trifle more patronizing in his demeanor toward her and the landlady. She had noticed the same thing in his manner with Amaziah at the cottage. When Am made one of his feeble jokes Bert used to laugh with him; now, Lavinia thought, he laughed at him. He told Mrs. Mayo that the Welcome Inn was a tip-top little place, but afterward he referred to it, the landlady not being present, as a "one-horse outfit." Even

Ethel resented this, but when she challenged the statement he laughed carelessly and said he was only joking, the Inn was all right enough, pretty dead-and-alive but not bad, really.

Lavinia was, and chided herself for being, perhaps over-suspicious, but she sometimes thought she perceived this attitude of easy superiority and patronage even in his manner toward Ethel. It seemed to her that he was more inclined to decide for himself where he and the girl should go or what they should do, rather than to leave the choice to her as he had formerly done. But, if this was so, Ethel apparently did not notice it. She was radiantly happy and, when he left on Monday morning, correspondingly wretched. Lavinia, in their farewell conversation, asked him how he thought he should like the banking business. He laughed carelessly.

"Like it as well as anything else, I guess," he said. "Got to like it, whether I want to or not. It's the old firm and Mother would throw a catfit if I went with any other. Well, good-by, Mrs. Badger. See you again before long, of course. Look out for this girl of mine and tell Am to give my regards to the gulls down at the Point."

In his next letter to Ethel he wrote that he was up to his neck in work and trying hard to get used to it. He had brought her a gold chain when he came and Lavinia often found her, when alone in her room at home, fondling it and the engagement ring and the gifts he had sent at Christmas with an adoring tenderness which, to her great-aunt, seemed almost pathetic. Lavinia wondered if he treated her little gifts with the same worshiping care. He had worn her locket on his watch-chain when he made his visit, and that was something. Probably he was all that he should be and she was just a cranky, crotchety old woman. She did not change her conviction that he was not good enough for Ethel, however. Nobody was.

Another winter. Ethel was now busy indeed. Mrs. Mayo was ill, confined to her room for several days of each week, and the care and management of the little hotel was upon the girl's shoulders. Miss Low was in the South and there was no one of experience to help. But Ethel did not seem to mind; apparently she enjoyed the burden.

"It is great fun, Auntie," she declared, "it really is. Aunt Tempy lets me do almost anything I want to do and I have all sorts of plans for improvements and changes. Oh, and we've got a new boarder. His name is Hunter and he is just out of law school. He has been sick and the doctors sent him out of the city to rest for a year. His father and mother are both dead and, as Judge Payne is a sort of cousin of his, the Judge suggested his trying Wapatomac. I guess he really came here because he could live cheaply. I don't think he has much money."

"A young chap, eh? Yes, course he must be if he's just finished studyin' law. Like him, do you?"

"Oh," carelessly, "he is rather odd, but seems nice enough. I had a letter from Bert yesterday. He is working frightfully hard. I do hope he doesn't wear himself out."

That Ethel wrote him daily Lavinia knew, but it seemed to her that he did not write quite as frequently as he used. Most of his letters were addressed in care of the Inn, of course, but occasionally one came to the Point and she noticed, or imagined, that it was not as bulky as those he had written the year before. Two and sometimes three stamps were necessary to pay the postage on those earlier letters, but now one was usually sufficient. Yet Ethel, if she too noticed this, said nothing about it. She was still fearful that he might be working too hard.

"And he is worried about something, Auntie," she confided, on one occasion. "I know that. It is something about the business, I am sure, but he won't tell me what it is. Oh, dear!"

Lavinia patted her shoulder. "There, there," she said. "Don't you fret yourself about his business. You've got enough of your own and Tempy Mayo's to attend to. I'm a good deal more worried about you wearin' yourself out than I am about his doin' it. Maybe hard work don't agree with him as well as it would if he'd ever been used to it."

This observation was not too tactful and Ethel resented it. Her great-aunt had to do a good deal of explaining and what she would have called "backing and filling" before peace was restored.

And Ethel's worry continued. She was much less cheerful than her wont and, although Lavinia was careful not to make too many inquiries, she was certain that the source of the sorrow lay in Chicago.

On a Saturday in April Amaziah came back from a trip to the village and when he entered the dining-room, where Lavinia and her grand-niece were setting the table for supper, he was obviously much excited.

Lavinia, who had watched his approach from the window, demanded to be told what was the matter.

"There's somethin'," she vowed. "You traveled up from that skiff as if the Old Harry was after you. I haven't seen you scratch gravel like that since the time you stepped on the hornet's nest. What are you wavin' that newspaper for?"

Her nephew had a folded copy of a Boston daily in his hand. When she tried to take it he held it out of her reach.

"Wait a minute," he ordered, importantly. "Wait a minute. Say, Ethel, what's the name of them Chicago brokers and bankers, the concern Bert Thornlow works for?"

Ethel looked at him. The color slowly left her cheeks.

"Name?" she faltered. "Name? Why—oh, what is wrong, Uncle Am? What—"

"You tell me first. What's the name of Bert's brokin' concern out in Chicago?"

"Thornlow, Semms & Co. Is there anything—"

"Ah ha! I thought so! Thornlow, Semms & Co. Well then, about everything's wrong with 'em. They've gone bust."

Ethel reached backward for a chair and sank into it. Lavinia glanced at her and then at Amaziah.

"Bust!" she repeated. "Bust?"

"Yes, sir-er-ma'am! Bust is what they are. Failed up, gone broke, gone plumb to smash. It's all there, right in the paper."

Lavinia seized the paper. It was there, the head-lines screamed it at her.

FAILURE OF WELL-KNOWN CHICAGO BANKING FIRM.
HOUSE OF THORNLOW, SEMMS & CO. CLOSES ITS DOORS.

The article beneath the head-lines was brief. Evidently an Associated Press dispatch received just before the early, out-of-town edition of the paper went to press. It stated merely that Chicago financial circles were shocked late this afternoon—the afternoon of the previous day, of course—by the announcement that Thornlow, Semms & Co., one of the city's oldest and supposedly strongest banking and brokerage houses, had gone into bankrutpcy. Few particulars were as yet obtainable, but there were many rumors, none of which could as yet be verified. The firm was founded shortly after the Civil War by Jonathan Thornlow and Nathan Semms and, later, carried on by Charles Thornlow, the former's son, who died in 1904. The surviving partners were—etc., etc.

Lavinia skipped much of this, but she read the concluding paragraph.

"The Thornlows are one of the city's oldest families and have been for many years identified with its history and growth. The Thornlow home in Lakeside is now occupied by Mrs. Charles Thornlow and her son, Albert. The latter, it is understood, has recently become a partner in the firm founded by his grandfather. Thornlow, Semms & Co. were regarded as an eminently conservative investment house and, if the failure is as disastrous as it is rumored to be, many Chicago fortunes will be affected by it."

Lavinia heard an exclamation behind her. She turned her head. Ethel was standing there and had evidently been reading over her shoulder. She would have spoken—have said something, she scarcely knew what—but the girl spoke first.

"I don't believe it!" she cried. "Oh, I don't believe it! It can't be true, it can't be! Why, Bert has told me, he told me ever so many times, that Thornlow, Semms & Co. were as—as strong as—as anything.... And see," excitedly, "it *isn't* true, Auntie. It says there that Bert was a partner. He wasn't at all. He expected to be pretty soon, but now he was only—only—"

Lavinia put an arm about her.

"There, there, dearie," she said, gently, "don't go to pieces. Keep cool. We don't know much about it yet; we don't really know anything. The papers don't always get things straight."

"The *Advertiser* does," vowed Amaziah. "Yes, sir, that's a newspaper, the *Advertiser* is. *It* don't make mistakes, no *sir!* Why, that time when the *Thomas Belgrew* struck on the Hog's Back shoal all the other papers gave out she was a two-masted schooner, but the *Advertiser* said she was a three-master, and she was, too. You can depend on the *Advertiser*. Now as to Bert's bein' a partner—how do you know that ain't right? A smart young fellow like him is liable to get made a partner any time, 'specially when he's his father's own son. Now—"

"Oh, for mercy sakes!" Lavinia interrupted, "whose son would he be—his uncle's? Am, you go and take a walk. Come, Ethel, you mustn't give up the ship and you mustn't cry, either. If it's true you must be brave for Bert's sake; that's what he'd want you to do. And if it isn't true—and very likely 'tisn't—we'll know that by to-morrow. Now let's you and me go on gettin' supper. Folks have to eat, no matter what's happened or hasn't happened. Most likely you'll hear from Bert right off. He'll either telegraph or write, of course."

But he did not. Ethel telegraphed him the next day—Amaziah took her message when he drove to the village for the Sunday paper—but he returned without the hoped-for word from Bert Thornlow to his fiancée. She wrote him a long letter that same morning, but almost a week elapsed before she received a reply. And that reply was very brief. She did not show it to Lavinia but the latter judged, from her grandniece's manner, that its contents was far from reassuring.

"Does he say anything about his mother?" she asked.

"Yes. He says the doctors are worried about her. The failure was a terrible shock."

"I guess likely. It was her husband's old firm and she was terrible proud of her husband and the family name and all. I suppose he told you to keep up your courage, everything would come out all right?"

Ethel did not answer, and Lavinia inferred that Bert had said nothing of the kind.

"Oh, well," she added, consolingly, "you mustn't mind. He is all upset just now, of course, and most likely can't think of anything except what's happened. You'll have to excuse him for not writin' as he usually does."

"He doesn't need excuses, from me or from any one else. He—he—oh, Auntie, if I could only do something to help him! If I were only there with him. He needs me, Auntie, I am sure he does, and I am away off here. It makes me feel almost wicked. If only I could go to him . . . But," sadly, "I suppose if I did it would only make more trouble; his mother would not like it."

Lavinia promptly agreed that she probably would not. "You couldn't do anything, dearie," she added. "He'll have to fight it through. In the end the fight may be good for him. He's had an easy time in this world, up to now he has, and it won't do him any harm to learn that life isn't all smooth water and a fair wind. This'll help stiffen up his backbone."

She spoke with confidence but inwardly she was not so sure. How much "backbone" Bert Thornlow actually possessed had been a question in her mind since her first acquaintance with that young gentleman.

The newspaper was giving a good deal of space to the Chicago failure, its causes and consequences. The latter were disastrous. Hundreds of investors had intrusted the custody of their money to Thornlow, Semms & Co. and their chances of salvage from the wreck looked slim indeed. As to the causes, the rumors concerning them increased and varied day by day but grew more and more disquieting. There were intimations of carelessness, of private speculation by the senior partner, even of actual dishonesty. Lavinia read all these, but she never referred to them in conversation with Ethel, although she was certain that the girl read them also. She thanked God that the summer season at the Welcome Inn was now well under way and Ethel increasingly busy in consequence. Lavinia no longer looked forward to the week-ends with her grand-niece; she was coming to dread them. Ethel was pale and very solemn, talking little and eating almost nothing.

During one of these week-end visits Lavinia ventured to ask a personal question. Her doing so was unusual; she seldom mentioned the Thornlow name unless Ethel mentioned it first.

"What does Bert say about his mother's health these days?" she inquired.

Ethel did not reply immediately. When she did it was without looking at the questioner.

"He—he hasn't said anything," she faltered, chokingly. "I haven't heard from him for—for over a week."

That ended the interview, for Ethel went to her room a few minutes later. Lavinia would have followed her, but changed her mind. The affair was going as she had for some time feared it might. Poor girl! Well, better to have an aching tooth out and done with than to prolong the ache for months or perhaps years; she tried to find some consolation in that bit of philosophy.

A fortnight later the newspapers gave them another important item of news. Mrs. Charles Thornlow, widow of the former head of Thornlow, Semms & Co., was dead. She had been seriously ill for nine weeks and a sudden acute heart attack had proved fatal. The concluding paragraph of the press dispatch was to the effect that the loss of practically the entire Thornlow fortune seemed certain.

"The Thornlows were reported to have been very wealthy during James Thornlow's lifetime, but, as all of Mrs. Thornlow's investments were made by the now bankrupt firm, it is assumed that the family losses are as complete as are those of the other unfortunate individuals who trusted their money to its care."

It was on a Wednesday that Amaziah rowed home from the village with the paper containing this dispatch and he brought Ethel with him. The girl was white and trembling but she was neither hysterical nor helplessly stricken. Her first words to her great-aunt proved that.

"Now I *shall* go to him, Auntie," she declared. "I have saved quite a lot of money and I shall use it. Now I understand why he has not written. I shall go to him. I must."

Lavinia did not try to dissuade her. She merely offered a suggestion.

"All right, dearie," she said. "I know how you feel and I don't blame you. Only—well, don't you think you had better telegraph him before you·start? He would want to meet you at the depot and—and all like that, I should think."

So Amaziah once more rowed over to town with the telegram while his niece and Lavinia packed the suit-cases. The reply to the telegram came that night; the operator intrusted it to Ben Crowell, Amaziah's fisherman crony, who brought it to the Point, making a special trip in his own dory. The message was short but emphatic.

DO NOT COME YET　WILL WRITE　BERT

Ethel went back to the Inn next morning to work harder than ever and to wait for the promised letter. Days passed before that letter came and when Ethel came home for that weekend she handed it to Lavinia without a word. Lavinia, before she took it from the envelop, looked at the girl's face and then, regardless of Amaziah, who was hovering about like a gull waiting to pick up a fish thrown away by an angler, she put her arms about her.

"Oh, my dear!" she cried.

Ethel put her gently aside. "Read it, Auntie," she said. "Uncle Am may read it, too, if he wants to. It doesn't make any difference now. I—I'll talk with you about it later."

She hurried upstairs. Lavinia took the letter from the envelop. It was a long one this time, seven closely written pages, altogether, four of them filled with explanations, excuses for what she must have considered neglect, pleas for forgiveness. But the final three contained the meat of the matter. The engagement was at an end; Bert had broken it arbitrarily. He was ruined—"almost stony broke," he said. His mother's fortune had dwindled rapidly since his father's death and the failure of the banking firm had taken the remainder. Even the Thornlow home would have to be sold.

"I shall have almost nothing when the whole mess is cleaned up. I don't know what I shall do or where I shall go, but probably somewhere on the Coast, in California or perhaps farther north. I have cousins in business in Oregon and I may go there, I am not sure. At any rate, I can't stay around here where every one knows me and is talking about me. I know you would be willing to wait, but I don't intend for you to do it. The prospect of my ever being in a position to marry is too vague and ridiculous even to dream about. Nothing could ever come of our engagement, so for both our sakes—yours, of course, particularly—it had better end now. Forgive me, if you can, and forget."

There was more, but Lavinia's patience was exhausted. The tone of the letter irritated her, a dozen words for the writer to one for the girl he was leaving. It confirmed her belief that Bert Thornlow lacked a "backbone." He was not standing up to face his trouble to fight it through, he was running away from it. Ethel was well rid of him.

But, when she ventured to hint something of that sort to Ethel, she discovered that the hint was a mistake. Ethel did not feel that way at all. She was not thinking of herself but only of him. What would become of him? All alone in the world, with no money and practically no relatives, his friends turning against him because he was poor and because misfortune and disgrace, for which he was not in the least responsible or to blame, had fallen upon the firm of which his father had been so proud—oh, it was dreadful! She pitied him so. She loved him more than ever, she would always love him.

"If he had wanted me to I would have gone to him this minute and gone with him anywhere. We would have got along somehow. I wouldn't have minded being poor. Why, we have always been poor, haven't we, Auntie?"

"Poor compared to what he and his folks used to be—yes. Only we are used to it and he isn't."

"If he had only said he wanted me, but he wouldn't do that. He is thinking of me, of course. I understand, I should feel the same way if I were he. You don't think I should go to him, in spite of it, do you, Auntie?"

Lavinia's reply was kind, but it was prompt and firm.

"No," she declared, "you shouldn't. And you sha'n't, if I can help it."

"But I shall always love him. Always—always till I die. I can't help it."

"I know, dearie. There's a good many things in this world we can't help—or think we can't until we find out different."

Ethel did not hear the last sentence. She was sobbing miserably.

"Oh, what shall I do?" she moaned.

Lavinia patted her bowed shoulder.

"Do?" she said. "Do? Why," sadly, "what some of the rest of us have had to do, I guess likely. That's just face the music and do the best we can."

Amaziah never was permitted to read Bert's farewell letter. Lavinia returned it to Ethel with the proviso that he, nor any one else except her grand-niece and herself, should ever see it or learn of its contents.

"And be thankful, girl," she added, with a breath of relief, "that that engagement of yours has been kept a secret. Now you won't be talked about, nor have to do any explainin'. And you won't be sympathized over, either. There's nothin' harder to put up with than the average run of sympathy. And I know what I'm talkin' about."

CHAPTER XI

ETHEL went back to her work as usual on Monday morning. Her whispered words, as she kissed her great-aunt good-by, were, to the latter, reassuring.

"Don't worry about me, Auntie," she said, "I shall be all right. I have a great deal to do and shall be busy every minute. As for the rest of it—well, I shall try to believe—yes, I do believe—that this isn't really the end. I am going to live and act—yes, and try to think—as if all this was just a—a postponement and that he and I will be together again some day —and happy. And we will, too; something tells me we will."

Lavinia's agreement was, outwardly at least, prompt and hearty. This was exactly the right philosophy, the right way to act and live and think.

"As for what's goin' to happen by and by," she added, "that nobody knows, but work and hope are about the two best things in this world to keep folks goin' and those that can hang on to both of 'em at the same time are lucky. Humph! That sounds like somethin' out of a book, doesn't it? Or a meetin' sermon or somethin'. You better trot along before I start to take up a collection."

On Wednesday of that week she drove up to the village, ostensibly to do some shopping but really to call at the Welcome Inn and learn at first hand how the girl was getting on. She found Ethel at her desk and her manner and speech were very encouraging.

"I'm awfully glad to see you, Auntie," she declared, "but you mustn't stop long. We've got a houseful and more coming to-morrow. Where I am going to put them, goodness knows.

Mrs. Mayo isn't well enough to be bothered—or at least I won't bother her—so I must plan for myself. I am a business woman now," with a brave attempt at a smile, "and 'strictly business' is my motto. I'll see you Saturday—or Sunday, anyhow."

On the way home Lavinia dropped in on Judge Payne. The Judge was out, but the housekeeper said he would be back soon and asked his caller to wait in his office.

"Mr. Hunter's there," she added, "but he won't mind."

"Mr. Hunter? Who is he?"

"Second or third cousin of the Judge's. He's helpin' the Judge a little with his work lately. He's stoppin' down at the Welcome Inn."

Lavinia dimly remembered that Ethel had mentioned that a young man, a distant relation of Payne's, had come to board at the Inn. She entered the office. Mr. Hunter was seated at a small table by the window, a pile of papers before him and a pen in his hand. He rose when she entered. He was a stocky, broad-shouldered young fellow of medium height, gray-eyed and with an unruly mop of reddish brown hair. He wore a gray suit, somewhat wrinkled, and a soft shirt with a bow-tie, one loop of which was untied and hanging. Ethel had said that he was "rather odd." Well, he looked it.

"Good morning," he said.

Lavinia returned the good morning. "Now sit right down," she added, "and don't bother about me. I'm waitin' for Judge Payne. You go ahead with whatever 'tis you're doin'."

He smiled and thanked her. He had a pleasant smile, she thought. She took the arm-chair reserved for clients beside Judge Payne's desk and he went on sorting and checking the papers before him on the table. She noticed that he had large hands, with thick, square-topped fingers. As he became engaged in his work he hummed a popular tune between his teeth.

Lavinia decided that, whatever his other accomplishments might be, he could not sing.

The bell at the front door rang and she heard the footsteps of the housekeeper as the latter hurried through the hall. A moment later she appeared at the door of the office. She seemed troubled.

"Mr. Hunter," she said, "that Dan Wixon is here and he wants to see the Judge. I told him he wasn't in, but he says he's goin' to see him if he stays the rest of the week. He's been—"

Before she could finish the sentence she was pushed aside and Mr. Wixon himself stood in the doorway. He was a gangling individual, with a flushed, unshaven face and a moth-eaten mustache. His expression was anything but agreeable.

"Say," he said, addressing Hunter, "she," indicating the housekeeper with a jerk of his head in her direction, "says the old man ain't around. Is that right?"

Hunter nodded. "Judge Payne is out but I expect him soon. Is there anything I can do?"

Wixon looked at him. "Who are you?" he demanded.

"My name is Hunter. I am—well, in a way I suppose I'm the Judge's—er—assistant."

"Humph! No, you can't do nothin' for me. I've come to see old Payne and I'm goin' to see him, too. Him and me have got a bone to pick."

He slouched into the room, his cap on one side. Lavinia knew him, of course, but she was not proud of the acquaintanceship. He and his wife lived in a three-room shanty by the shore at the west end of the town. He picked up a haphazard living by clamming, oyster-raking and, occasionally cod-fishing, when he chose to work at all. His wife was a hard-working, decent woman and his treatment of her had been town talk for years. Amaziah had recently heard and repeated a story to the effect that she had left him, had gone away after he had knocked her about while he was drunk. Drinking was his favorite amusement and it was evident that he had been drinking now.

Lavinia did not speak to him, nor he to her; in fact, he did not seem to be aware of her presence. She had risen from the arm-chair when he entered and now he seized that chair by the back, jerked it out into the middle of the floor and flung himself into it. Hunter gazed at him; then he spoke.

"I beg pardon," he said, deliberately, "but I guess you didn't notice that this lady was sitting in that chair."

Wixon merely grunted. Hunter spoke again, a little louder this time.

"That was this lady's chair," he repeated. "There is another over there by the wall."

Wixon turned his head. "What lady?" he growled. "Oh," apparently noticing Lavinia for the first time, "how are you, Mrs. Badger? Hotter'n the devil and all, ain't it?"

"That chair—" Hunter began again, but Lavinia interrupted. "Oh, never mind," she protested, hastily, "I can sit in the other chair just as well as not."

She did sit in it. The young man at the desk seemed far from satisfied but she shook her head meaningly and he subsided. Wixon crossed his long legs and fumbled in his pockets.

"Guess likely you know what I'm here for, Mrs. Badger," he observed. His eyes were a trifle glassy and his enunciation not too clear. "Been a lot of cheap talk goin' 'round about it, I suppose. Well, that's all right. Let 'em talk, I'm talk. I'll have my say bimeby. Man's wife's his wife, ain't she? All right, then where's she b'long? Why, along with him, don't she? I say she does."

He relapsed into gloomy mutterings, still fumbling at his pockets. Lavinia said nothing. He was drunk, that was plain, and when drunk he was always ugly, or so it was reported. She had no desire to converse with him, to say nothing of getting into an argument. It was Mr. Hunter who spoke next. He had been regarding the soiled cloth cap still cocked over the Wixon left eyebrow.

"There is a hat-rack over there in the corner," he suggested, pleasantly.

Wixon paid no attention, he continued to mutter. Suddenly he broke out in a savage growl.

"I say she does," he repeated, his voice rising almost to a shout. "I say man's wife b'longs where he is. And where's my wife now, eh? Don't know. Don't know, but I'm goin' to know. Old Philander Payne knows. He's the one put her up to it; he's one told her to quit me and go off some'ere else. All right, he's goin' to tell me where she is and I'm goin' get her back. Ain't his wife, is she? No sir, she's mine! He'll get her back for me or I'll put him in Ostable County jail. Don't care if he is a lawyer. I can get 'nother lawyer, can't I? Bet your life I can."

He relapsed again into mutterings. Hunter looked at Lavinia, but again Lavinia shook her head. Wixon seemed to find what he had been searching his pockets for. He produced from one of them a somewhat tattered cigar, stuck it in his mouth, scratched a match on the varnished arm of the chair, lit the cigar and blew a cloud of malodorous smoke.

This time Mr. Hunter did not look at Lavinia. He looked at the cigar. Then he rose deliberately—apparently he was always deliberate, both in speech and action—came around the corner of his table and approached the smoker. He touched the latter on the shoulder.

"Eh?" queried Wixon, startled from his mutterings. "Wha' you want?"

Hunter pointed to a small placard on the wall opposite the official desk. It read "PLEASE DO NOT SMOKE."

"You didn't notice that, did you?" he drawled.

"Eh? Notice what? Wha' you talkin' about?"

"That sign. Can you read it?"

"Eh? Course I can read. Think I'm a darn fool?"

"I haven't thought. Just read it now, please."

Wixon read. Then he snorted.

"To hell with it," he observed.

The next moment the thick, square-tipped fingers of Mr. Hunter's large left hand encircled the back of his neck. Those of Mr. Hunter's large right hand snatched the cigar from between his lips.

"Get up," said Mr. Hunter, still deliberately.

Wixon sputtered and struggled. He tried to turn his head but could not. He rose a few inches from the chair seat and, when he did so, the chair was kicked from beneath him. It was on casters and slid across the floor. Lacking its support Mr. Wixon sat down upon that floor with emphasis.

"Ugh!" he gasped.

"I said 'Get up,' not 'Get down,' " observed Hunter.

Wixon, an authoritative push accelerating his movement, struggled to his feet, but he did not stand erect. The grip on the back of his neck prevented that. The square-tipped fingers did not slip, instead they sank deeper into his leathery hide.

"Leggo me," he howled and added a richly embroidered characterization of his captor.

"Now get out," ordered Mr. Hunter.

Wixon swung wildly with both arms but Hunter was behind him and out of reach. He felt himself propelled toward the door but he hung back and struggled. Hunter still held the confiscated cigar in his right hand and now he knocked the ashes from it, leaving the end red-hot and glowing. Then he bent forward and whispered in his captive's ear.

"Hi!" bellowed Wixon, in a paroxysm of rage and alarm. "You will not! If you do I'll break— *Ow!*"

"Better go," suggested Hunter.

Mr. Wixon went. He swore and he threatened but he went.

Hunter opened the office door with the hand holding the cigar and Lavinia heard the pair move through the hall. A moment later she heard the outer door slam. Hunter returned, deliberate as ever, and smiling cheerfully.

"Sorry," he said. And then, "Will you excuse me while I wash my hands?"

He went out, but was back again almost immediately.

"Perhaps we had better open another window," he suggested. "That cigar was—er—fragrant."

He opened the window and then reseated himself in the chair by the table. Lavinia, who had not spoken during the astonishing performance just ended, drew a long breath. Then she asked a question.

"Won't he come back again?" she asked.

"Guess not. I told him we didn't need him."

Lavinia sighed. *"Well!"* she exclaimed. "Well, I must say!"

Mr. Hunter smiled. "Sorry to have made all this fuss," he observed. "Seemed to be necessary, though. Hope you weren't frightened."

"Humph!" with a sniff. "It takes more than Dan Wixon to scare me an awful lot. He may bully and knock his wife around but I never heard of his hurtin' anybody that stood up to him. But I am surprised some, that I will say. I didn't expect to see you get him out of here so quick. He was all for stayin' one minute and the next he was steppin' lively toward that door. What did you say to him when you whispered in his ear?"

The smile became a chuckle. "I told him if he didn't go I should put the hot end of that cigar on the end of his nose."

"You did! My soul and body! And then—?"

"Oh, then I did it—and he went."

Lavinia stared for an instant. Then she began to laugh and laughed until she was obliged to fumble for her handkerchief. Hunter laughed, too, but quietly.

"Oh, dear!" gasped the lady. "I wouldn't have missed this for anything. And you— Didn't Ethel tell me you was a—a kind of invalid, Mr. Hunter?"

He had taken up a sheet of paper and the pen and was dipping the latter in the inkwell.

"Ethel?" he repeated, absently. "Ethel? Oh," with more interest, "you mean Miss Holt, the young lady at the Inn?"

"Yes. I'm her great-aunt. Maybe you've heard her speak of me. My name is Badger."

"Oh," he put down the sheet of paper but still held the pen in his fingers, "oh yes, of course. I have heard her mention your name. Heard the Judge mention it, too. How do you do, Mrs. Badger?"

Lavinia's lip twitched. Ethel had made no mistake when she described this young chap as "odd."

"Why, I'm pretty well, thank you," she replied. "But then, I gen'rally am. Besides, I've been doin' nothin' but sittin' still and lookin' on. You're the one whose health ought to be asked about, seems to me. 'Specially as I understand you've come to Wapatomac on account of it."

He grinned. "Somebody has been exaggerating, I should say. I never called myself an invalid exactly. My legs and arms are all right; it is my head and nerves that are supposed to be shaky. After I finished law school I had a bad breakdown and when I came out of the hospital they told me I must rest for a year. Resting in Boston is expensive—and noisy. Cousin Philander—Judge Payne, I mean—suggested that I try Wapatomac. He said there wasn't much excitement here. He's right."

"Humph! As a general thing I'd say he was. But a few minutes ago, in this office—well, what's been goin' on here may be your notion of a dead calm, but 'tisn't mine."

She shook her head. He chuckled, quietly.

"The doctors told me to take a little gentle exercise occasionally," he observed. "This is the first I've had."

"And you call it 'gentle,' eh? I doubt if Dan Wixon would agree with you. And as for bein' a help to shaky nerves—good land of mercy!"

Another chuckle. "That fellow shook up my temper, not my nerves. You live down at the—er—at Long Cove Point, don't you, Mrs. Badger? Some one—Mrs. Mayo, I think it was—told me you did."

"Yes. The lightkeeper down there is my nephew. His name is Holt, he's Ethel's uncle."

"I see." She judged that he knew this. Probably Tempy Mayo had told him about the family. She wondered if she had told it of her own volition or in answer to his questions. Probably the former, he did not appear to be of the prying kind.

"Know much about lighthouses?" she asked.

"Nothing, except that they are lighted at night."

"You ought to come down to ours sometime. Amaziah—or Ethel, if she's there—will be glad to show you 'round."

"Thank you, Mrs. Badger. I will."

Obviously he meant it. He was a queer one, no doubt about that. She asked him why he selected the Welcome Inn as a lodging- and boarding-place.

"Principally because I could get a good-enough room there without paying much for it."

"Oh—yes, yes. How do you like it there?"

"First rate."

That ended the conversation. He picked up the sheet of paper and bent over it. A few minutes later Judge Payne came in and Mr. Hunter went out to the dining-room, carrying the papers, ink and pen with him.

The Judge had little that was new to communicate concerning Occidental Mines, but that little was good. The new workings were in operation and the outlook was promising. The stock was selling at two dollars a share now.

"Not that there has been a great deal sold," he added. "There hasn't and that is a favorable sign, too. Shows that its possibilities are realized and that those who own it are holding on, just as you and I are, Lavinia."

"Humph! Just as you are, you mean. Two dollars a share? Why, that means ten thousand dollars for what I've got. Good land of love, Philander! And you won't let me sell yet?"

"Not yet, nor even soon if I have my way. How does it feel to be growing rich?"

"Let me feel the money and then maybe I'll tell you. Speakin' of tellin', you haven't let out a word about it to anybody?... No, no, course you haven't.... Now I want to talk about this young man you've taken aboard here in this office. I know his name's Hunter and that he's a cousin of yours and that he's stoppin' at Tempy Mayo's Inn. What else is there about him?"

"I take it you and he scraped acquaintance while you were waiting for me just now."

Lavinia laughed; she laughed so long that the lawyer ordered her to stop and let him in on the joke. She wiped her eyes.

"Scraped acquaintance," she repeated. "Why yes, I cal'late you might call it as much as that. Listen, Philander."

She told him of the arrival and departure of Dan Wixon. Payne heard the story, at first with indignation when Mr. Wixon's behavior and threats were mentioned and then with amusement when the application of the "hot end" of the cigar was described.

"Well, well," he chuckled. "It must have been funny enough. I wish I might have been here to see it."

"I don't. You'd have been dignified and starchy, Philander, and that would have spoiled everything. No, no, this cousin of yours handled things a lot better than you would. Now tell me about him—what I don't know already, I mean."

There was not a great deal to tell. William Hunter—friends of his own age called him "Bill," of course—was the son of Payne's wife's sister. The family had lived in Iowa until Hunter Senior died and then William and his mother had come East. The mother died soon after their arrival. She left him a little money, but William had worked his way through college and law school in Boston and was expecting to be admitted to the bar. Then, as a consequence of his hard work and over-study he had suffered a complete collapse and nervous break-down. He was just out of the hospital and had been ordered to the country for quiet and rest.

"That was when he wrote to me," went on the Judge. "I had scarcely seen him since his mother's death and knew nothing of his trouble and sickness. Even then he didn't ask me for help; wanted my advice as to a quiet place in the country where he could sleep a lot and spend very little. I ordered him to come down here and we would talk things over. He came—and decided to stay. That's about all."

"I want to know! Wonder you let him go to the Inn, Philander. That don't seem like you. You've got spare bed-rooms in this big house."

"So I have and I offered him one of them, but he wouldn't take it. Wanted to be independent, I suppose. He's a queer bird, if I ever saw one, but I must say I like him—so far, at least."

"I liked the way he took care of Dan Wixon. I like the way he talks, too—dry and slow and good-natured. And he's got an awful catchy grin. But what is he doin' in your office? Fussin' with your papers don't look like rest to me."

Judge Payne rubbed his chin. "It doesn't to me, either, but that's what he calls it. He hadn't been in town a fortnight when he was around begging for something to do. 'Just let me sharpen pencils or lick postage-stamps or something,' he said. 'All I do there at the Inn is sit and count the boarders and think what a loafer I am.' I didn't want to, but he insisted and, when I talked it over with Dr. Hardy, Hardy seemed to think something to take his mind off himself and occupy a little of his time might do him more good than harm. I hope it will; I should feel guilty enough if it didn't."

Lavinia looked at him through her spectacles. "Philander," she declared, "you're a lawyer and the ways of lawyers are supposed to be hard to see through; but I can see through you as if you was a pane of glass. You've got a notion in the back of your head that this young Hunter critter may turn out to be the one to take some of your law work off your shoulders. In time, I mean. That's it, isn't it?"

Her friend shook his head in half-grudging admiration. "You ought to have been a lawyer yourself, Lavinia," he observed. "Why yes, I may have some such idea. You, yourself, told me I needed an assistant."

"So I did and so you do. Well, good-by."

"Where are you going now?"

"Home, of course. Lighthouse folks have the eatin' habit like everybody else and I've got to see to gettin' supper."

She rose, shook out her skirt and moved toward the door. The Judge smiled.

"Lavinia," he said, "you've got at least ten thousand dollars of your own now and—"

"Oh, no, I haven't."

"Oh, yes, you have. That stock of yours is just as good as that much money even now. And later on, perhaps—"

"Now, now, Philander! You've heard the old story about the boy who said he'd just as good as had a horse given to him that day. He asked the man to give it to him and the man said no; if he'd said yes he'd have had him. Poor Judah had a tin box full of china nest-eggs that never hatched and I lived with him quite a spell; don't forget that."

"But, confound it, Lavinia, this egg has hatched.... Oh well, never mind. Good-by."

Ethel did not come to the Point on Saturday. The Inn was so crowded and she was so busy that she could not leave, but she did come the following week and on that Sunday afternoon, as she and her great-aunt, having finished with the dinner dishes, were chatting in the sitting-room, there came a knock at the door. Amaziah had gone to his room for a nap.

"Now who on earth can that be?" demanded Lavinia. "Never heard a team comin', did you?"

Ethel shook her head. "Perhaps it is Mr. Crowell to see Uncle Am," she suggested.

"Ben Crowell would come to the back door.... No, no, you sit still. I'll go."

She rose and went to the door. Ethel heard her exclamation of surprise.

"Why, Mr. Hunter! Well, well! Come right in."

He entered the sitting-room. He was wearing the same wrinkled gray suit he had worn when Lavinia met him in the Judge's office and his thick reddish-brown hair was as rumpled as it had been then. Ethel was astonished to see him there. Her great-aunt had told her of the amusing adventure with Dan Wixon, but she had said nothing concerning her invitation to visit the light or Hunter's prompt acceptance of it. That invitation had been rather perfunctory and Lavinia had forgotten it altogether.

"Why, Mr. Hunter," exclaimed Ethel, "how in the world did you get 'way down here?"

"How do you do, Miss Holt?" said Mr. Hunter. "I walked."

"Walked!" Lavinia and her grand-niece uttered the word simultaneously. Their caller nodded.

"Yes," he said.

"But," cried Lavinia, "it's all of four mile from the Inn— that is, if you come over the road."

He took a clean, but much rumpled handkerchief from his pocket and wiped his forehead.

"I came about a mile over it," he observed.

"Oh. Then how did you come the rest of the way?"

"Through it. Will you excuse me a minute? I think I'll go outside a minute and take off my shoes."

"Take off your—" began Ethel. Then she paused and looked at her aunt in utter amazement. Lavinia was as astonished as she was. Hunter apparently noticed their expressions, for he smiled.

"As an offhand estimate," he observed, "I should judge there was about two pounds of sand in each shoe. The doctor told me he wanted me to gain weight, but—"

He left the sentence unfinished and went out by the door he had entered. Ethel put her hand to her mouth. "Did you ever see any one like him in your life?" she whispered, as soon as she could speak. "I told you he was odd, Auntie."

Lavinia shook her head. "And that wasn't stretchin' the truth any," she agreed, with emphasis. "Sshh! Here he comes."

He returned and, accepting their invitation, sat down upon the sofa. Lavinia asked concerning Judge Payne's health.

"The Judge is very well, he replied. "He has a new house-keeper—but perhaps you knew that."

Lavinia exclaimed in astonishment. "A new housekeeper!" she repeated. "Why, what on earth for? Where's Martha?"

"She has gone to Worcester. Her sister who lives there is very ill."

"You don't say so! Isn't she comin' back at all? Why, she's been workin' for Philander years and years."

"So I understand. If her sister recovers she will come back. Otherwise she will probably feel that she must stay and take care of her brother-in-law."

his must have been awful sudden. I was up there
s only a little more than a week ago, wasn't it?—
she nor Philander said a word to me about it

dn't know. It was sudden. Martha got the news
and left Tuesday afternoon. The new housekeeper
xt day. She is a widow; her husband was a distant
Martha's, I believe. She was living in Wellmouth;
nat is the name of the place. Martha telegraphed her
ne came at once."

"Well, well! Poor Martha, I'm sorry for her. How do you
like this new woman who's just come?"

"The Judge says she seems to be a good cook. Her name
is Pail. P-a-i-l."

Ethel burst out laughing. "Pail!" she exclaimed. "Why,
what a funny name."

"It's not common. There is a person named Bucket in one
of Dickens's novels, I remember. This one is a large Pail, more
like a tub."

Lavinia had been thinking. "Pail?" she repeated, slowly.
"Pail? Why, yes; I knew I'd heard of somebody by that name.
He lived in Wellmouth, too, and he married— My soul and
body! Don't tell me this woman's first name is Octavia?"

The corner of Mr. Hunter's lip twitched. "I am afraid I
shall have to," he said. "She told me her name was Octavia,
but she wished I would call her 'Ocky,' because her friends
always did. I haven't—as yet."

Ethel was laughing, but Lavinia was serious enough, serious
and, apparently, a trifle disturbed.

"That's who it is," she declared. "It must be. I've met her.
Her last name used to be Devitt and she was livin' in East
Wapatomac when I first came to this house to stay. Why,
before that, she and Amaziah—"

She paused. Even Ethel knew nothing of her Uncle Ama-

ziah's only serious love affair. He had been smitt[en by the]
charms of the Devitt young woman and, at one t[ime]
were, as Wapatomac would have expressed it, "keepi[ng com-]
pany." There had been some sort of a lover's quarrel a[nd the]
affair was broken off. Then Octavia's people moved to [Fal-]
mouth and the girl had married there. The husband's na[me—]
she remembered it now—was Pail. Simeon—or was it Silas [—]
Pail.

"Well, well, well!" she mused.

"What is it, Auntie?" asked Ethel.

"Nothin'. Nothin' to amount to much. . . . What was you
goin' to say, Mr. Hunter?"

"Why, simply that—er—Mrs. Pail told me she knew who
you were. I happened to mention that I was coming here this
afternoon and she seemed interested. She said that there was a
time—that is the way she put it—there was a time when she
knew Mr. Amaziah Holt very well. She wished to be remembered to him."

"Oh," observed Lavinia and then changed the subject.

Their visitor remained the entire afternoon. Amaziah came
in and was introduced. He volunteered to show Mr. Hunter
the lighthouse and the lantern and the invitation was accepted.
Refusing to remain and join the family at supper, the young
man bade them farewell and set off on his long walk back to
the Inn. His good-by was brief.

"I've had my best afternoon since I came to Wapatomac,"
he declared. "Thank you both very much. And you, too, Mr.
Holt, of course."

"I don't feel right about your trampin' all that way through
the sand," said Lavinia. "If you get down sick again on account
of it I'm sure your Cousin Philander never'd forgive me."

"I sha'n't be. Sand in the shoes is a relief after water on
the brain. Good night."

"You must come again," said Ethel. He turned to look at

was exactly what he had given Lavinia when
to call.

," he returned. "I will."

departure Amaziah expressed an opinion.

ueer critter," was Amaziah's estimate. "Kind of
ed, almost, seems so. Never can tell what crazy
say next. When we was goin' aloft to the lantern-
plained to him that them windin' steps was called
pinal staircase. He said it looked to him like a bad case of
curvature. I suppose likely he was jokin' but I give you my
word he looked solemn as a funeral. I couldn't make him out.
I tell you one thing, he ain't a patch on that Thornlow young
chap. When Bert Thornlow joked he laughed and that gave
other folks a chance to know 'twas time to laugh with
him."

Lavinia was watching him intently. Now she wiped her
spectacles and readjusted them.

"Did he tell you any—er—well, 'special news?" she asked,
with deliberation.

Amaziah, apparently, did not hear her. He muttered something about going outside to look at the weather and left the
room, rather hurriedly his aunt thought.

"Deary me!" she muttered. "As if I didn't have enough to
fret me already."

"What do you mean, Auntie?" asked Ethel. "I can't see why
Mr. Hunter—"

"Mr. Hunter's all right. It wasn't him I was thinkin' about.
There, there, never mind; I seem to have got in the habit
of chasin' bugbears and, nine times out of ten, when I catch up
with 'em there aren't any there. . . . I kind of like that Hunter
boy. He's funny but I believe a body could count on him right
along through. He'll make a good helper for Philander or
I miss my guess. Don't you like him, Ethel?"

"Why, yes, I guess I do. Only I am like Uncle Am; I'm

never sure what he will say next. Why do you sup̄
'way down here, Auntie?"

"Because I asked him to, I presume likely. That anď
he said he would come. He acts to me like a perso
sticks to his word."

"Well, he said he would come again. I wonder if he wı̄
Lavinia turned to look at her. "I shouldn't be surprised,
she observed, drily. "Why? Would you rather he wouldn't?"
Ethel laughed. "I'm sure I don't care whether he does or
not," she replied, lightly. Her tone expressed complete indif-
ference. Lavinia was a trifle disappointed. Later, when she
passed the door of the girl's room, she glanced in. Bert Thornlow's photograph was on the table and Ethel sat before it.
The ring he had given her was on her finger and a packet of
letters—his letters, Lavinia was sure—were in her lap. Lavinia
heard a sigh which was almost a sob.

She, herself, was sighing when she reached her own room.
Was this to continue forever? Was Ethel's life to be wrecked
by a dream and a memory? There were as yet no signs of
forgetfulness. "Always," Ethel had said. "Always." Well, as she
had said in return, always was a long time. This was only
the beginning.

CHAPTER XII

STILL another winter was at hand. Mrs. Mayo's health was no better; she was confined to her room most of the time and the care and management of the Welcome Inn now rested entirely upon Ethel's shoulders. The girl did not complain, on the contrary she seemed to enjoy the responsibility. Her week-end stays at the Point cottage were things of the past. She usually came down for Sunday dinner with Amaziah and Lavinia but returned to the Inn the same afternoon. Mrs. Mayo owned a horse and buggy and Ethel was given permission to use them whenever she wished, consequently the skiff, except when Amaziah used it for his own purposes, lay idle at the landing below the lighthouse.

Mr. Hunter—Lavinia addressed him as "William" now and Amaziah as "Bill"—called occasionally. Usually his calls were made on Sundays and he sometimes dined with the lighthouse group. Better acquaintance had not changed Lavinia's favorable opinion of the young man. He was just as odd as ever, just as deliberate in his manner and speech, and his dry comments concerning persons and happenings were always amusing. Lavinia liked him, and Ethel declared him "good fun."

He casually explained that the reason why his visits to the Point cottage were made on Sunday was because Sunday was his "day off."

"We're commanded to rest on the seventh day," proclaimed Amaziah, solemnly. "That's law and gospel."

"Ye-es," somewhat doubtfully. "That is the commandment. The lawyers—most of them obey it. The gospel people apparently don't. They work harder on that day than on any other. Hum...that's interesting. It never occurred to me before. It seems to prove that—once a week anyhow—a minister is more wicked than a lawyer. That is a point to remember."

"Do you call walkin' 'way down here 'rest'?" demanded Lavinia. "Because if you do, I don't."

"Well, that's another question. Six days a week my head is busy and my legs are on a vacation. On the seventh day my legs work and my head loafs.... That is, unless I get into an argument such as this promises to be. Suppose we talk about something else—clams, for instance, I think I'll have a little more of that chowder, Mrs. Badger, if I may."

Lavinia was beginning to have her own idea as to the cause prompting the Hunter calls. Amaziah was outspoken on the subject.

"That young fellow frogs it down here just for one thing," he vowed, contemptuously. " 'Day off'—nothin'! He comes Sundays 'cause he knows Ethel's liable to be here then. If she was here Fridays he'd come Fridays, you can bet your life on that."

Lavinia was secretly inclined to agree with her nephew, but it was against her principles to admit it.

"Stuff and rubbish!" she sniffed. "He boards and rooms at the Inn, don't he? He can see her there every night and every morning if he wants to."

"How do you know he don't see her? Oh well, now don't fly off the roost. I realize, same as you do, that it's all foolishness, fur's his chasin' her is concerned. 'Tain't likely she'll pay attention to a poor, fog-minded red-head like him, without a cent to his name. A girl that's had a millionaire takin' her to ride in his own automobile! Bosh! She'll send him about his business when she gets good and ready. And what is his business? Why, nothin'; he ain't even a reg'lar lawyer yet."

But he became one soon afterward. The next time Judge Payne drove down to the Point he informed Lavinia that Hunter had passed his examinations and had been admitted to the bar. "And that will be a great help to me," he added. "I intend turning over some of my less important cases to him and see what he can do with them. He is a droll stick, as I told you before, but he is a clever young fellow. It may be, Lavinia, that when I am gone he will be handling your law business for you."

"Um—yes, I guess likely. Long afore you've gone I'll be where the lawyers cease from troublin'. And, even if I shouldn't, the amount of trade I could give him wouldn't fix him so he could keep hired help. And, now that we're speakin' of hired help, how's your new housekeeper gettin' along?"

The Judge shrugged. "She feeds me well enough," he said. "She isn't another Martha, by any means, but she will have to do for the present. Good housekeepers like you, Lavinia, are scarce; they aren't to be caught every time a line goes over. If she didn't talk so much—"

He shrugged again. Lavinia smiled. "She had the name of doin' that when she was a girl, so I've heard. Somebody, I forget who, told me that that Wellmouth husband of hers was hard of hearin'. Most folks figure deafness is an affliction, but maybe he got more reconciled to his after he was married."

"He should have been thankful. Amaziah isn't deaf, though, is he?"

Lavinia turned to look at him. "Amaziah?" she queried sharply. "What made you think of him? What has he got to do with your housekeeper?"

"I don't know."

"Now, now, Philander Payne! You wouldn't have dragged Amaziah in unless you had some reason. Out with it."

"Well, it isn't any of my business, of course."

"Maybe it isn't mine and perhaps that's why I'm curious about it; I've lived in Wapatomac a good many years, you know. Has Amaziah been callin' at your house lately?"

"He was there last Monday evening; that I know because I saw him, myself. And Friday Mrs. Pail went to the entertainment at the town-hall. She may have gone alone, but I doubt it."

Lavinia was thinking. "Monday night he told me he was goin' to lodge-meetin'. And Friday—why, Friday evenin' he went to see Ben Crowell, who is laid up with the rheumatics. He asked me to keep an eye on the light while he was out. . . . And now you tell me— Why, the poor simpleton! You don't suppose—"

"I don't suppose anything. If I remember correctly he and she were—well, very good friends years ago. That was a little before your time in Wapatomac, Lavinia. Probably they are just renewing old acquaintanceship. I shouldn't worry, if I were you."

"And I shouldn't if I were you. And if Amaziah was somebody else—but, there, he isn't. Philander, if I drop in at your house some of these days pretty soon don't get the notion that you're goin' to make money out of me, because you ain't. I shall be there just to see what that woman looks like. Yes, and hear her talk, if I can."

"If she is there you will have no trouble in hearing her talk. If you can find a way to keep her from talking and let me in on it I should be much obliged."

The following Sunday when Ethel came to the Point she announced that her stay this time must be even shorter than usual. Her report concerning Mrs. Mayo's health was far from encouraging. "Aunt Tempy," she was beginning to fear, was in a serious condition. "Dr. Hardy says she must not be bothered with any business at all and I don't like the way he looks when I ask him about her. It is lucky that the summer season is over and we have only our regular all-the-year boarders, for I have to look out for everything."

"You've been doin' that for a good while, haven't you?" suggested Lavinia.

"Ye-es, but I have been able to talk things over with Mrs. Mayo sometimes. Now I can't and I have to make every decision just as if the place was mine. Of course, if it was my own I shouldn't mind so much, for then if I made a mistake the consequences would be mine alone. And the idea that I'm just a hired hand, as you might say, holds me back so. If I owned the Welcome Inn there are so many improvements I should like to make, so many experiments I should like to try. Some day, Auntie, I mean to have a little hotel, or a gift-shop, or both, of my very own. It may be the tiniest kind of one, but I will have a good time with it—yes, and I will make it pay; you see if I don't."

Her eyes shone when she said it. Her great-aunt liked to see her like that. It was the intervals of silence she dreaded, the absent look, the sudden announcement that she was going to her room for a little while, or for a walk alone on the beach. Lavinia knew what those meant only too well.

Mr. Hunter walked to the Point that Sunday afternoon, but his stay, too, was short. It may have been because he found that Ethel was leaving early, but, at any rate, after an hour or so, he announced that he must be moving on to what he called the metropolis.

"It looks like rain," he said. Then, as a spatter of drops dashed against the window, "In fact, it is rain. . . . Well, good-by."

But now Lavinia, as she would have expressed it, "put her foot down."

"You sha'n't tramp home in a pourin' down rain-storm," she declared, with emphasis. "Ethel's got Tempy Mayo's horse

and team right out in the barn and she can take you along
with her well as not, can't you, Ethel?"

Ethel, who had been sitting quietly on the sofa, with the
previous day's newspaper in her lap, but a faraway expression
on her face, started and looked up.

"You've forgotten, Auntie," she said, "Mrs. Mayo's horse is
lame just now and I didn't like to drive him. It was such
a pleasant day that I borrowed a boat and rowed over.... And
now—why, good gracious, it's raining, isn't it? Never mind,
I must go back just the same; I can't be away any longer."

"That's all right. I had forgotten, but it's all right. You can
harness Major onto the buggy and go that way. You can leave
'em in the Inn stable and Am can get 'em next time he rows
across.... Am! Am! Why, where's he gone to? Come to think
of it, I haven't seen him since dinner."

She went to look for him, but he was not to be found. A
sudden suspicion seizing her she threw an apron over her head
and went out to the barn. The barn was empty. Major and
the buggy were not there.

She came into the house, fuming, to find Ethel and Hunter
arraying themselves in oilskins and sou'westers which the girl
had brought from the closet in the shed behind the kitchen.
As Lavinia began to tell of the mysterious absence of the horse
and buggy Ethel broke in.

"Don't bother, Auntie," she cried. "Mr. Hunter and I are
going to row over to town. I borrowed that boat and I want to
return it promptly. As you see, we are rigged for rough
weather, I don't mind a little rain, and Mr. Hunter says he
doesn't."

"Well, for a sick man—" began Lavinia, but Hunter interrupted.

"I'm not a sick man," he declared. "I am thinking of sending
a bill to the Board of Selectmen. As an advertisement for
Wapatomac as a health resort I should be worth their paying

for. Especially if I included a couple of photographs. 'Bill Hunter before and after taking.' You will notice," he added, in an impressive drawl, "that the Christian name is 'Bill.' "

"Don't worry, Auntie," put in Ethel. "Come on, Mr. Hunter."

He, apparently, did not hear her. "Well, Mr. Hunter?" she urged.

He shook his head. "Evidently you did not notice," he said, sadly. "I must send you a copy of the ad."

"What? ... Oh, all right," with a laugh. "Come along—Bill."

"Much better. At your service, Ethel." He followed her out. Lavinia stood at the back door to watch them. Under ordinary circumstances she would have made a strenuous protest against their taking the boat trip in such weather, but now her mind was occupied with something more important. There was but one person who could have taken Major and the buggy. That person, of course, was Amaziah. And he had taken them without asking her permission, something he had never done before. Moreover, he had gone away without saying a word to any one of his intention or his destination.

She had said nothing to her nephew of the disclosures concerning him and Octavia Pail made by Judge Payne. Her knowledge of his dodging of the truth with his tales of lodge-meeting and Ben Crowell's "rheumatics" she had so far kept to herself, awaiting the next occasion when he applied for leave of absence. Then she meant to, as she would have said, have it out with him. But he had not given her the opportunity. He had absented himself without leave. In all the years they had lived together she had managed him as she might have managed a small boy. She had taken over practically all his responsibilities, such as they were, and he had been only willing to shift them to her shoulders. She was the actual er of the light as well as mistress of its keeper's cottage.

And now, all at once, he was beginning to be secretive and independent. The independence could not be real; she could not imagine him doing anything entirely on his own initiative. No, this meant that there was a rival manager at work. Dear, dear! And the man was over fifty years old.

Five o'clock came and then six, and still he had not put in an appearance. It was raining hard now and the wind was beginning to blow. Getting dark, too, time to light up. She climbed the "spinal" staircase—it was not for her quite so easy a climb as it had been two years before—and lighted the great lantern. She would have gone out on the railed gallery and peered along the stretch of sand leading toward the village, but the rain and wind were so severe that she gave up the attempt. She descended the winding stairs, entered the house, and sat down in the rocker by the stove in the sitting-room. There, for another thirty minutes, she sat and fidgeted. Her resentment at her nephew's behavior was beginning to be overshadowed by anxiety concerning his safety.

She was on the point of rising and going to the front bedroom to look out of the window, when she heard a footfall on the step by the side door. Then there came a thump upon that door, followed by what sounded like a groan.

She hurried to the door and opened it. Some one—in the dark and rain she could make out little but a bulky shape— was standing there.

"Oh, my Lord!" wailed a voice, a feminine voice. "I—I'm drownded! I'm dead!"

Lavinia did not believe in ghosts, so she did not accept this statement literally. Nevertheless, she was decidedly surprised and startled. She had expected to find her nephew on that step and she had a greeting ready for him. He might not have fancied that greeting, but he would have understood it. But now the greeting was not spoken. Lavinia stood still, stared, and was, for the instant, speechless.

But the shape on the step was not speechless.

"I'm drownded!" it wailed again. "I—I— Oh, what *is* the
[ma]tter with you? Ain't you goin' to— Oh, for the land sakes,
[do]n't stand there starin'! Let me in!"

Lavinia, still in a daze, stepped aside. The shape pushed
[past] her and rushed into the sitting-room. When she followed it
[wa]s standing by the stove and unwrapping what appeared to
[be] a soaked carriage-robe from its head and shoulders. From
[un]der the robe emerged a hat with a limp feather dangling
[lik]e a rat's tail, a disheveled mass of hair and a flushed face.
[Th]e lower part of the face was in rapid action, its owner had
[no]t stopped talking for an instant.

"Oh, my soul! I'm wet right straight through. I don't believe
[the]re's a dry rag on me; I know there ain't. And what ain't
[dr]ownded is froze.... Oh, don't that fire feel good! I've got to
[sit] down—I've got to."

The robe fell to the floor with a sodden flop, disclosing a
[tal]l, broad figure wearing a broadcloth cape with a fur collar
[an]d bead trimming, a bedraggled gown and sodden shoes and
[sto]ckings. Lavinia came out of her daze and sprang to the
[res]cue.

"Yes, yes, yes," she cried. "Course you'll sit down. Take this
[roc]ker. My, my, you're awful wet! Put your feet right up on
[the] stove. That's right."

The apparition obeyed orders. It collapsed into the rocker,
[wh]ich creaked in protest. Lavinia's fingers were busy.

"Let's get that hat and cape off first thing," she said. "Mercy
[m]e, they are wet, that's a fact. And your shoes, too. You sit
[rig]ht still and I'll make some hot tea. Won't take but a jiffy,
[the] kettle's boilin' this minute."

She rushed to the kitchen. When, not more than three
[mi]nutes later, she returned with a cup and saucer in one hand
[and] the teapot in the other, the occupant of the chair was

still talking; Lavinia was under the impression that she had been talking continuously during her absence.

"I presume likely you're wonderin' who on earth I am and what I'm doin' down at this fag-end of nowhere on a night like this. Well, I'll tell you soon's ever I can get my breath. . . . My, don't that tea taste good! . . . You're Mrs. Laviny Badger, ain't you?"

"Yes. But—"

"Um-hm, of course. I knew that's who you must be. He says to me, 'You keep right on walkin' straight ahead and you'll get there. Don't wait for me,' he says. 'I'll come soon as I can.' 'But how'll I know when I do get there?' I asked him. And no wonder! Couldn't see a thing! Black as a nigger's pocket, and the rain a-pourin' down! 'You'll know 'cause it's the only place there is,' says he. 'You can't go no further 'count of the water.' 'Which water?' says I. 'Salt water,' says he. So off I started and left him there. Well!" with a groan. "Don't talk!"

Lavinia had had no opportunity to talk so far but she broke in with a question.

"Left who?" she asked.

"Why, him. He was the only one there was to leave. I left him unharnessin' the horse and—"

"Wait! Wait! Who was it you left?"

"Why, Amaziah. Amaziah Holt. He's your nephew, ain't he? You see, he took me to ride this afternoon. I says to him afore we started, 'Don't you think it looks a little mite like rain?' and he said no, he didn't. And then, after a spell, I told him I thought 'twould be kind of nice to ride down along the beach. You see, he'd talked so much about this everlastin' lighthouse of his that I was kind of curious to see what it looked like. It and this house. He's always sayin' what a nice house he owns. And we'd got part way down, maybe a couple of miles or so, when it did commence to rain. So then he started to turn around, and the road was awful narrow and the ruts awful deep. I says to him, 'Oh, do be careful, Ammie!' And—"

But Lavinia broke in once more. " 'Ammie'?" she repeated, involuntarily.

"Eh? Oh yes! Well, you see," with a simper, "I call him that because 'twas what I used to call him back when we was such good friends. Before I married Simeon—Mr. Pail that was, of course—I used to call him 'Ammie' and he used to call me 'Ocky.' My name's Octavia—Ocky is short for it. Well, I declare! I haven't so much as told you who I am, have I, Mrs. Badger; I guess you thought 'twas pretty funny of me. I'm Octavia Pail, and I'm keeping house for Judge Philander Payne. You know him—course you do."

Lavinia had already guessed her identity. She did not comment upon it; she was, just then, interested in other things.

"Where is Amaziah?" she demanded.

"Oh, he's somewheres along the road, I suppose. He said he'd follow right along with the horse, soon's he could get him unharnessed."

"Unharnessed! What horse are you talkin' about?"

"Why, Ammie's horse; Major, seems to me his name is. Don't you understand, Mrs. Badger? Amaziah was takin' me to ride with his horse and buggy. And we'd have been all right only for that wheel comin' off."

"The wheel? Look here, Mrs. Pail, maybe it's my fault, but I seem to be kind of mixed up. Suppose you tell me the whole of it right from the beginning."

This suggestion was a mistake, for Mrs. Pail accepted it literally and proceeded to go back to the beginning—or, so it seemed to Lavinia, to somewhere even before that. She talked and talked. From the mass of verbiage Lavinia gathered that, when Amaziah attempted to turn for the drive back to the village the left rear wheel of the ancient buggy had come off and Mrs. Pail and her escort slid more or less gracefully from the seat into a puddle. Then the lady had walked on until she reached the lighthouse and Amaziah was to follow, leading Major. As for the buggy, that was to be abandoned where it was until morning.

Now that buggy was one of Lavinia's most cherished possessions, the horse being the other. The idea of the precious vehicle being left on its side all night in a pouring rain was one which she could scarcely bear to think about. There were many things she would have liked to say and all her will power was needed to prevent their being said. As a consequence she said little or nothing. Mrs. Pail, however, her spirits rising under the influence of the external heat from the stove and the internal warmth from the tea, talked on and on.

She pulled up in the middle of a sentence with a sudden exclamation. "My soul!" she said. "I'm settin' here runnin' on like this and it's just come over me that I must look like the Evil One himself. My hair's all stringin' down and the red from that buggy robe has all run onto my face and I'm sand from stem to stern, as Simeon—Mr. Pail, my husband as was, I mean—would have said. He was in the fish trade, you understand, Mrs. Badger, and he was always talkin' about a person as if that person was a boat. Why, if Amaziah, or anybody else, was to see me now I don't know what they would think. Do you suppose I could go to a—a bedroom or somewheres where there's soap and water and a comb and brush and get fixed up a little mite? I so hate to put you to so much trouble, Mrs. Badger, but—well, there, you understand, don't you?"

Lavinia did not trouble to say whether or not she understood. She lit a lamp, conducted her visitor to her own bedroom and left her there. Then she came downstairs and went to the front window to watch for her nephew and her horse. Of the two, just then, she was more interested in the welfare of the latter.

The night was now so black and the rain so heavy that she could see nothing. The first intimation of the wanderer's return was the slamming of the barn door. Then squelchy footsteps plodding to the back of the house. She hurried to the kitchen and, just as she reached it, the kitchen door opened cautiously. She stepped back into the shadow and Amaziah tiptoed in.

"Whoo! Whoosh! Godfreys mighty!" she heard him ejaculate in a muffled splutter.

She stepped forward and confronted him. In the lamplight he actually glistened, like a tinsel figure on a Christmas tree. As she told Ethel afterwards, "All I could think of was that woman in the fountain in the Public Garden up to Boston. He had on his best Sunday suit and his new overcoat and the water was pourin' from the edge of that coat and from his pant legs and his sleeves and his mustache and the end of his nose. I declare it looked to me as if both ears were full. And he was all wet sand and dirt up above his knees. He hadn't been in that kitchen but half a minute, but there was a little puddle around each of his feet already."

She stared at him and he stared back at her. She was the first to speak.

"Well!" she observed. Amaziah's red face turned an even more violent crimson under its watery coating.

"Well!" said Lavinia again. Amaziah's mouth opened and closed. Suddenly he lifted both hands and waved them in the air. A shower of drops flew about the kitchen.

"I-I-I—" spluttered Amaziah. "I— Oh, shut *up!*"

He rushed past her into and through the dining-room and on into his own bedchamber. She heard the door close with a bang. Lavinia stared after him. Then her sense of the ridiculous got the better of her righteous anger. She put the lamp down upon the table by the sink and, leaning against the wall, laughed and laughed.

When she returned to the sitting-room she found Mrs. Pail already there. Octavia had managed to make some improvements in her appearance during her brief stay in the bedroom. She had removed her hat, her face was clean and her hair arranged, after a hasty fashion. The upper half of her body had been protected by the carriage-robe and, although her skirt was still wet and draggled, her stockings were dry and their toes were crowded into a pair of slippers very much too small. Lavinia was certain she recognized both stockings and slippers.

Mrs. Pail apparently noticed the direction of her gaze, for she said, "Um-hm, I see you're lookin' at 'em. They're yours; I found the slippers in the closet and I rummaged the stockin's out of a drawer in the bureau. I didn't believe you'd mind, Mrs. Badger. My own stockin's was nothin' but wet rags, as you might say, and as for my shoes—don't talk! There they be, behind the stove. I hope they'll dry sometime or 'nother, but I vow I don't know."

Lavinia's just resentment against the cool appropriation of her property was secondary to her incredulous surprise. Bill Hunter had suggested that the Payne housekeeper looked more like a tub than a pail, but, seen as now without the extra wrappings, Mrs. Badger thought that a hogshead would have been a better comparison.

"You're wearin' my stockin's!" she exclaimed. "Why—why, I wouldn't have believed you could get 'em on."

"I couldn't—only part way," was the calm reply; "but, far's they go, they are a good deal better than nothin'."

When Amaziah, washed, combed, and dressed in dry garments, appeared from his own room fifteen minutes later he found his aunt and Mrs. Pail seated by the stove. Octavia was talking volubly and, judged by her attitude, and expression, Lavinia was either listening resignedly or falling asleep. He was inclined to favor the latter surmise, but she looked up just then and the glance she gave him caused him to shiver slightly and look in the other direction.

"Um-hm!" he observed, with a brave attempt at cheerfulness, "here we be, anyhow. This is consider'ble better than outdoor a night like this. I tell you, Aunt Lavvy, if you'd seen us when that wheel fetched loose—"

Lavinia interrupted. "Where's my horse?" she asked.

"Eh? Oh, he's out in his stall eatin' his supper. I rubbed him off best I could and to-morrow mornin' I'll—"

"Where's my buggy?"

"Well—well, you see, Lavvy, I—well, there wasn't nothin' I could do with that buggy—not to-night, there wasn't. I just had to leave her where she was. First thing in the mornin' I'll row acrost to the village and get a hold of the blacksmith and him and me'll cruise down together and fix her up in no time. She wasn't hurt any to speak of. . . . That buggy needed a good washin' anyhow." The last sentence had evidently come to him as a happy thought.

Lavinia said "Humph" and that was all. Mrs. Pail sighed contentedly and shifted the position of the Badger slippers on the base of the stove.

"I presume likely the Judge will be wonderin' where on earth I've gone to," she observed. "Well, he'll have to wonder, that's all. Nobody's goin' to coax me out into that rain again this night; not to walk they ain't."

Lavinia's mouth opened, but she said nothing, she swallowed instead. Her nephew glanced at her once more and then hurriedly looked away.

"I cal'late," he stammered hastily, "that you was some surprised, Aunt Lavvy, when Ocky showed up at the door here, eh? Yes, yes, I guess so! Ha, ha!"

Lavinia shrugged, "I've had more than one surprise this afternoon and evenin'," she remarked. "The first one was when I went out to the barn about three o'clock."

Amaziah seemed to understand perfectly. At any rate he asked no questions. Mrs. Pail's eyes were closing; she nodded. The old clock's striking aroused her.

"Well!" she exclaimed. "Is that eight o'clock? Now if I was at the Judge's supper would be over and I'd be washin' the dishes. I suppose you've had your supper long ago, Mrs. Badger? I should if I'd been you."

Lavinia sat up straight in the arm-chair. For an instant she seemed to be on the point of energetic action. Then her chin thrust forward and she sank back. She had not had supper, but she would go without it—and so should they. There were limits.

Mrs. Pail waited for an answer but none was forthcoming. She sat up in the rocker and clasped her hands.

"Ammie," she announced, vivaciously, "I've got an idea. Your auntie's tired, I can see she is. She's been sittin' here, worryin' about you and she wants to rest. Now let's you and me get the supper. It will be fun. You tell me where everything is; it's your house, so you know, of course. You fetch the things for me and I'll do what cookin' and warmin' up there is. Come right along to the kitchen. Mrs. Badger, don't you stir. You sit right where you are until Ammie and I call you. . . . No, no, you just must let us do it. Don't think about me; it'll be no trouble for me at all. It won't be the first time I've cooked for you, will it, Am? Remember that hot spider-bread I used to make for you in the old days when you came to see me cold winter nights? My, how you did used to love that!"

She was shuffling toward the kitchen already. Amaziah was divided between beaming anticipation and apprehension. He hesitated. His aunt did not hesitate. She was at the kitchen door a full step before the others.

"Indeed you sha'n't!" she snapped. "I've done the cookin' in this house for twenty-odd years and I'm still able to do it, I guess."

But she was not permitted to do all of it. Mrs. Pail insisted that she was going to make that spider-bread. "You'd like to have me make it, wouldn't you, Ammie? It will be just like old times."

Lavinia, for the first time since her début as cook and housekeeper in that kitchen, found herself, if not second fiddle, at the most only a member of the orchestra. She was permitted to set the table and open the jar of beachplum preserve, but Octavia Pail presided at the range and, when she needed assistance, it was Amaziah and not Mrs. Badger who was called upon.

"Now, Ammie, if you'll get me the butter."

"Yes, Ocky, it's in the pantry. I'll fetch it."

"Thank you. You have everything real handy in this little house of yours, don't you. I don't wonder you love it, I should think you would."

His house! Lavinia squirmed. That house was hers, or she had long ago accepted it as such. Of course, as a matter of fact, the house belonged to the Government, but she had ruled it so long that she had almost forgotten that. At any rate, it was much more hers than Amaziah's. He used it only as a convenience, a place in which to eat and sleep, where his meals were provided and his bed made—provided and made by her, Lavinia Badger. She had cooked for him and washed and mended and, in return, had neither asked nor received payment other than her own board and lodging. And now, for this evening at any rate, there was some one else in her shoes— figuratively as well as literally. Could it be possible—really possible—that he would be such a fool as to—

He might be. Such things had happened and to men of far greater intellectual capacity than Amaziah Holt.

Through the open door from the dining-room she watched the pair in the kitchen. This Pail woman must have been rather pretty, in a large way, when she was a girl. She was not ill looking, in a larger way, even now. But her chin, under its folds of flesh, was square and determined and, when she scorched her fingers with the hot frying-pan her black eyes had snapped for an instant in a manner which, so Lavinia decided, indicated that she possessed a temper. Oh, Amaziah, you—you fool!

During the supper Mrs. Pail was gracious urbanity personified. She apologized for the spider-bread. It wasn't just what it should be. You see, she was not used to the stove—yet. It was the "yet" which stirred Lavinia; if she could be sure that it was used with intention. But she could not be sure; she could not be quite sure of anything. And Mrs. Pail was so polite and so smilingly genteel. And, after all, she was a guest. Wait—only wait—until she had gone and Lavinia and her nephew were alone. Then things would be said—indeed they would.

But, so far as Lavinia could see, this interview was not likely to take place until the following day. The wind was still screaming about the gables of the little house and flinging the gusts of rain against the windows. Even this woman could not be put out of doors a night like this. The only way she could get to town would be on foot and that was out of the question. She would have to remain all night. Lavinia went up to Ethel's room to prepare it for a stranger's occupancy. The vigor with which she pounded the pillows was expressive of her feelings.

The room was not destined to be occupied that night, however. Lavinia, as she descended the stairs, heard the front door open and Amaziah's voice raised in surprise. A masculine voice replied. When Lavinia reached the sitting-room she found Bill Hunter, oilskin-coated and rubber-booted, standing and dripping on the rug by the stove.

"Why, Mr. Hunter!" she exclaimed. "Where on earth did you come from?"

He brushed the water drops from his eyebrows.

" 'Out of the nowhere into here,' " he quoted. "The last mile of this road on a night like this is as near nowhere as anything can be—and still be somewhere."

"But what brought you 'way down here—again?"

He explained that he had come with Judge Payne's horse and buggy in search of Mrs. Pail. He and Ethel had made their water trip safely, if not comfortably, and about seven o'clock he had gone up to Judge Payne's house.

"I"—he hesitated an instant—"I had an errand there. I found the Judge rummaging in the refrigerator. He was looking for his supper. He was worried about that, but more about you, Mrs. Pail. You had told him you would be back early and, considering the weather, he was afraid some accident might have happened."

Mrs. Pail broke in. "Well," she announced, "he was right, I'll say that. If he had seen me and Am sailin' head over heels out of that buggy like a pair of—of I-don't-know-what's, he'd have—"

Lavinia interrupted now. "Yes, yes," she snapped, impatiently. "You can tell him all that by and by. I want to know how he ever thought of looking for you here."

Hunter smiled, his one-sided smile. "Sherlock Holmes stuff," he said. "I remember that you said your horse and buggy had gone—er—somewhere this afternoon. Amaziah—Mr. Holt here —had, apparently gone somewhere, too. Mrs. Pail, you had told the Judge you were going for a little ride with a friend. The rest was pure deduction; you know my methods, Watson."

"Eh?" This from Amaziah. "Who's Watson? What's he got to do with it?"

"Nothing at all. Old medical friend of mine, that's all. Now if you will get your things on, Mrs. Pail."

Mrs. Pail did not appear eager to get her things on; she seemed, so Lavinia thought, rather disappointed. Amaziah grumbled that it was a devil of a night to go out in. Neither made any open protest, however, and the Payne housekeeper departed to Lavinia's room to prepare for the journey home.

Lavinia's curiosity was still not quite satisfied. "But I don't just see yet," she said, "why you thought they had come down here to the Point."

"I didn't know that they had, but I thought perhaps they might. As a matter of fact, the person who lives in the last house before the beach road begins told me he had seen a horse and buggy headed this way. So I kept on."

"Humph! Speakin' of buggies, did you happen to run across mine on the way down?"

"Pretty nearly. I stopped just in time." He coughed and there was a significance in that cough, which caught Lavinia's attention. She looked at him. He returned the look and then moved his head slightly in the direction of Amaziah, who was filling his pipe at the moment. Lavinia took the hint.

"Am," she suggested, "don't you think you'd better run out and take a look at the light? You haven't been nigh it since you got home. . . . Oh," impatiently, "don't worry. I'll call you afore she leaves."

Amaziah started guiltily, dropped his pipe, stooped to pick it up, and then, muttering something to the effect that maybe he had better, now was as good a time as any, went out through the kitchen. Lavinia turned to Hunter.

"Well," she asked, "what is it? . . . Why, what makes you look so queer? Is anything wrong? Ethel——"

"No, no. Ethel is all right, but my coming here to-night was not entirely on account of the Pail woman. Mrs. Badger, I have some bad news for you."

"Bad? Very bad?"

"Yes. Mrs. Mayo was taken seriously ill just after we got back to the Inn this afternoon. Her heart has been weak for some time, as you know. The doctor came at once, but——"

"Oh? . . . She—she is dead?"

"Yes. She died about six o'clock."

Lavinia sat down in the rocker. She said nothing. Tempy Mayo had been an old and firm friend. Hunter, too, was silent. Afterward, when Lavinia thought of it, she liked him for that. The average person, she reflected, would have said a great deal, altogether too much. He seemed to know when to talk and when to be quiet.

For a moment she sat there. Then she sprang to her feet.

"I must go there right away," she exclaimed. "Ethel will need somebody to help. I'll go the first thing to-morrow mornin'. Oh, I wish I could go to-night."

"You can. That was another of my reasons for driving down. You can ride up in the buggy with Mrs. Pail and me."

"Eh? Why, so I could. Only—only," remembering the bulk of the Payne housekeeper, "there won't be room on the seat, will there?"

Bill Hunter's answer was characteristic.

"Not horizontally," he said, "but we can manage it in layers. You can sit on Mrs. Pail's lap."

CHAPTER XIII

SO Amaziah was not, that evening, obliged to listen to the "talking to" which his aunt had promised herself the privilege of giving him. That he had expected and dreaded it and was correspondingly relieved by its postponement was proved by his eagerness to assist in her preparations for hasty departure.

The postponement was destined to be a long one. During the weeks which followed Lavinia's brain was busy with problems so important to her and to Ethel that she scarcely gave a thought to her nephew's attack of Indian summer love-fever. On the few occasions when she did mention the name of the Payne housekeeper Amaziah was so meek and non-resistant, accepting her sarcasm without retort and appearing so sheepishly ashamed of himself, that she dismissed the subject from her mind. He realized, she imagined, what an idiot he had been and was cured.

Octavia Pail paid no more visits to the Point cottage. The Badger buggy was rescued and repaired and, on occasions when old Major drew it to Wapatomac and return his rightful owner held the reins. If Amaziah rode in that buggy it was only as a passenger; he never borrowed it again, with or without leave. When he did beg for leave of absence, either for an afternoon or evening, he invariably used the skiff as a means of transportation. And, to account for each of such absences he had always a plausible excuse. Lavinia took pains to check up on the first two of these excuses and found them valid and truthful; after which, being preoccupied with the important matters before mentioned, she accepted those that followed at their face value. Which, as it developed, was a mistake.

She remained at the Inn with Ethel until after Mrs. Mayo's funeral. Then she returned to the Point, but drove back and forth to spend at least a part of every other day with her niece. There were so many things to do at the present and so many complications clouding the future.

Temperance Mayo's will, when it was read, disclosed the fact that she had, aside from a few hundred dollars in her account at the Wapatomac bank, almost no property except the Welcome Inn and the six acres of shore front land upon which it stood. Her relatives in Brockton were her sole heirs and they were located there and had no wish to leave. The Inn, with its outbuildings, furniture and fixtures, was to be put upon the market and sold as soon as possible. The price named was twenty-five thousand dollars. Of this sum twelve thousand was represented by a mortgage held by a Brockton investment trust. The terms of sale were thirteen thousand in cash to be paid the heirs and the taking over of the mortgage by the new owner. The mortgage had two years still to run and could, in all probability, be renewed at that time.

Ethel and her great-aunt figured it out. Seven hundred and twenty dollars' yearly interest, beside cost of repairs and insurance. To say nothing of running expenses.

"That's a lot of money, Ethel," said Lavinia. "No wonder that Tempy didn't leave much outside of this hotel. Wonder to me she could keep it goin' at a profit."

"But, Auntie," Ethel was very earnest about this, "she did keep it going and she did make a profit, even if it wasn't very big. It is the summer season that pays. Every year more and more people are coming to Wapatomac to spend the summer. More and more people are going to own automobiles, too, and go about in them, you see if they don't. If I owned the Welcome Inn it is to those summer people and the automobile trade I should cater especially. Of course I couldn't afford to build on, add more rooms—that would cost too much, for the present anyhow. And that isn't really essential—yet. What I should do is repaper and decorate and furnish—the lobby and dining-room especially. The dining-room should be just as attractive as it could be. Then I would serve the very best food in the county. Mrs. Mayo's food was always good, but there was nothing very distinctive about it. Mine should be. Every person who ate in my dining-room would go away and talk about what they had had to eat; that is the very best kind of advertising. Then I would— Oh, but what is the use? I can't do any of it. It isn't mine and never will be."

She sighed. Lavinia tried to be comforting.

"Well, I don't know," she said. "Even if you was rich and had all that money to buy the place with—which the Lord knows is foolish even to say 'if' about—even if you had I don't know as I'd like to see you do it. Ownin' and runnin' a hotel must be an awful worry and responsibility."

"Responsibility—yes, of course. And worry—well, that too, I suppose. But I would have a wonderful time while it lasted even if I went to smash in the end. And I don't believe I should smash. You see, Auntie, I'd never try to make it a big hotel. What I should try to do is make it the very best little inn in this section. Even that would be lots and lots of work, but it is the kind of work I love. And I'll bet I could make a go of it, too. . . . But there, I'll never have the chance to try. I ought to think myself lucky to still have my job as manager. The Brockton people have asked me to keep on with that until they are able to sell out."

That ended the discussion of the subject for the time, but, on the following Sunday, it was resumed. Ethel had, it was evident, been thinking of little else during the interval. After dinner, when she and Lavinia were alone and busy with the dishwashing, she broke in on a chatter of town gossip.

"Auntie," she said, "I want you to listen. Listen and not laugh, because what I am going to say will sound perfectly ridiculous. . . . What would you think of my trying to borrow enough money to buy the Welcome Inn?"

Lavinia dropped her dish-cloth. "What!" she said. "Borrow twenty-five thousand dollars! What would I say? If I thought you meant it I wouldn't say anything. I'd send Amaziah to fetch the doctor."

Ethel shook her head. "I suppose you would," she agreed. "But you don't understand. Twenty-five thousand is the asking price, but I believe I could buy the place for—well, perhaps twenty-three thousand. In that case all the real money I should need to borrow would be about ten thousand. I might —I might be able to do that."

"For the land sakes where and how?"

"Oh," rather vaguely, "somewhere. Perhaps Judge Payne might let me have it—or part of it."

"Philander Payne! My soul, girl, what are you talkin' about? Philander isn't rich, although I presume likely he's got some money put by, but he's got a business head, he's a smart lawyer. Do you think he'd hand you, or anybody else, ten or twelve thousand dollars without any security?"

"Perhaps I could give him a second mortgage on the property. It is—I am sure it is—or would be after I had run it by myself a few years—worth more than twenty-five thousand. Why, Auntie, good shore property in Wapatomac is getting scarcer and scarcer. Those six acres where the Inn stands is one of the best locations in town."

Lavinia held up her hand. "Don't!" she protested. "You talk the way your Great-Uncle Judah used to run along when I was livin' with him. Don't say another word like that. The very sound of 'borrow' makes me think of him. No, no, child, no. In the first place I very much doubt if Philander, or anybody, would give you a second mortgage for ten thousand and, even if you could get it, I'd still say no. You would have the interest on two mortgages to pay then and every time the sun came up all you could see was DEBT across the face of it."

"Well," sadly, "I suppose it is foolish—but, oh, dear!"

"I know. But an 'oh, dear' over things that might be isn't half so heart-breakin' as one over things that are and you've come to wish wasn't."

So again the subject was dropped. Lavinia sympathized with the girl's disappointment. If she, herself, were wealthy she would enjoy buying the Welcome Inn for Ethel and sitting by to watch what the latter made of it. To do that, however, would mean being so rich that the loss of every cent invested was a matter of no consequence. There were, doubtless, people in the world who could afford to throw away money like that, but it was hard to imagine such people.

Besides, Ethel was, after all, just a girl in the early twenties. Smart and clever and enterprising, a wonderfully good business-manager for one her age, but a girl, just the same. Youth was always ready to run risks and take chances. It was the duty of age and common sense to say no when no was necessary. It was fortunate that she, Lavinia, was alive and well to insist upon prudence and caution. She must be careful of her health; she was needed now as much as she had ever been.

And she was careful, or thought she was. Nevertheless, she woke one morning with aching limbs and a feeling of lassitude which was as unusual as it was uncomfortable. That afternoon she had a chill and that evening Amaziah, in spite of her protests, drove to Wapatomac to summon Dr. Hardy. The latter, when he came, ordered his patient to bed and insisted that she remain there.

"But, Doctor," protested Lavinia, "who's goin' to run this house if I'm not around? I can't go to bed, I tell you. Nobody's goin' to put me there."

The doctor smiled. "Nobody will have to," he replied. "You

are there already. And there you are going to stay till I tell you to get up. Amaziah, you can cook your own meals, can't you?"

Amaziah sniffed. "I've cooked plenty in my day and time," he boasted. "Yes sir-ee, I can cook my own vittles and hers too, if it's needful."

"Ugh!" This from the occupant of the bed. "Cookin's one thing and eatin's another. Who'll eat what you've cooked? That's what I want to know."

"Eh?" Amaziah was indignantly resentful. "Is that so? Well, I tell you I've seen folks take my cookin' and be thankful to get it."

"By the time they did get it they'd be thankful for anything, I presume likely. It takes you about half an hour to get the oven hot. At that rate we'll have to-day's breakfast to-morrow. Now, Doctor—"

But Dr. Hardy interrupted. "We-ll," he said, thoughtfully, "of course if Ethel could come over and stay—"

"Ethel! Stay here! With that Inn on her shoulders!"

"No," hastily. "No, of course she couldn't. But perhaps we could hire a woman to help out. I'll try and see what I can do."

"Indeed you won't! Am and I'll get along without spendin' any money on hired women."

And get along they did—somehow. After the first day or two Lavinia knew nor cared little about it. Her cold developed into an attack of influenza and, for the first time in many years, she was really ill. Three weeks had passed before she was well enough to leave her room. Ethel came over twice, and sometimes three times, a week to sit with her for short periods. It was during the second visit of the third week that Lavinia thought she noticed something peculiar in the girl's manner. She seemed, or so her great-aunt thought, excited and—yes, elated. She laughed when there was no apparent reason for merriment and there was an unwonted sparkle in her eyes.

Lavinia, characteristically, did not ask point-blank the cause of this excitement. Instead she led up to it by a circuitous route. She inquired first how things were going at the Inn. Conditions there, so Ethel informed her, were very much the same. A number of people from out of town had come to look over the property, but she was sure it had not yet been sold. Yes, Judge Payne was well and so, apparently, was Mr. Hunter. Oh, yes, indifferently, the latter was as odd as ever. Had anything of especial importance happened in Wapatomac? No, nothing important ever did happen there after the summer people left.

Nevertheless, Lavinia was certain that something had happened somewhere. An idea, a worrisome idea, came to her mind and she ceased beating about the bush.

"Dearie," she said, earnestly, "I've been sick, I know, but I ain't sick now. I'm well and I'm goin' to stay well. Now then, what is it you're holdin' back from me? You—you haven't heard anything from him—from Bert Thornlow, I mean, have you?"

Ethel's obvious surprise at the question was answer sufficient.

"From—from him?" she repeated, slowly. "Why, what do you mean?"

"Oh, nothin', nothin'," hurriedly. "I just thought maybe— I'm sorry, Ethel. Dear, dear, what a fool an old fool can be when she sets her mind to it."

Ethel did her best to smile. "That's all right, Auntie," she said. "No, I haven't heard anything from—of that kind."

"Well, you've heard somethin' or you know somethin', and you've had your orders to keep it from me. Now I'm past the place where I'm goin' to stand— Who's that at the door?"

Ethel hastened to answer the knock. Lavinia waited impatiently for her return. Whoever the caller might be it was not the doctor, for he did not come up to the room. After five minutes or so she rose from her chair and tiptoed to the little hall and the head of the stairs. She could hear a buzz of voices in the sitting-room but she could not understand what was being said. She waited a moment or two and then, instead of going back to her own room, tiptoed into Ethel's, the window of which commanded a view of the front walk and the road.

Beside the Inn horse and buggy another was standing there and Lavinia, who could recognize most of the horses in Wapatomac by sight, recognized this one as belonging to Isiah Black, the livery-stable keeper. As she stood there a young man came down the walk and climbed into the buggy. She did not recognize him; he was a stranger.

The young man called from the buggy seat.

"Thank you very much, Miss Holt," he called. "Hope I haven't troubled you too much. Naturally people are interested and our paper does its best to give them the news. I'll run down again in a few days; perhaps Mrs. Badger will be well enough to see me then. Give her the *Post's* congratulations, please. Thanks. Good morning."

When Ethel came back to her great-aunt's room she found that lady in the chair where she had left her.

"Who was it?" inquired Lavinia, casually.

"Oh—er—just a stranger—er—asking questions. It didn't amount to anything. Really, Auntie, I must be going. I'll see you again in a day or two. I'm so glad you're better. I'm glad for"—with a little catch in her breath—"for everything. It is *wonderful!*"

A hug and kiss and she was gone. Lavinia did not urge her to remain. She leaned back in her chair and waited until she was sure the girl was well on her way along the road. Then she rose and, in wrapper and slippers, went slowly down to the sitting-room. It was the first time she had been in that room since her illness began, but she was determined to go this time and no one should stop her.

Amaziah was out on a clamming expedition. He should have been back by this time, but Lavinia was thankful for his absence. She looked about the room. It was badly disarranged, things thrown hither and yon, but, although she sniffed disgustedly at the confusion, she had expected it and was not greatly disturbed. On the center table lay a clean, neatly folded newspaper, left, she was sure, by the young man who had just driven away. She picked up the paper and opened it.

It was the New Bedford *Morning Post,* dated the previous day. In black letters heading a column on the front page she read her own name.

OCCIDENTAL MINES IN ANOTHER SENSATIONAL RISE. STOCK GAINS SEVEN POINTS IN DAY'S SESSION. OSTABLE COUNTY RESIDENTS PROFIT. MRS. JUDAH BADGER AND JUDGE PHILANDER PAYNE AT WAPATOMAC LARGE HOLDERS.

When, a half-hour later, Amaziah, his arms full of bundles, came into that sitting-room he stared in amazement. His aunt was seated in the arm-chair by the stove, the paper in her lap.

"Well, for godfrey mighty sakes!" gasped Amaziah and dropped at least four of his bundles.

Lavinia asked a question. "Where have you been?"

Amaziah apparently did not hear her. "What are you doin' here?" he demanded. "How did you get downstairs?"

"Walked. Did you think I tumbled down?"

"Did the doctor say you could do it?"

"No. What have you got in those bundles?"

"Why—why, one thing or 'nother. I've been over to town."

"To town? Thought Ethel told me you'd gone clammin'."

"Well—well, I did start to, but I changed my mind. I'm kind of sick of clams, had to eat so many of 'em in my lifetime."

"I see. Yes, yes. And what *are* you cal'latin' to eat? What have you got there?"

For an instant Amaziah hesitated. Then he squared his shoulders.

"Chicken, for one thing," he announced. "Chicken and cranberries and sweet potatoes and a punkin and—oh, I don't know what all. We're through with clams in this house from now on. We're goin' to live like the rest of the big-bugs, that's what we're goin' to do."

"I want to know! Who said so?"

"Who said— Oh, Lordy, I forgot! You don't know anything about it, do you. And Ethel said I mustn't tell you yet. . . . But," suddenly noticing the newspaper in her lap, "but you must know. You've been readin' that paper where it's all printed out. You must know. We're rich. We're worth more'n a hundred thousand dollars, Lavvy Badger. I guess nobody's goin' to stop us eatin' what we've a mind to—no, nor doin' what we've a mind to. That's what I said to 'em up to the store and you'd ought to seen the way they hustled to wait on me. Eh? Ho ho!"

His excitement was choking him. Lavinia drew a long breath. "How much was that chicken a pound?" she asked, crisply.

CHAPTER XIV

D R. HARDY came the next morning. He was surprised and concerned to find his patient fully dressed and in the living-room. More surprised still when Amaziah told him that she had read the New Bedford paper.

"Dear, dear, Mrs. Badger!" he exclaimed. "I'm sorry. Oh, of course," hastily, "I don't mean I'm sorry for your good luck, or anything of that kind. I'm delighted—we all are; but I didn't want you to learn of it until you were stronger. Too much excitement just now might be—"

"There, there, Doctor! If I can stand the excitement of tryin' to live nigh eighty year on next to nothin' I guess likely findin' out that I've got more'n that won't kill me right off. Besides, I don't believe it."

"Believe it! Why, my dear woman, of course you believe it. It is the truth. It is in the papers. You read it, yourself—or Amaziah says you did."

"Humph! If I believed everything I read in the papers I'd have been up in the Taunton asylum afore this. Everybody in Wapatomac has read it, too, I suppose?"

"Yes, certainly they have."

"And they are all talkin' about it, of course?"

"Yes, indeed. Your ears and Judge Payne's must have burned for the past few days."

"I don't know about Philander's ears but if mine burned any more than the rest of me while I had that pesky fever I didn't notice it. Doctor, you go right by the Judge's place on your way home, don't you? ... Yes; well, ask him to come down here and see me right off, won't you, please? To-day, if he can make it convenient."

Dr. Hardy looked doubtful. "Really," he demurred, "I don't think you should discuss business affairs just yet."

"Sshh! There, there! what will I do? Sit here and talk to myself? Or listen to Amaziah thinkin' up new ways to spend my money for me? You tell Philander I want to see him this very afternoon."

And that afternoon the Judge came. His face was beaming as he entered the sitting-room. He crossed the room and took Lavinia's hands in his.

"It is good to see you up again, old friend," he vowed. "What do you mean by getting sick and frightening us all? I'm ashamed of you, Lavinia."

"I'm ashamed of myself. And if you get frightened every time somebody you know catches cold I'm ashamed of you, too. Take off your things and sit down. Am, you clear out. Judge Payne and I have got things to talk about."

Amaziah was disappointed. "What have I got to clear out for?" he demanded. "You can talk just the same if I'm here, can't you?"

"No. We wouldn't get a chance. Go away."

"But there's no place to go."

"Then go and try to find one. And don't forget to shut the door after you."

Amaziah muttered something about its being a healthy note when a man was ordered out of his own house. He obeyed orders, however, and his parting remark was peculiar.

"Well, anyhow," he grumbled, " 'twon't last forever."

The door slammed behind him. Judge Payne was puzzled.

"What in the world did he mean by that?" he asked. "What won't last forever?"

"I don't know and I don't imagine he does. All this foolishness in the paper has gone to his head; there was plenty of

empty room there for it to go to. Never mind him, Philander
Payne, he isn't what I got you down here to talk about. Now
then, what is all this craziness? This Accident Mines stuff?
How much truth is there in what that paper printed? If any,
I mean."

It was all true, so the Judge informed her, or practically all.
His was a long story, but, shorn of detail and trimmings, it
amounted to this. The engineers and mining experts had been
practically certain that the workings of the Lost Prospect
were rich if they could be developed and carried on. That was
why Occidental had taken them over. There was a certain
amount of speculation in it, of course, but it was speculation
based upon sound deduction and scientific reasoning. There
had been delay, due to renovation and the installation of new
machinery, but active mining had been going on for some time.

And, only a short time before, new and extraordinarily rich
deposits had been opened. So rich were they, and, judging by
present conditions, of such extent and ease of operation that
Occidental Mines promised to become one of the most profitable mining companies in the country. News of the great strike
had leaked out, as it was bound to, and the stock had been
flying upward for a fortnight. The shares had risen by leaps
of two and three dollars at a time. During one of these flurries
they had touched thirty-two. Even now the current market
price was twenty-eight. And—

But Lavinia broke in here.

"Wait!" she commanded. "Wait a minute! Philander Payne,
let me get this—or some of it—into my head. Do you mean
that, while I've been shakin' and sizzlin' and sneezin' upstairs in that bed, that stock of mine you've got put away in
your safe has been sellin' for thirty-two dollars? Just one
share of it?"

"It has sold for that—yes. It has fallen off a little since, but
that is only because the first wild rush is over. There may be

another one, and when it comes, the price will almost certainly go higher."

"But—but it's twenty-eight now?"

"Yes. Or it was this morning. My brokers wired me."

"Twenty-eight dollars for one share! And I've got five thousand of 'em!"

"Yes. Your holdings are worth about one hundred and forty thousand dollars now, Lavinia. I told you you would be a wealthy woman some day. That day came a little sooner than I expected, but that only makes me out a better prophet. Congratulations, Mrs. Badger. I trust your present attorney may continue to have the honor of handling your legal business."

Lavinia ignored the pleasantry. She leaned back in her chair and shook her head. "Well," she said, after a moment, "it may be so, but I guess likely that influenza has taken away my appetite; anyhow I can't seem to swallow it all at one time. Maybe you'd better tell me the rest later on, Philander—if there is any rest. I'm goin' up to my room now and lie down a spell. If you wasn't a good friend of mine I shouldn't feel 'twas polite to send you off this way, but that's one good thing about friends—you can treat 'em worse than you can anybody else. You'd better come again to-morrow—yes, and keep comin'. If this—this mince-pie dream *is* true you and me'll have a lot to talk about and settle between us."

He bade her good-by and promised to call again the following day. At the door he turned.

"What?" he asked. "You spoke to me, didn't you?"

She smiled slightly. "Not to you I didn't," she replied. "I was beggin' Judah's pardon, that's all. Looks as if I'd have to be doin' that the rest of my life."

The following week was a strange one for her and for Amaziah. The difference between them was that Amaziah enjoyed it and she did not. Long Cove Point, in the fall and winter season usually a lonely and deserted spot, suddenly became a center of attraction. Acquaintances in the town who had not visited there for years called to inquire concerning her health. The reporter from the New Bedford paper came again; so, too, did a reporter from one of the Boston dailies. Their interviews with the lady they had come to see were brief and not very satisfactory, but Amaziah was always on deck and happy to tell all he knew and a good deal which he guessed. His photograph, a snap-shot taken by the enterprising New Bedford man, appeared in smudgy half-tone and Amaziah bought four copies of the paper that day. Lavinia, when it was suggested that a flash-light likeness of her would be very acceptable, declined with such emphasis that the suggestion was not repeated. She read the article accompanying her nephew's portrait, however, and her criticism and comments were pointed.

"What's all this about your not knowin' for sure whether you'll stay on keepin' light?" she demanded. " 'Mr. Holt was non-committal concerning his plans for the future.' What kind of plans were you talkin' about, I'd like to know?"

Amaziah, rather red in the face, hesitated, stammered and then became, for him, oddly defiant.

"Well," he blustered, "I don't know's I've got any 'special plans—not yet. But after a man's been slavin' all his life, the way I have, it's kind of natural he might think of easin' off some now that he can afford it."

"Who can afford it?"

"Why, I—we can, can't we? Now we've got all this money."

"What we?"

"Eh? Why, you and me, of course. Lavvy, what's the matter with you? You don't seem to take this serious. With all them barrels and barrels of money—"

"Sshh! I haven't seen so much as a lard pail of real money yet. Time enough to take it serious when I do."

"But we're goin' to see it. That newspaper man told me—"

"Did he? I judged by what I've just been readin' that most of the time you was tellin' him."

"But, Lavvy, with all them shares of Occidental we've got—"

"There's that 'we' again. How much have you got?"

This was a sticker. Amaziah's chest deflated. "Why—why," he stammered, "course I ain't really got any, not myself, I ain't. But you—"

"Hush! Tell me this. How long have you known I had any stock? And who told you about it, in the first place?"

The answer was unsatisfactory. Amaziah fidgeted and hemmed and hawed. Why—well, he didn't know. It was all over town. Everybody knew it. Didn't know's he could re-member when he learned about it first, or who told him. It had just come to him, same as it had come to everybody else. Of course, the newspapers—

"But how did the newspaper folks find out that Philander and me were the biggest stockholders down here? Who told them?"

He could not tell her, or did not. She and Judge Payne dis-cussed the question a good deal, but never solved the puzzle. Their opinion, arrived at some time afterward, was that Octavia Pail, the Payne housekeeper, might have overheard some of the conversation in the lawyer's office—either between Lavinia and the Judge, or between the latter and Hunter— and had repeated what she heard to Amaziah. If that were true, the rest was easy enough to understand. Amaziah could never keep the whole of a secret; he would be sure to at least hint concerning a part of it.

Payne called frequently and, as soon as she was well and strong enough, she drove up to the village to confer with him. The market-price of Occidental remained about as it was, fluctuating between twenty-five and thirty. The conferences between the two friends were often long and sometimes a trifle heated. The lawyer's advice was not always accepted, Lavinia was not easy to convince. One lengthy interview ended in a partial compromise.

"All right," agreed the Judge, at last, "it's as you say, of course. But I do think—"

"Tut, tut! You've been tellin' me what you think over and over again for a fortnight. Now you know what I think. That's the way it's goin' to be, Philander, so we'll stop talkin' about it.... How is young Hunter gettin' along handlin' your business—what you let him handle, I mean."

"Very well indeed. First rate. I intend turnin' over practically all the new work to him. I shall look out for my old clients personally, of course, but for the rest—well, I'm getting lazy in my old age, I suppose."

"There's that age foolishness again. When I tried to get you talkin' about something else I didn't mean that."

"Umph! It won't stand talking about; that's a fact. Lavinia, why don't you give up hard work? Take it easy for the rest of your life. You can afford it now."

"Seems to me I've heard you say that before. I notice that you aren't retirin', yourself—only part way, anyhow—and, accordin' to the papers, you can afford to just as well as I can. Besides, you haven't got an Amaziah on your hands. Who do you think would look after him if I sat down and folded my hands?"

"He could hire a housekeeper. Or you could hire one for him."

"Um ... yes. And then all I'd have to do is sit and watch the way she kept house. I wouldn't sit long, I'll bet you. Not in that house, I wouldn't. Why, that time when your precious Ocky was makin' spider-bread on my stove 'twas all I could do to keep from snatchin' the fry-pan out of her hand.... By the way, Philander, Am hasn't been callin' on her lately, or takin' her to ride, has he?"

"Not so far as I know. She has her regular afternoons and evenings out, but where or how she spends them I have no idea. I haven't heard of Amaziah's being with her."

"Guess likely that upset in the puddle soaked a little common sense into both of 'em. I only asked because I can't be sure of all that went on while I was laid up in bed. I haven't heard anything either, so probably they've got over their silliness. Hope so, anyhow. I was a little worried there one time."

When Ethel came down to the Point the following Sunday her great-aunt questioned her concerning the condition of affairs at the Welcome Inn. She asked if there were any new developments or possible purchasers for the property. Ethel had refused to discuss business with Lavinia during the latter's illness, nor, in truth, had the older woman been well enough or sufficiently clear-headed to show interest. Now, however, she was her keen self again and, before her first question was answered, she could see that the girl was troubled.

"Why yes, Auntie, there is something new. It may be nothing but gossip, no truth in it, but they say that some Boston people—I don't know who they are—are thinking of buying the property. If they do, so it is said, they will tear down the Inn and build cottages to rent for the summer season, a sort of land-development scheme. That will end my dream of being a genuine hotel proprietor. I shall have to look for another position. Oh, well, I can find one, I guess; but it is too bad. There is a splendid chance there at the Inn. I know it."

She said no more on the subject, nor did Lavinia. Ethel had been very happy and very much excited at the news of her great-aunt's rise to riches. And not once—Lavinia noticed this particularly—had she even hinted that a little of the money might be used to buy the Mayo property. If she had suggested that Lavinia lend her the necessary ten thousand, or whatever the amount in cash might be, Lavinia would not have been surprised, in fact she rather expected her to do that very thing. But she did not; instead she faced the prospect of losing her position and her opportunity if not cheerfully, at least calmly and without complaint.

Lavinia, for her part, did not suggest anything. She had given the matter much thought, but her customary caution and her prejudice against anything akin to a gamble or a risky speculation outweighed her sympathy for the girl's ambitions. Better not take the chance. After all, Ethel's being out of employment would not be a great calamity. There was money enough now—at least Judge Payne and the newspapers assured her that there was—and what was hers would be Ethel's some day. Until that day came the latter did not really need to work; she, Lavinia, could look out for her and provide for her liberally, generously. It might be for the best. Ethel was bound to marry—as pretty and attractive a girl as she was was certain to do that when the right man came along. Of course there were no signs of anything like that in the immediate future. Bert Thornlow's photograph was still upon the girl's dressing-table, the chain he gave her she still wore, although not where it could be seen, and all of Lavinia's hints concerning Hunter or any other eligible young man were either ignored or carelessly laughed at. She was still true to her first love, there seemed to be no doubt of that.

So, that Sunday afternoon, after Ethel had gone, Lavinia sat in her favorite rocker, thinking, thinking. Her conscience troubled her a little. It should not, of course, but it did. Reason and common sense told her that she was right in her decision to keep her newly acquired fortune and that Ethel would, in the end, be far better off without the ownership of and responsibility for the Welcome Inn on her shoulders. The trouble was that Ethel wanted that ownership and responsibility very much indeed and she, Lavinia, could now afford to give them to her. Yes, she could; she was rich. It sounded like a joke, but apparently it was the solemn truth.

But even rich people could not afford to waste money. That, too, was the solemn truth.

She heard Amaziah enter by the kitchen door. She glanced at the clock. Five minutes to six! Where had the time gone?

And where had Amaziah been? It occurred to her then that she had not seen him since dinner. He said nothing about going away; as she remembered it now he had simply disappeared while she and Ethel were still at the table. He had not been about while she and the girl washed and wiped the dishes. It was a cloudy afternoon, not rainy, but threatening and raw and disagreeable. And now it was almost dark. The light— Yes, no doubt that was it, he had been in the tower all this time. Asleep, perhaps—but, if so, he must be chilled through.

And then she heard his voice. He was speaking in a low tone, but she could hear what he said.

"You go right in where it's warm, dearie. I've got to hustle out and light up. It's way past time. I'll be right back."

Another voice answered. "All right, Ammie, dear, trot along. I'll make myself to home. Now don't run up those awful stairs. I'm glad I don't have to do it; they must be dreadful hard for fleshy folks. Be careful for my sake."

Lavinia recognized that voice. She sprang from the chair. An instant later she was standing in the middle of the dining-room floor and Mrs. Pail—Mrs. Octavia Pail—who should have been in Judge Payne's kitchen preparing his supper, was standing before her.

Octavia spoke first. "Oh," she exclaimed, "you scared me! I didn't hear you comin' and you flew in here so fast you took my breath away ... Er—er—how d'ye do, Mrs. Badger? Surprised to see me, I guess likely, ain't you? Well, I don't wonder."

Lavinia was surprised—very much so. Her feelings were a mixture of astonishment, resentment and vague apprehension. So this was what Amaziah had been up to. The "silliness" was not over. It had been going on all the time, except that it had been carefully hidden from her. While she had been sick— yes, and no doubt before that, her nephew and this woman had—had—

And they called each other "dear" and "dearie"!

"Now, Mrs. Badger," purred Octavia. "No, I sha'n't call you that any more. I'm goin' to call you 'Aunt Lavvy' same as Ammie does. Now, Aunt Lavvy, you go right back into the sittin'-room and sit down and rest. You ain't been well at all and you mustn't stand too long on your feet. You go right in and set down by the stove. I'll come with you. Here, you lean on me. I'm real handy with sick folks; everybody always says that about me. Now take your time."

The solicitude with which she placed her hand beneath the Badger elbow was tenderly sweet. Perhaps it should have been appreciated but it was not. The elbow was jerked away.

"I ain't so feeble but what I can hold myself up without proppin'," snapped Lavinia. "Now what in the world—? Where's that—that nephew of mine?"

"He's gone out to 'tend to his lighthouse, but he'll be right back. Don't stand there. Please let's go into the sittin'-room. Soon's Ammie comes we'll tell you all about it. There's a lot to tell," archly. "Indeed and indeed there is!"

Lavinia, more or less in a daze but with her apprehension already succeeded by a very real alarm, led the way to the sitting-room. Mrs. Pail, still purring solicitude, panted beside her. She patted the chair cushion and breathed a sigh of relief as the older woman sank down upon it.

"There," she announced, "now we're comfy, ain't we? No, you mustn't say anything till Ammie comes. He'll hurry, I know. He's so impatient to tell you about it."

She went on talking but Lavinia heeded nothing of what she said. Instead of listening she looked. Octavia was arrayed in her best, that was evident. The gown she was wearing looked as if it had just come from the dressmaker's. Her hat was new, also. And—Lavinia gasped when she saw it—there was a new and shining band of gold encircling the third finger of her left hand.

She was gazing at that ring when they heard the back door close.

"There!" exclaimed Octavia. "Here he is now. Oh, Ammie! We're waitin' for you."

Amaziah entered. He, too, was dressed in his best. Lavinia noticed that at once. Also she noticed that he looked embarrassed. Meeting his aunt's eye his own faltered. He was more than embarrassed; unless she was very much mistaken he was frightened.

"Am Holt," snapped Lavinia, "what's the matter with you?"

Amaziah tried to smile. It was not a successful attempt, the smile was sickly.

"Eh?" he stammered. "Matter with me? Why—why, nothin's the matter. I—I'm fine. How've you been this afternoon, Aunt Lavvy?"

"Never mind how I've been. Maybe I'll be better when I know what's goin' on here. Where have *you* been? What have you been up to?"

"Eh? Up to? Why—"

"Yes, up to. You heard what I said. Look at me. No, no, I'm not over there in the corner, I'm right here. Look at me, I tell you! Now what have you done that you're ashamed of?"

Octavia put in a word. "Oh, now, Aunt Lavvy," she protested, "you mustn't talk that way. Ammie ain't ashamed. At least," with a titter, "I should hope he wasn't. Dear me, no!"

Lavinia paid not the slightest attention to her. Her gaze was fixed upon her nephew's face. Amaziah wriggled, started to speak, seemed to think better of it, started again and again stopped. Once more Octavia came to his rescue.

"He don't know how to begin, I guess," she explained. "He knows you're goin' to be surprised and he's wonderin' how to break it to you. Never mind, Ammie dear, I'll tell her. Probably it'll be a little mite easier for me than 'tis for you. You see, Aunt Lavvy—"

"Be still!" Lavinia's command was a sharp as a whip crack. "I'm talkin' to him, Mrs. Pail, and I'm waitin' for him to answer me. . . . Well, Amaziah Holt, out with it."

Amaziah's red face was distorted with another feeble smile. He gulped, glanced at the bulky figure beside his aunt's chair, and then gave utterance to an astonishing statement.

"You're makin' a mistake, Aunt Lavvy," he blurted. "She ain't Mrs. Pail any more. She's Mrs. Holt. She and me got married this afternoon."

During the minutes which followed Lavinia said not a word. She sat in the rocker, her hands gripping its arms and her eyes closed. Her nephew and his bride talked continuously, sometimes singly and sometimes together. Octavia, of course, said by far the more. Amaziah's contributions were mainly confirmations and exclamations of agreement. "Yes, that's how 'twas, Lavvy." "Um-hm, that's the way we looked at it." " 'Twas much for your sake as 'twas anybody's. You see, we realized that you was gettin' pretty old and feeble and runnin' this house all alone was more than you'd ought to tackle from now on, so—" et cetera.

"Course we'd fixed it up to do it some time," gushed Ocky, her tumult of words running like a mill-race in flood. "Ammie and I always thought an awful lot of each other and— Oh, do let me tell it, Ammie. We'll get her all mixed up if you don't— Let's see, where was I? Oh, yes, well—and then we had a sort of—of lovers' quarrel, I s'pose you might call it.

That's what they call it in books, you know. And so he went
away mad and I went away mad and I married Mr. Pail and
that, naturally, you'd think was the end. But 'twasn't, oh, no!
When I came back to Wapatomac to do housekeepin' for Judge
Payne one of the first old friends I met was Ammie. And,"
with a simper, "it didn't take either of us long to find out
we'd never forgot each other, and so—"

Lavinia heard it all, but heeded very, very little. She sat
motionless in the rocker, trying to face the situation and to
realize what it meant, and would mean, to her. At last, a long
last, the sermon, with its punctuations of "That's so" and
"That's just how we felt, Aunt Lavvy," drew to its end.

"And so," was Octavia's peroration, "when you was layin'
here so sick I said to Ammie, I said, 'That poor soul needs
somebody to take the load off her back and needs 'em right off.
We're goin' to get married some day, why not do it now, without sayin' a word to a livin' soul, and go down there to
that house on the Point and start in takin' care of it for her
and lettin' her fold her hands and set around and do nothin'
for the rest of her life—although how long that'll be, of course
the good Lord only knows.' That's just what I said, wasn't it,
Ammie?"

"Yes, sir-ee, those are the very words. And now," triumphantly, "you see we're all fixed, Aunt Lavvy. You won't have
to do no more housework; you won't have to run things any
more. You won't have to feed me nor—nor help me to do this
and that, because there's somebody else to do it. Ocky, she'll
cap'n the ship from now on. You'll be just a passenger, that's
what you'll be. 'Tain't," with another happy thought, "as if we
couldn't afford it. We're rich, we've got as much or more money
than anybody in town. How much longer I'll stick to keepin'
light is one of the things we haven't made up our minds about
yet, but we can decide it when we get around to it. Rich folks

don't have to work 'less they want to.... Eh? Did you say somethin', Aunt Lavvy?"

Lavinia's eyes opened. She raised a hand and motioned vaguely toward the door.

"Go away," she moaned. "Oh, go away!"

"But we ain't told you half of it yet. There's lots more. About what we've planned and all."

"I don't want to hear it—not now, anyhow. Go away and let me alone."

Amaziah might, probably would, have protested against this unceremonious dismissal, but his wife took him by the arm.

"She's tired," she said, in what was obviously meant to be a whisper, but which would have been audible in the next room. "She's tired and the surprise has sort of—of numbed her, as you might say. You and me will go out in the kitchen and see what we can find for supper. We'll fetch hers in to her when it's ready. It'll be the first real whole meal I've ever got for you, Ammie. Won't it be fun, dearie? Now let's go. Maybe she'll take a nap while we're gone. I hope so, poor dear old thing. Come along."

They tiptoed out. Lavinia remained where she was for a time. Then she rose and taking her hand-lamp from the corner table, climbed the stairs to her own room. When, later on, Ocky knocked at the door to announce that her supper was ready to be "fetched up" she was informed that it need not be, that Mrs. Badger was not hungry, but did wish to be left alone.

At eleven o'clock on Monday morning Ethel, at her desk in the office of the Welcome Inn, was, as she glanced out through the open door, astonished to see her great-aunt crossing the lobby. Sim Baker, the Inn porter and handy man, was behind her, a suit-case in one hand and an old-fashioned valise in the other. Ethel recognized both suit-case and valise. They were her Aunt Lavinia's property.

"Why, Auntie!" she cried. "What are you doing here? Did the doctor say you might come out? I don't believe he did; it looks as if it might rain or snow any minute."

Lavinia's first remark was addressed to the Baker boy. "Put those in behind the rail there," she ordered, pointing to the bags. "There'll be a couple of trunks here by and by. I'll tell you where to put them when they come....No, no, Ethel, I won't talk to you out here. Can't we go inside?"

Ethel, more astonished and puzzled than ever, opened the gate in the rail and led the way to the little private office. Lavinia looked about her.

"Shut that door," she commanded. The door was closed. Ethel pushed forward a chair.

"Auntie," she begged, "do sit down. You frighten me. You look as if you had been up all night."

Lavinia sank into the chair. "I have, the first part of it," she announced. "And wide awake the other part. Ethel, have you got a good-sized, comf'table room to spare in this place— one that won't cost all creation, I mean?"

"Certainly. A dozen of them at this time of year. But who wants it? Who are you getting it for?"

"I'm getting it for myself. I'm goin' to live in it for the rest of my days, I hope. Ethel, those Boston folks haven't made a decision about buyin' this Inn land, have they?"

"Not so far as I know. They hadn't yesterday and I don't believe they have since."

"All right. Then they won't have the chance. You'd like to buy it yourself, wouldn't you? You haven't changed your mind?"

"*Auntie!*"

"All right, all right. You can. I stopped in on Philander Payne just now and he's goin' to fix it so I can get the nine or ten thousand, or whatever 'tis, cash that's needed. He'll fix it about renewin' the mortgage, too.... There! don't ask me any more questions now. There's plenty to tell you, goodness knows, but can wait until I feel like talkin'. Just now I want you to take me up to that room I'm goin' to have and show me a bed to lie down on. I'm tired."

CHAPTER XV

IT was not until after supper that evening that Lavinia told Ethel the whole story—of Amaziah's plunge into matrimony, of her night of consideration ending with a decision, and of what she had so far done to put that decision into effect.

"Yes," she concluded, "it's settled and done with. You're goin' to buy this Inn and I'm goin' to live in it till I die. The minute that poor, helpless, mouse-in-a-trap of an Amaziah told me his precious Ocky was goin' to be cap'n of the ship and I was goin' to be passenger I knew somethin' would have to be done. And when she commenced to call me 'Auntie' I made up my mind to do it, whatever it was. My head wasn't clear enough then to know just what I was goin' to do, but I knew what I shouldn't do—and that was stay there. When I booked as passenger 'twouldn't be aboard *her* craft, not while there was anything else afloat."

Ethel's own head was not too clear at the moment. All this was so sudden and so amazing that she could scarcely grasp it in its entirety.

"And Amaziah is really married!" she mused. "Why—why, it doesn't seem possible."

"I know it doesn't. But it is. He's really married all right enough, and, unless I miss my guess, it won't be long before he begins to find out how much married he is. I—I declare I'm too provoked with him to pity him and yet I can't help it. . . . Well, well! Let's forget him for now. There's lots more important things for us to talk about."

Ethel was quite as eager as she to discuss the more important things, but she could not leave the subject of her uncle and his bride without one more question.

"Do they know you are coming here to live—always, I mean? Did you tell them, Auntie?"

"No. If I'd told 'em that I'd have told 'em a lot more and I wanted to cool off a little before that happened. I said I was comin' over to see you and I didn't know when I'd be back. They were still callin' after me to know what that meant when I drove off. I spent from one o'clock till daylight packin' my trunks. I don't think I left much out, I hope I didn't. We'll send for 'em to-morrow and I'll send a letter at the same time. ... And now about your buyin' this property."

She had ordered Judge Payne to sell a sufficient number of shares of Occidental Mines to provide funds for the cash payment. The mortgage held by the Brockton Trust Company was to remain undisturbed, if possible.

"Nobody hates debts more than I do," Lavinia had told Judge Payne in her brief conversation with him that morning, "but I've seen too many young folks spoiled by things bein' made too easy for 'em. The way Ethel feels now she'll work her head off to make a go of that Welcome Inn, but, by and by, when the edge has wore off the new broom, she might not work quite so hard if she knew the place was all hers. With that mortgage interest to pay and the mortgage itself hangin' around she'll have to keep up steam. That'll be good for the Inn and it won't do her any harm."

The Judge agreed with her in the main, but he offered a suggestion. "Why not let me see if I can't get the Brockton people to give up the mortgage? I mean for you to pay them and take over the mortgage yourself."

Lavinia shook her head. "No, no," she said, decisively. "That wouldn't work. There might come a time when gettin' that interest together would be hard scratchin' for her. Then she'd tell me about it and I'd be soft enough to say, 'Never mind; let it go a spell,' or somethin' like that. And from then on it would be paid whenever was easiest instead of on the due date. Oh yes, it would; that's human nature."

"But I am sure that Ethel—"

"Hush, hush! It isn't Ethel's human nature I'm talkin' about as much as 'tis mine. Better, a whole lot better, have that mortgage held outside the family. It's a business matter and business matters in families 'most generally make trouble. You ought to know that better than I do, Philander Payne— you're a lawyer."

Ethel's gratitude for her great-aunt's generosity was deep and sincere.

"You'll never regret it, Auntie. I'll see that you don't. And we'll make this Inn the—the very best— Oh, I can't believe it! It's the chance I've dreamed about. Oh, Auntie, you darling!"

The arms which she threw about Lavinia's neck were trembling with excitement. Lavinia, too, was excited and almost as happy. Now that she had taken the plunge the misgivings and doubts were cast aside. She was in for it—and glad that she was.

"It'll be a good thing for me," she declared. "Somethin' to keep me interested now that I haven't got Amaziah to look after.... Oh, dear!" with a sigh, "if it wasn't for that poor foolish critter and what he's let himself in for I guess likely I'd be dancin' around the way you are. He'll think I'm a selfish, cantankerous old woman—and that wife of his will take care that he keeps on thinkin' so. Well, I must do somethin' for him and I shall, though I haven't decided just what yet."

By the following morning, when Amaziah himself came to the Inn, she had made that decision. Amaziah was in what he would have called a state of mind. Anxious, nervous and shaken, he did not look like a happy bridegroom. Of Ethel, at the desk, he inquired concerning his aunt.

"She is expecting you, Uncle Am," said Ethel. "She is up-stairs in her room. I'll have the boy take you there."

"But, but, Ethel—say, look here! You don't cal'late she—she's really run off from—from Ocky and me, do you? Yesterday, after she'd gone, we went up to her room and I vow if there wasn't her trunks all packed and locked up."

"She'll tell you all about it, Uncle Am. Oh, I must congratulate you, mustn't I. I almost forgot. I hope you—and Mrs. Holt—will be very happy."

Amaziah grunted an absent-minded acknowledgment and followed the boy to the second floor of the Inn where, in a pleasant sunny corner room overlooking the sea, Lavinia was busy superintending rearrangement of some of the furniture. The porter was doing the actual shifting and she was giving orders.

"Oh," she observed, when her nephew appeared in the doorway, "it's you, Am, eh? Well, I rather thought you'd heave in sight pretty soon. That'll be all just now," addressing the porter. "We'll 'tend to the rest later on."

The porter departed and Amaziah, at his aunt's invitation, sat down on the edge of a chair. He seemed to lack sufficient confidence to occupy the whole of it. Lavinia also sat.

"Well, Am," she began, cheerfully, "good mornin'. You rowed across, I presume likely? Well, it's a nice day for a row; little mite chilly, but just right when you're exercisin'. How's your wife?"

"Why—why, she's fine. Only she's—she's— Say, Lavvy, what in the nation are you doin' over here? Up in this room and—and shovin' the furniture 'round! I swan a body'd think you was goin' to live here all the time."

His aunt smiled. "If they think that they think just about right," she observed. "That's what I'm goin' to do, Am. Has the express-cart man come for my trunks yet? He started couple of hours ago."

At this confirmation of his worst suspicions Amaziah's face expressed woe unspeakable. He groaned aloud. Lavinia went serenely on.

"You've got a wife now," she said, "and you don't need me any more than a cat needs an extra tail. Your—what's-her-name—Ocky will keep house for you and look out for you and I don't doubt she'll do it better than I could. She ought to, she's a whole lot younger."

"But—but Aunt Lavvy, we never expected this. We wouldn't have drove you out for anything. We never thought you'd get mad."

"I'm not mad. This is just common sense. You and she ought to be thankful. It won't be nigh as expensive to feed two folks as 'tis three. Your salary ain't as big as the President's, Amaziah."

"I know that, but—but there was three of us for a long time, when Ethel was there, I mean.... Course," he added, "I realize you always paid a little somethin' towards runnin' expenses, and—and now—"

"And now, you figured—or she figured—that, bein' as I had more money than I used to have, I'd pay consider'ble more than a little. Your wife would be skipper, you'd be fo'mast hand, and I'd be what she called me—passenger. And the passenger would pay first-class fare—with extras.... There, there! I didn't mean to bring money into it. Sorry if I did. Am, I couldn't be passenger in that house; I wouldn't know how, I was skipper there too long. Inside of a fortni't I'd be interferin' and givin' orders and there'd be a first-class row. I've thought it all out and my mind's made up. You and she'll live there and I'll live here and there'll be peace in the family. At least," drily, "if there isn't it won't be my fault."

Amaziah was far from satisfied. He begged and coaxed and pleaded. Lavinia remained firm.

"It won't seem like home without you around to—to boss me," he wailed, almost tearfully.

"Shh! That's no way for a man that's just got married to talk. When I was first married I don't recollect wantin' anybody around but my husband. As for the bossin'—well, maybe there'll be some of that left. No, it's settled. Sorry you and Ocky don't like the tune. Maybe I sha'n't like it any too well, either, but we'll have to face the music, all hands of us."

Amaziah's temper flared momentarily.

"All right for you to talk," he burst forth. "You're richer'n fruit cake all of a sudden and so you ain't got any use for poor folks any longer."

"And you mustn't talk that way, either. My bein' rich, as you call it, hasn't anything to do with it. That doesn't count. What does count is independence, and independent I mean to be, rich or poor. I'm goin' to talk it over with Philander Payne and I'm goin' to have him pay you fifteen dollars every week as an allowance from me. That'll be ever and ever so much more than I was able to pay toward the runnin' costs while I lived with you. I'll pay that as long as I can afford it. If the time ever comes when I can't afford it I'll stop. And I'll fix my will so that when I die you'll get somethin' out of what I leave—if I leave anything."

"If you leave anything! What kind of talk's that! You, worth a hundred and fifty-odd thousand of money! Fifteen dollars a week! And me the only nephew you've got! My godfreys mighty!"

"I've got a niece by marriage, though. I can hardly realize it."

He went away in a tantrum, neglecting to thank her for the promised allowance. She saw Judge Payne that afternoon and arranged for the payment of the allowance.

"It's all—and maybe more—than I ought to give him," she said. "If I allowed him another dollar he and she would be

for givin' up keepin' light and livin' on the interest of whatever debts they could run up. I know Amaziah and, although
I don't know her very well, I've known her kind. With Am's
wages and that allowance and a house rent free they ought to
be able to live in comfort. If he is ever took sick I'll help
more, of course, but not so long as he's well. That's for his
sake—not mine. . . . Now talk about somethin' else. Have you
looked into those other matters I told you to, Philander?"

"Yes. I have a list here. But, Lavinia, as I told you before—"

"Yes, yes; but I told *you* before. Have you done what I
told you? That's what I'm interested in now."

Considering that the present owners of the Welcome Inn
wished to sell and that Ethel Holt was eager to buy it would
seem that the transfer of ownership might have been a simple
and prompt procedure. But it was not quite that. Some travel-
ing was involved and Judge Payne, who traveled very little of
late years, turned the preliminaries over to his assistant, Mr.
William Hunter. And Mr. Hunter proceeded to show himself
a keen trader. He journeyed to Brockton a number of times
and he made bids and refused counter-bids until Ethel, who
was impatient, and Lavinia, to whom his ability as a business
man had yet to be proved, became fearful that his delay in
closing the deal might result in their losing the property
altogether. When they ventured to remonstrate he only
laughed.

"Leave it to me," he said. "They're as anxious to sell as
we are to buy. They'll come down to a respectable figure
pretty soon; every time I see them they have slid a little
further down the pole. Two-thirds of their talk about offers
from other people is bluff. We'll get it. Leave it to me."

And, in the end, they did get it and at a figure which caused
Lavinia to open her eyes.

"Is it really so?" she demanded. "They let you have it for
as little as that?"

"Yes."

"But why? Is there somethin' the matter with the property? Somethin' we don't know about? Title mixed up, or anything like that?"

"No, no. I've had the title searched and it's clear. It was just a matter of shaking the bait in front of their noses. They were getting closer at every shake; I knew they would snap at it finally. They wanted the money and didn't want the hotel, that's all. An easy job, any one could have done it."

"Humph! Maybe so, but I'd hate to have trusted it to the average one. Ethel, you and I ought to be a whole lot obliged to this young man, did you know it?"

"Indeed I do. Bill, I can't begin to thank you. Why, you're a wonder."

"Make it a 'freak' and you'll be nearer the mark. Now I want to fix up that mortgage transfer."

He attended to that also, finally succeeding in having the mortgage taken over by the Wapatomac bank.

"They know you here at home," he explained. "Much better to deal with home folks than strangers."

As a consequence of these strokes of business Lavinia's opinion of him, favorable from the first, became still more so. Ethel, too, was impressed. He was tremendously interested in her plans for renovating and improving the Inn and he and she consulted and agreed and argued together. Their evenings, after working hours, were spent in making sketches for alterations, selecting wall-paper, deciding upon color schemes, all sorts of things.

"He is the greatest help you can imagine, Auntie," the girl declared. "He is full of ideas, and they are almost all good. His taste is good, too. You wouldn't believe it to look at him. He wears the funniest neckties and his clothes are usually every-which-way, but he knows how a room ought to look, even if he doesn't seem to care how he looks himself. I told him that the other night."

"You did! Well, I should call that pretty close to cheek, myself. What did he say?"

"Oh, he didn't mind. He said it was only the important things that interested him. Besides, if his clothes looked too well the kind of clients that come to him now wouldn't come any more, they would think he was getting ready to raise his fees. I noticed, though, that he was wearing a new tie the next day. He's lots of fun."

"Humph! A good-sized cargo of horse sense behind the fun, too. Philander tells me he's gettin' on fast in the law business. You like him better than you used to, I take it, eh?"

The reply was not as satisfactory as Lavinia hoped it might be. It was too prompt and a little too careless.

"I always liked him. What made you think I didn't? He's lots of help and he makes me laugh. He's queer and he says funny things in the most solemn way. Any one with a sense of humor couldn't help liking him. I wonder if he'll ever get married. I doubt it. He's exactly like the 'confirmed bachelor' you read about in books."

When the plans for the making over of the Inn were completed they were sent out for estimates. Ethel was glum enough when she showed the resultant figures to her great-aunt.

"I had no idea everything would be so expensive," she said, with a sigh. "Of course this is ridiculous. Bill says things like this remind him of what the Irishman said when they asked him what his pig weighed. 'Well,' he said, 'it didn't weigh as much as I thought it would. Of course I thought it wouldn't.' He says we should have thought our improvements would have cost too much, then we could say 'I told you so.' Oh, dear—well, I must cut out a lot of things, of course. Perhaps I can do them later on—if I'm lucky."

But, the Inn property having been bought for a good deal less than she had expected to pay, Lavinia was inclined to be generous; for her almost reckless.

"Go ahead with what you've planned, dearie," she said. "I had laid out about so much to spend on the place and, thanks to friend Bill and his sharp dickerin', I haven't spent it all. Go ahead with your plans. Only," with emphasis, "don't go ahead with any extra ones, mind that. If you do you'll have to plan how to pay for 'em."

So the improvements were begun immediately. When the summer season opened the Welcome Inn was a lighter, brighter, and far more up-to-date establishment. The stiff Victorian parlor was transformed. Only a little new furniture had been added, but the dingy old arm-chairs were gay with chintzes and the ancient art squares replaced with hooked rugs. There were new curtains everywhere and the lambrequins and stuffy portières had disappeared. The dining-room had been made longer and more small tables added. Ethel had arranged for a daily supply of inexpensive flowers from some local gardeners and each table had its vase and candles. The new paper and fresh paint made the bedrooms more inviting.

"There!" said Ethel. "It doesn't look quite so much like the regulation boarding-house, does it, Auntie?"

Lavinia's approval was qualified. The Welcome Inn, under Tempy Mayo's management, had been successful; she, herself, like the majority of Wapatomacites, had spoken of it with pride, and these changes and novelties were but experiments, after all.

"No-o," she agreed, "it don't. But it is a boardin' house just the same and—well, I hope the folks who used to like it the way it was won't feel homesick when they see it switched around."

"They won't. You mustn't be old-fashioned, Auntie. Besides,

I am not going to be satisfied with just keeping the old boarders; I mean to attract a lot of new ones."

"Don't get too fancy, that's all. Tempy's meals were plain, but they were about as good of their kind as you'll find any-where and folks liked 'em. If you're goin' to have a lot of citified cookin'—"

"But that's just what I'm not going to do. My meals will be plain too, but they will be good. My clam chowder will be the best clam chowder in the county. And my broiled lobsters will be broiled, not burned. I know what I'm going to do, Auntie. People who appreciate the best will find it here and, when they find it, they will tell their friends. That is the very best kind of advertising, so Bill says. And the changes I made this year are only a beginning. I have hundreds of ideas I haven't told you or any one else about yet. You wait and see."

"All right; I'll wait long as the Lord'll let me. Only don't work yourself sick. You're flyin' around all day and layin' awake plannin' all night. That don't pay, even if your clam chowder does."

Amaziah's opinion of the new Welcome Inn was not a high one. He told his aunt that he didn't think much of it. "Looks like a whole lot of fuss and flumadiddle to me," he declared. "All them old-timey hooked mats on the floor! Why I can remember them kind of things in our house when I was a boy. And every last one she's got is second-hand. If you're goin' to buy new things why not buy 'em when they are new? That's my notion—but my notions don't seem to count much now-adays."

Amaziah was not in the brightest spirits, for some reason or other. He was more subdued, less assertive and less ready with his opinion on any subject. Lavinia and her grand-niece had several times driven down to the Point cottage to call upon the newly wedded pair, but the calls were not altogether happy social events. Mrs. Holt was not overcordial. She seemed disgruntled and, though she talked as much as ever, her conversation was mainly in the nature of complaints about something or other.

"Well," was her greeting on one occasion, "how d'you do? I didn't know as we'd see you much or any this summer. Must be quite a come-down visitin' this little one-horse place after havin' everything so big and grand up to the hotel. All I hear when I get up to town—which ain't often with all I have to do 'round this shanty—is how much money has been spent fixin' over that Inn of yours, Ethel. I hope you'll get some of it back, but I presume likely it won't make much difference if you don't. Must be grand to be rich, especially when it's kind of a new experience, as you might say. Ha, ha!"

She told Lavinia that she hoped living up in all that whirl and stir was agreeing with her. "Seems to me you're a little mite thinner lately. Don't you think she looks more kind of peaked, Ammie?"

Amaziah hesitated and then muttered that he didn't know as he'd noticed, 'special. Octavia straightened in her chair.

"Nonsense!" she snapped. "Why, course you do. You said so yourself only the other day. You know you did. What does ail you?"

Her husband's only acknowledgment of the question was a rather sickly smile. Lavinia's tone was sweetness itself as she admitted that perhaps she had lost a pound or so. "I always said this Point was about as healthy a place as there is," she added. "It agrees with you, Ocky, anybody can see that; *you* haven't fell off any."

Both she and her grand-niece were silent for the first few minutes of the ride home. Then Ethel spoke.

"Poor thing," she sighed. "I'm so sorry for him."

Lavinia did not ask for whom she was sorry. She had been thinking the same thing.

"I know," she said. "So am I."

"Well, after all, he has only himself to blame. It is his own fault."

"And that's about the only thing he'll be let to call his own, I'm afraid."

CHAPTER XVI

THAT first summer of the Welcome Inn under its new ownership was a very real success. July was a profitable month but August was far better. The weather was exceptionally fine, every room was occupied, and—one of the best indications that their occupants were pleased—a number of the July tenants pleaded to be allowed to remain through the remainder of the season. The fact that they could not be accommodated made them only more eager, and, in consequence, they made bookings for the following summer. The transient trade grew in volume. Parties stopping for luncheon or dinner, told their friends who, after their visits, told friends of theirs. The Inn's reputation for charm and good food, appetizingly cooked and well served, spread. A correspondent of a periodical devoted to summer travel called and, no doubt inspired by a bountiful dinner, wrote an article entitled "Welcome Indeed" which, with its accompanying photographs, carried the fame of the Welcome Inn far and wide.

It was a remarkable triumph for a first season and Ethel was, of course, very happy. She was very tired also, for, in spite of her great-aunt's remonstrances, she worked all of every day and a part of every night. She was already planning for the year to come. Lavinia, almost as happy as she was, suggested that the dining-room be still further enlarged, but Ethel disproved the suggestion.

"No, Auntie," she said. "Some day, perhaps, but not yet. If people come here and find that they can't get in that will make them only more determined to try again some other time. I may raise my rates a little—not much, but a little—

for I've learned already that the kind of customers I want are willing to pay for the best if that best is given them. And I am going to open a sort of shop in connection with the Inn. People are buying antiques now—old things, I mean. There is a real craze for them; I could have sold those hooked rugs that Amaziah thought I was crazy to buy for twice what I paid for them—yes, and more. You know that tiny little old house on the Silas Webster property? It is more than a hundred and fifty years old and has the dearest little paneled rooms and fireplaces in it. Well, Bill has made inquiries for me and it can be bought for almost nothing. It is falling to ruin where it is. Bill's idea is to buy it and then have it taken to pieces—like a card house, you know—and carted down here and set up beside the Inn in the little pine grove. That will be my antique-shop."

"Where are you goin' to get the antiques to put in it?"

"From all around this neighborhood and in Bayport and Denboro and Harniss. I shall be hunting for them in my spare time all winter long. And Bill is going to help me. He is as much interested as I am, and, in his law business, he meets lots and lots of elderly people who have wonderful things stored away in their attics. That antique-shop will be my baby this coming year."

Lavinia shook her head. "Well," she observed, drily, "I did kind of hope I might live long enough to be a great-great-aunt, but I never expected to be one to a second-hand store."

Ethel laughed. "Sorry, Auntie," she said, "but you see how it is. This," indicating the Welcome Inn with a wave of her hand, "is my only love."

Her expression changed immediately after she said it and she walked away. Lavinia realized that her own pleasantry, had, perhaps, been a mistake; that when sleeping dogs were sleeping it was better not to disturb them even with as mild a joke as hers had been. Ethel, during those busy months, had been happier, in far better spirits. Her great-aunt had hoped that she was forgetting the Thornlow experience. There were certain encouraging symptoms—yes, there were.

The friendship with William Hunter was the most encouraging of these, or so Lavinia was beginning to believe. That young man's interest in the Inn and his coöperation in its welfare were the leading causes of the friendship, of course. But friendship meant closer association and understanding. From tolerating him and finding amusement in his oddities Ethel had progressed as far as a genuine liking for him. She admitted that. And that his feeling toward her was very much more than a liking Lavinia was now certain. Not that he had ever intimated anything of the kind, or that his behavior was in the least lover-like. He was just a good pal, which was very good policy on his part, according to Lavinia's judgment, and, if he had consulted her, she would have told him so.

He was making progress in his profession. Judge Payne relied upon him more and more. He was a partner of the Judge's now. The old gentleman still handled the business of his older clients—of whom Lavinia was one—but Hunter took care of almost everything else. He had handled a number of minor civil cases in the Ostable court. He was popular with the townspeople, particularly with the middle class, those not possessing an over abundance of money. He had championed the causes of several of these against influential opponents and his clients said he wasn't scared of the big-bugs. He had spoken in the town-meeting against certain privileges which the local "ring" had granted to several of its adherents and his drawling, good-natured sarcasms were repeated and chuckled over from one end of Wapatomac to the other.

Yes, Bill Hunter was getting on, there was no doubt of that.

The little old house on the Silas Webster property was purchased and taken to pieces, precisely like a house of cards, as Hunter had said. The cards—meaning the walls, sections of roof, strips of paneling and wooden mantels—were piled one upon another in trucks and brought to the grounds of the Welcome Inn, where they were put together again. The only new portions of the structure itself were the chimney and the foundations. With reproductions of old-fashioned paper and genuine old Currier and Ives prints on the walls, hooked and braided rugs on the floors, and old furniture and knick-knacks in profusion, even Lavinia Badger, who partially shared her nephew's prejudice against buying "cast-offs," was obliged to admit that it was attractive.

"I declare it looks like Cousin Jabez's house in West Den-boro, that I remember goin' to with Mother when I was a little girl," she said. "If you could shut the front parlor and the front hall up tight for a couple of years, so they would have the right smell to 'em, it would be just like it."

The antique-shop was ready for the opening of the summer season in mid-June. The winter season had been a good one; all the regular year-around lodgers and boarders had remained and there were a few new ones. Bill Hunter had been a wonderful help in the scouting for antiques. In fact it was owing to his sharp eye and his tactful diplomacy as a purchaser that the majority of the best pieces were located and acquired.

"It's funny how he does it, Auntie," Ethel confided. "He seems to be able to get things that I can't get at all. There was that old Davis couple over in East Harniss. They had the darlingest curly maple side table. They weren't using it and I had heard that they were willing to sell it; the person who told me said they wanted to sell it very much. But, when I went to see them, would they sell it to me? Indeed they wouldn't! I raised my bid twice and that just seemed to make them more stubborn. They said they had changed their minds—guessed they'd hang on to it for a spell. So I gave up. But Bill called a day or two later and when he came out of that house, he had the table on his shoulder. He had bought it at the same price I offered, too."

"Did he tell you how he did it?" Lavinia asked.

"Oh, he told me, but it was mostly nonsense. It is awfully hard to tell whether he is joking or serious. He said he did it by using the yes method. Old Mr. Davis talked politics and Bill said yes to everything. Then Mrs. Davis talked about what a nuisance the neighbors' hens were in her garden and he said yes to that. By and by—a long by and by, too, I judged—he mentioned that that was a rather odd old table. They said yes, so it was. He said that it was a pity tables like that had gone out of fashion, and, of course, they said yes again. After another half-hour or so he offered them so much for it. 'By that time,' that is the way he put it, 'they had forgotten there was a no in the language and said yes from habit.' He makes me laugh, but he does seem to get what he goes after, I'll say that for him."

Lavinia agreed that he did. Inwardly she wondered—although she was careful not to say it—if he would eventually get what she believed him to be after in another instance.

CHAPTER XVII

THE first batch of summer guests had arrived. The Sunday following their arrival was a beautiful day and, after dinner, Lavinia urged her grand-niece to go out into the air.

"Go to ride, go for a row—go somewhere. You couldn't have stuck closer to this place if 'twas a jail and you was servin' sentence in it. You've worked and planned till you're right on edge of comin' down sick and sick is what you will be if you don't get out door. Now go this minute and stay till dark. You hear me?"

Ethel heard and, obviously, was tempted, but she demurred.

"How can I, Auntie?" she said. "There are so many things to look after. I ought not to even think of such a thing."

"You hadn't ought to think of anything else. And what is there to look after that that Crowell girl can't attend to for a few hours, I'd like to know? She was bookkeeper and clerk at that Hyannis hotel long enough to be some use, I should think. What did you hire her for if 'twasn't to take a little of the load off your shoulders? And I'm here, too, ain't I? I don't know much about keepin' hotel, but I can say yes or no to boarders when it's necessary. Oh, run along, Ethel, do. The few cents you might lose by not bein' on deck aren't a patch alongside what you'll have to pay the doctor if you don't do somethin' of the kind once in a while."

Ethel was wavering, but still reluctant.

"But where shall I go, Auntie?" she queried. "If I wander around all by myself I shall be thinking of nothing but the

Welcome Inn every minute of the time. There'll be no rest or change in that."

Bill Hunter happened to be present while this conversation was going on and he offered a suggestion.

"I was thinking of borrowing a boat and rowing across to the Point," he put in. "I haven't dropped in on Mr. and Mrs. Amaziah for more than a month. The last time I was there she told me that, between washing and scouring and raking and scraping enough victuals together to fill up that man of hers—that is what she called him, 'that man of mine'—she was wearing herself to the bone. None of her bones was within a foot of the surface then, so far as I could see, but they may be showing through the upholstering by now. At any rate it ought to be interesting to find out. Why don't you come with me, Ethel?"

Lavinia nodded emphatic agreement.

"Just the thing," she declared. "Am was sayin' you never came near him and his wife these days and that Ocky was hintin' that since you owned a city folks' hotel you didn't associate with the common run. You go there."

The bay was calm, the sky blue and Ezra Bearse's dory, although fishily fragrant, was comfortable and seaworthy. The water trip was a pleasant one. Ethel, to whom the Welcome Inn, its present and its future, were all-absorbing topics, would have talked of them, but her companion would not let her do so.

"This is supposed to be a pleasure excursion," he warned her. "Business, boarders and bills are taboo. They are not to be mentioned. Those were my orders from the Admiral before we set sail."

"Aunt Lavinia being the Admiral, I suppose. All right, but you don't expect me to keep quiet all the way across, do you?"

"Not at all. Any unimportant subject may be brought before the court."

"Thanks, your Honor. What unimportant subject would you suggest?"

"Oh, the weather, or the morning's sermon—anything like that."

"We couldn't possibly argue over weather like this. And neither of us went to church, so we don't know what the sermon was about. Anything else?"

"Oh yes, plenty. The price of eggs—or politics—or me."

"Do you consider yourself unimportant?"

"Privately—no. For publicity purposes I strive to preserve a becoming modesty. It was the mention of politics which reminded me of myself. Did you know that I may be elected a Selectman of what last week's *Item* referred to as our enterprising and flourishing community? You didn't? Dear me! I supposed the town was ringing with the news."

"What are you talking about?"

"About myself as an addition to the Board of Selectmen. It was suggested to me, a few days ago, that my name be presented as a candidate. No, I didn't suggest it; I merely listened and blushed—oh, yes, and laughed. You may laugh, too, if you like. Don't bother to turn your head, I sha'n't mind."

"I'm not laughing. I don't understand, that's all. I thought the Selectmen were elected at the town-meeting and that is in February, isn't it?"

"Ordinarily it is. But it seems there is to be a premature vacancy. Mr. Nathan Smalley has served for—ah, twenty years at least. He is seventy-nine now and his eightieth birthday is in September so he has decided to resign. Wants to give up public work while still in his prime, I understand. There is to be a special town-meeting late in August to elect his successor and transact other pressing town business."

She regarded him for a moment. Then she shook her head.

"I do wish I could tell when you are joking and when you

are serious," she declared. "Do you really mean that you are going to run for Selectman?"

"Oh, I sha'n't run. The most I shall do is sit still and permit myself to be pushed. I haven't decided to do even that—yet. . . . What do you think about it?"

He did not stop rowing but he looked her straight in the face as he asked the question. He was so grave and his look so searching and direct that she colored.

"Why—why, I don't know," she replied, rather hurriedly. "Being Selectman in a little town like this isn't such a great honor, of course. It is flattering to have them think of you as a possibility. After all, you haven't lived here very long. Would you like to serve?"

He nodded. "Sometimes I think I should," he admitted. "There are things going on in and about Wapatomac that I don't like, and that many others don't like. They think they should be stopped and that they could be if the Board woke up and got after the people who are responsible for them. Our present Selectmen are honest old gentlemen but they have been in office so long and have always been so sure of reëlection that they have grown—well, lazy. A good many of our people think new blood, young blood, on the Board might help toward improvement. I agree with them. Whether I could furnish the right kind of blood is a question. I hope I could, but I'm a long way from feeling sure."

"But wouldn't it interfere with your law work—your practice, I mean?"

"No. In fact it might help it. We lawyers aren't supposed to advertise our particular circus on the bill-boards, so we have to find publicity in other ways. Politics is one of those ways. I always had an idea that I might enjoy politics—in moderation, of course. And being a candidate for Selectman in Wapatomac is as moderate as anything I can think of."

"Then you are going to let them make you a candidate?"

"I don't know. I am asking your opinion."

"But my opinion isn't worth anything."

"It is to me," with sudden emphasis.

She did not ask him why. She had a strong feeling that it would be unwise to do so. She devoutly wished that their voyage might end before another word on that subject was spoken by either of them. And, as it happened, that was almost exactly what it did. From the shore ahead of them came a hail.

"Hello, there! Hey! Hello!"

"Oh, it is Uncle Am!" she cried in relief. "There he is, waiting for us. Hello, Uncle Am!"

"How be you? Seen you comin', Ocky and me did. Fetch the boat in abreast me, Bill. Best water's right along here when the tide's out."

Amaziah seemed very glad to see them, so glad that Ethel was a little puzzled. She found a part of the answer to her puzzle—or guessed that she did—in a remark which he made as he led the way up the beach to the cottage door. She had inquired concerning his wife's health.

"Oh, she's fine," he said. "Nothin' the matter with her that way. She gets kind of lonesome by spells, or says she does.... Say," turning suddenly and speaking as one with a grievance, "you wouldn't say 'twas my fault there was next to nobody comin' down here this time of year, would you? No, course you wouldn't. And I tell her so. Says she don't have a chance to talk to a livin' soul but me. I can't help that, can I? I don't have anybody to talk to but her, far's that goes. Spoilin' a whole Sunday afternoon jawin' away because—"

The remainder of the sentence was a growl. He did not speak again until he ushered them into the little sitting-room. Mrs. Holt, as bulky as ever, was there, sitting in the rocker.

"Here they be, Ocky," announced Amaziah.

Octavia rose from the chair. Her bow and smile were

impressively genteel, but the effort was a trifle spoiled by the fact that the chair was of the ordinary size and she had some difficulty in separating herself from it.

"Why, how do you do, Ethel?" she said. "And Mr. Hunter, too. Well, well, this is a surprise. I didn't expect to see you 'way down here, even if it is a nice day to be out in. Not that that makes any difference far's I'm concerned—the gettin' out, I mean. I'm one of the kind that never do get out and have given up expectin' to."

Hunter and Ethel were rather at a loss for a reply. Amaziah, however, was moved to protest.

"Why now, Ocky," he expostulated, "how you talk! 'Twas only last week—Tuesday, wasn't it?—that you was up to the village 'most all day. I had to stay to home 'count of the light."

"There, there! Do be still. What do you suppose they care what happened to us last Tuesday? Why don't you ask 'em to sit down?" Then, with a resumption of the genteel manner: "It's real nice of you both to call. We appreciate it, your takin' so much trouble on our account. Make yourselves to home, do. Am, why don't you take care of their things? What are you standin' there for?"

Her husband hastened to relieve them of coats and hats.

"Now get chairs for 'em," his wife ordered. "I guess likely, Mr. Hunter," with a sigh, "you must think we don't have callers very often, the way we act. Well," with another sigh, "we don't. Nobody ever comes here except once in a dog's age, and I, for one, don't blame 'em."

The call was not a pleasant one. The remainder of it was much like the beginning. Ethel and her escort did their best to be agreeable and entertaining, but it was hard work for Mrs. Holt was evidently in a fractious frame of mind and determined not to get out of it. That their coming had interrupted a family jar was plain and explained the cordiality of her husband's greeting. He welcomed the interruption and she, obviously, did not. Ethel, glancing about the familiar room, said that being there seemed just like coming home again. Octavia observed that she could not see why it should.

"If I was livin' in luxury, where there was people comin' and goin' night and day, people that had everything and was used to everything, seems to me I'd be glad enough to call that home and not hanker for a two-for-a-cent place like this. But there," turning to Hunter, who was absently gazing at a framed photograph on the mantel, "I presume likely nobody's really satisfied with what they've got; they always think they'd be happier if they had somethin' different. Don't you think so, Mr. Hunter?"

"Eh? . . . What? Oh, yes, yes indeed, Mrs. Holt."

"Um-hm. And when they've got that somethin' different," with a glance in the direction of the sofa, in the corner of which her husband was slumped like a bundle of old clothes, "a good many of 'em are liable to wish they'd been contented where they was. Oh, dear me, human nature's a queer thing, isn't it, Mr. Hunter?"

"Well, my own is the queerest I've ever had, I'll admit that."

"Yes. . . . Now really, ain't you funny. He, he! You make me laugh and it's a great comfort to laugh once in a while. If you had to live down here on this Point all winter I guess you'd think 'twas. You'd almost forget how to laugh—you would so."

Bill Hunter nodded. "I have no doubt I should," he agreed, solemnly. Ethel, catching his eye as he said it, choked, coughed and turned her head. Amaziah seized the opportunity to get in a word.

"I saw you lookin' at that photo on the mantelpiece," he observed. "Know who 'tis, don't you?"

The photograph showed the upper half of a tall, rather bony damsel wearing the tight-fitting, tightly buttoned jersey of the late eighties. The hair across her forehead was "banged" and the pose suggested that her back hair had been jammed into the forks of the photographer's headrest.

"Know who 'tis?" repeated Amaziah.

Hunter swallowed and glanced at Ethel, apparently seeking help. It came from another direction.

"Why, of course he does," squealed Ocky. "It's me. 'Twas taken over at Ostable one time, on Cattle Show day. I don't think I've changed such an awful lot, considerin'; do you, Mr. Hunter?"

Bill swallowed once more and again he glanced at Ethel. There was a mischievous twinkle in her eye.

"Why—er—why—well, I—" he hesitated. And then, gravely, "What do you think, Ethel?"

Ethel, taken by surprise, stammered that she wasn't quite sure. "But no," she added, regaining composure. "I should say there was not much change—considering."

"Um-hm, that's what I say. Of course," with a simper, "I guess likely I am a little mite fleshier than I was then, but I truly don't think I look much *older*."

Amaziah seemed to believe this an opportune moment to edge into the conversation.

"Younger, if anything," he declared, stoutly. This diplomatic effort got him nowhere. His wife tartly ordered him not to be silly.

"If I don't look like Noah's wife in her last days it's a miracle," she snapped. "Planted down here all sole alone from mornin' to night. Nobody to say a word to from the time I get up till I go to bed. And I go to bed same time the chickens do. And why not?"

Amaziah was understood to mutter that they hadn't got any chickens, but, as this statement of fact was ignored, he slumped back again into silence and the sofa corner.

It was a little after five when Ethel announced that she and Mr. Hunter must be going. They would be late for supper if they stayed longer, she said. Octavia evidently felt it her duty to say the customary thing; she begged them not to hurry.

"Of course," she added, "I'd be real glad to have you stay to supper, but the kind of supper you'd get here wouldn't amount to much to folks used to eatin' at the Welcome Inn every night. However, there's somethin' in the house to eat— at least, I suppose there is."

Amaziah came out of his trance. "Why, course there is," he proclaimed, indignantly. "There's plenty. A body'd think I starved you to death, Ocky. You don't look as if you was starved, I'll leave it to Bill and Ethel if you do."

His helpmate was still quivering from this jab from an unexpected quarter when Ethel hurriedly averted the return thrust by declaring that she and Mr. Hunter were ever so much obliged, but that they couldn't possibly remain. Octavia did not press her invitation.

"Well, if you've got to go I presume likely you've got to," she said. "It's real nice of you to put yourselves to the trouble of comin' way over here to see everyday folks like Am and me. Come again, whenever you feel like it—and haven't got anything better to do."

"Oh, we will. And you and Am must come to the Inn. Come often. Aunt Lavinia and I would love to have you."

"I've told her that up'ards of a dozen times," vowed Amaziah. "Told her that Aunt Lavvy wanted us to come and have dinner with her, but she won't go."

"I'm waitin' till I can afford to buy clothes fit to wear in a place like that. When that'll be the Lord only knows.... Well, good-by, Ethel; good-by, Mr. Hunter. See you again some time—I hope."

Amaziah accompanied them to the dory. He was muttering to himself most of the way.

"She could buy new clothes if she wanted to," he grumbled. "There's money enough for that, and she knows it. Trouble is she don't want to buy 'em. If she did she'd lose that much to growl about. Seems as if she can't be happy unless she's miserable."

As Ethel was just about to step into the boat he added a word in her ear.

"I guess likely I'd ought to beg your pardon, Ethel," he whispered. "You must have had a devil of a call. Well, she ain't always like that; sometimes—once in a while, that is—she's pretty nigh all right. I—I— Oh hum—well, so long."

He turned and moped back up the slope of the beach. Ethel looked sadly after him.

"Poor Uncle Am," she sighed. "What will become of him?"

Bill Hunter shook his head. "They tell us the way of the tough transgressor is hard," he observed. "Sometimes it seems to me that the way of the tender innocent is a darned sight harder. . . . Well, it is early yet, and there will be a beautiful sunset. Shall we row about a while before we land?"

They rowed up the bay toward the mouth of the creek, where the marshes, bright with new green, hedged them in on either side. The sun, sinking lower in the west, turned the lightly drifting clouds to purple galleons, edged with gold, floating in a flame-colored sea. The gulls were busy everywhere, dipping, darting, calling. There was scarcely breeze enough to stir the tops of the pines on Henderson's Hill. Bill swung lazily at the oars and they chatted of this and that. They moved on up the creek until they reached the spot where it widened a trifle. Ahead of them, at the bend, was the stretch of white shell-covered beach, with the gray, weather-beaten cluster of scallop shanties huddled against the bank behind them. Their conversation had grown more and more idle and fragmentary and now, for a minute or two, it had died away altogether.

Suddenly Bill stopped rowing and pulled the oars inboard. "Ethel," he said.

She had been day-dreaming, her thoughts far away, and when he spoke her name she scarcely heard him.

"Oh—what is it? Did you speak?"

"I said 'Ethel.'"

"Yes, I know. Why have you stopped rowing? Is anything the matter?"

"Not yet, but I'm afraid there is going to be.... May I talk to you?"

"Of course. Why not? You have been talking, haven't you?"

"Probably I have, I'm not quite sure. At any rate, I haven't talked the way I want to now.... Ethel."

"Yes. Go on. What is it?"

"Ethel."

"Bill, if you don't stop repeating my name over and over I think I shall scream."

"Don't. Let the gulls do that.... Ethel—oh, all right, all right! I'm making progress; it may not seem so, but I think I am. Just before we landed over there at the Point—before we called at the—er—Holt love-nest, I mean—I told you a little about myself, about my letting them put up my name for the Board of Selectmen—that sort of thing. Remember?"

"Of course I do."

"Well, that of itself doesn't amount to much one way or the other. It might lead to something more important, that's all— but I think I told you that, too. I am getting on pretty well at the law—as a green hand, I mean. I think I can honestly say that; you mustn't get the idea that I'm tooting my own horn without any fish in the cart. It isn't all noise—or I hope it isn't."

He paused, drew a long breath, and, apparently forgetting that he was wearing a hat, lifted a hand toward his hair, the characteristic movement which she had seen him make so often when very earnest or very much engrossed. This time, however, the hand encountered the hat brim and the hat was knocked overboard. The outgoing tide was running swiftly just then and the hat sailed jauntily away. He paid not the slightest attention.

"Oh, Bill!" she cried. "Your hat!"

"Eh? . . . Oh, never mind. I need a new one anyway. You told me so, yourself. . . . Ethel—er—er—oh, *damn* it!"

"Why, Bill!"

"Sorry. I'm getting desperate. Something's the matter with me. I—I can't talk. Think of it! A lawyer who can't talk! Oh, Lord!"

He ran his hand through the mop of tawny hair, causing it to stand up like the neck feathers of a belligerent rooster. She was sitting, facing him, on the thwart just in front and he leaned forward and took her hand in his. By this time she was almost as nervous as he and she tried to snatch her hand away, but he clung to it tightly.

"Ethel," he blurted, "I'm making a blithering idiot of myself, but—but I never did anything like this before and—and I can't seem to help it. You see—oh, don't you see? . . . Ethel, will you—could you—"

"Oh, Bill," desperately, "please don't say it. Please don't."

"I've got to. Haven't made a very good job of it, I know; but—oh, well, I guess I've made it plain enough, even at that. . . . I love you, Ethel. Have ever since I first saw you. Don't you think you could—could—"

"No, Bill. No. . . . Please!"

"I don't mean marry me right away, or anything like that. I want to get ahead a little further before we marry. But I think I can get ahead. With you to work for I know I can. Ethel—Heavens and earth, don't *cry!* Have I made you feel as bad as all that?"

She was fumbling for her handkerchief with her free hand. She found it and pressed it to her eyes. He dropped the hand he had been holding and sat erect on the seat. His face, which had been very red, was pale.

"Sorry," he murmured. "Ought to have known, I suppose. More or less of a fool at every turn—but to-day it seems to be more. Don't cry. If I've hurt your feelings—"

"Oh, hush!" she sobbed. "Hush! You haven't hurt my feelings. You've just—just—oh, Bill, why did this have to happen? Now everything is spoiled."

He sighed. "I suppose it is, if you say so," he agreed, "but I'm afraid I don't understand."

"But it is. It is. I like you, Bill, I like you ever and ever so much. You've been the best friend I've had—you and Auntie are my only two real friends. I could always count on her and during the last year I've been counting on you almost as much. And now you have to go and spoil it all. Why—why—*why?*"

His smile was a rather forlorn one, but it was a smile.

"Couldn't help it, I guess. Spoiling things comes natural to me, maybe. . . . I take it then, that you can't—you won't—"

"I can't. I can't. I like you—oh, I do like you; but not that way."

"I see. . . . Somebody else, then? . . . He's a lucky man."

"No, there isn't anybody else. That is—well, there used to be, but now—I'm beginning to realize that is over. I am never going to marry. Never."

"Never is a long time, Ethel."

"Oh, don't!" impatiently. "That is what Aunt Lavinia is always saying and I'm tired of hearing it. I don't care how long it is, I know my own mind. I shall never marry."

"I see. That does seem to settle it. Of course—probably I didn't make it very plain—of course you realize I didn't expect you to—didn't dare expect you to say yes this minute. I hoped you might be willing to think it over and, perhaps, by and by—"

"No, Bill—no."

"I see. . . . Well, thank you for listening. Just friends again then, you and I, same as always, eh?"

"Oh, Bill," eagerly, "do you want to—to keep on that way? Do you really?"

"Why not? That is, provided you can forgive me for—for upsetting the apple-cart just now."

"Forgive you! I haven't anything to forgive. And I'm dreadfully sorry. Truly I am. Very, very sorry. If I could I would, but—"

"But you can't. Then you shouldn't, of course. . . . Well," stooping to pick up the oars, "shall we cruise a little further or head for home?"

"Bill, you're not—you won't hold it against me?"

"Nothing to hold on my side of the line. On yours—well, if you'll forget my—er—presumption—cheek—whatever you want to call it, we'll start over again."

"And you'll still be my friend?"

"Give me the chance to prove that I am, that's all. . . . Well, here we go. Which way?"

"Home, I think. It must be supper time now."

The long row through the winding channel of the creek and across the bay seemed interminable to Ethel. It was easy to say forget and start over again as if nothing had happened, but by no means easy to do. It had happened and neither of them could forget it. It would never be forgotten. They might not speak of it, but it would always be there, between them. The old frank, whole-hearted comradeship would never be the same; how could it be? They might pretend, they were pretending now, but that was the trouble—there would always be that element of pretense in their relationship. She felt guilty, almost wicked and yet she had done the only thing she could do.

Bill, swinging back and forth with the oars, was the more talkative of the two. He even joked occasionally, in his dry way. They caught up with the hat, on its outward bound voyage, and he rescued it and laid it to dry on the seat beside him.

"Come aboard, castaway," he said. "A penny saved is a penny earned. I can wear you for a while yet."

"But, Bill, you can't. It will be all out of shape."

"It has been out of shape for a year. Now it will be in another shape, that's all. Blocked in the cradle of the deep."

He grounded the dory on the beach by the wharf at the harbor end and helped his passenger ashore. He took her hand as he did so and she noticed that his was trembling. There was no tremor in his voice, however, and his words were as matter of fact and everyday as if nothing out of the ordinary had taken place since they left there early in the afternoon.

"You run along to the Inn," he said. "I know you are in a hurry to get there. I've got to make this craft of Ezra's fast and take the oars and rowlocks up to his shanty. I may catch you before you get home—will if I can—but don't wait for me."

Not a word of reproach, not a look of complaint or resentment. He was even smiling as she turned to go. A wave of contrition, of tenderness, of pity, swept over her. She turned back.

"Oh, Bill," she pleaded, "you won't let this—all this spoil our friendship, will you? You won't?"

"It shan't be spoiled so far as I am concerned."

"You see, I—I—well, as I said, I haven't so many friends, real, true friends. If I thought that I had lost one of them I should be wretched."

"You can't lose this one. I promise you that."

"Bill," impulsively, "you are a dear fellow."

"Thank you, ma'am."

It was supper time when she entered the Inn and the lobby was almost deserted. Lavinia was not in sight—she was with the others in the dining-room, probably—and Miss Sarah Crowell, the new clerk, was at the desk behind the rail. She looked up when Ethel came in. There was, so it seemed to the latter, a peculiar expression on her face as she saw her employer.

"Oh, you're back, are you?" she said. "Mrs. Badger said not to expect you for supper. She thought likely you'd have that over at the Point."

"I know. They asked us, but I thought I had better come back. Anything happened since I left?"

Miss Crowell seemed to hesitate. Her expression was even more peculiar.

"Why—" she replied, "why, nothing except that the Baileys came a day ahead of time. We wasn't expecting them until tomorrow, you know. They were visiting some relations over in Ostable and the folks they were visiting with drove them down."

"I see. Well, that doesn't make any difference. They had reservations."

"Yes.... Somebody else came, too. Somebody we wasn't expecting. The name's on the register."

Ethel turned to the register. She read the names of Mr. and Mrs. Carlton M. Bailey, Brookline, Mass. Then she read the entry below.

"Albert Thornlow, Spokane, Washington."

CHAPTER XVIII

"ALBERT THORNLOW." Ethel read the name, looked up and across the vacant lobby, then looked down and read it again. Yes, it was his writing. It was he—it must be. She stood there, motionless. Behind her, Sarah Crowell was evidently expecting to hear at least an exclamation of surprise, but there was none. Her employer did not speak, nor turn, nor move.

Sarah could stand it no longer.

"Yes," she said, "it's him, all right. Looks just the way he used to look, too. A little older, maybe, but that's all. I guess you're some surprised, ain't you, Ethel? The rest of us were, I know that."

There was no reply. Miss Crowell tried again.

"He asked about you first thing. Asked about everybody, he did. Said he was awfully glad to get back to the old town and was looking forward to seeing all his old friends. He's in the dining-room now. If you go in you'll find him there. Better hurry, hadn't you? Supper's most over."

Ethel spoke then. She did not turn.

"I'm going up to my room for a few minutes," she said. "Look out for everything till I come down, will you, Sarah?"

She went out, through the gate in the rail, and moved toward the stairway. Miss Crowell, very much taken aback and tremendously disappointed, called after her.

"But your supper, Ethel. Mrs. Badger told 'em you might not be back and if you don't go right in now I don't know what you'll get to eat."

"Never mind. I'll get something—if I want it. I'm not very hungry."

She went on up the stairs. She was doing her best to speak calmly, not to appear disturbed, not to make a show of herself. She met no one in the upper hall and was grateful for that. She reached the door of her room, opened it and went in. There, without removing her coat and hat, she sat down in a chair. The room was whirling about her and her world was whirling with it.

He had come back. She had heard nothing from him, nothing of him, for three years. She had long since given up expecting to hear. And now he had come back. Soon—very soon, she and he would meet. What did it mean? What could it mean? Why had he come?

There was a rap on the door. She heard it but made no sign. Then the door opened.

"It's only me," said Lavinia. "Shall I come in? If you don't want to see me you needn't, you know."

Ethel looked up. "Oh, yes, Auntie," she said, absently. "Yes, of course. Come in."

Lavinia entered, closing the door behind her. She walked over and put a hand on the girl's shoulder.

"I wasn't sure you was here, after all," she said. "Sitting all alone in the dark. . . . Well, dearie, Sarah tells me you know what's happened. She says she showed you the register."

Ethel nodded. "Yes," she said, slowly. "But I can't believe it. I—I don't understand. Oh, Auntie, what does it mean? *Why* has he come?"

"There, there, dearie. I'm sure I don't know what it means. Perhaps it doesn't mean much of anything. I talked with him just a few minutes. He seems just the same as he used to. He didn't tell me much about himself, except that he had been out West practically all the time since—well, since we heard from him last. I asked him what business he was connected with and he said that he wasn't connected with any just now. At present he was prospectin', more or less—whatever that means. He did say somethin' about havin' had a stroke of luck lately, but he didn't say what kind of luck, or where it came from. He don't look poor; I'll say that."

"But why did he come here? Why?"

"I asked him, but the answers I got wasn't very much help toward findin' out. He had quite a lot to say about the Inn here; had read about it in that magazine and some folks he knew had told him how nice it was and what a success you had made of it. And he congratulated me about the Occidental Mines doin' so well. He read about that in the papers, too—or so he said. He'll most likely tell you a whole lot more—about everything."

"Did he—did he ask about—about—"

"About you? That was the first thing he asked—how you were."

Ethel made no comment, nor did Lavinia continue. There was an interval of silence. Then Lavinia turned away.

"Well, I'll run along," she said. "You haven't had any supper, I suppose?"

"No, and I don't believe I want any.... Auntie—"

"Yes, child. What is it?"

"Oh, nothing. I want to—to think a while, that's all. I'll be down by and by, probably. Yes, I will; I'll be down. If he asks you may tell him that."

Lavinia, at the door, paused momentarily.

"I will, if I see him," she said. "Ethel, don't—don't be too— Oh, well, never mind.... Heavens and earth, what a mess *this* is!"

The last sentence was a low-voiced but fervent soliloquy, spoken after the door had closed behind her. She walked slowly toward the head of the stairs, then, changing her mind, went on to her own room. She did not leave that room until breakfast time next morning, so she was not present at the meeting of her grand-niece and Bert Thornlow, after the years of separation.

If she had been present she would have witnessed nothing startling or sensational. Miss Crowell, who remained after hours on purpose to witness it, was again disappointed. Sarah was a romantic soul and, being a native of Wapatomac and having heard many local stories and rumors concerning the former intimacy between the two, had made up her mind that young Thornlow had returned to Wapatomac for one reason only—to see Ethel. "He was drawn to her as the iron is drawn to the lodestone"—that was a sentence in a story she had recently read and, although not precisely certain what a lodestone might be, she did feel confident that the comparison fitted the present situation. But, when Ethel came down the stairs and Bert Thornlow rose from a chair in the lobby and came forward to meet her, the behavior and speech of the pair were as unromantic and everyday as speech and behavior could possibly be.

"Why, Bert," said Ethel, "how do you do? This is a surprise! Auntie told me you were here, but I could hardly believe it."

"And," said Miss Crowell, describing the meeting to a bosom friend later that evening, "all he said was, 'Well, well, Ethel! How are you?' And that was all. Then they shook hands and walked over and sat down on the sofa in the corner. What they said after they got there of course I don't know, but, if 'twasn't more interesting than the first part, I'm sure I don't care."

The interview in the corner was a long one. Bert said a great deal. Ethel not so much. Her part in the conversation was mainly in the form of questions. Some of the answers to those questions she repeated to Aunt Lavinia at breakfast next morning.

"Yes, he told me a great deal, Auntie. All about where he

had been since he wrote me that last letter and what had happened to him. He has had a hard time, poor fellow. He has been in San Francisco, and Portland—the Oregon Portland, of course—and Los Angeles and Denver and Spokane—even in Vancouver; that is in Canada, you know. He has tried his hand at all sorts of things, clerking in a bank, and with a lumber firm, and for eight months he was on a steamer in the Pacific, going to Honolulu and Tahiti and even as far as Manila. He was a sort of purser—I believe that is what they call it—on the steamer. Some of these positions he knew would not be permanent or amount to much even when he took them, but they were something—they gave him a little self-respect while they lasted, so he says. And the others—well, they promised more, but they all came to nothing in the end."

"I see. Hard luck, that's a fact. And now—what's he doin' 'way East again?"

"I was coming to that. It seems that he was living in Spokane, in a cheap boarding-house, I gathered, when he had word that a Mr. Harland of Portland, a cousin of his mother's, had died and left him a little money. Not a great deal, but enough so that he can, as he says, manage to scratch along for a while. So he decided to come East and see what he could find here. He was in Boston and—well, he took the train for Wapatomac. It was just an impulse, so he says. He hadn't meant to do it—but he did."

"Um-hm. Yes, yes. How long is he going to stay?"

"Only a day or two. He will go back to Boston then.... Auntie, I must leave you now. I have so many things to do."

She hurried away, leaving Lavinia to finish her breakfast alone. Ethel looked pale and tired, as if she had slept but little. But, or so her aunt thought or imagined, there was an air of excitement about her, almost elation. Dear, dear. This was a mess! And what would come of it?

Thornlow, himself, entered the dining-room just then, saw

Mrs. Badger at her table, and came over. She asked him to sit down and he did so. They had met and conversed the evening before, but she was glad of this opportunity, especially as there was no third person present. She meant to draw him out, if possible, get him to talk about himself. After a little she realized that no drawing out would be necessary; he seemed to be eager to talk.

He told her of his wanderings since he left Chicago, a little of his various attempts to find satisfactory and permanent employment, of the small legacy which had come to him and of his determination to come East and see what, if any, opportunity he could find there. He was, as always, a good talker, his manner had lost nothing of its charm, and, except that he was a trifle thinner and a little less exuberantly boyish, Lavinia found little change in him. As handsome as ever, and as likeable, she found herself listening to and laughing with him just as she used when he came to the Point cottage. He had been telling a humorous story of a happening on his voyage to the South Seas, but, when it reached its end, his manner changed. He became suddenly grave.

"Mrs. Badger," he said, "or Aunt Lavinia—that is what I used to call you and, if you don't mind, I'm going to call you so now. Sitting here, you see, talking with you, makes me feel as if I hadn't been away at all. Aunt Lavinia, I know you are wondering just why I came to Wapatomac. What my real reason for coming was. You are wondering that, aren't you?"

It was more of an assertion than a question, but he seemed to expect an answer. She—and it was unusual for her—was a trifle embarrassed.

"Why—why, I wouldn't say that, hardly," she equivocated. "Lots of folks do come here. This place wouldn't last long as a hotel if they didn't."

He smiled. "You're dodging," he declared. "Of course you are wondering. I wish I could give you a satisfactory reason,, but I can't. You see, I don't know. I was in Boston and I was lonely. The few people I do know up there were going home for the week-end. I hadn't any home to go to—haven't had for a hundred years, or so it seems to me sometimes. I was thinking of Wapatomac and—well, it did somehow seem like home. It always has ever since I left it. I had the best times of my life down here."

He paused, momentarily, and then added.

"So—well, I jumped the train and came. As I said in the beginning, I had no good excuse for coming—considering everything."

It was charmingly said, with just the right tone of depreciation and apology, but Lavinia Badger did not like it. It sounded sincere, but her common sense told her that it was not.

"Nonsense, young man," she said, almost sharply. "I know what you came for and so do you. You came to see Ethel, of course. Why not own up to it?"

He did not seem to resent the tone or the statement.

"Did she tell you I said that was what I came for?"

"No. Do you think likely she would, even if you had told her?"

"I don't know, she might. I imagine she tells you most things. But that makes no difference. And you're right; it was to see her that I came. I did not tell her that, in so many words, but I suppose she guessed it, just as you did. Probably I shouldn't have come; I'm sure you think I shouldn't. I am a failure, of course. A flat failure."

"Here, here! A young man your age shouldn't talk that way —not yet."

"Why not? It is true. Oh, now, wait a minute. I mean it is true so far. Perhaps it won't always be true, certainly it won't if I can help it. The reason I speak of it is just this: I don't want you to think that I have come here with the faintest idea that matters between Ethel and me are going to be as they were before I went away. I am not fool enough to expect that, or, for her sake, even wish it. Why, for all I knew I might have found her married to some one else."

"Yes? ... Um-hm. ... Well, she isn't. Unless you want to call it that she's married to this hotel. She's devotin' her life to that and she's makin' it go, too."

"So I understand. I had heard of its success before I came East at all. She is a clever girl, a wonderful girl, and I am what I said I was—a failure so far. Now, Mrs. Badger—Aunt Lavinia, I mean—I am going to be honest with you. My feelings toward Ethel have not changed—they never will. Hers toward me have changed, I suppose; there is no reason why they shouldn't."

He paused, momentarily. If he was hoping to find an answer in Lavinia's expression, or if he expected her to speak, he was disappointed. She was thinking, however, and her thought was: "So she hasn't told you whether they have changed or not. Well, that's something, anyhow."

He went on.

"That makes no difference, so far as what I am trying to tell you is concerned," he said, earnestly. "If my coming back into her life is worrying you, Mrs. Badger, it need not. I am just another transient, that's all, and you may consider me just that.... There! Now I've spoiled your breakfast, I am afraid, but at least we understand each other."

He rose and moved on to another table. Lavinia finished her cup of coffee. It was cold by this time, but she was scarcely aware of it. She was not too confident of that mutual understanding. He might understand her, apparently he did, but did she thoroughly understand him? He had seemed entirely frank and open, the soul of candor and self-abnegation; he should, perhaps, have been entirely convincing, but she was not entirely convinced. It was as it had always been since she first knew him. While he talked she was inclined to believe every word; but afterward the disturbing doubts began to creep back into her mind. If he was so determined that the old love affair was a thing of the past, something never to be renewed, why had he come there at all? He had given her an answer to that question. He had come to see Ethel, but only as a friend. . . . Well—maybe. . . . But all that about half expecting to find Ethel married to some one else. Rubbish! He had read the article in the magazine and that had referred to her as "Miss Holt, the charming young hostess." And those friends who had praised the Welcome Inn in his hearing—they must have known she was not married. Bosh! Stuff and nonsense! So much of it, at any rate.

Dear, dear, dear! Man born of woman is of few days and full of trouble. It was Job who said that, wasn't it? Well, if Job was a married man—she could not remember whether he was or not—and had asked his wife's opinion of that bit of wisdom, the lady could have told him that a woman's troubles were quite as plentiful and that the most troublesome trouble was the man himself.

Bert Thornlow kept his word. He remained at the Inn but two days; then he returned to Boston. Lavinia's breath of relief was not a deep one, however. Her prophecy, made only to herself, was that he would be back again before long. He was; the train on Friday evening brought him, and this time he stayed until the following Monday.

"I just can't help it," he told Miss Crowell. "Boston is as dead as Copps' Hill at this time of year. And hotter than the sub-cellar of the hereafter, besides. All I could think of was the ocean breeze blowing the curtains of my bedroom window here at the Inn. And then—*you* were here, you know. Oh, I had to come!"

Sarah giggled and exclaimed, "Oh, you get out!" She did not want him to get out, however. In her opinion he was "just as nice as he could be and so full of fun." Her gaze followed him admiringly as he turned away from the counter.

He came again the following Friday and, on Saturday, Lavinia was surprised to find the porter delivering a trunk marked with his initials at the door of his room at the end of the corridor. It was one of the smaller and least expensive rooms in the house; he had taken it, so he told her during their conversation at the breakfast table, because it was cheap and because his stay was to be so short. She spoke to the porter about the trunk.

"Um-hm, it's Mr. Thornlow's," so the porter told her. "He's goin' to stay with us a spell, seems so. No, he never said how long. I wish 'twould be all summer. He's a fine man; give me half a dollar when he went away last time."

Lavinia casually mentioned the trunk when she and Ethel met at luncheon. Ethel was quite willing, even eager, to explain.

"He says that, so far as he can see, he might as well be here as anywhere else for the present. His friends in Boston are looking about to find an opening for him but, of course, they aren't likely to find the right thing immediately and the summer is the worst possible season. They believe, so he says, that something really good may turn up in the fall."

"And he's goin' to put up here till the fall comes? Is that it?"

"Why—I don't know. He may. It will cost him no more here than in the city. That room of his is about the lowest priced one we have, but he says it will do perfectly well and is certainly all he can afford."

"Hum! So he's contented to sit down here in Wapatomac and wait."

"Of course he isn't contented," almost sharply. "I don't see why you say that, Auntie. He isn't contented and he isn't happy. He is miserable, I know he is, but he doesn't complain. And when you think that, only a few years ago, he had everything he wanted and now has nothing, I think he is pretty brave. If he wants to stay here, and pays his board like other people, I see no reason why he shouldn't. Do you?"

Lavinia believed she could see at least one very important reason, but she made no reply. She found a ray of comfort in the fact that, so far at least, she had noticed nothing to indicate that, on the part of the new boarder, there was any attempt to reëstablish himself in Ethel's affection. They met frequently, of course, but almost always when others were present, and, to all appearances at least, he was merely what he had told Lavinia he intended to be, a friend. Whether or not this was simply tactful diplomacy on his part she had no means of knowing. As to Ethel's feeling toward him she was equally uncertain, although it had not been so very long since her grand-niece had vowed that she still loved him and would always love him.

There was nothing she, Lavinia, could do—except wait and watch, and what good would come of waiting and watching she could not see. Ethel was a girl no longer; she was a woman, with a mind of her own. But then, Lavinia, too, had a mind of her own.

Thornlow was already popular with the other guests at the Welcome Inn, and their number was increasing daily. He had lost none of his old charm and good looks and, not only the younger set but their elders as well, enjoyed and cultivated his society. Amaziah and his wife called one afternoon and both yielded to the spell. In Amaziah's case it was merely a revival of the old adoration, but for the discontented and cantankerous Ocky to join the chorus of laudation was something of a surprise—to Lavinia at any rate.

"Well, sir," declared Amaziah, "to see him around Wapatomac again is enough to make you believe that there's a barn in Gilead, as the fellow said. If he ain't an example of what a gentleman ought to be then I never saw one. Knew me the minute he laid eyes on me, he did, and come right across the room and sang out my name. "Why, if it isn't Mr. Holt!' he says. And if I'd had a million dollars right in my fist he couldn't have grabbed for my hand any quicker than he done. Could he now, Ocky, eh?"

Octavia, although evidently as favorably impressed as her husband by the Thornlow condescension and cordiality, could not forego the opportunity to make one disagreeable remark.

"I don't know, I'm sure," she snapped. "I never saw you with as much as twenty dollars in your fist, all at one time."

Amaziah, for once, ventured a retort. "I can't go to bed with fifty cents in my pants pocket without findin' it gone when I turn out in the mornin'," he grumbled. "And there's no holes in them pockets either—except at the top."

His wife ignored the innuendo. "Mr. Thornlow is a gentleman," she announced. "He is coming down to have dinner with us next Thursday. Considerin' that he is—well, just a stranger, as you might say, and we ain't even—ahem—poor relations of his, I think it is very nice of him. Our own flesh and blood relations don't come to see us *too* often. . . . Oh, and that reminds me, Ethel. How is Mr. Hunter, these days? Are he and Mr. Thornlow good friends?"

Ethel, taken by surprise, colored slightly. "Why, yes," she replied. "They seem to be. Why not?"

"Oh, nothin'," with a smile. "I just wondered, that's all."

Hunter and Thornlow were friendly enough, judging by outward appearances. Ethel had introduced them the day after Bert's first arrival, which was also the day after she and Bill had rowed home from the Point. When she and Bill met that morning there had been some embarrassment on her part, mingled with a little doubt and trepidation. In spite of their agreement to continue to "go on as if nothing has happened," the fact that it had happened made the meeting a trifle awkward—at least, it seemed so to her.

But Bill did not seem embarrassed. His good morning was as cheery and his manner as easy as if there had been no proposal and no rejection only a few hours before. He appeared almost as if he had forgotten the affair already. Of course that is precisely what she should have hoped he would do, but she could not help feeling a twinge of resentment. A heartbroken lover should not joke—not so soon after sustaining the fracture. Such casual good humor, even if only pretense, was not flattering to one's vanity. She had told Aunt Lavinia nothing of the proposal. It was not a thing to tell any one—even her. And Bill, she knew, was a favorite of Lavinia's. She felt a little guilty, which was ridiculous, because she could have said and done nothing else. And why should she trouble herself when, apparently, the other party concerned was concerned very little?

Nevertheless, the feeling of guilt persisted and possibly that was the reason prompting her statement to Thornlow a short time afterward. Thornlow and Hunter had been introduced, had chatted a few minutes, and then the latter had departed for the law office. Bert watched him go, a smile lifting a corner of his mouth.

"He's an odd dick, isn't he?" he observed.

Ethel did not smile. "He is one of the finest fellows I know," she said, almost sharply.

Thornlow looked at her, then in the direction of the closing door.

"Oh, yes, of course—no doubt," he agreed. "Well, Miss Welcome Inn, I suppose you are going to be very busy this morning. Is there anything I can do to help? Carry trunks or dust off the ink? No? I expected as much. I seem to be more or less useless wherever I go."

There was just a touch of bitterness in the last sentence. Ethel noticed it, but he walked away before she could speak again.

CHAPTER XIX

JUNE was over and July came in. The first of the month brought with it a new flock of boarders to the Welcome Inn. Every room was taken and the bookings for August were to capacity. The antique-shop was doing a good business. This meant, of course, constant replenishing of the stock and consequent excursions throughout the surrounding districts in search of new finds and treasures. One thing Lavinia, the ever watchful, noticed about these antique hunts—that is, that, whereas during the winter months it had been Hunter who usually accompanied her grand-niece, now her companion was much more likely to be Thornlow.

Of course there might be various reasons for this. Bill Hunter was busy in the Payne law office a great deal of the time and it was hard for him to leave in the daytime. He was getting on famously with his work there, was coming to be known at the Ostable court-house and throughout the county. His hint to Ethel that he might possibly be candidate for the Wapatomac Board of Selectmen was a hint no longer. He was a candidate, open and avowed, and rumor whispered that his chance of election was good. The local "ring"—meaning the handful of well-to-do and ultra-conservative citizens who had handled and managed political affairs in the town for years— disapproved of his "new-fangled" ideas and had a candidate of its own, but Hunter was growing in popularity. He was young, but he had horse sense and played a square game, so people said. "Wouldn't do a mite of harm to put a new punch in that dead-and-alive Board, anyhow," that was the word passed about through the gathering at the post-office at mail time. And Judge Payne confided to Lavinia, during one of their conferences in his private office, that he should not be surprised if the boy won out.

"It would be a rather good joke on the old crowd if he did," he chuckled. "They have been having things their own way so long that they are about due for a surprise."

"You goin' to vote for him, Philander?" Lavinia asked.

"Guess so; that is, if I get up to the town-meeting. And I shall get there if I'm feeling all right and the weather is good."

The Judge was not, as Lavinia would have put it, as spry as he used to be. During the past year or two he had aged perceptibly. He was much more careful of his health and seldom went out of doors in inclement weather. His mind was alert enough, however, and he and Lavinia had some sharp arguments concerning business matters. They often disagreed, but Lavinia usually had her own way.

"I think you'll be sorry," he told her.

"Maybe, and then you can always have the comfort of sayin' 'I told you so.' The way I look at it, Philander, I'd rather be sorry and safe than just sorry."

If Hunter noticed that Bert Thornlow was gradually taking his place as companion and adviser on the searches after antiques he said nothing about it. If he noticed that Ethel and the new boarder were together more and more often he did not appear to do so. He must have heard of their former attraction for each other—Amaziah Holt, for one, took pains to tell him all about it—but it did not seem to disturb him, outwardly at least. His manner toward Ethel had changed not at all. He was friendly, good-natured and, as ever, eager to oblige when he could. With Thornlow he was always agreeable. They were not close friends—they never would be, for two people were never less alike—but they chatted pleasantly when they met and there were no signs that Hunter regarded the other as a hated rival.

Lavinia was inclined to resent this attitude on his part. She was certain that he was in love with her grand-niece and for him to step aside and let another fellow walk away with his girl without making the slightest effort to help himself was irritating. Knowing nothing of what had taken place in the dory that Sunday afternoon, she lost patience with him. She could see what was happening, didn't like it, but could do nothing to prevent it. If she were William Hunter, however, she would, at least, try to do something, indeed she would. She had half a mind to tell him to wake up before it was too late.

Always provided, of course, that it was not too late already. She was beginning to fear that it was.

And, one evening, early in the month, she learned that her fears were justified. Ethel and Thornlow had been out attending a meeting of the local Dramatic Club. Ethel, ever since her high-school days, had been interested in amateur theatricals. The Club was planning to give its annual production of a play early in August and at this meeting the play was to be reread and the parts definitely assigned. Hunter was to take part—he had a talent for comedy and characterization—and Ethel, if she could spare the time, was to play the young heroine. She was not as yet certain that the time could be spared. If she accepted the rôle, she told Lavinia before she went out to the meeting, hers would be only a tentative acceptance. If, after a week or two, she found that she was likely to be too busy to attend rehearsals, they must find some one else for her place.

Bert Thornlow, too, might take part in the play; in fact it was quite possible that his was to be the leading rôle. The young man who would ordinarily have been chosen for it had been taken ill and Dr. Hardy emphatically declined to permit his leaving his room for at least a month. In this emergency the Club was desperately searching for some one to take his place when a member suggested that perhaps Mr. Thornlow might be persuaded to try it. He had already attended several of the preliminary meetings, acting as Ethel's escort, and, when questioned, admitted that he had done a good deal of amateur acting in his college years. He had asked for a little time to consider the matter but was expected to give his answer at this particular meeting.

The meeting was a protracted one and it was almost midnight when Lavinia, awake as she usually was when her grandniece was out—a habit carried over from the latter's girlhood—heard the front door of the Inn open and close. The lower floor of the Welcome Inn, except on Saturday evenings, was invariably dark and deserted by eleven, so there was no doubt in Lavinia's mind as to the identity of the late arrivals. A few minutes later she heard Ethel's step on the second-floor corridor. She opened the door a crack and whispered her name.

Ethel heard the whisper and turned. She opened the door and entered.

"Good gracious, Auntie!" she exclaimed. "You up and with the lamp lighted at this hour! What is the matter?"

"Nothin' at all. I couldn't sleep, so I cal'lated I might as well set up and read for a spell. Well, how did the play-meetin' go? Made up your mind not to take that part, I hope. You shouldn't, with all you've got on your hands already."

Ethel laughed. She seemed in high good spirits. There was color in her cheeks and her eyes were very bright.

"Sorry to disappoint you, Auntie," she said, "but I have taken it—that is, I am going to try to take it. I may have to turn it over to some one else by and by, but I hope not. It's an awfully good part."

"How about Bert? What did he decide?"

"Oh, he is going to be the hero. He didn't really want to very much, but he finally said he would if I would. So the whole cast is made up now. And he'll be splendid, too; you see if he isn't. He would be good at anything."

"Except hard work." It was not often that Lavinia Badger spoke impulsively, but she did so then. The thought was in her mind and the words were uttered before she realized her great mistake. Realization came quickly enough. Ethel turned like a flash.

"Why, what do you mean?" she said, hotly. "How can you say that? After all he has been through—and suffered—and— Oh, you ought to be ashamed of yourself!"

"There, there, child! I'm sorry. I didn't mean—"

"I wouldn't have believed it of you! Of course I always knew you never really liked him. You pretended to, but I was sure you didn't, just the same. Well, *I* like him. And I believe in him. No matter if everybody else in the world hated him I should always— Oh, how could you! . . . Good night."

She was at the door, but Lavinia hurried after her and caught her arm.

"Ethel, Ethel!" she pleaded.

"No, I don't want to talk to you. I don't want to hear another word. You have said enough. It shows—"

"Ethel—wait. Please wait. I am sorry—awfully sorry. Don't go. You and I haven't ever gone to bed, either of us, with hard feelin's against the other—not in all our life together we haven't. We mustn't do it now."

Ethel remained where she was, a hand upon the door knob. She did not turn—but neither did she open the door. Lavinia tried once more.

"Ethel, dearie, come back and sit down for just a minute. I think it is time we had a talk. I shouldn't have said what I did, I know. You can put it down to jealousy, I guess. I've lived long enough—or so any sensible person would think—not to be jealous of anybody or anything, but where you're concerned I can't seem to get over it. The notion of anybody comin' between you and me is—well, it seems to fetch out all the spite in me. I'm an old woman and gettin' childish and silly, I presume likely. You mustn't mind me too much; call it that I ain't responsible. . . . Now shall we come back and sit down?"

She turned toward the chair. Ethel hesitated an instant and then followed her, sitting on the side of the bed.

"Well, here I am," she said. The color was still in her cheeks, but she spoke calmly enough.

"Thank you, child. Mercy me, I raced across that room like a kitten chasin' a spool. And goodness knows I'm no kitten. Whew! I'm all out of breath."

She closed her eyes momentarily. Ethel's resentment vanished and anxiety took its place. She leaned forward.

"Auntie," she cried, "you're not— You're all right, aren't you?"

"Yes, yes, I'm all right. Don't worry about me. Now let's have that talk, shall we?"

"Why, yes—if you feel like talking. If you think you should talk—to-night. It's awfully late."

"When it's too late for me to feel like talkin' it will have to be consider'ble later than this; anybody that knows me will tell you that. Besides, it is you that will probably have to talk most."

"Very well. What do you want me to talk about?"

"About you—and Bert."

"Well, what about—us?"

"That's just it—I don't know what about you. Fact is, I can't seem to get along without pokin' my nose into other folks's affairs. I've been watchin' you two and wonderin' ever since Bert came back here. Do tell me—that is, tell me if you want to—are you and he engaged again?"

A moment's wait. Then Ethel nodded.

"Yes," she said, "we are."

"I see. Well, I rather thought, by the looks of things lately, that you was or were goin' to be. That's settled. Now I shall know whether to treat him like a boarder or an in-law, sha'n't I. That's been botherin' me a little."

She sighed, as if pleased at having solved a puzzle. Ethel could not help laughing.

"Auntie," she exclaimed, "you are funny; did you know it?"

"Shouldn't wonder. I know I laugh at myself often enough."

"But you mustn't think I have been hiding anything from you. You see, we didn't decide anything—Bert and I—until to-night. He pretended, even to me, that he came back here merely because Wapatomac seemed like home to him. That was what he told me."

"Um-hm. He told me that, too."

"He said he did. You see, he had made up his mind that he was a failure in life, that he must not dream of our ever being—being what we used to be to each other. He meant never to even hint at such thing."

"I see. And to-night he did hint. Was that it?"

"Well, to-night it—we—oh, I don't know, it just seemed to say itself. Auntie, you know how I have always felt toward him. I told you I should never change. And—well, he was like that, too. He had not spoken—or hinted—for my sake. If he had had anything to offer me it would have been different, but he considered himself a failure. As if I cared about that!"

"I know. You wouldn't."

"I didn't—and I don't. . . . Auntie, I—I can't tell you any more about it. You can't tell things like that."

"Course you can't. Well, what next? Are you goin' to be married right off?"

"Certainly not, and we are going to keep our engagement a secret, just as we did before. He is going to stay here at the Inn, for a while, anyway. And help me with the management and everything. He is as interested in the Welcome Inn as I am. He really is. He is full of ideas and good ideas, too. Even if he can't find a worthwhile opening in the city in the fall—

even if he never finds one—he could be such a help here. A hotel like this needs a man's help; there are so many things he could do that I can't. And if business keeps on as it is now—and it looks as if it would—there would be a comfortable living here for both of us. Oh, Auntie, it will be wonderful! I have so many plans for the future. With him to help me we can make this little Inn known as the best of its kind anywhere. Yes, I mean it. Why—"

And so on. Lavinia did not interrupt, nor do anything except listen and agree. It was only after Ethel had gone and she was alone again, that she settled back in the chair to face the situation as it was. She had seen it coming, she had expected it, it was inevitable from the moment that Bert Thornlow entered the door of the Welcome Inn and wrote his name upon the register.

So much for all his noble self-sacrifice and renunciation. He had returned to Wapatomac for just one purpose, of course—that was proven now. But what was the real reason prompting that purpose? Love for Ethel? Why, in a way, perhaps, but that, to Lavinia's mind, was not reason enough. According to her estimate, an estimate made during their earlier acquaintanceship and which she had since seen no excuse for changing, Bert Thornlow was far more fond of Bert Thornlow than of any one else and she could not picture him as sacrificing his own ease and comfort merely for love of another person —even of Ethel Holt. Nor could she believe that he would ever be contented to spend the remainder of his life as assistant-manager of a summer hotel in the country. Of course that would mean ease and comfort and security without too much work. That thought might be in his mind, perhaps it was—but there must be something more than that.

It was almost three o'clock when Lavinia Badger went to bed and, after a little, to sleep. And she fell asleep with the growing conviction that she had found the answer to her question. She believed she knew the real reason for Bert Thornlow's return to the girl he had run away from.

"Humph!" she said aloud. "I guess that's it. Of course it is. And you may be sure Ethel will never think of it—she wouldn't. . . . Humph! Well, there's a little time yet. I'm pretty average healthy."

Then she blew out the lamp.

CHAPTER XX

BY the middle of July the summer season at the Inn was in full blast. Some of the early arrivals had gone but always new ones came to occupy the rooms they had vacated. Among the new-comers were the Oakbridges, mother and daughter. Mrs. Oakbridge was a languid person, whose clothes and jewels were the talk of the Inn and who never appeared on the lower floor before noon. She breakfasted in bed and the waiters were kept busy obeying her numerous commands. She was the widow of a St. Louis brewer and was reported to be very wealthy indeed. Some friends of hers had spent a short time at the Welcome Inn the previous summer and their enthusiastic recommendation had been the cause of her coming there.

"They knew I wanted a quiet place," she condescended to explain to Ethel. "Estelle and I have had a hectic winter abroad and at home and we both need a rest."

"Wapatomac is a wonderful place to rest in," Ethel told her. "At least so every one says."

"Yes," with a sigh, "so I should judge by what I have seen of it. Oh, well, it is no doubt just what I need, but what Estelle, at her age, will find to do heaven only knows. We went to Athens last year to see the ruins, but we could have seen more ruins right here in this hotel for less money. Isn't there *any* one on your register under seventy?"

Estelle, the daughter, was pretty, vivacious, a born flirt, and as elaborately gowned and bedecked as her mother, by whom she was idolized. She did not appear to find life among the "ruins" at all boring. Although the majority of the guests at the Welcome Inn were middle aged or elderly there were young people there and with them Miss Oakbridge became immediately popular. At the dances on Saturday evenings she never lacked partners and the young fellows swarmed about her like gulls about an incoming fishing-boat. She was agreeable and friendly with all of them and, so far at least, played no favorites. If she showed any partiality it was toward Bill Hunter and Bert Thornlow and that, perhaps, was because neither of them showed any symptoms of being susceptible to her fascinations. She was a young person accustomed to having what she wanted. If what she happened to want seemed to be hard to get that made her want it still more. Neither Hunter nor Thornlow nibbled at her hook; therefore she took pains to dangle it under their noses.

In Bill Hunter's case her bait dangling was prompted largely by pique and the desire to solve a puzzle. He was like no one she had met before. He was, outwardly at least, so naïve, so unconscious, so oddly innocent, and yet so provokingly stubborn. She gave him opportunities for tête-à-têtes, for exchange of confidences, for strolls together along the porches on moonlight nights. Sometimes he accepted these opportunities, but he never appeared to realize that they were especial and valuable privileges. When she leaned forward to ask questions, her eyes raised to his, he, as likely as not, leaned backward and looked, not into those eyes, but at the teacup in his hand, or the flowers in the bowl on the next table and said yes or no or "I guess so" in the most matter-of-fact tone. She tried to flatter him by asking him about his boyhood, about his law-practice, about his ambitions. He answered most of her questions frankly enough, but, so far as evincing any evidence that her interest pleased him he might have been talking to a spinster aunt. She could not make him out at all.

"He is the queerest thing," she confided to a fellow-guest of her own age and sex. "He fascinates me, he is so ridiculously matter of fact. He isn't a bit good-looking and he doesn't seem to care how he is dressed, even whether his hair is combed or not. And yet he isn't just a country gawk. I shouldn't call him stupid either—really. Would you?"

"No-o. But I don't know him very well."

"Well, I'm sure he isn't stupid, but he likes to make people think he is. He must. And yet every once in a while he says the brightest things—out-of-the-way things. He makes me laugh, even when he makes me mad. Of course you understand I don't really care what he does or says, goodness knows he is nothing to me, but he does provoke me. Do you know, he hasn't danced with me yet and I have all but asked him. Never mind, he will. He shall—if I have to pull him out on the floor by main strength. Just wait and see."

With Bert Thornlow her tactics were entirely different. Bert danced with her often enough, chatted with her frequently, sometimes strolled with her in the moonlight. But never once did he permit her to think him innocent or naïve. If she looked into his eyes the look was returned with interest, an amused interest, which she read as implying that he knew exactly what her game was and could play it as well as she could. He was an antagonist worth conquering. Her interest in him was far more real than in Hunter, in fact just how real it was becoming she was not quite sure. At any rate he was a tantalizing, if perhaps dangerous, subject to work upon and the current rumor that he and the pretty young proprietor of the Welcome Inn were very friendly indeed made him still more attractive.

To the same young person in whom she had confided her perplexity concerning Hunter she spoke of Bert Thornlow.

"Do you suppose there is any truth in the story that he and that Holt girl are really in love with each other?" she asked. "I, for one, don't believe it. Why, she isn't his kind at all. She is well-enough looking in a sort of way, but that isn't his way. He is what Mother would call a man of the world. He has been everywhere and—and—oh, you know what I mean. It is easy enough to see how she could fall for him, but for him to really, seriously care for her—that's just stuff and nonsense, I'm sure of it."

The confidant sighed. "He is one of the most—most interesting men I ever met," she agreed, wistfully.

"Yes, he is. The trouble is that he knows it. But, so far as he and Ethel Holt are concerned, I am going to find out the truth about that, if I die for it."

And so, perhaps in pursuit of that truth, she put herself very much in the Thornlow way. They were together a good deal. Lavinia Badger's sharp eyes noticed it, but she said nothing. Ethel noticed it—she could not help it—but she, too, said nothing. It was Bert, himself, who first mentioned Miss Oakbridge's name in a conversation with his betrothed.

"That Oakbridge girl is a man-chaser, if I ever saw one," he observed, with a laugh. "She would try to flirt with a clothes-horse if it wore trousers. She has been after poor old Bill Hunter. Have you noticed it?"

Ethel nodded. "I notice she seems to be after—several people," she said, a trifle more tartly than she intended. He laughed again.

"Meaning me, of course. Oh, yes, she would like to add me to her string, if she could. Well, don't worry. I wasn't born yesterday; I've seen her kind before."

"I don't worry. Why should I?"

"You shouldn't. See here, Ethel—you're not— You trust me, don't you?"

"Certainly I do."

"Well, then. I have to be—oh, decently agreeable to her, of course. I can't help that. She and her mother are really our star boarders. Her father was old Samuel Oakbridge, the beer baron. My own father knew him. The story was that old Sam was worth at least two million. A prospective sub-assistant hotel-keeper can't be too frigid to a couple with all that money to spend. Mrs. Oakbridge bought about two-thirds of our antique stock last week. I'm going to do my best to see that she keeps up the good work. Business is business—eh, dear?"

In mid-August were scheduled two events of importance to Wapatomac in general and the inhabitants of the Welcome Inn in particular. On the evening of the fourteenth the Dramatic Club was to give its first performance of the new play at the local town-hall. There was to be a second performance, in aid of a county charity, in the hall at Denboro the following evening. Ethel, very reluctantly, had been obliged to resign from the cast. She was too busy at the Inn to give the necessary time for rehearsals. There had been difficulty in finding some one to take her part but at last that matter had been satisfactorily managed. Estelle Oakbridge had been persuaded to play the heroine's rôle. She, so some of the Inn guests discovered, had had much experience in amateur acting, and impromptu charades given in the hotel lounge had proven that she was surprisingly able. So she was asked and had accepted. Bert Thornlow was the leading man, the young, romantic hero of the play, and Bill Hunter was the character comedian. Rehearsals had gone well and every one in the know predicted a success.

The second event of importance to Wapatomac was its "special" town-meeting on the afternoon of the sixteenth. The new member of the Board of Selectmen was to be chosen at this meeting and Hunter's chances of election were reported to be very good indeed. Ordinarily the choosing of a new Selectman was a matter of only minor interest, but this time was an exception. There had been considerable agitation in Wapatomac and neighboring towns concerning the illegal sale of liquor, particularly to minors. At this period practically the whole of Ostable County was "dry" and those using alcoholic stimulants were accustomed to procure them by keg, jug or bottle from

Boston. The sale of liquor by the drink was forbidden and the law regarding its sale to those under voting age was, or was supposed to be, strictly enforced.

Of late, however, and particularly during the months of current spring and summer, the juvenile group—its would-be "sporty" element, at least—had been served with drinks or supplied with hip-pocket flasks on more than one occasion. From the high-school picnic several groups had returned late and suspiciously hilarious. Angry parents had complained and threatened. Questionings had proved futile; none of the culprits professed to know where the whiskey came from. Of course some one did know—probably several knew—but they professed ignorance and would not confess. There were strong suspicions of a barber in Denboro, of a billiard-room keeper in South Wapatomac, and, more particularly, of several small inns or road-houses located along the roads between the villages. That these latter sold liquor to favored patrons there was practically no doubt, but also no proof. The favored patrons were, of course, silent and others guessed but could not be sure. So long as no one but known alcoholics among the adult population over-indulged there was little more than whispered criticism and comment, but when the sons and daughters of respectable families began to be talked about the whispering changed to outspoken fault-finding and threats.

Something must be done about it. What did Wapatomac pay its Sheriff for, anyhow?

The Sheriff's name was Jabez Williams. He was a middle-aged citizen, good-natured, easy-going, and, generally speaking, popular. He made his living in the oyster and shell-fish trade and his small salary as Wapatomac's Sheriff was a side-line perquisite. So long as his professional duties consisted in locking up an occasional tramp or keeping a fair amount of order along the main road on the night before the Fourth of July he was equal to the situation. Now, however, he found himself the center of criticism and his popularity—even his office—in danger. Jabez did not like the change, but he was not quite certain what he could do about it. He loudly proclaimed that he was just about ready to do something—something drastic that would make all hands "set up and take notice," but so far he had done nothing. The special town-meeting would soon be held and there would be a lot of talk then. Jabez knew this quite well.

Bill Hunter, in his office-chair campaign for the Selectman's position, had expressed himself rather forcibly concerning the sale of liquor and gambling. It could be stopped, he believed, and it was the sheriff's duty, backed by the Board of Selectmen, to see that it was stopped. On one occasion, at a meeting of the Town Improvement Society, he had said as much in a brief informal address. "If those fellows—you all know who I mean—are making their places public nuisances they should be put out of business. Proof? Well, that shouldn't be so very hard to find, it seems to me."

As this expressed the opinion of a majority of Wapatomac's citizens it was received with applause and quoted. It would go a long way, so local prophets predicted, to put Mr. William Hunter on the Board.

The first performance given by the Dramatic Club in the Wapatomac town-hall was a great success. The hall was crowded with permanent residents and summer visitors and the applause at the final curtain amounted to an ovation. Bert Thornlow, Estelle Oakbridge and Hunter made the outstanding hits and the town buzzed next day with praise of their performances.

Mr. Amaziah Holt announced that he didn't know as he ever see a better show anywheres in his life—unless maybe 'twas up to the Howard A-thee-ne-um one time in Boston. "And, of course," added Amaziah, "them actors up there was paid to do their jobs. And they wa'n't so terrible much better, even at that."

Lavinia Badger liked the play. She said so. "But," she added, in her conversation with her grand-niece, "I know you would have done that girl's part better if you had had it instead of the Oakbridge one."

Ethel laughed. "Nonsense, Auntie," she protested. "Estelle was wonderful. No one could have been better. The way she played up to Bert in the big scene at the end of the third act was perfect. You know it was."

Lavinia nodded. "Yes," she admitted, "it was pretty good, that's a fact. When it comes to playin' up to anybody, especially a man, she's hard to beat, I will say. Bert did his part in the playin' up too, I thought. I never saw a couple make love more natural."

Ethel changed the subject. She praised Bill Hunter's acting highly. Her great-aunt's agreement was hearty and unqualified now.

"He is good at anything he does, that young man," she declared. "And always will be, or I miss my guess."

Ethel's laugh was a trifle impatient this time. "I declare, I believe you have fallen in love with Bill, Auntie," she said. "He is perfect in your eyes. Well, he isn't half as good an actor as Bert—no, not half."

"Perhaps you're right, dearie. Don't be cross. Goodness knows I'm no judge of play-actin'. You're goin' over to Denboro to see it all again to-morrow night, I suppose?"

"Yes—if I can get away, and I think I can. Bert has hired the automobile at the livery-stable and we are all going over in it with him, Estelle and Bill and I."

The local livery-stable keeper had added a second-hand motor-car to his string of vehicles for rental purposes and was very proud of it.

The next afternoon Mr. Hunter at his desk in Judge Payne's

office, had an unexpected caller. Sheriff Jabez Williams, no less. The Judge was taking his afternoon nap and the pair had the office to themselves.

"Hello, Sheriff," was the Hunter greeting. "What brings you around? Glad to see you, of course. Sit down? You look as if you had something on your mind; what is it?"

Mr. Williams did not immediately accept the invitation to be seated. He did so only after he had tiptoed back to the office door and made sure that it was tightly closed and latched. Then he drew a chair close beside the Hunter desk and leaned forward.

"Somethin' on my mind?" he repeated. "Yes sir, I have got somethin' on my mind and mine's the only mind it is on so far. That is," as an after-thought, "except, of course, the half-dozen or so fellows I've swore in to help me. And even they don't know exactly what 'tis yet, you understand."

He paused, apparently to let the importance of this communication sink in. Mr. Hunter nodded gravely.

"Yes, yes," he agreed. "I understand everything—"

"Eh?" in astonishment. "What are you sayin' that for! How can you understand when I haven't told you yet?"

"I can't. You didn't let me finish. I was going to say that I understood everything except what it was all about. What is up, Sheriff?"

"That's what I'm here to tell you. Look here, Mr. Hunter; you've been sayin' considerable about nothin' bein' done to get after the scamps who've been sellin' rum and runnin' gamblin' games around here, haven't you? Sayin' 'twas high time they was put a stop to and—and all like that, eh?"

"Yes. Maybe not considerable, but some."

"I know you have and that reflected right back on me and my job as Sheriff of this township, didn't it?"

"Possibly."

"Darned sure it did. Well, about all hands seem to be certain you're goin' to be put in as Selectman at the town-meetin' to-morrow and I didn't want you to go on the Board with any wrong notions about me not doin' what I'm hired to do. I ain't been loafin' on my job, but, on the other hand, I didn't want to go off half-cocked. I've been lookin' around and questionin' around and layin' my plans. Now I'm ready to hit and hit hard. You get that, don't you?"

"Yes, and I'm glad to get it. More power to your muscles. Who is going to be hit and when and how?"

"I'm here to tell you that, too. And you're the only one that's been told or is goin' to be told. Mr. Hunter," impressively, "I'm goin' to head a raid and searchin' party on the Oak Leaf to-night. About twelve o'clock or so me and my crowd is goin' to land on 'em and land heavy. That's business, ain't it, Mr. Selectman? You nor the rest of the Board can't say I'm layin' down on my job after that, eh?"

He leaned back in his chair with an air of triumph. Hunter rubbed his chin and reflected. He knew what the "Oak Leaf" was and where it was. It was one of the larger restaurants and road-houses located by the main highway between Wapatomac and Denboro villages, but, in this case, just inside the Wapatomac township line. Its proprietor, Elnathan—or Nate— Briggs, had been under suspicion of illegal liquor-selling but, so far at least, there had been no actual proof of his doing so. During the summer months the Oak Leaf did a flourishing business. It specialized in sea-food and the younger groups among the summer visitors often patronized it on their way back from dances or straw rides. Briggs, himself, had lived in Wapatomac all his life and had many friends among the fishermen and the rougher element alongshore. He dressed well, spent money generously, and was popular in his set. Hunter had not credited Jabez with the pluck to undertake a raid of this importance. His opinion of the Sheriff rose, in consequence.

"Good work!" he exclaimed. "Hope you catch the rascal

with the goods. But," with the caution of his profession, "better make sure your warrant is all right before you start."

"It's in blank—names of two or three places on it—but it's all right. You wait till to-morrow mornin' and you'll hear some talk, Mr. Hunter. And the Wapatomac Board of Selectmen won't have to be lookin' 'round for another sheriff neither. Just you keep quiet and don't let out a word of what I've told you, that's all."

He rose. Hunter lifted a hand. "Just a minute, Williams," he said. "Why did you tell me this?"

"Because you've been doin' a lot of fault-findin' and because you're goin' to be Selectman. I want to keep on bein' sheriff and 'twon't do me no harm to have somebody on the Board to stand by me. After the raid's over there might be some of the members to say I wasn't responsible for it at all. If they do you can tell 'em you know better because I told you about it before it happened—told you my plans and everything; see?"

Bill Hunter chuckled. "I see," he said. "But, of course, you know you haven't told me your plans. Said you were going to raid the place to-night, that's all."

"That's enough, ain't it?"

"Seems to be. Well, I hope you have good luck."

"Expect to. The only thing that'll make a hash of it is for somebody to tip Nate off ahead of time. You're the only one that can do that, because you're the only one, except me, who knows. If he should be tipped off—why—well, it would be plain enough who did it, wouldn't it?"

"Looks that way. But—er—well, I don't think you need worry on that account."

"I don't. So long, Mr. Hunter. See you to-morrow at the meetin'. I'm cal'latin' to vote for you."

When Ethel Holt and Estelle Oakbridge left the Inn in the hired car early that evening, with Thornlow at the wheel, and

bound for Denboro, Hunter did not accompany them. He had
planned to do so, but Judge Payne asked him to stop on his
way at the house of a client to leave some papers and briefly
discuss a business matter, so he left before supper, a sandwich in his pocket and driving a livery-stable rig. Every
buggy in the stable had been already engaged, so he was
obliged to be content with an ancient "carryall" and a horse
almost as ancient. He might have borrowed the Payne horse
and buggy, but the Judge had mentioned that the animal had
lost a shoe the previous day and there had been no time for
a visit to the blacksmith. The carryall would do well enough;
Bill was neither fussy nor proud in matters of that kind.

The Denboro performance was as successful as that of the
previous evening in Wapatomac. There was a crowded house,
much applause, and praise of the play and the actors. The other
participants started homeward soon after it was over, but
Hunter lingered for half an hour. He was treasurer of the
Dramatic Club and the Denboro committee in charge there
asked him to remain until the receipts had been counted and
the expenses reckoned. It was a few minutes after eleven
o'clock when he climbed aboard the carryall and picked up
the reins.

It was a damp, cloudy night and there were few stars. In
Denboro village most of the homes were dark, their occupants,
even those who had attended the town-hall performance, were
already in bed. The road beyond the village wound through
the woods and was black and silent and deserted. The old
horse plodded along at a jog-trot, the carryall swayed and
squeaked, and Hunter drowsed and nodded on the worn leather
seat.

His drowse was becoming a genuine nap when he was
aroused by the gleam of lights ahead. For an instant he thought
that he must have been asleep for an hour or more and was
entering Wapatomac. Then, shaking himself into full wake-

fulness, he realized his location. There were still several miles to go before he would reach the thickly settled part of the town. He was inside the township borders—yes, but only just inside. The building on his right, sitting back from the road, the windows of its lower floor ablaze, was the Oak Leaf, the road-house owned and managed by Elnathan Briggs—the establishment which Jabez Williams had informed him was to be raided by the Sheriff and his posse that very night.

He pulled the old horse into a walk and leaned forward to look. Nate Briggs and his patrons were in for a surprise and that very shortly. Apparently it would be a real surprise, for, judging by appearances, the Oak Leaf was running at full blast. Also it was evident that there were a goodly number of patrons, late as it was. At least a dozen vehicles were drawn up in the yard or by the fence. Well, well! there would be something for Wapatomac and Denboro to talk about next day, just as Williams had prophesied. And names would be mentioned, too—and talked about. The county papers of the following week would be eagerly read.

He was moving on when he noticed the tail-light of an automobile just beyond the Briggs front gate. Automobiles, although now far more numerous than a few years before, were still something of a rarity in that section. The light shone upon the license-plate at the rear of the car and he idly glanced at it. It was a Massachusetts plate and the number was—

He jerked the horse to a standstill and sprang from the carryall to the ground. He hurried to the side of the car and looked in. Yes, there was no doubt about it. The car was that owned by the Wapatomac livery-stable keeper, the car in which Thornlow and Miss Oakbridge—yes, and Ethel Holt—had left Denboro only an hour before.

Ethel was—she must be—inside there now, at that moment. He took his watch from his pocket, and, stooping to the head-lamp of the car, looked at the time. It was a quarter to twelve.

And Jabez had told him that the Oak Leaf was to be raided at twelve or thereabouts.

The old horse attached to the carryall was standing placidly where he had left him in the middle of the road. He seized the bridle, led the animal to a vacant place by the fence just beyond the automobile and, unbuckling the reins, tethered him to a fence-rail. Then he hurried up the path to the door of the Oak Leaf, opened the door and went in.

CHAPTER XXI

THE OAK LEAF, before Mr. Briggs bought it and turned it into a house of entertainment, had been a good-sized dwelling of the ordinary middle-class New England type. The front door opened into a small hall, with stairs leading from it to the upper floor. From that hall two other doors opened, one to the right and the other to the left. Both were closed; that on the left, he ascertained by turning the knob, was locked, but from behind it he could hear laughter and loud conversation, in masculine and feminine voices. He tried the door to the right, it was not locked and he opened it and looked in.

This, evidently, had once been the dining-room of the old house and was still used for that purpose. Instead of one large table, however, there were now several smaller ones. At two of these were seated parties of three or four, chatting, smoking and eating. The occupants of the chairs were strangers to him, they were not Wapatomac people, certainly. They looked up when he entered, but did not seem greatly disturbed nor in the least alarmed. There was nothing illegal going on here, so far as he could see, but that did not concern him at the moment. He hurried through the room and out at the door at its rear.

There was another hall here with doors leading from it. He was trying one of these doors when some one seized his arm. He turned, to find a shirt-sleeved person with a white apron tied about his waist and an empty tray in his hand. This person did seem disturbed.

"Well, Mister," he growled, after a moment's scrutiny,

"what is it? What do you want? Who you lookin' for?"

Hunter smiled. "Some friends of mine, that's all," he replied, easily. "Don't trouble. I'll find them all right."

His hand was on the knob of a door on the opposite side of the hall and he turned it as he spoke. He caught a glimpse of a group at a table. Red-faced men, coatless and at ease. There were cards and chips on the table, also bottles and glasses. The room was thick with tobacco smoke. His glimpse was but momentary, for the person with the apron jerked the door shut again and put his back against it.

"You can't go in there, Mister," he declared angrily. "Them rooms are private. Say, who are these friends of yours, anyhow?"

Hunter did not answer. There was still another door leading from that hall and he opened that. This time he was successful. There was a table in this room, also, and seated in chairs beside it were Bert Thornlow, Estelle Oakbridge and—yes, Ethel Holt. There were plates of sandwiches on the table and before Thornlow and the Oakbridge girl were wine glasses partially full. A bottle stood on the floor beside Thornlow's chair.

The trio stared at him in amazement but he gave them no opportunity to speak. Instead he spoke, sharply and to the point.

"Out of here, quick!" he ordered. "Quick! Don't stop to talk. Quick, *quick!* Get your things and come with me."

He darted to the other side of the table and, seizing Ethel by the arm, lifted her to her feet, almost by main strength. She was pale and frightened. Estelle Oakbridge, however, laughed.

"Why, it's Bill Hunter!" she exclaimed. "How nice of you to come! But what's the hurry?"

"Hurry enough! Don't talk, I tell you, we haven't time. Come!"

Estelle's laugh broke off in the middle. His manner and his

evident agitation were having their effect. She rose from her chair.

"Bert," she faltered, "Bert! What is this? What is it! Don't you think perhaps we—"

But Bert Thornlow had not stirred. His face was flushed and his fist clenched.

"What the devil's the matter with you, Hunter?" he demanded, angrily. "Who asked you to jam in here? What do you—"

Hunter did not wait for him to finish. Behind him, in the hall, the aproned waiter was shouting, "Nate! Nate!" They could hear him running, evidently in search of the proprietor.

"Shut up!" broke in Hunter, savagely. "Look here, Thornlow! Unless you want to see these girls' names in the papers along with yours and have them talked about from one end of Wapatomac to the other you'll help me get them out of here now—this instant. Oh, don't you understand? This place is going to be—"

He paused. Sheriff Williams! He had promised, or as good as promised.

"Never mind," he concluded, with an earnestness that, at last, carried conviction, "you can take my word for it that if you don't get out now you won't have a chance. And you'll be mighty sorry afterwards. Ethel, come with me."

He led her toward the door. She had not spoken since he came in and she said nothing now; but she went with him, willingly, eagerly. Estelle Oakbridge caught at Thornlow's sleeve.

"Oh, Bert!" she pleaded, hysterically, "do come! Please! I—I don't know what he means, but—but I'm frightened, Come!"

And Thornlow came. Hunter led the way, through the dining-room, where the parties at the tables were on their feet, the girls clinging to their escorts' arms and whispering. In the front hall the waiter was thumping the door of the locked room. "Lemme in! Lemme in quick!" he was whispering hoarsely. Bill Hunter stepped back to let the other three pass out into the yard, when a hand was laid heavily on his shoulder. He turned. Elnathan Briggs, owner of the Oak Leaf, was beside him. Recognition was mutual.

"Oh!" exclaimed Briggs. "Oh-oh, I see! Mr. Hunter, ain't it. Well, well! Selectman Hunter, gettin' busy ahead of time. Yes, yes! Well, good night, Mr. Hunter. Hope you've enjoyed yourself. We'll all remember you was here. Yes, indeed! We won't forget—unless you do."

At the front gate Hunter took command. He glanced anxiously about him, but saw no signs that the raiders were in the neighborhood. He listened, but, except for the increasing hubbub in the road-house, there was no sound. He detained Thornlow momentarily to whisper in his ear.

"Get them into that car," he ordered, "and get away hell for leather. Take the back roads if you can and make for home. And, look here, whatever else you do, don't tell, or let them tell, that any of you were within a mile of this place to-night. Now go!"

Bert Thornlow hesitated. "I don't know that we can go," he muttered. "That's one reason why we're at this joint. That confounded push-cart," with a wave toward the livery-stable automobile, "is out of kilter or out of gas, or something. We just managed to crawl opposite the fence here when she stopped dead. Maybe you can start her, but I swear I couldn't. The fellow inside told me he would have his man look her over —but I suppose that's off now."

Bill Hunter stared at him. Then he shook his head. The night had been full of unexpected complications, but this was the final and most unexpected. And at any moment—

He drew a long breath. "Whew!" he sighed. And then, quickly: "All right, leave the car to me. Maybe I can do something with it. There's my rig there—that horse and carryall. Take it and clear out. Hurry, that's all."

He helped them into the carryall. Thornlow took the reins. As the wheels began to turn the door of the carriage opened. Ethel Holt leaned out and spoke to him. It was the first time she had spoken to him since he entered the room and found her and the others there.

"Bill," she said. "Oh, Bill, I—I—"

"You mustn't stop to talk now. Please!"

"I—I don't know what this means—any of it—but— Tell me! You're not going to be in any trouble yourself—on our account?"

"I? Not a bit. I'll be all right. See you to-morrow. The back roads will be best, Thornlow, don't forget. And," with emphasis, "none of you must tell any one that you were here tonight."

The old horse picked up his hooves and the carryall disappeared in the darkness. Bill turned his attention to the automobile. He tried this and he tried that, but the motor refused to come to life. Bert had said they might be out of gas. Well, if that was it, there was no remedy—yet. Mr. Elnathan Briggs would be doing him no favors. The contrary, if anything.

The door of the Oak Leaf opened and closed. Groups hurried from it, boarded their vehicles and drove hastily off. A few minutes later he and that motor-car were alone by the border of the road. The lights in the road-house were extinguished, one by one.

And then, a quarter of an hour afterward, a group of men emerged from the blackness of the woods and moved steathily across the yard. There were whisperings, followed by a resounding bang on the Oak Leaf's front door.

"Open up here!" ordered the voice of authority. "Open, in the name of the law."

Sheriff Williams and his raiders. Too late—but that might have been expected.

CHAPTER XXII

LAVINIA had promised Ethel that she would go to bed early.

"We shall be late, it will be almost twelve when we get back from Denboro," said Ethel, "and if I find you awake when I come in I shall have no patience with you. You can't seem to get used to the idea that I am old enough to take care of myself. Nothing is going to happen to me—or, if it does, you can't prevent it by sitting up and looking out of the window. Now, mind, I expect you to go to bed by ten o'clock—and stay there until morning."

Lavinia remained downstairs, sitting in the lobby with the week's issue of the Weekly *Item* in her hand, until ten o'clock. Then she walked over to the desk and addressed Miss Sarah Crowell, who was reading a library book.

"Everything all right, Sarah?" she inquired.

Miss Crowell, torn reluctantly from a particularly tender and thrilling interview between young Lord Eastley and the beautiful and mysterious young American girl on the moonlit terrace at Monte Carlo, looked up.

"Eh?" was her startled query.

"I asked you if everything was all right."

"Huh! Just as all right as it usually is, far's I can see. Why?"

"Nothin', except that, if you don't need me any longer, I'm goin' to bed."

"Wish *I* could. I've got to hang around back of this counter for another hour. Good night."

Lavinia said good night and moved toward the stairs. Sarah

looked after her with marked disapproval. She told the night-watchman afterward that that old woman seemed to think she was running the Welcome Inn.

"The minute Ethel Holt steps out of that door she goes on watch," declared Miss Crowell. "I can't sit down a minute without feeling those spectacles of hers owling at the back of my neck. No matter if there's no work to do she makes me feel as if I ought to jump up and begin doing it. Ugh!"

The night-watchman chuckled. "For a body her age," he agreed, "there ain't much she don't see, that's a fact. I'd like to think I'd be as up and comin' as she is when I get as old as that."

Lavinia, in her room, prepared for bed. She blew out the light with the comforting feeling that her promise to Ethel had been kept. After a half-hour of tumbling and tossing she began to realize that it was only half kept and that the second half was not likely to be kept for some time. She did drop off to sleep at eleven, but was wide awake again at twelve. She got up then and looked out of the window. The light by the drive at the front door was still burning, so it was evident that Ethel and the Denboro party had not yet returned. According to her old-fashioned idea it was high time they did. Nothing had happened, of course—her common sense told her that—but for twenty years she had worried about Ethel and a twenty-year habit is hard to break. She went back to bed again, but sleep was out of the question. When the tall clock in the lobby struck one she was still wide awake and her vague apprehension was becoming a real alarm.

At last, however, she heard the sound of wheels on the drive. She rose and, drawing aside the window-shade, peeped out. Yes, there they were. Ethel and the "Oakbridge one" and Bert Thornlow. They were whispering and the Oakbridge girl was giggling. They were all right, nothing untoward had happened.

She ought to have known it would not. She was an old fool and the older she got the more foolish.

But—wait a minute—there was something queer. Why, yes, of course that was it. They had left the Inn in an automobile and they had come back in a carryall. She could see the carryall plainly and the old horse between the shafts. Now why in the world? Unless the automobile had broken down and refused to go. The dratted things were always getting out of kilter, everybody said so. Well, Ethel was safe, anyhow, and that was all that mattered. The rest she could find out in the morning. She went to bed once more and this time slept soundly.

During her interview with Ethel across the breakfast table, however, she did not mention what she had seen from the window. Sober reflection during dressing had caused her to decide not to speak of that. Ethel would want to know what she, Lavinia, was doing out of bed at that hour and there would be a lot of unnecessary talk. So she began by asking how the Denboro people liked the play, if the seats had all been sold, how much money the two performances were likely to clear, and the like. Ethel answered the questions, but volunteered no details; in fact—and Lavinia could not understand it at all—she seemed to have lost all interest in her hitherto beloved Dramatic Club. Her answers were rather vague and absently given, and that she was troubled and worried about something was, to the shrewd eye of her great-aunt, increasingly obvious.

Any one other than Lavinia Badger would probably have demanded point-blank to be told what was the matter, but that was not Lavinia's way. That something was wrong she was now sure, but she was just as sure that Ethel did not mean to mention it. The nearest she came to a direct question along that line was when she asked if everything had gone all right during the ride to and from Denboro.

Ethel's answer this time was promptly, even hurriedly, given. "Oh, yes—yes, of course, Auntie," she said. And then, "Why? Why should you think it didn't?"

"Oh, I don't know. You went in one of those pesky automobiles and, judging from what I hear and what I read in the newspapers, 'most anything's liable to happen to one of them."

Here was the opportunity for the girl to explain their return in the carryall instead of the car, but no explanation was given. Ethel changed the subject, she began to speak of matters connected with the Inn and its management.

By the time breakfast was over Lavinia was certain that something had happened the previous evening, something which, to Ethel's mind at least, was seriously disturbing and which, for some reason, she intended to keep to herself. As they came out of the dining-room they met Mr. Hunter, who was just coming in. Lavinia heard Ethel catch her breath as she saw him. Bill's good morning, however, was cheerful and casual.

"Home safe and sound, I judge, all of you," he observed. "That's good. Make pretty good time on the trip?"

Ethel nodded. "Yes," she replied. "And—and you?"

"Oh, I came along all right. I was a little late in getting started, but I got here eventually. Well, no more dramatics this season. Now we can settle down to hotel-keeping and the law. High time, so far as I'm concerned."

Ethel said nothing. She and Bill looked at each other and Lavinia, who was looking at both of them, saw the latter's eyebrows raised as if in question and a barely perceptible shake of the head by the former. So, whatever the secret might be, Hunter was in it. What he had asked was, of course, if she, Lavinia, knew, and Ethel had signified that she, Lavinia, did not know.

"This is your busy day, Mr. Hunter, seems to me I remember," she observed. "Town-meetin' this afternoon. We'll have to call you 'Selectman Hunter' when you come home to supper, I presume likely."

Bill Hunter smiled. "Well—maybe," he said, and moved on to the dining-room.

Ethel went into the office to look over the mail. There were many things needing her supervision and Lavinia scarcely saw her the rest of that day. She, Lavinia, remained in the lobby for a time and so happened to witness the meeting between Bert Thornlow and Miss Oakbridge, when, just before ten, the latter came down to breakfast. Thornlow, who had already breakfasted, happened to be standing by the foot of the stairs as she descended. Estelle spoke to him and he walked toward her. Their greeting was casual enough, but, a moment later, their voices dropped almost to a whisper and they appeared to be holding a confidential and rather lengthy conversation. Once, when the girl giggled vivaciously and spoke a trifle louder, Lavinia saw Thornlow glance over his shoulder as if to make sure they were not overheard, and he obviously cautioned his companion.

"So you are in it, too," thought Lavinia. "Well, of course you would be."

The thought of a lover's quarrel between Ethel and Bert, with Miss Oakbridge as a focal point, came to her mind. It was the most natural thing to infer. But Ethel's manner and behavior did not fit in with that idea. If Ethel had been jealous she would have kept her feeling under cover. She was far too proud to let any one suspect her of a feeling of that kind. No, it was not jealousy—at least not altogether.

The day was a long one for Lavinia. She saw little of Ethel, nothing of Hunter and she made no effort to see or talk with Thornlow. As for Miss Oakbridge, she and that care-free young lady were never intimate. They exchanged nods or good mornings and that was all. Estelle was not at all interested in elderly people.

As she passed by the desk on her way in to luncheon she overheard part of a conversation between the Inn errand-boy and Sarah Crowell. The boy had been up to the post-office after the hotel mail and had, apparently, picked up an item of news. She judged, by the little she overheard, that the post-office loungers were laughing at what they considered a joke on Sheriff Williams. The latter had led a raiding party some time during the previous night upon a place on the outskirts of the town, in search of evidence of gambling and illegal liquor selling.

"And, as near as anybody can find out," she heard the boy say, "it just amounted to nothin', the whole of it. Never found so much as a pack of cards or an empty rum bottle. They're all pokin' fun at Jabez and he's mad as hops. Vows he'll have his say pretty soon and then they'll hear somethin'. Don't know what he means, do you?"

Lavinia had known Jabez Williams ever since she came to Wapatomac to live and her opinion of him as an enforcer of the law was not high. She forgot the scrap of conversation almost as soon as she heard it and it was not until some time later that it was recalled to her mind.

Several of the male guests of the Welcome Inn went up to the village that afternoon to attend the town-meeting. It was a dull, rainy day; there was little amusement inside the hotel and any town-meeting might usually be counted upon to furnish mild entertainment.

At five, or a little after, Lavinia was in her room, knitting and looking out of the window at the rain-splashed road and the trees bending before the easterly wind. From where she sat she could see the corner where the road from the village joined the Shore Road and, as she looked, she saw a pedestrian turn that corner and come splashing through the puddles toward the Inn. The collar of his oilskin was turned up and his sou'wester pulled down, but she recognized him instantly. Amaziah Holt walked like no one else on earth.

Why was he coming there, on such a day and in such a hurry? Was there trouble at the lighthouse? Was that wife of his sick? Perhaps. She went out into the hall and was half-way down the stairs when he entered at the front door, shaking the water from his coat-sleeves and stamping with wet boots on the rug.

She called to him. "Amaziah! Am! Do you want me? Here I am—on the stairs."

He saw her and came clumping across the lobby. "Hello, Aunt Lavvy!" he hailed. "Ethel anywheres around? Say, she ain't heard the news yet, has she?"

"News? What news?"

"Why, what's just happened up to town-meetin'. About Bill Hunter and all. Ain't any of you heard it? Well, you will. 'Tain't all over yet—the meetin', I mean—but I got out soon's that part was settled and hustled down here. I knew you folks—'specially you and Ethel—would want to know. Both of you been talkin' up Hunter as if he was somethin' wonderful. Wapatomac ought to be thankful to have a man like him S'lectman, and so forth and so on. Good as elected, that's what you told me last time I saw you, Lavvy. Maybe you've forgot what I said. 'There's many a slip,' says I, 'betwixt and between.' That's what I said, and now maybe—"

He was too excited to lower his voice and the occupants of the chairs and divans in the lobby were looking in his direction and grinning broadly. Sarah Crowell had left her stool by the bookkeeper's desk and was approaching the counter. Lavinia sharply interrupted.

"Hush!" she ordered. "Anybody would think you was peddlin' fish, to hear you yell. Stop it, this minute. Here! you come upstairs with me. Come up to my room, where you can do your talkin' to me and not to all creation. Don't say another word. Now come!"

Amaziah obeyed, but with some hesitation.

"Ethel," he said. "Don't you think maybe Ethel will want to hear it, too?"

"She can hear it later—if it turns out to be worth hearin' at all. Come straight along."

In her room, with the door closed, she turned to face him. "You look as if you'd been dredged up off back of the bar," she declared. "Take off those wet things and put 'em on the floor yonder in the corner. . . . There! Now sit down in that chair—that one there. Mercy on us, don't walk right across the middle of the rug! Go 'round the edges where the mud can be wiped up. . . . All right, now then. What is it that ails you?"

Amaziah was a trifle subdued by this time, but only a trifle. He leaned back in the chair she had assigned him and nodded several times, portentously.

"Selectman William Hunter!" he sneered. "Yes—yes! You don't say! Well, he ain't Selectman and somebody else is. That's what ails me, if you want to know, Aunt Lavvy."

Lavinia stared at him. "Somebody else is!" she repeated. "Who?"

"Sam Doane, that's who, and Bill Hunter isn't."

She pumped the story out of him, as she would have said, a stroke at a time. The business of the town-meeting had moved along smoothly enough until the matter of nominating candidates for the new member of the Board of Selectmen came before it. Even then, when Eldridge Baker offered the name of Samuel Doane, brother of Gustavus Doane, the postmaster, and the nomination was seconded, there was no excitement— and, so Amaziah admitted, "not a terrible sight of hand-clappin' neither." Then Dr. Hardy put the name of William Hunter before the meeting.

"There was hand-clappin' then," declared Amaziah. "Yes— and hollerin', too. Looked then as if the election was over about as soon as it started. Those was the only nominations and the chairman, 'Lisha Hamlin 'twas, give out the meetin' was open for discussion. Baker he had a little to say about what a fine man Doane was, how he'd always stood up for the best interests of Wapatomac and the like of that, but he never got much attention. Folks was beginnin' to holler 'Vote! Vote!' the way they do in town-meetin', when Jabe Williams stood up.

" 'Mr. Chairman,' says he, 'I'd like to say a word.'

"All hands had a big laugh, 'cause the yarn about Jabez's big raid had been goin' around and 'twas a town joke by this time. Hamlin he rapped for order and give out that Sheriff Williams had the floor. Jabe wasn't laughin', he was scowlin', but he waited until the rest of us had quieted down and then he commenced to talk.

" 'If,' he began, scowlin' harder than ever, 'there's anybody here that thinks I don't know what's bein' said about me to-day he'd better get that notion out of his head. I know it all right, and don't you forget it. I haven't said much in answer to it, although maybe some of you heard me promise to say somethin' later on. All right, now I'm goin' to say it and all I ask of you is to sit still and listen.'

"He got far as that when Dr. Hardy stood up and called for point of order. 'Mr. Chairman,' says he, 'we're supposed to be gettin' ready to elect a Selectman. That's the business afore us just now, as I understand it. I judge Mr. Williams wants to talk about somethin' which hasn't anything to do with that business. No doubt we'd all like to hear from him later on— I'm sure I should; but just now I suggest we'd better stick to what we're supposed to be doin'.'

"All hands laughed and 'Lisha pounded the table some more.

" 'Dr. Hardy is right, of course,' he says. 'Mr. Williams, if you will postpone your remarks for a few minutes—'

"He only got as far as that when Jabe cut in on him. 'Postpone nothin'!' he sang out. 'How do you know, any of you, that what I'm goin' to say has nothin' to do with who we vote in as Selectman at this meetin'? 'Cordin' to my ideas it has a whole lot to do with it. If, after you've heard what I've got to tell you, you still want to elect one of the men that's been nominated here this afternoon to run town affairs for you—if you do—well, I can't help it, of course. But I give you fair warnin' that you'll hear me now, or, maybe, be sorry afterwards.'

"Well, that was a kind of staggerer, as you might say. Nobody knew what he meant—at least, if any of 'em did know they hadn't let on—waitin' for the bomb-shell to be hove, maybe. Anyhow, there was a grand old hubbub. Some was hollerin' for Jabez to sit down and others for him to heave ahead and talk. It took 'Lisha consider'ble time to get it quiet enough so's he could hear himself. Then he says:

"'Does the chair understand, Mr. Williams, that the statement you wish to make has a bearin' on the question before the house? That is the fitness of one of the nominees for the office of Selectman of this town to hold that office. Is that it?'

"'You bet your life it's it;' says Jabez, thumping the back of the settee in front of him with his fist. 'That's just what 'tis.'

"'Then you may go on,' says 'Lisha. And Jabez went on. And the further he went the more the rest of us pricked up our ears."

Amaziah's story, as he told it, was lengthy, rambling and spattered with "I tell you's" and "You'd better believes." Lavinia listened, interrupting only to drag him back to the subject when his ramblings carried him too far afield. Sheriff Williams's story dealt with the raid on the Oak Leaf roadhouse. He admitted that it had been unsuccessful, that he and his posse had found no liquor-selling or gambling going on, nor any direct evidence that such breaches of the law had been made on the premises. If there was liquor there it had been hidden where neither he nor his men could find it. He admitted that Briggs and the latter's employees had not hindered the search.

" 'Twas as flat a fizzle, that raid was," admitted Jabez, "as ever anything could be. And we left Nate Briggs talkin' big about suin' for libel on his reputation and stuff like that. And yet I know—blast it all! half of you fellows sittin' here listenin' to me know—that Nate Briggs has been sellin' rum and lettin' cards be played for money in that place of his for more'n a year."

Dr. Hardy once more rose and mildly mentioned that, so far at least, the Williams remarks had had no bearing upon the question before the meeting.

Williams whirled upon him. "I know that," he snarled. "I know that well as you do; but here's where they're goin' to have that kind of bearin'. Right here! And they'll bear down hard, too. Listen!"

And then, accordin' to Amaziah's tale, he fired his big shot. He knew, he declared, as soon as he led the raiding party within sight of the Oak Leaf that the raid was destined to fail. The road-house was dark, not a light anywhere. There were no horses and carriages hitched along the front fence although an hour before, when he himself had passed that fence, there were a "couple of dozen of 'em." Briggs, when he answered the knocks on his front door, was in his night-shirt. "And I'm tellin' you," vowed Sheriff Williams, "that Nate ain't in the habit of turnin' in afore three o'clock, let alone quarter past one." And the interior of the house was as orderly and quiet and respectable as any dwelling along that road.

There was just one answer, of course; the Oak Leaf had been "tipped off," its proprietor and his employees warned that the raid was to be made and, consequently, they were ready. The question, therefore, was who had given them the tip.

"Now," Amaziah quoted Jabez as saying, "I'd never so much

as told the boys in my gang that we was goin' to land on the Oak Leaf last night. When we got together and started they didn't know where we was goin' till we fetched up there. There was only one other human bein' on earth except me who knew that. That other one knew because I told him—told him myself—yesterday afternoon. I ain't makin' any accusations, I'm just givin' you the facts. You can draw any conclusions from 'em you've a mind to. I said there wasn't any horses and buggies or carriages alongside that fence. There wasn't, but there was one automobile there and when we came out it was still there. I guess likely it wouldn't have been there only the machine had run dry of gas and the fellow at the helm of it couldn't get it started.

"And he," went on Williams, with deliberate emphasis, "the fellow in that automobile, was the one I spoke of, the only one besides me who knew the raid was due to come off last night. I had told him and I did it because I cal'lated if anybody could be trusted he could. He's been doin' lots of talkin', on the quiet and out loud in public, about places like that Oak Leaf and how they'd ought to be showed up and put out of business. I told him because I wanted him to know I was onto my job. All day to-day I've heard myself laughed at and made a monkey of for messin' up that raid. What I'm sayin' now is that it wouldn't have been messed up at all, I'd have caught Nate Briggs with the goods on him, if he hadn't been given the tip in time. Who gave it to him? I know who I think did. What was this fellow—supposed to be a law-abidin', high-minded citizen, always preachin' about gettin' after such places —what was he doin' there himself—last night of all nights? Only one reason that I can see. Oh, he was there; I've got half a dozen witnesses to prove it. And if you want to know why he was there, what made him come there, I'd say you'd better ask him. He's right here in this hall this minute, so I'll leave the rest of it to you."

He sat down, mopping his forehead. The hall was in a tumult. The first part of his speech had been interrupted by laughter and cries of derision, but the latter part of it was listened to with excited and eager attention. Now there was a general roar. "Who is he?" "Tell us his name, Jabe," and the like. Sheriff Williams was rising to his feet once more but some one else was ahead of him. William Hunter stood up and, shouting in order to make himself heard, claimed the chairman's attention.

"Mr. Chairman!" he shouted. "Mr. Chairman! May I say just a word?"

He was given the floor, as soon as the persistent pounding of the gavel restored a semblance of order. There were still a few cries for Williams, but Hunter's first words stilled them.

"Gentlemen," said Bill Hunter, "I can give you the information you seem to want. I was the man in that automobile. Yes, and I was the man the Sheriff told yesterday afternoon that he intended to raid the Oak Leaf. Mr. Williams is quite right, so far as that part of it goes."

He paused, smiled and looked about him. The hall hummed like a disturbed wasp's nest. And yet no one said anything, no one spoke. It was the rustle as every one in that crowded room leaned forward to stare at the speaker which caused the sound. A second later, however, some one did speak. Some one said "Aha!" in a tone of triumph. This person, needless to say, was Sheriff Jabez Williams.

Bill Hunter kept them waiting only an instant. Then he continued. "I was in the automobile—yes. And Mr. Williams is quite right in his guess that if the blessed thing would have run without gas I would have run with it. As it wouldn't I— well, I stayed. But," still smiling, "he is dead wrong when he intimates that I went there to warn Briggs of the raid. I didn't do that."

Again he paused. The hum in the hall had ceased; every one

had been listening intently, fearful of missing a word. But now it broke forth again, rising, breaking into a murmur, a babel of exclamation, cries of indignation, of disbelief, of angry questions. Williams was on his feet now. Chairman Hamlin's gavel thumped and thumped.

"It's all right, 'Lisha," shouted Jabez. "I'm not goin' to make a speech. I've said what I had to say. I just want to ask Mr. Hunter there one or two questions, that's all. Considerin' how all hands have been layin' into me seems as if I had a right to do that much. And," with grim emphasis, "if he's square and has got nothin' to hide, seems to me he'll be willin' to answer 'em.... Eh? How about it, Hunter?"

The Chairman hesitated. It was Hunter himself who spoke. "All right, Sheriff," he said, "go ahead and ask."

"I'm cal'latin' to, don't you fret. To commence with, then: You say you didn't go to the Oak Leaf last night to tip Briggs off?"

"Yes, that is what I say."

"And you didn't tip him off?"

"No."

"Then why was you there at all?"

"It just happened. I had been over to Denboro, took part in the play the Dramatic Club gave; you know that, every one knows it. On the way home I—well, I stopped."

"What did you stop at that particular place for?"

"Because—well, never mind. I stopped."

"Know darned well you did. And you won't say why?"

"No."

A voice from the rear of the hall offered a suggestion. "If his automobile had run out of gas he had to stop somewhere, didn't he? Got to do better'n that, Jabe."

Jabez ignored the comment. "Maybe you'll answer this one then," he went on. "Had you been inside Nate's place—inside the house, I mean—afore me and my crowd got there?"

"Yes."

"Um-hm. And that's no surprise neither. What did you go in for?"

"For a reason of my own. It was not to warn Briggs of the raid, I give you my word."

"Humph!" sarcastically. "Your word! Well, let that slide for the minute. Did you see Nate when you was in there?"

"Yes. I saw him, but I didn't speak to him."

"Maybe that wasn't necessary. Now—"

But Hunter did not let him finish, he broke in sharply.

"There is no need of all this cross-examining," he said. "I have told you that I went into the Oak Leaf. I did. Why I did is my own affair. I was there only a few minutes and I did not warn him or any one working for him. That is all I can say."

"All you will say, you mean. Well, just one thing more. You know Nate Briggs pretty well, don't you?"

"No. I've met him and, a year or so ago, I did a little legal business for him. His cow was killed and I managed the settlement made him by the railroad company. I never met him before then and I haven't since."

"Except last night. Well, you can bet your life I'd forgot you was his lawyer when I told you I was figurin' to raid his place. All I remembered then was that you was the one doin' most of the talkin' about gettin' after the rum-sellers. Awful holy and righteous you was when you talked that way. Long's 'twas no friend of yours and no customer of yours you—"

The chairman's gavel descended. "There, there, Mr. Williams," he protested, "that's enough. Mr. Hunter, have you anything further to say?"

Bill Hunter looked about him, at the faces all turned in his direction, most of them troubled and dismayed, some scowling and vindictive. He was smiling once more and his tone, when he replied, was calm.

"Why, yes, Mr. Chairman," he said, "I have. All the morning I have been thinking over this situation and trying to make up my mind what I ought to do. Let me say here that I don't blame Sheriff Williams for feeling as he does and believing what he does. If I were in his place I should probably believe and say pretty much the same things. I can't explain— there are reasons why I can't. To me they are good reasons, but I can't tell what they are. I did not visit the Oak Leaf with any idea of informing its owner of the raid and I did not give him such information. And," impressively, "Briggs is no friend of mine and I had never been in his place before. That's all the defense I can offer just now—probably all I shall ever offer—and it is pretty lame as it stands, I admit.

"So much for that. I realized that something like this might happen here this afternoon and I decided that, if it did or did not—my duty was plain. When I allowed my name to come before this meeting as a candidate for Selectman of Wapa-tomac I meant, if elected, to do my best for the town. It did seem to me that there were things to do and I meant to try and do them. That is why I permitted my friends to work for me and—if this trouble had not arisen—I would have permitted them to vote for me. It has arisen and, as I see it, it changes everything. If I were one of those friends, after hearing what they have just heard I wouldn't vote for a man who seemed to be a hypocrite and a double-crosser. I know that I'm neither, but there is no reason why they should know it. So, until this matter is cleared up—if it ever is—I shall not permit them to vote for me, even if they still want to. Mr. Chairman and fellow-citizens, I hereby withdraw my name as a candidate."

There was a tremendous sensation now. Some cries of "No, no," but they were comparatively few. The majority seemed to be too amazed and bewildered to be certain of anything. Only Sheriff Jabez Williams was serenely triumphant. He leaned back on the settee with chest expanded. "Aha!" he said again, and it was a crow of triumph and vindication.

Arguments broke out here and there. An incipient fist-fight started in a far corner, but was instantly suppressed. Elisha Hamlin thumped and pounded.

Hunter was still on his feet. Evidently he was going to say more, so they bent forward to listen. His concluding sentences were brief and to the point.

"This," he said, emphatically, "is final. I can't begin to say how grateful I am to you good fellows who have been working for me and who have believed in me. I appreciate your belief and backing more than I can tell you. I am sorry for just one thing; that is, that I did not withdraw my name before the nominations were made. I considered doing it. I think now that it might have been much better if I had.

"However," with decision, "that is off the subject. I am no longer a candidate. No one must vote for me—providing," with a one-sided grin, "any one should be fool enough to still want to do it. Even if elected I should not serve. I'm out—out. I trust that is understood. Sorry I've taken so much time and a lot sorrier for the trouble I seem to have got you all into. . . . That's all."

He hesitated and then, his smile broadening to a grin, he added, addressing Mr. Williams: "Satisfactory, is it, Sheriff? . . . I hope so."

A moment later he was on his way out of the hall.

Amaziah, panting with excitement and flourishing his fist in a farewell gesture, had at last arrived at his peroration.

"And so," he said, "they elected Sam Doane Selectman. Lots of folks didn't vote and only a few of us paid much attention to what was goin' on, but the special meetin' had been called for for just that election and practically nothin' else, so what else was there to do? My soul to heavens, Lavvy, you'd ought to have been there! Why—"

His aunt lifted a hand.

"Sshh!" she ordered, impatiently. "Humph!...Well, I don't believe it."

"Eh? Don't be*lieve* it! Haven't I been sittin' here tellin' you? Think I made it up all out of my own head, do you? All right! If you think I'm a liar ask anybody else you've a mind to. Ask Bill Hunter, himself, he couldn't deny it if he wanted to. Ask—why, ask Mr. Bert Thornlow, he'll tell you. Maybe you'll believe him."

"Oh, so he was there, was he?"

"Certain sure he was. Him and two or three more men-folks from this Inn, sitting in the back row. I saw him myself. And if you don't believe me—"

"Oh, *do* be still! Of course I believe what you've told me. Why shouldn't I? What I mean is that I don't believe Mr. Hunter ever went to that Oak Leaf place to tell Briggs that the raid was comin'. That, or anything like it."

"But he was there last night, Aunt Lavvy. He owned up that he was; Jabez made him own up to it. And if it wasn't for that why was he there at all? He wouldn't say why, couldn't think of any good reason, most likely. Well, I own up I never thought any too much of him and Ocky didn't neither, but I never thought he'd do a thing like that. Just because Nate had hired him to get pay for a dead cow. And now look where he is. Wanted to be our Selectman! Him!"

"Oh, rubbish! What do I care about that? What do you suppose he cares, either? A body would think bein' Selectman of Wapatomac was like bein' President of the United States. I don't believe that worries him a bit. He only let 'em put up his name because a lot of folks begged him to and because he honestly thought, same as a good many of us did, that he might be able to get things done if he was on the Board. That's nothin'—nothin' at all. But, as for the rest of it—well, I don't believe it. There's somethin' behind it that we don't know about yet. Maybe we never will know, but, anyhow, I for one am sure that it isn't anything mean or underhanded on his part. Yes, and you can tell your Ocky I said so, if you want to. Bah, how she will crow! Yes, and so will a lot more like her. . . . There, there, go along home. I want to think all this over. Yes, and don't stop downstairs to tell Ethel or anybody else."

"Why not? She'll hear it soon as Bert and the rest of 'em get back. I just thought—"

"Never mind what you thought. You go right along and don't stop to talk to anybody."

To make sure that he obeyed orders she accompanied him to the front door of the Inn and watched him splash away in the direction of the landing where he had left his skiff. Then she went back to her room and sat down in the rocker. She was disturbed, of course. Not because Hunter had not been elected to the Board; that was a small matter and, from things he had said and knowing him, she was certain that his disappointment would not be keen. But, knowing the town she lived in, it troubled her to think of the things concerning him which would be said—which were being said already.

There was something behind it, of course, something she did not understand at all. It was, she was convinced, a part of the mysterious happenings of the previous night. There was that unexplained incident of the departure in the motor-car and the return in the carryall. Ethel had not explained that —had not mentioned it.

And—why yes—she remembered now. It was Hunter who had driven over to Denboro in a carryall. Ethel, before she and her party had gone in the automobile, had mentioned that Bill was not going with them, that he was driving over in a rig hired from the livery-stable. And, when the Sheriff had reached the Briggs road-house, he had found Hunter there tinkering with a car which would not run. Was it the car the

Thornlow party had left in? And, if it was, then Bert and Miss Oakbridge and—yes, and Ethel—were somehow involved in the Hunter mystery.

She had been sitting there, puzzling and planning, for nearly an hour when some one knocked at her door. Ethel, no doubt. Well, her coming was opportune; there were questions to be asked and answered.

It was not Ethel, however, who opened the door in answer to her "Come in." It was Hunter, himself. And the expression upon his round, slightly freckled face was very grave. Lavinia knew the reason, of course, but she had not expected him to take it as hard as this. She had expected him to grin and treat the whole affair as a joke.

"Why, Mr. Hunter!" she cried, "glad to see you. Take a chair. Mercy on us, you look as if you'd lost your last friend. I didn't know you cared as much as all that. The town is the one to feel bad, the way I look at it. It has lost the chance to get a good Selectman, that's all. Too bad, but I guess there's just as many fools here, accordin' to population, as there is anywhere else. And Jabez Williams is up in the front row of 'em."

When she began to speak he did not appear to understand. Now, however, the grin for which she had looked was in evidence.

"Oh, that," he said. "You mean the town-meeting rumpus. That's nothing; that doesn't bother me in the least. You see, Mrs. Badger," the grin had gone as quickly as it came, "it wasn't that which brought me. You see," he hesitated—"well, something has happened. I'm mighty sorry to have to say it, but I have bad news for you."

She looked at him. "Bad news?" she repeated. "Is it—is Philander—?"

The Judge had not been well for some time and so, naturally, she thought of him. But Hunter shook his head.

"Judge Payne is in bed just now and the doctor was called from the meeting to be with him. He has had a bad shock."

"Shock! You mean he's had a stroke?"

"No, no. Nothing of that kind. He has had a shock to his nerves, but that is bad enough. As soon as I came in he sent for me and told me the news. Knowing what I knew, or had heard, of your affairs I—well, I—"

"Come, come, Bill Hunter! I'm not so dreadful feeble yet that bad news has to be broke to me in what they call 'easy payments.' What is it you're tryin' to say?"

"Mrs. Badger, Cousin Philander's brokers telegraphed him from Boston this afternoon. The Occidental Mining Company—"

Again he hesitated. Lavinia prodded him on. "Yes, yes," she snapped. "Accidental Mines, I've always called it. What about 'em?"

"The company went into a receiver's hands to-day. There have been some rumors of trouble, but they were always denied. The stock has been pretty feverish on the exchanges, but no one expected this."

"Hum! Receiver's hands, eh? Just what does that mean, young man?"

"Well, of course we have heard no particulars, but the brokers seem to believe it means, in this case, pretty nearly a complete smash."

CHAPTER XXIII

HUNTER had not meant to impart his bad news quite as bluntly. He had meant to lead up to it gradually, to be tactful. His hurrying to the Inn with the tidings had not been done entirely on his own initiative, although he had not said so. He, of course, knew that Lavinia Badger was a holder of Occidental stock. Ethel had told him that and he judged, from what she told him and the gossip he had heard since he came to Wapatomac, that the larger part of her fortune was invested in the mining company. The tale of her inheritance of the Lost Prospect shares and their conversion into those of Occidental Mines was common property in the town. No one seemed to know just how large was the windfall—Ethel did not mention any figures—but Amaziah Holt was not at all reticent and boasted openly of his aunt's smartness and good luck. Wapatomac credited Mrs. Badger with being a rich woman.

Hunter's knowledge of her affairs, other than that derived from the rumors and Ethel's disclosures and Amaziah's boastings, was practically nil. Judge Payne attended to the Badger business, as he still did to that of his older clients and friends of long standing, and the Judge was always close-mouthed. Even now his cousin would not have ventured to interfere had it not been that Payne himself had asked him to do so. The old gentleman had beckoned him to the bedside and whispered in his ear.

"Tell Lavinia," he whispered, "tell her about the telegram. She ought to know. Tell her—tell her perhaps it isn't as bad

as they think it is. Tell her to—to come and see me and—and
not to worry about—about me."

Dr. Hardy had interfered at that moment. The doctor was
grave and his expression and brief word of caution led Hunter
to infer that it might be a good while before the Judge would
be permitted to see any one. Bill had dreaded the task before
him. Mrs. Badger was old, older than Philander Payne, and
he had seen the effect of the ill-tidings upon the latter. The
Judge, too, although a heavy investor in Occidental, must have
other resources, other investments. Whereas Lavinia Badger's
financial eggs might well be in that one basket.

He had meant to be tactful, had even tried to be, but she had
forced him to speak out. And, having spoken, he waited, fear-
ing the reaction. And that reaction, when it came, was far, far
different from what he had expected. For a moment she said
nothing at all, merely looked at him intently, then adjusted
her spectacles and looked again. It was he who spoke first.

"Mrs. Badger," he faltered, "I—I can't begin to tell you how
I hated to have to bring you news like this. I—"

She interrupted. "Shh, shh!" she said. "Course you would,
anybody would. Just let me get it clear, that's all. A complete
smash, you say. That means it's all gone to pot. Nothin' left.
You are sure?"

"Why, no, not absolutely sure. Perhaps I shouldn't have
said that. The telegram stated that the Occidental Company
had gone into a receiver's hands and that, from what had been
learned so far, matters seemed to be pretty bad. The brokers
were certainly not optimistic, they weren't hopeful—that was
plain enough. But the news had only just come to them and it
may be that, when we learn more particulars—"

"Yes, yes, I know, I know. It may be better or it may not—
most likely not.... Tut, tut!... Well, well!... Hum! I can't
say as I'm so terrible surprised."

He had expected almost anything but that.

"What!" he gasped. "You're not *surprised!*"

"Why no, not altogether. Easy come, easy go is a pretty true sayin', 'cordin' to my experience. I never could really make myself believe that anything poor Judah was mixed up in would make money and keep it for long. I've been more or less expectin'— But that don't change things, does it? I'm awful sorry for Philander. I've told him a good many times not to count chickens ahead of time, but he wouldn't listen. Dear, dear! Poor soul!"

Apparently she was much more concerned about the Judge's loss than her own. Her next words seemed to prove it.

"It struck him right down sick, you tell me? Dear, dear! How is he now?"

"Pretty weak and very much shaken. Dr. Hardy has told me little; he is with him now—or was when I left. The Judge has not been at all well for some time and this—" he shook his head. "I ought to be getting back to him, I suppose," he added.

"Yes, certain sure you had. Tell him I'll be up to see him first thing in the mornin'. And tell him I'm thinkin' about him, won't you? Oh, dear, if he only hadn't been so sure he was right. Now, run along, Mr. Hunter—Bill, of course, I mean. Thank you for comin' down in the rain to tell me."

"That was the least I could do, Mrs. Badger. I'll let you know the moment we hear anything further. I—I realize what this must mean to you. Ethel will—"

"Ethel? Oh, yes, yes; she will be upset, that's a fact. Perhaps—yes, I'd rather you wouldn't tell her to-night. She couldn't help any and maybe to-morrow's news will be some better, though I must say I doubt it."

He rose and turned to the door. There was much he would have liked to say, but her attitude made the saying hard.

"If I can help you in any way," he stammered, "about your business affairs—if Judge Payne should not be well enough to do it—I hope you will call upon me. You will, won't you?"

"Shouldn't call on any one else, if Philander was laid up. And if he is worse, if you or he need me, just send word. Thanks again. Good night."

He had opened the door when she called his name.

"I declare," she said, "I don't know what you must think of me, Bill Hunter. I haven't hardly told you how sorry I am about what happened at town-meetin'. Never mind, the truth'll come out some time or other, it's bound to."

"The truth? Oh, then I take it you don't believe I tipped off friend Briggs."

"Don't be silly. And don't think I am either—not so silly as that, anyhow."

He went away, marveling. She was a wonderful old woman and an absolutely uncomprehensible one also. How she could have taken the news that might—no doubt did—mean utter ruin to her, how she could have taken it as she did was beyond his understanding. She had said scarcely a word about herself. She had been greatly troubled about Judge Payne and had even remembered to sympathize with him because he had not been made a Selectman.

By the way—the thought occurred to him for the first time —who had told her about that? Ethel? No, Ethel could scarcely more than have heard it by this time. But Ethel must be very careful, or the true story of the happenings of the previous night would come out and her name would be talked about. He must see Ethel and caution her. She must keep still, for her own sake. Telling the truth would not help him—he was past help. Jabez Williams had seen to that—and it would hurt her. He must make sure that she did not speak. As for Thornlow and Estelle Oakbridge, they would keep quiet, he was not afraid of their telling anything.

The next day brought more details of the Occidental collapse. The Boston brokers wrote Philander Payne and the Boston morning papers, when they arrived at noon, spread the tidings. For some time, so it was stated, there had been disquieting rumors concerning Occidental Mines, but those rumors had always been emphatically and authoritatively declared to be false. The market-price of the stock had varied, slumping heavily when the rumors were most rife and rising again when their truth was denied. For several months there had been little active trading and although the bid and asked price was considerably lower than the high peak of a year before, it was—up to the news of the crash—at a fairly satisfactory figure. Small dividends had been declared and paid with regularity and the company's reports were encouraging.

And now, without warning, Occidental Mines had gone into bankruptcy, or what amounted to that. The full story was not made public until months afterwards and, when, at last, the reports of the investigating committees were ready they were not pleasant reading. The new workings taken over from the Lost Prospect had proven rich, but only temporarily so. They, it developed, had gradually petered out. There were debts, all sorts of discreditable and shady transactions, hitherto carefully covered by the "insiders" who had, unquestionably, been unloading their own holdings on a gullible public. Later still there were to be law-suits, criminal prosecution, a great deal of ill-smelling scandal for the newspapers to waft abroad. But all these did come later, much later. Just now the only certainty was that Occidental Mines had gone to the dogs and that, consequently, the greater part, if not all, of the money invested in it by the public at large had gone with it.

Wapatomac gossip had plenty with which to busy itself. Besides the astonishing result of the election at town-meeting, the revelations of Sheriff Williams and the resignation, under a cloud, of Mr. William Hunter, there was now this thunderburst which had, so it was reported, brought financial ruin to two of the town's supposedly wealthy citizens. Every one knew that Judge Payne was a heavy holder of Occidental stock. He had made no secret of his interest in it and his belief in its future. Having been credited with making at least a hundred thousand dollars by his shrewd investment he was now given credit with having lost practically everything. He was very ill indeed, the doctor was worried about him, he might die. And with no one but "that young Hunter fellow" to look after his affairs, he was in a bad way, that was a fact. "If what Jabe Williams says about Bill Hunter is true—and he wouldn't explain anything in that meetin', remember—I'd hate to have him look after anything of mine."

All comment was not as ill-natured as this, of course. Generally speaking, there was much sympathy for Philander Payne. And Hunter, in spite of his refusal to explain or to add anything to his flat denial that he had warned Briggs of the raid, still had staunch friends. The latter refused to believe him either a traitor or a hypocrite. "There's something behind this and it'll come out some day," they declared. "Some day the crowd who have been throwing bricks at him will feel pretty sick, see if they don't."

Lavinia Badger was by far the more talked about of the three. Payne had been well-to-do for years; Lavinia's fortune had been hers only a comparatively short time. She had been lucky and, consequently, those whose luck had not been of that kind, were envious. Now, although she, too, had sympathetic friends and acquaintances, there were a number whose comments were touched with spite. "Judge Payne earned what he had, the heft of it anyhow. That Badger woman got hers from the husband she hadn't had anything to do with goodness knows how many years. She was awful lucky and now the luck's turned. Too bad, but, after all, she's no worse off than she was before the money was poured into her lap."

Hunter, when he left the Welcome Inn, after his interview with Lavinia, had taken care to depart unseen by Ethel. He did not return to the Inn that night, for Judge Payne was still in a critical condition and Dr. Hardy remained at the bedside until the small hours of the morning. Consequently Ethel heard nothing of the calamity which had befallen until her great-aunt herself told her. Lavinia called the girl into her room as she was passing the door on her way to breakfast and told the story, calmly and tersely. Ethel was overwhelmed. She was white and speechless, Lavinia was cool and matter of fact.

"Now there's no use your lookin' like that, dearie," she declared. "What is is, and cryin' over spilt milk won't pick any of it up. Thing to do, as I see it, is just to keep a stiff upper lip and, whoever asks you questions, just tell 'em you don't know."

"But we do know, Auntie. Bill told you it was true. Oh, this is terrible! Is—is it all gone?"

"Those Occidental Mines have gone to smash, I'm afraid there's no doubt of that. Anything more than just that we, as I say, don't know. And 'don't know' is what I'm goin' to say and keep sayin' and I want you to say the same thing."

"But, Auntie, what will you do?"

"Just about what I've been doin' for quite a spell, I guess likely. Stay here in this Inn long's I can pay my board. When I can't I'll go somewheres else, if it isn't too far to walk."

Ethel's woe changed to indignation. "Indeed you will not!" she declared. "You have taken care of me ever since I was a baby and now it will be my turn to look after you—mine and Bert's."

"Bert's? Oh, yes—yes, of course. After you're married, you mean. But maybe Bert won't feel the same way about it as you do; I never took care of him, you know."

"Auntie! Please don't say such things. I don't want to be cross with you now, of all times. But perhaps this—all this that Bill told you—may not be as bad as those brokers think it is. Oh, you can't have lost everything. That would be too wicked!"

"I know, but seems to me I recollect hearin' this called a wicked world.... Now, now, dearie, we won't say any more about it; not till we know more anyhow. And don't talk about it to other folks, no matter how much they talk to you. I ain't down to my last copper quite yet. There ought to be a little somethin' in the corner or somewheres, enough to keep Am's and Ocky's pension goin' for a few weeks longer.... Hum! They'll be surprised, won't they? And scared, too, I guess likely. By the way, have you seen Am lately?"

"Not for two or three days. Why?"

"I wondered. He was here to see me yesterday afternoon, came down to tell me about the town-meetin'. You've heard what happened up there, I suppose?"

She was watching her grand-niece intently as she asked the question. Ethel's reply proved that she had heard very little.

"I heard them talking about it in the lobby, but I was too busy to pay attention. I went to bed early last night. Bill was elected to the Board of Selectmen, I suppose?"

"Oh, no, he wasn't. The new Selectman is Mr. Sam Doane."

"What! Why, I can't understand it. I thought Bill was sure to win. Oh, I am so sorry!"

"So am I. And Wapatomac ought to be—will be later on, or I miss my guess."

"But I don't understand it at all. Every one was sure Bill would win easily. Why—why, Auntie! Are you sure? What happened?"

"A good many things, 'cordin' to Amaziah's tell. Wonder you haven't heard 'em. The whole town must be talkin' about it this minute."

"But I haven't seen any one. I went upstairs at nine last evening; I was so tired. I saw Bert for a few minutes, but he couldn't have known—at least he didn't mention it."

"Hum! Maybe he forgot. Well, it's the big news—and will be until they hear about the Accidental business and commence to figure how soon Philander and I will land in the poor-house.... There, there! I shouldn't have said that. Don't worry about me, dearie, I don't want you to. Wait till we hear more and then you and I will have another talk. Go and get your breakfast now; I had the boy bring mine up here half an hour ago."

Ethel left a moment later, but under protest, and convinced, as Hunter had been when he left that room the previous evening, that her great-aunt was a wonderful woman. It was easy to promise not to worry but hard indeed to keep that promise. She tried to find comfort in the faint hope that, perhaps, the brokers had exaggerated, that perhaps the disaster was not as total as they feared. It was a very faint hope, but she clung to it, she would have been ashamed to do anything else. Poor, poor Aunt Lavinia!

Well, it would be her task—hers and Bert's—to see that comfort and peace of mind were Auntie's to the end of her days. They would see to that, indeed they would.

Fortunately there were many things to be done that forenoon, new guests were to arrive, others were leaving. She was too busy to do more than wave to Bert from behind the desk. She wanted to talk with him, wanted to ask him what he had heard concerning the happenings at the town-meeting, for she could not understand that at all. Hunter, himself, had not been at the Inn since the previous day. Word had come from him that Judge Payne's condition was still critical and that he must remain with him. Dr. Hardy forbade his patient's seeing callers, so Lavinia did not go there as she intended.

At one, with the arrival of the Boston papers, came the public disclosure of the Occidental catastrophe. There were no flaming head-lines, but a half-column in the financial section gave the details so far known. Most of the male guests at the

Welcome Inn read that section with care and one or two of them owned Occidental stock. Ethel saw a small group with papers in their hands and their heads together and she shivered. She could guess what they were talking about. She remained in the private office, but she saw one of the hotel boys bring the paper to Sarah Crowell, point to a page and whisper excitedly. She saw Miss Crowell turn to look in her direction and then Sarah and the boy both looked toward the stairs. That meant they were talking of Aunt Lavinia, saying something disagreeable and spiteful, no doubt. And, before night, all Wapatomac would know and talk—and talk. Why couldn't people mind their own business?

"Well," she overheard one gray-haired man say to another as the pair strolled by the counter, "I managed to dodge that punch, anyhow. I had a couple of hundred shares of that stock but I got rid of it about a year ago. I'm always pretty leery of mining stuff."

"They say," she heard the other reply, "that that old woman —what's her name?—oh, yes, Badger—has about all her money tied up in Occidental. She's an aunt or something of the Holt girl, the one who manages this place. If it's so she is going to be pretty well cleaned out, I'm afraid. Why is it that widows and orphans always invest their savings in the shakiest securities? Seem to smell 'em out and run after 'em the way a dog chases a skunk. And usually with the same disastrous results. Eh? Ha, ha!"

Ethel closed the office door. She did not want to hear any more and she did not want to talk to any one, even Bert, just then.

But it was Bert himself who opened that door a few minutes later. She had scarcely seen him during the forenoon and had not spoken with him since the previous evening. He opened the door without knocking, hurried in and, with scarcely a word of greeting, held a copy of the Boston newspaper before her eyes. He seemed very much excited and distraught.

"Look here!" he demanded, sharply, "have you see this?"

He was pointing to the column on the financial page.

She shook her head. "No," she said sadly, "I hadn't seen it. What does it say?"

"Say! It says—well, read it and see for yourself."

He thrust the paper into her hands. She read the first paragraph, then she put it down.

"I—I don't want to read any more," she faltered, woefully. "It—it is as bad as we feared, isn't it? Oh, poor Auntie!"

He stared at her in amazement.

"Bad as you feared?" he repeated. "You knew about it before—before this?"

"Yes, Auntie told me this morning. Bill Hunter came down last night to tell her; Judge Payne had had a long telegram from his brokers. Auntie made me promise not to tell any one. We hoped it might not be quite so bad, you see."

"Bad!" He snatched up the paper, crumpled it and threw it violently into the waste-basket. "It's as bad as it can be. The fellows out there," with a jerk of his thumb toward the lobby, "are saying it is just plain ruin, that's all. See here, Ethel! has your great-aunt got everything she owns tied up in that stuff? I know she used to have, you told me so, but has she now?"

"I—I guess so. I suppose so, Bert. Judge Payne was such a great believer in it and he attends to Auntie's business affairs. I am so sorry for him, too. He must have lost a great deal."

He seemed not in the least interested in the Judge or his loss. He was walking up and down the office, scowling, his clenched fists jammed in his trousers pockets. Ethel waited for him to speak, but, as he did not, she asked a question.

"Does this mean that the stock is—is worth—"

"Worth!" he broke in, savagely. "It may be worth a cent a sheet as waste paper, but no more, if that. Your aunt had five thousand shares of it, didn't she? That is what you wrote —or told me, or something, wasn't it?"

"She did have five thousand shares, but she sold a little, I know, to buy this Inn for me."

"Yes, yes, I remember that. But she hung on to the rest? Didn't sell it when it was up at the top?"

"I suppose she didn't. Why should she? Judge Payne was so sure—"

"Oh, damn Judge Payne! The old fool ought to have his head examined."

"*Bert!*" She sprang to her feet. "Bert!" she cried again. "How can you talk so! Judge Payne is very sick—very sick indeed! And for you to—"

"Oh, bosh! What do I care? Serves him right."

He was flushed and furious. She was white, but almost as angry as he.

"I don't know what is the matter with you," she said icily, "but I do know that you ought to be ashamed of yourself. I thought, when you brought that paper to me and I knew you knew, that you had come to sympathize, to say how sorry you were for Auntie. I was about to suggest that you and I go up and see her now. But I'm sure she wouldn't want to see any one who behaved and spoke as you have been behaving and speaking. No," sharply, "and neither do I. I think you had better go—and not come back until you are ready to beg my pardon and behave decently. Perhaps I shall be willing to see you then—I don't know."

That seemed to bring him to his senses. He took another stride up and down the office and then turned. She had seated herself at the desk and he came over and laid a hand on her shoulder.

"Ethel," he said, "I'm sorry, honest I am. I have gone off

half-cocked, I guess. This—this thing in the paper knocked me over, that's all. I know what it must mean to you—"

"To me. It means nothing to me except what it means to Aunt Lavinia."

"Of course, of course. That is what I tried to say. I'm sorry enough for her and I shall tell her so. Look here, you don't suppose she has got anything left—anything except what is sunk in this Occidental stuff, do you? Anything to amount to anything, I mean."

"I don't know whether she has or not, I haven't asked her."

"Well—er—why don't you? She's a pretty keen old girl and perhaps—"

"Oh, stop! Of course I sha'n't ask her—not now, at any rate. I told her this morning that she was not to worry. That you and I would look out for her always and be proud and glad to do it.... And we will, won't we, dear?"

Her tone changed as she asked the question. There was no anger in it, it was a plea for support and encouragement. Bert Thornlow's reply was prompt, almost too prompt and his agreement too casual to suit her. She had expected enthusiasm and he appeared scarcely to realize what she was saying.

"Oh, yes, yes, sure," he said, absently. "Humph! The devil! ... Well, I won't bother you any longer. We'll go up and see Aunt Lavinia by and by. Just now I want to talk with some of those old boys who know the stock-market. They may sight a gleam somewhere in this mess, but I'm afraid not. See you in a little while. So long."

He stooped to kiss her. She accepted the kiss, but she did not return it. Her feelings had been hurt and resentment still lingered. Long after he had gone she still sat at the desk, her work unheeded, thinking, thinking.

Another knock at the door aroused her from her disturbing reverie. "Come in," she said.

It was Amaziah who opened the door, a very much shaken

and agitated Amaziah. His leathery countenance was as pale as its habitual coat of tan and sunburn would permit it to be, and his chin was quivering with emotion. He looked at her, then over his shoulder, and he carefully closed the door behind him before he spoke.

"Hello, Ethel," he stammered. "I—I— Say, oh, my Lord above, ain't it awful!"

So he had heard the news already. She nodded.

"Bad enough," she agreed, "but there is no use wailing over it. That doesn't do any good. Have you seen Aunt Lavinia?"

He groaned. "Yes, yes, I've seen her. I was up to the post-office and all hands was readin' the papers and talkin'. I hurried right down. I've been up to Lavvy's room talkin' to her— that is I was talkin' much as she'd let me. I never see such a woman," he added, his voice rising in righteous indignation. "I declare to man she ain't half as upset as I am. Losin' everything she's got don't seem to fret her hardly at all. She— she's a darn sight cooler about it than I am—a darned sight. I give you my word I was just about ready to cry like a young one and all she did was make fun of me for doin' it. Made me kind of mad, that did, spite of my feelin' so broke up about her and—and all the rest of us."

"All the rest of us? What has it to do with the rest of us? It is her money that has gone—not ours."

Amaziah gaped in astonishment.

"Why—why, how you talk, Ethel!" he exclaimed. "Course it's her money now, I know that."

"Now? What do you mean by now?"

"Why—well, I don't mean nothin'. Only—only—well, the way I've always looked at it—the way me and Ocky have looked at it—all them thousands of hers was a sort of family affair, kind of what they call a trust, as you might say. And Aunt Lavvy she looked at it the same way, course she did. Look how she helped you out along with the Welcome Inn.

Look at how she's been—er—payin' me and Ocky kind of—er—weekly wages for bein' her relations, so to speak. And—"

Ethel broke in impatiently. "I don't think you and your wife need worry about your weekly wages," she said. "Auntie, herself, told me that she had enough in the savings bank to pay that—for a while, at least."

"Yes, I know. She told me that much. 'Twas a relief, too, I own up. But it's a whole lot more'n that, Ethel. You must see 'tis, yourself. Aunt Lavvy's pretty far along in years, 'tain't likely she's going to live forever. Well, then, after she's gone—why—why then—"

"Oh, good heavens!" Ethel's impatience was scornful this time. "So that is what really troubles you. You're not thinking of her, the loss of security and comfort this means to her. All your crying and the rest of it is because you're afraid there will be nothing left for you when she dies. Uncle Am, you—oh, you make me sick!"

"Don't know why I should," stoutly. "Just common sense, ain't it? She'd have it long as she was here, abidin' amongst us, as the fellow says, but after she was gone somebody else was bound to have it. She can't take it with her, can she? Course me and Ocky didn't know how much she'd leave us, but, bein' as I'm her only nephew, I was bound to get some. So, naturally, Ocky and I have kind of counted on it, made some plans about what we'd do with it. No hurry for it, you understand, but—"

"Oh, be still! You had better go. I—I'm not in the mood just now to hear any more. I'm busy. Go away."

"Humph! Don't see what there is for you to get mad about. I'm just as sorry for Aunt Lavvy as you are. Course I am. It's only—well, Ocky's goin' to be terrible disappointed."

"I'm glad she will be."

"Eh? Well, that's a nice thing to say!"

"What I say next may be worse, so I think you had better go.... Oh, go, please!"

Amaziah, evidently considering himself a deeply injured man, rose to his feet.

"All right," he said, with dignity, "I'll go. When you see Aunt Lavinia you can tell her I didn't have a chance to tell you what she asked me to tell. I promised her I'd tell it—that's part of what I came in here for—but a hint is as good as a kick; I know when I ain't wanted. Good-by. I'll tell Ocky what you said about her."

Ethel had paid little heed to this declamation, but she did hear a part of it.

"Wait!" she ordered. "What was that? Aunt Lavinia asked you to come here and tell me something? What was it?"

"Never mind. Let somebody else tell you."

"No, you are going to tell me. Stop looking like—like the Statue of Liberty and tell me. What is it?"

"Well, I promised Lavvy I'd tell you about what happened up to the special town-meetin'. She said you hadn't heard about Bill Hunter's bein' showed up as a disgrace and all. But, of course, I don't have to tell it and, long as you've as good as fired me out, I—"

"Stop! You do have to tell it; I want you to. Sit down in that chair again. Mr. Hunter a disgrace, you say? What do you mean?"

Bert Thornlow and Miss Oakridge had been playing tennis. They were resting between sets, cozily ensconced in a swinging seat at the farther end of the Inn porch. Estelle had selected the seat and the location, possibly because of their comparative privacy. They were deep in conversation, laughing and chatting, when approaching footsteps sounded upon the porch tiles. Miss Oakridge peeped over the canvas side of the swinging seat

"Here comes your pet landlady, Bert," she whispered. "And looking for some one—probably you. My, she looks cross! Have you been a naughty boy, or what is it?"

Ethel saw the pair and came up to them. She may not have looked cross, but she certainly did look determined.

"Sorry, Estelle," she said, "but can you spare Bert a minute? I have something to say to him."

Estelle jumped from the seat. "Surest thing you know," she declared. "See you later, Bert. Ta ta! Be good, both of you."

She waved a farewell, and tripped away. Thornlow looked after her, then he turned to look at Ethel.

"Well, dear?" he queried, smiling. And then; "I say, what's up? What's the trouble? Anything new about the Occidental business; is that it?"

"No. Bert, you know about what happened at that town-meeting? About Jabez Williams accusing Bill Hunter of being a—a liar and a traitor to his friends and backers, all that? You know it, don't you?"

Thornlow smiled. "Why—er—yes. I know it, of course," he admitted. "Every one does."

"I didn't, until a few minutes ago. How long have you known?"

His hesitation was a trifle longer this time.

"Oh—well," he replied, "I knew it yesterday, of course."

"Why didn't you tell me?"

"Haven't seen much of you since it happened. Besides, I didn't consider it very important. Hunter wasn't made Selectman, or whatever you call it, but that isn't exactly front-page news, is it? I don't imagine his heart is broken, or anything like that."

"Perhaps not; but I know he wanted to be a member of the Board because he believed that he could get things done that would help the town.... But his not being elected doesn't matter so much."

"Humph! As a matter of fact he didn't give them a chance to elect him; he withdrew his name before the vote was taken."

"I know he did. And you know why, don't you?"

"Oh—er—I understand that some one—the Sheriff, I believe—accused Hunter of double-crossing him, or something like that. It seems he told Bill that this—er—speakeasy place was to be raided and that, therefore, as Bill was the only outsider who knew it and Bill was caught there when the raiders came, and the raid fizzled—well, the Sheriff naturally inferred that Bill had passed the word along in time. I don't know that you can blame the Sheriff much for that. Natural enough he should think so."

"But we—you and I and Estelle—we know it isn't true."

"Do we? We know that Hunter came there and shoved us out in a hurry. Good thing he did. We might have had some unpleasant publicity if he hadn't."

He chuckled.

Ethel gasped. "And you can laugh at it!" she exclaimed. "You know perfectly well why he came there—why he stopped there that night. He saw our car, the car we had left Denboro in, standing in front of—of that place. It was the only car there and he would recognize it, of course. And he knew the place was to be raided that very night, almost at that very time. He came in there for just one reason, to get us out and away, to save us from that publicity you talk about. And then, when he found our car wouldn't run, he sent us home in his carriage and stayed there himself and—and all the rest happened. . . . Oh! And you seem to think it is funny!"

He shrugged. "So it is, in a way," he said. "The joke is on him, I admit, but it is only a joke, after all. It will be forgotten before long; things like that always are. By the way, Ethel, how do you know all this? Did Hunter tell you?"

"No. I haven't seen him since it happened. Uncle Am was at the meeting and he has just been telling me about it. As to why Bill happened to come to the Oak Leaf and all the rest, I didn't need any one to tell me. It is plain enough. You and Estelle must know it, just as I do. He came to get us out of trouble and he did that very thing. And now look at what it got him into!"

He shrugged once more. "Well," he observed, "admitting that your guess is true, what can we do about it? We're a whole lot obliged to him and all that, but—well, any decent fellow would have done the same thing—if he had known the raid was to be pulled off, as Hunter did."

The look she gave him was unlike any he had before seen in her eyes. She started to reply, then hesitated, and then asked another question.

"When you heard all this—you haven't told me how you heard, but never mind—when you heard it what did you do?"

"Do? Why, nothing, of course. What was there to do?"

"What did you say?"

"Say? I said nothing, you can bet on that. The milk was spilled and, unless I wanted it spilled all over you and me and Estelle, I realized I must keep mighty quiet. And so must you. You understand that, dear? Of course you do."

She did not answer. He went on, very earnestly, "It is for your sake, it is you I am thinking of. It wouldn't do the Welcome Inn any good to have it known that its owner and—er—well, call me its assistant-manager, escaped being caught in a raid on an illegal gin-mill by the skin of our teeth. I shouldn't have taken you girls there at all, I realize that now, of course."

"But you had been there before, hadn't you?"

"Why—well, yes. Once or twice, just as a lark. Some of the fellows here at the Inn—"

She interrupted. "I see," she said, slowly. "I see. We must keep still. Keep still, save our own skins, and let the fellow who really saved them be talked about and called a sneak and a liar and—and a mean two-faced scamp. Uncle Am says it is going to hurt him in the town and county, his reputation, his law-practice—everything. And you heard the story and didn't deny it, didn't say one single word."

"Now, see here, I told you—"

"Hush! Well, *I* am going to deny it. I'm going to see that every one knows it. I'm going to tell the truth."

"Ethel! For heaven's sake—"

"Oh, don't! Truly I—I didn't believe any one could be such a—a coward."

She turned and walked briskly away. He took a hurried step after her.

"Ethel!" he urged. "Ethel, don't be an idiot."

She did not reply, nor did she pause. He watched her until she entered the Inn. Then he drew a long breath, whistled softly, and, with his hands in his pockets, strolled across the lawn by the tennis-court. Miss Oakbridge hailed him and he walked over to where she was standing.

CHAPTER XXIV

LAVINIA came down to dinner that evening, but she went up to her room again as soon as the meal was over. She had expected that Ethel would join her at the table, as she usually did, but Ethel did not appear. Sarah Crowell, when questioned, informed Lavinia that Ethel had been shut up in the private office most of the afternoon.

"Mr. Holt was in there with her for a while," said Sarah, "and after he'd gone she went out on the lawn, or the porch or somewhere, for a few minutes. Then she came back and shut herself up again. She's upstairs in her bedroom now. Said she had a headache and didn't want any dinner, guessed she'd lie down a few minutes. She did look kind of—of white and used up, I thought. She works too hard; I've told her so, and more than once, too."

Lavinia did not linger in the lobby or the lounge. The guests, those with whom she was acquainted, bowed and smiled, but none of them came over to speak with her. For this she was thankful, for she did not feel inclined either to listen to or take part in casual conversation. She noticed that people, some of them, were looking in her direction and that, as she passed, heads were turned and voices lowered. She could guess what they were saying, "Poor old woman! Tough luck, at her age, to lose every nickel. Why, I hear there was a time when she was worth—" and so on.

So long as they did not say it to her, that was all right. She was smiling as she climbed the stairs.

She did not go immediately to her own room but kept on along the corridor until she reached Ethel's door. She rapped lightly. No response, so she knocked again, a little louder this time.

"Yes? Who is it?"

"Just me, dearie. May I come in?"

Ethel was not lying down; the bed was uncrumpled, so it was obvious that she had not done so. She was sitting in the chair by the table and, in the lamplight, her face did look white and very serious.

"I'm glad you came, Auntie," she said. "I was just about to go to your room and see if you were there. Sit down. I want to talk to you."

Lavinia sat. Ethel wasted no words, her first sentence indicated what the talk was to be about.

"Uncle Am came to the office to see me this afternoon," she said.

Lavinia nodded. "I made him promise he would."

"Yes; he said you did. He told me about the town-meeting and what happened there."

"Did, eh? All of it?"

"I think so. I'm pretty sure I didn't let him leave out anything. Auntie, I—I am ashamed."

"Why? It wasn't your fault."

"Of course it was," sharply. "You know it was.... Oh—well, no, perhaps you don't know yet, but I'm going to tell you. Auntie, the real reason why Bill Hunter was at that dreadful Oak Leaf place that night, at that time of night, was because he knew I was there."

She paused, plainly expecting her great-aunt to exclaim, to express astonishment, to profess disbelief. But Lavinia did none of these things, she merely nodded.

"I was wonderin' if somethin' like that might not be the reason," she said.

"You were—*what?* Why should you? You couldn't have."

"I know, but I did, just the same. Course all that stuff of

Jabe Williams's was bosh and fiddle-de-dee, all that about Hunter's bein' there to tip off Nate Briggs. That was too silly to even think about, let alone believe. Bill Hunter may be a queer one, in some ways, but he isn't a mean one, that I'll swear to. Besides, before I heard about the town-meetin' at all, I knew somethin' mysterious had been goin' on that night and that you and Bert Thornlow and that Oakbridge flip-gibbet were mixed up in it—and Bill Hunter, too, of course."

"You did? Why, we all swore to say nothing at all, not one word. I was so careful."

"Indeed you were! Pretty nigh too careful. The way you dodged tellin' me anything except about the play would have made me suspicious, if nothin' else had. But you see, there was somethin' else. I was lookin' out of my bedroom window when I saw you and Bert and that Oakbridge one come home. You had gone away in an automobile and you came home in a carry-all. That, of itself, was odd enough, but when you didn't mention a word about it—and the land knows I gave you chance enough—then it got odder still. And after Amaziah told me about Bill's bein' caught by Williams and his gang, caught out in front of Nate Briggs' dive in an automobile that wouldn't go—well, then, I began to guess hard. Some of the guesses were wrong, I don't doubt, but some of 'em maybe were right."

She chuckled. Ethel looked at her in wonder.

"Auntie," she declared, slowly, "you are—well, I'm sure there is no one like you in this world."

"Hope not, for the world's sake. One of my kind ought to be plenty."

"You won't have to guess any more. I'm going to tell you the whole thing. I'm ashamed of myself, I ought to have known better. I didn't really want to go in to that Oak Leaf, the stories I had heard about it were not good ones, but the car had run out of gas, or something was the matter with it, and Bert and Estelle—"

She went on to explain. The Oak Leaf windows were a blaze of light, there were many horses and carriages by the fence, it was evident that the road-house was still open for business. Bert said he was sure they could buy gasoline there. Then he suggested that they all go in for a minute or two. "Don't like to sponge on them for gas and buy nothing else," he said. "Come along with me. We'll have a sandwich and some ginger-ale or something."

Ethel had demurrred. What she had heard of Elnathan Briggs and his establishment were not to their credit; but Estelle had been wild to go—she declared that she was hungry, and thirsty—and Bert had insisted. So Ethel yielded, against her better judgment, and they went in.

"Was the ginger-ale good?" inquired Lavinia, innocently.

Ethel looked at her. "How did you know that?" she asked. "Oh, well, you guessed, I suppose; you seem to have guessed everything. But I did have ginger-ale, I really did. The others— oh, Bert whispered to the waiter and gave him money and he brought a bottle of something—wine, they said it was. I didn't taste it. I'm not a crank or a fanatic or anything of that kind, but all I could think of was what I had heard about Elnathan Briggs and how he was one of those suspected of selling liquor to the high-school boys."

Again she paused. "Yes, yes," urged Lavinia, "go on. This is the most interestin' part."

"There isn't any more to tell. Bill came bursting in then and hurried us out."

"Did he say anything about the raiders comin'?"

"No, not a word. But any one could see, by the way he acted and the state he was in, that something was going to happen. I was frightened—I guess we all were. And that waiter must have heard him telling us to hurry and it frightened him, I'm sure. He ran and found Briggs and—yes, that was why the raid was a failure, I suppose. But Bill was not to blame—not really.

He saw our car outside, knew we must be inside there, and came to get us away. Oh, Auntie, suppose he hadn't! Suppose we had been arrested, our names printed in the paper—everything!"

"I know, dearie. Well, they weren't printed there, and now they won't be."

"No, they won't. But Bill's will be. And now the people of this town—yes, and the people all through the county—are calling him a hypocrite and traitor and—oh, everything that is mean. And Uncle Am says that he didn't attempt to explain or excuse himself at the meeting at all. Didn't say why he was at that Oak Leaf, merely denied that he had warned Briggs. Oh, if I had only been there! I should have told them the truth, indeed I should. Well, I shall now."

"Indeed and indeed you won't!" Lavinia's tone was sharply earnest. "That would upset the whole calabash. You wouldn't help Bill Hunter to amount to anything and you'd only get yourself into hot water. You haven't committed any great crime, but you'd be talked about and whispered about almost as much as if you had—and laughed about a good deal more. You were foolish to go into a place of that kind, but I sometimes think the fools have to pay a bigger price for their foolishness than the bad ones do for their badness. No, you mustn't say one word."

Ethel's eyes flashed. She sprang from the chair.

"Why, Aunt Lavinia Badger!" she cried, fiercely. "How can you! Do you think I am going to keep still and let Bill be called everything that is mean, let him lose his reputation and his practice and—and—"

"There, there, child! Take it easy. That's one trouble with young folks, they fly off the handle so. When they get older they come to realize that it pays to look and see if there's a place to light when they're through flyin'. Bill Hunter isn't goin' to lose much, not in the long run he isn't. He'll be talked about for a while and, maybe, lose a few half-way friends; but his real friends, after they've thought it over, are goin' to stick by him. Pretty soon they'll begin to hunt 'round and try to find out what really happened at that Briggs place. There were other customers there that night; I judge from what you say there was a good many of 'em. Somebody'll begin to whisper pretty soon, see if they don't. Some of the truth'll leak out some day, it usually does, and, even if it doesn't, there won't be much harm done."

"Harm! With poor Bill—"

"He won't be poor Bill long, I tell you. All he'll have to do—and, if I know him, all he will do—is just keep on smilin' that twisted smile of his and keep on denyin' that he tipped off Briggs about that raid. It won't take the smart folks, the sensible ones, long to realize that there is somethin' behind it all. Bill Hunter will come out all right."

Ethel, it was plain, was still far from convinced.

"But it seems so mean," she protested. "And it is mean, too. What will he think of us? What must he think now? No, I can't do it, Auntie. I am going to tell the truth."

"Better ask him before you do. I know what he'll say. He'll be for makin' you swear on the Bible that you'll tell absolutely nothin'. He got himself into this mess to help you out of one."

"To help all of us—Estelle and Bert and me."

"No, to help you. Don't try to fool your oldest relation, dearie. Not that way, anyhow."

Ethel made no reply to this insinuation. She was thinking.

"Oh!" she exclaimed, after a moment. "Oh, if I had only been at that town-meeting! Then was the time to speak out. If only some one who knew had been there!"

Her great-aunt looked at her. "Umph!" she observed. "Have you talked with Bert Thornlow about this?"

"Yes."

"What does he think about this truth-tellin'?"

Ethel was silent. Lavinia drew her own inferences from the silence.

"I judge he isn't in favor of it," she said. "Well, I could have told you he wouldn't be. He had his chance to speak out and wouldn't take it, so I'd have been surprised if he'd changed his mind."

Ethel turned quickly. "His chance!" she repeated. "When?" What do you mean?"

"At the town-meetin'. Didn't he tell you he was there?"

"At the meeting? He wasn't there!"

"Oh, yes, he was. Didn't Am tell you? He was there, he and two or three other men from the Inn. Amaziah saw him."

Silence, a long interval of silence. Ethel had turned away. Lavinia started to speak, then thought better of it and waited. At last the silence was broken.

"Auntie," said Ethel, slowly and with evident effort, "would you mind going now? I don't think I want to talk any more."

Lavinia rose. "Course I won't mind, child," she said. "I'll trot along. See you to-morrow mornin'."

She went out quickly. As she was closing the door she remembered that she had not kissed her grand-niece good night. She turned and looked into the room. Ethel was still sitting there, her fingers twisting and untwisting in her lap. If she heard the door open she made no sign. Lavinia closed the door softly and tiptoed away.

In her own room she sat down on the edge of the bed, fumbled for a handkerchief, and held it to her eyes. After a moment, however, she threw the handkerchief impatiently aside, rose and, walking over to the bureau, regarded her own reflection in the glass.

"What a feeble-minded critter you are," she muttered aloud, apparently addressing the reflection. "Work and contrive and hope for just one thing and then, when it looks as if 'twas liable to happen, sit down and cry about it."

Bert Thornlow and Miss Oakbridge were in the lobby next morning after breakfast. Their tennis rackets were under their arms and they were about to go out to the courts. Ethel Holt, emerging from behind the office rail, saw them and walked toward them.

"Good morning, Estelle," she said. "Will you excuse me if I borrow your partner for a few minutes? I want to talk with him."

Estelle's consent was not too gracious. "I hope you won't be very long, Bert," she demurred. "Our court will be taken if we don't hurry."

Thornlow, also, seemed a trifle peeved. "What is this, Ethel?" he queried. "Business?"

"Yes. At least I think it is."

"Can't it wait until we've had our game?"

"I had rather it didn't."

"Oh—well, all right. Back in a jiffy, Estelle. Save the court for us if you can."

He followed Ethel to the private office. She sat in the chair by the desk; he lounged against the wall.

"Perhaps you had better sit down, Bert," she said. "This talk of ours may be rather long." She paused an instant and then added, "Or it may not."

He lit a cigarette. "Hope it won't be too long. I had promised Estelle to play a set or two with her."

"Yes, so I gathered. You play a good deal with her, don't you?"

"Why—I don't know. I like tennis and she plays a good game. What of it? You don't mind, do you?"

"Not at all—now."

"What does the 'now' mean? See here, Ethel, you're not—"

She lifted a hand. "Let's not get off the subject," she interrupted.

"All right, suits me. What is the subject? Business, you said. Nothing gone wrong with the Inn, has there?"

"No. It isn't the Inn business I want to talk about. By the way, you're not as greatly interested in the Inn as you were, or professed to be, a while ago, are you?"

"Eh? Why, certainly I am. Only everything seemed to be going well and I considered that making myself agreeable to the guests was as good a way for me to help things along as any I could think of just now. I'm not much good at the figuring and buying and the rest. You do all that fifty times better than I could do it."

"Yes, I imagine that is true."

"Well, then?" he grinned and added, "What is all this mysteriousness? Not giving satisfaction, am I? Is that it? Sorry, Boss. I'll try to do better in the future."

He reached over to take her hand. She drew away.

"It is the future you and I are going to talk about," she said. "For some time I have been—well, uncomfortable. I have noticed things, things I didn't like. I was ashamed to notice them and more ashamed of my feelings concerning them, but —well, there they were. However, in a way they don't amount to much just now. Bert, why didn't you tell me you were at that town-meeting?"

He had not expected this and the question disconcerted him. He looked at her sharply, hesitated, shrugged and answered.

"What good would it have done if I had? I was going to, but you blazed away about Bill Hunter's martyrdom and called me a coward and a few other pet names. I didn't like them any too well and—and so, perhaps, I wasn't in the mood to tell any more. I'm human, after all. Frankly, Ethel, when you said those things to me I—"

"Oh, don't, *don't!* . . . You were at that meeting?"

"Oh—why, yes, I was there."

"And you heard all that Williams man said?"

"Yes."

"And you knew they weren't true—any of them and you

could see—of course you could—what effect they would have upon Mr. Hunter."

"Mister Hunter! Why the sudden formality? Come, come, Ethel!"

She ignored the joke and the laugh which accompanied it. She went on.

"I called you a coward when I thought you had heard about all this after it happened, heard it from somebody else. What do you think I should call you now, when you admit that you were there, could have stopped it all, could have told the truth, explained everything—and didn't do it?"

"Oh, don't be ridiculous! If I were the only one concerned I might have done some explaining. Probably should. But when you and Estelle were mixed up in the mess—you, especially— I— Look here," sharply, "you haven't been fool enough to tell, have you?"

She went on as if he had not spoken.

"It is bad enough to be a coward, hiding and letting another man take the blame that belonged to you. But when, besides, you lie—lie to *me*—"

"Here! That's enough. I didn't lie. If you had asked me if I was at that meeting I should have said yes. Told you when you asked this time, didn't I? . . . I'm getting about sick of this. Huh! seems to me you're taking a whole lot of interest in Bill Hunter. A whole lot. Very touching, but a little over-enthusiastic, isn't it? When I first came here I heard whispers about how friendly you and he were. Didn't pay any attention to them then. But now—after this!"

"If you care to listen you may hear whispers about yourself and—some one else. But there," quickly, "that is nothing. I don't care about that. Bert, when you came back here I didn't ask you many questions, did I? I didn't insist that you explain why you hadn't written to me all those years? I was doubtful and I was troubled, but I trusted you and made up my mind to believe that, just as you said, you had come to me because you couldn't stay away any longer. I would have waited for you forever, so perhaps I was too anxious to believe that you had been waiting for me."

"Well, I was. You know I was."

"Perhaps—yes, perhaps in a way you were. But I wonder—for some time I have been wondering—if you would have come back to me if you hadn't known—"

"Known what? What did I know?"

She did not answer. Her mind was made up, but she was debating whether or not to explain further. There was nothing to be gained by it, nothing but more words and the prolonging of this sordid, wretched, miserable game of accusation and denial.

"Bert," she said slowly but firmly, "this might as well end. All this between you and me. I have seen the end coming, but I wouldn't face it. Now, within the last few days, I have had to face it. I don't think your heart will break. And even I shall not feel as badly as I should have only a little while ago. Bert, our engagement is off."

His expression was a curious one. His face was crimson and his lips drawn back from his teeth. But, when he spoke, there was no consternation or dismay in his tone. He was angry, that was all.

"Ugh!" he snarled. "So that's it, eh? Well, all right. Maybe I can stand it if you can."

"I rather thought you could."

"Oh yes, I can. Don't worry about me. But what is all this about the last few days? Your precious Billy boy, I suppose? Good God? If you can fall for *him!*"

"I wasn't thinking of him when I said that. Your sitting there in that town-meeting and treating the disgrace of the fellow who got you out of trouble as a joke, that and your lying to me might have been enough. But there was something else, something else I didn't like at all and that made me suspicious. Bert, I didn't like the way you took the news of Aunt Lavinia's losing her money in the Occidental failure. I didn't like your manner and the things you said. They set me to thinking—and I didn't like my thoughts."

He scowled. "What are you talking about now?" he demanded. "I was sorry for the old woman, naturally I was."

"But a good deal more sorry for yourself, don't you think?"

He gazed at her for a moment, his eyes half shut. Apparently he was tempted to say something, but hesitant whether or not to say it. Then, with another shrug, he yielded to the temptation.

"Very well," he said, defiantly, "maybe you're right. Probably I was sorry for myself—and for you. Why shouldn't I be? You told me this was to be a business talk, didn't you? All right, we'll make it strictly business. Sentiment is one thing and common sense is another and what I'm saying now is common sense. I care for you just as I always have; you may not believe it, but it is so. I came back here because I did care—and that is straight, too. I'd rather marry you than any one else on earth."

"Thank you."

"Oh, cut out the sarcasm. I want you to understand this, so listen. I didn't have a cent, I was a failure and I told you so. But—well, you seemed glad to see me and—and—I began to think things over and the way I looked at it was like this: This Welcome Inn was all right for a while, nothing I wanted to stick to all my life or that I would want my wife to stick to, but it would be at least a meal-ticket and a bedroom for us as long as we needed it. I knew about the old lady's lucky strike in Occidental. You wrote me about her inheriting the Lost Prospect stock and the rest of it everybody knows. Why, all I've heard since I've been back in Wapatomac is that she was worth anywhere from one hundred and fifty thousand up.

Of course that isn't a million, but it is a comfortable stake. Now she is old and you, and Jehosaphat—Amaziah, or whatever he is—are the only relatives she has. And you are the apple of her eye, so, naturally, the bulk of what she had would come to you. You and I, married, with nothing but this country hotel on our hands, might have to keep our noses to the grindstone and work and scrimp and plan the rest of our days. But, with a hundred and fifty thousand coming to us in a few years, we—"

She stirred, wearily. "Oh, please—please!" she protested. "You needn't explain any further. What you have said makes it quite plain. Go and have your tennis match. I am busy."

"Huh! Oh, well, all right. But I tell you this; some day you're going to remember those things I've been saying—"

"I hope not."

"You are, though. And then you are going to realize that they are the only things a sensible man could say. You asked for them, you know."

"That's true. Good-by."

"And some day you're going to be grateful to me for saying them."

"I am grateful now—and very thankful."

"Oh, bah! What's the use?... Well, it had to come some time. I've been realizing that for the past few days, but I'm sorry it had to come this way. I shall always think of you, Ethel, and be wishing you luck and happiness. I—"

He might have said more, but she had turned her back on him, so, after another instant of hesitation, he went out. She heard the door close, leaned back in the desk chair and closed her eyes. Her feelings were strange ones; she did not attempt to analyze them. After a little she took up a pen and set to work. That account was closed forever, but those on the desk must be audited. The Welcome Inn was a busy place in August.

CHAPTER XXV

BY the end of the first week in September, however, it was far less busy. And at the end of another fortnight it was, except for the dozen or two regular, year-around guests and the few transients, deserted. The table-girls, chambermaids and extra hands in the kitchen had gone and only the few who, like Miss Crowell, were permanent fixtures, remained on the pay-roll.

Bert Thornlow gave up his room two days after he and Ethel had their "business talk." His departure caused a small sensation, for the majority of the hotel inmates supposed him to be financially interested in the establishment and concerned in its management. His reply to questions was always the same. He, so he good-naturedly explained, had been spending the summer months at the Welcome Inn, partly because of his liking for Wapatomac and partly because Miss Holt and her aged relative had been kind to him during a previous summer which he had spent in the town. As to his having any financial interest in the Welcome Inn, that was a joke. As to his managerial interest—well, that, too, was a joke. His friendship with Miss Holt and her great-aunt had prompted him to advise a little now and then perhaps, and to offer occasional suggestions, but that was all. "No, no," he said, laughing, "I'm not a hotel-keeper; have no ambitions along that line." He was leaving a trifle earlier than he expected, that was true, but he had been called to Boston on a business matter and probably should not return.

To the larger number this explanation was satisfactory, but to others, and particularly to Wapatomac inhabitants who remembered his close friendship with Ethel Holt when she lived in the lightkeeper's cottage at Long Cove Point, it was far from convincing. There were guesses and speculations. Miss Sarah Crowell had some guesses of her own and she confided them to her friends, under the seal of strict secrecy.

"He was a whole lot too much interested in that Estelle Oakbridge," whispered Sarah. "Or she was interested in him—I guess that's nigher the truth. Anyhow they've been together an awful lot lately and maybe Ethel didn't like it and there was a row. Oh, I tell you a girl can see a lot when she's stuck behind a counter in a hotel the way I am. I keep my eyes open even if I do manage to keep my mouth shut. Say anything to Ethel Holt about it? Me? Well, I should say not! I've got my own self to think about and good jobs are scarce these days."

Mrs. Oakbridge and her daughter left a week later. They had intended staying until the end of the season, but Mrs. Oakbridge decided that the Wapatomac climate was too damp for her arthritis and so she and Estelle were going to spend the month of September in the city.

"Didn't say what city, did she?" asked Lavinia, when Ethel told her.

"Why, no, Auntie, I asked her but she said she wasn't sure."

"You asked the wrong one. I rather guess Estelle is sure and I'll bet you she does the plannin' for that family. Have they left a forwardin' address for their mail?"

"Yes. The Vendome, in Boston."

"Um-hm. I judged 'twould be somewheres in that neighborhood."

Ethel made no comment and Lavinia did not press the point. A fortnight later she read in a Boston daily an account of a supper party given by Miss Oakbridge at the Vendome. In the list of guests was the name of Mr. Albert Thornlow, Spokane, Washington.

Lavinia read it and smiled. "Um-hm," she soliloqized. "Well,

I presume likely beer money is just as good as minin' stock money—if you can get hold of it."

Ethel had volunteered no information concerning her break with Bert. "It is all over, Auntie," she said. "Bert and I are not engaged any longer. No, I had rather not talk about it, if you don't mind. It is settled, that is all."

Lavinia did not mind. Not the means to the end, it was the end itself, and the fact that it was the end, which mattered with her. She was very considerate and kind in her manner toward her grand-niece but she did not offer sympathy. There was one cloud less in the sky. Perhaps the sun would shine some of these days.

Judge Philander Payne's condition was still grave. He was confined to his bed, with a nurse in attendance, and the doctor had strictly forbidden his being troubled with business or professional matters of any kind. Hunter found his own position a little trying. He explained the situation to Lavinia.

"You see," he said, "the Judge has never permitted me to have anything to do with the affairs of his own small list of clients. You are one of those clients and everything connected with your investments or interests are locked up in your box in his private safe. The doctor says I must not mention business to him yet awhile. Of course things can't go on as they are; before long that safe will have to be opened and I, or some one else, will have to take charge, but I don't want to force matters until it becomes absolutely necessary. So far as I know, or can learn, there is nothing in that safe which requires immediate attention. As to your Occidental holdings—"

Lavinia interrupted here. "So far as that goes," she said, "from what I can make out from the newspapers that Accidental stock is dead as a last year's smelt and it might as well be buried in Philander's safe as anywheres else. As for whatever else there is there—well, that can wait, too, for a spell.

Don't risk upsettin' Philander on my account. There's still a few cents left up in the savin's bank, thank goodness."

He assured her that the wait would be but a very short one. As for the Occidental Mines and its future, he could give her little or no hope. The stock was practically worthless, for the present, at least. The investigation was going on and might not be concluded for months.

Hunter, during this distressful period, came to the Inn only late at night and left early in the morning. His meals he ate at the Payne home and remained in his office or in the Judge's room practically all of his working time. The sensation in town over the events at town-meeting was becoming an old story. Moreover, as Lavinia had prophesied in her talk with Ethel, a reaction was setting in, a reaction in Hunter's favor. Prior to the Williams *exposé* he had been popular in Wapatomac, had made many friends. Now those friends were quietly working in his behalf. They refused to believe him either a hypocrite or a traitor. Dr. Hardy was one of these and he expressed their feelings.

"It's rubbish, all that Williams stuff," he declared. "Anybody who knows Hunter ought to be sure it is. Use your common sense. If it had been true, if he was as mean a snake in the grass as Jabez says he was, he would be a liar too, wouldn't he? He'd have had a plausible, smooth lie ready to spring on us at the meeting. But he didn't lie. Just denied that he warned Briggs of the raid and let it go at that. Why? I don't know. Maybe we'll never know. He won't say a word, you can bet. But I'll bet right now that there is something behind it all and that, whatever that something is, it is to his credit rather than the other way. Bill Hunter is all right."

Ethel and Hunter saw little of each other. Their only conversation of moment took place on the evening following that when she and Bert Thornlow reached their final understanding. He came into the Inn about eleven o'clock and she came out from behind the office rail. He was on his way toward the stairs when she spoke his name.

"Bill," she said.

He turned. "Oh, hello, Ethel! Thought, of course, you had gone to bed long ago. What's the matter? Your Aunt Lavinia—"

"No, no. Auntie is all right. I've been waiting for you to come in. I have something to say to you. It won't take long. I know you must be awfully tired."

"Eh? Tired? Well, if I am I haven't had time to realize it. And no lawyer is ever too tired to talk. What's up?"

"Bill, I—I don't know what you must think of me."

"Hum. Seems to me I remember telling you a little of what I thought of you. But I ordered you to forget it, didn't I? Yes of course I did."

"Bill, don't joke; this is very serious."

"So was that, so far as I was concerned. There, there! I am serious as a judge—more so than some judges I've seen. I'm all ears—figuratively as well as literally. Go on."

"Bill, why didn't you tell the truth there in town-meeting? Why did you let that Williams man say those wicked things about you—lie about you as he did—and not defend yourself at all?"

He grinned cheerfully.

"So you've heard about it, have you? Naturally, you would, of course."

"Oh, don't be ridiculous! The whole town had heard about it. I didn't hear until the next day, but then I did. Bill, why did you sit there and say not one single word?"

"Oh, I did say several words. I said them very loud and clear, and I went and shouted in their ear, like—er—Humpty Dumpty in the Alice book. And then," with a chuckle, "also like Humpty Dumpty, I had a great fall ... Good gracious, don't look so disconsolate. It doesn't amount to anything."

"Amount to anything! How can you!"

"But it doesn't really. I should have rather liked to be a Selectman in this town. I imagine I should have had some fun at the job and, maybe, helped in some ways. But—"

"Bill, stop! I know why you didn't speak out, of course I do. And that only makes it worse, so far as I am concerned. Oh, as I said to Auntie, if I had only been there! I would have said things. I have half a mind—yes, almost a whole mind—to say them now."

His grin vanished. "Here, here!" he protested, sharply. "You'll do nothing of the kind. That wouldn't help me any and it would get you into the very mess I was trying to keep you out of. Ethel, don't do anything foolish. Behave yourself."

She shook her head sadly. "Oh, I don't suppose I shall speak—now. Aunt Lavinia, when I told her how I felt, flew at me just as you do. She said my telling would do no good and perhaps some harm. Probably you are right, both of you, but I am so ashamed."

"Nothing to be ashamed of. It was bad luck for all of us, that's all. I am glad I noticed that car and recognized it. That was good luck."

"Good for us, I suppose."

"Good for old Briggs, too. If he has another cow run over he ought to give me the case, just out of gratitude, eh? Now, now, don't worry any more about it. I promise you I sha'n't."

"But I shall. I do."

"You mustn't. Why, just suppose you and Bert had been caught in that raid. . . . Eh? What did you say?"

"Nothing. You mustn't trouble about Bert. I assure you he isn't troubled on your account. Not in the least."

The scorn in her tone was so apparent that he stared in surprise.

"But—but," he faltered. "I suppose—I know you and he—"

"You need not know it any longer. There is nothing to know."

"But—see here, Ethel, you haven't—just because you think I got into a jam on your account, you haven't—"

"You had nothing to do with it. That is—well, I am beginning to realize now that you hadn't—so far as what happened that night, I mean. I mean— Oh, I don't know what I mean. Bill, you—you have been pretty wonderful. I can't thank you— I'm not going to try. But you know— Oh, well, good night."

She hurried away toward the office. That good night had been a shaky one, it seemed to him. Was she crying? She mustn't do that—of course she mustn't. And what was all this about Thornlow?

Slowly he climbed the stairs. He was very tired, mentally and physically. He should have gone to bed and to sleep immediately, that was what he had meant to do. But it was more than an hour afterward before he made a move toward undressing. Instead he sat on the edge of the bed running his hand through his hair, thinking, guessing, wondering.

When, at last, he did put out the light, his head looked like a loosely piled hay-stack after a gale.

On an afternoon in the final week of September Lavinia was in her room alone. She had been alone but a few minutes, for Amaziah Holt and his Octavia had been making their regular weekly call and had just departed. They were much more punctilious in their calling than before the Occidental crash. So long as Aunt Lavvy was supposed to be wealthy the fifteen-dollar-a-week allowance was regarded as a certainty and an insufficient certainty at that. Now that allowance was all the pair might count upon from her and how long even it might be counted upon was problematical.

"We've got to go and see her right along," declared Ocky,

"and sympathize with her and feel sorry for her and soft-soap her every minute. If we don't she's just as liable as not to quit givin' us anything."

Amaziah agreed, of course. To agree with his wife was the easiest way to keep peace in the family and even that was not always too easy. He nodded, gloomily.

"Well, I am kind of sorry for her, anyhow," he observed. "After all, when you set down and realize how it must feel to be richer'n turkey soup one minute and poorer'n a shot herrin' the next a fellow can't help feelin' sorry. Poor old Aunt Lavvy! Tough luck, I call it."

Octavia sniffed impatiently. "If you've got any sorryin' to spare," she said, "you can hand it along to me. Your Aunt Lavinia's all alone in the world and she won't be here but a few years. I've got Lord knows how long to live and a husband on my hands. When I give in finally and said I'd marry you I figured, naturally, that she'd be here to help with the housework, if nothin' more. That's what you told me she'd do. And, instead of that, she clears out to live in a hotel and be waited on and here I am doin' dishes and scrubbin' floors."

Amaziah ventured a feeble protest.

"Why, Ocky," he said, "you haven't scrubbed a floor since you've been here; you always make me do that."

"And why not? My heavens alive! Do you want to see your wife down on her knees breakin' her back with a mop?"

"Course I don't! Never do see you that way, do I? 'Tain't your back that gets broke, it's mine. It aches like all get-out this minute. Between scrubbin' and scourin' and luggin' wood and climbin' lighthouse stairs—"

"You don't climb stairs on your back, do you?"

"I pretty nigh came down 'em on my back last night. I was so dog-tired last trip I made that I all but slipped on the top step. I might have been killed and then you'd have been a widow. There's somethin' for you to think about."

"I was a widow before I married you. I think about that sometimes, too."

The exchange of domestic pleasantries continued during the row across the harbor and the pair were in anything but an agreeable mood when they reached the Welcome Inn. There, however, all was sweetness and light, so far as Mrs. Holt's manner was concerned. All she had been able to think about, day and night, she declared, was their poor dear Aunt Lavinia and the awful thing that happened to her, but, as she told Ammie, this world was like that. Take her own case, for instance. She and her first husband had been so happy, makin' their plans and all, and then he had to die.

"But we're told it's all for our good," she added, "so we must believe it is, I presume likely. I tell Ammie that, but I'm afraid he can't always see the truth of it, same as I try to do. You must look on the bright side, Ammie. That helps a lot."

Amaziah muttered something to the effect that he would be darn glad to look on a bright side if there was one anywheres in sight. He was gloomily silent during the call. Octavia did practically all the talking.

He left his hat behind when they went out and returned, a moment later, in search of it. Lavinia regarded him commiseratingly.

"Too bad, Am," she said. "Awfully too bad. I'm sorry for you, goodness knows, but I'm afraid you'll have to make the best of it now. There's nothin' else to do."

Amaziah came nearer. He glanced at the closed door and then stooped to whisper.

"Say, Lavvy," he whispered, "what would you think of my gettin' a berth aboard a lightship?"

"A lightship!"

"Um-hm. One of the fellows I know over to Denboro has a brother aboard the Pollock Rip lightship. He says they're changin' hands every once in a while and he thinks maybe he could get me the chance if I wanted it."

"But you don't want it. Course you don't. The pay doesn't amount to much, from what I hear, and it must be an awful lonesome job, rockin' away off there, miles from land."

Amaziah nodded. "That's what I mean," he whispered. "A fellow on a lightship has to stay six weeks aboard, then he has six weeks ashore, and then six weeks back again. I ain't just sure about the six weeks, but it's somethin' like that, anyhow. For six weeks I'd have to be to home, but for the next six I'd be ten mile from everything, where nobody could get at me—nobody."

Lavinia, in spite of her compassion, could not help laughing. "I see," she said.

"Um-hm. Well, don't tell anybody. I'm considerin' it, that's all."

He moped dismally out. Lavinia shook her head. Poor Amaziah!

She was still thinking of him and wondering what, if anything, could be done to make an impossible situation less impossible, when she heard rapid footsteps approaching along the corridor. There was a sharp rap on the door. In answer to her "Come in" Hunter entered, with Ethel at his heels. Both were, plainly, very much excited.

"What's the matter?" demanded Lavinia. "House afire, is it?"

Hunter laughed. "Not exactly," he replied. "Mrs. Badger. I've come to talk business with you.... I brought Ethel along, because I knew she would be as interested as I am—and," with a whimsical smile and a shake of the head, "as surprised as I was. Of course, if you had rather she were not present, why—"

"Why, I'll go, of course," put in Ethel. "But Bill says he has just learned—he has just found out the most astonishing thing.

About you, so he says. And that it is good news, too. Naturally I am crazy with curiosity, but I can wait, I suppose, if I have to. Shall I go?"

Her great-aunt did not answer the question. Instead she looked keenly at Mr. Hunter.

"Humph!" she grunted, after a moment. "So you've found it out, have you? Philander has let you into that safe of his, I suppose, eh?"

"Yes. The doctor permitted me to talk with him for a few minutes this morning. He is better, but he realizes that he won't be able to practise law or to attend to any business for a long time, if ever, so he has turned everything over to me. You haven't been aware of it, Mrs. Badger, but I have been your attorney since about ten o'clock. However, you can give me my walking papers whenever you like. That is your privilege."

"Sha'n't give 'em this afternoon, anyhow.... No, Ethel, you don't have to run away. Go on, Mr. Hunter—Bill, I mean."

Hunter hesitated. Apparently he scarcely knew how to begin. Ethel spurred him on.

"Oh, hurry up, Bill!" she urged impatiently. "Don't stand there sputtering. What is all this?"

Bill Hunter grinned. "Well," he began, "all this is so—so astonishing that I haven't got over the shock. I couldn't believe it when I discovered it and—and, by the Lord Harry, I can hardly believe it yet. Ethel, this Aunt Lavinia of yours has been fooling us. We have all been pitying her and sympathizing with her because she had lost the money that came to her when she inherited those Lost Prospect shares. Well—well, you see—"

"Oh, I don't see at all. Why should I? Do hurry up and say something!"

"I'm trying to say it. Our sympathy has been wasted, that's

all. She has lost practically nothing. She is almost as well-to-do as she ever was."

Ethel gasped, stared, and gurgled inarticulately. Hunter's grin widened.

"Yes, I know," he observed. "That is the way I felt when I looked over the contents of that box with her name on it. It is true, however. Isn't it, Aunt Lavinia?"

Lavinia's eyes twinkled behind her spectacles.

"Why, I shouldn't wonder," she replied. "I don't cal'late that I'm headed for the poor-house—not yet awhile, anyhow. Unless, of course, everything else goes to pot the way Accidental did."

Ethel was still gurgling. "But—but the Occidental—" she gasped.

Bill shook his head. "That's the joker in the deck," he announced. "She has only two hundred shares of Occidental stock. At least that is all I can find."

Lavinia nodded. "Two hundred is right," she agreed. "I kept that much just because—well, because of poor Judah. Sort of sentimental about it, I presume likely. More sentiment than sense even that was, as it turned out."

"But—but, Auntie, you had ever so many shares. I supposed—I thought all you owned was in that Occidental company. What did you do? I can't understand. Oh, why doesn't some one tell me something?"

"There, there, child! Stop cacklin', do. Stay on the roost and I'll tell you, of course. From the minute I got those Accidental certificates I was suspicious of 'em. Anything that Judah Badger had anything to do with I couldn't believe in. I would have liked to, but I just couldn't. I hung on for a spell, even against my judgment, but then, when the stock got to sellin' at those ridiculous big prices, I began to peddle it out—or have Philander's brokers peddle it for me—four or five hundred shares at a time. Poor Philander fought with me about every sale. He was certain sure I was makin' an awful mistake, wreckin' my chance of bein' worth a million and all that. But, the way I looked at it, a hundred-odd thousand on earth was a whole lot more dependable than any amount of millions up in the sky. I sold out everything but those two hundred shares. Now I wish I'd sold them along with the rest."

"But, Auntie, what has become of your money? Where is it?"

Bill Hunter broke in. "I'll tell you where it is," he said. "Of course I haven't checked up on the list, you and I must do that together, Mrs. Badger; but, as far as I can make out from a pretty superficial looking-over, it is in Government bonds and Class A securities and in half a dozen savings banks in Ostable County and Boston. . . . Tut, tut, tut! Aunt Lavinia, you certainly are a wonder."

"Nothin' wonderful about me. I've had a lifetime to learn to be careful on, that's all. Ethel, seems to me the time to cry was when you thought I was dead broke, not when you find out I'm not."

Ethel was dabbing at her eyes with her handkerchief, but she was laughing, too.

"Oh, Aunt Lavinia," she gasped, "you—you— Oh, I don't know what to make of you! Why did you let us all be so sorry for you? Why didn't you tell us?"

Lavinia tossed her head. "Should have told you pretty soon. Why didn't I tell you before? Well, dearie, I didn't mainly for your sake. I'd been wanting a chance to—er—test out a—er—certain party for a good while. This Accidental breakdown gave me that chance. And," with a satisfied nod, "the test turned out just about as I thought it would."

Ethel was silent. Bill looked at her, then at Lavinia; obviously he did not understand.

"Best thing that ever happened to this family, that Accidental blow-up was," Lavinia went on. "Couldn't have come at a better time. I'm awfully sorry for poor Philander though.

I'm afraid he's lost an awful lot. Bill, when he's able to see folks I want to come up right off. I don't suppose there's anything I can do to help him, but, if there is, I'm goin' to do it, whether he lets me or not. And he needn't be afraid of my sayin' 'I told you so,' either."

Ethel's mind was still in a whirl, but she happened to think of others who would be affected by this astonishing disclosure and mentioned their names.

"Uncle Am will be surprised—and delighted," she said. Lavinia held up a protesting hand.

"Neither your Uncle Amaziah, nor his wife either, will have a chance to be delighted that way, not for a while, anyhow. It won't do either of 'em any harm to think that fifteen dollars a week is all they're ever goin' to get out of me. You mustn't tell 'em and, so far as that goes, you mustn't tell anybody at all. What's my business is mine and not the town of Wapatomac's. Don't tell one single word."

She chuckled. Then she added: "Am was tellin' me that he might ship aboard a lightship. Said aboard a lightship he could be where nobody would get at him for six weeks at a stretch. By 'nobody' he meant that Ocky of his, of course. Well, I shouldn't wonder if it was a good notion. Let him go to his lightship. I would be the last one to interfere with any chance for peace and comfort he could find anywhere—indeed I would. And the longer they think I haven't got a cent the better it will be for him, I'm sure of that."

There was much more of this, but at last Hunter declared that he must go. "I'll see you this evening, Mrs. Badger," he said. "I want to go over your list of securities with you and listen to any instructions you may wish to give me. And let me say again that—that—well, I can't seem to say it, but perhaps you can guess how glad I am for you—and Ethel."

The door closed behind him. Lavinia sighed.

"There goes about as likely a young fellow as ever I ran

across in all my born days," she declared, with emphasis.

Ethel nodded. "He is, isn't he?" she agreed.

"Well, well! I'm glad to hear you own up to it. Was a time when about all I could get out of you was that he was 'queer.' You didn't seem to notice the good stuff that was underneath the queerness."

"I know," sadly. "I'm afraid I didn't notice a good many things in those days."

"Needn't blame yourself for that. You aren't very old yet. It takes years and hard knocks to make most of us realize that it isn't the shell of the nut that counts, it's the meat. When I was a little girl I saw a pretty kitten in the field back of our house. If I'd been contented with lookin' at him I'd have been all right. But no—I had to run across and pat him, and that turned out to be a mistake. It was a tryin' experience but it did learn me somethin'. I had on a brand-new dress and I thought my heart was broke. But it wasn't. And, by and by, I got a new dress that I liked lots better than the old one."

Ethel had heeded only the first part of this reminiscence. "Well," she observed, with a sigh, "I may not have the years but I certainly have had the hard knocks."

"Stuff and nonsense! What you've had is the best thing that could happen to you. That dress is spoiled—yes, but you'll have a new one. At least, I do hope you will. See here, child, you understand why I didn't tell you or anybody that I wasn't poverty struck when those Accidental Mines went up?"

"Yes. I suppose I do. It was a test, you said."

"So it was and it worked out just as I expected 'twould. If I hadn't kept still we'd have had that Thornlow—er—kitten smellin' 'round our door-step yet. You're not sorry to get rid of him?"

"No," sharply. "I'm glad—and thankful."

"You ought to be. And— Oh, let's talk plain while we're at it. I sha'n't be here forever, but I don't want to move off this earth till I feel sure that you're goin' to have a happy life, and the right man to look after you, and, we'll hope, children of yours and his. I never had any children of my own and, as it turned out, I picked the wrong man. You've been like my own child to me and I've been awfully afraid you were goin' to pick wrong. It has worried me night and day. But that's over and over for good this time, I guess likely."

"You needn't guess. It is over."

"Well and good. And now, I suppose, you're thinkin' that you'll never marry anybody. Stay an old maid till you die, eh?"

"Oh—oh, I don't know. What are you talking about, Auntie?"

"If you don't know what—or who—I'm talkin' about you aren't as smart as I think you are. Ethel, Bill Hunter is head over heels in love with you. You know that, don't you?"

"Oh—well, yes, I suppose I know it. He said he was."

"Said it, did he? When?"

"Some time ago. Before—before Bert came back."

"Hum! That's news. And what did you say?"

"I said I couldn't marry him."

"Why? Didn't you care enough for him?"

"I cared for some one else—then."

"Then? . . . But there, there, I understand. You had a picture in your mind, as well as in your room, and you felt it would be wicked to stop lookin' at it. You have stopped—and in time, too, thank the Lord. How do you feel about Bill now?"

"I don't know. Oh, Auntie, won't you please stop! Please! I don't know how I feel about anybody or anything. I am wretched, that's all. As for believing and trusting any one ever again I—I—please don't talk about it."

"I won't. I've said my last word. Or the next to the last one, anyhow. The last one is just this: Don't you throw away the good apple in the measure just because the one you took first turned out to be specked. Pickin' the specked one was a mistake, but losin' the second one would be a whole lot worse. Just think that over. You've got time enough to think in. Now kiss me and trot along."

It was December, a clear, brisk forenoon, sunshine and a cloudless sky, a light breeze stirring the bare branches of the lilac shrubs by the gate. Lavinia stood by the window of her bedroom, looking out. From that window she had watched Bill Hunter and Ethel drive away in the former's buggy. They were on their way to East Bayport where, in a cottage on a side road, Hunter had, the previous day, discovered a hundred-year-old gate-leg table which might possibly be bought at a reasonable price by the right man—or woman.

Ethel, when she boarded the buggy, was in good health and gay good spirits. Her cheeks were flushed, her eyes sparkled, she was laughing. Bill, when he stepped forward to greet her, was the picture of adoring happiness. Lavinia was standing there, peering after them, when Mary, the housemaid, came in.

"Morning, Mrs. Badger," said Mary. "Lovely day, ain't it?"

Lavinia paid no attention, so Mary tried again.

"I say it's a fine day. Guess you didn't hear, did you, Mrs. Badger?"

Lavinia turned. "Eh? No, guess likely I didn't. I was thinkin'."

"Um-hm. I get to thinkin' myself, sometimes. What was you thinkin' about this time?"

Lavinia smiled. "Well," she replied, "I was thinkin' that I really believed the time had pretty nigh come when I could face the idea of dyin'."

Mary was shocked. "Dyin'!" she repeated. "Why, what a notion that is for you, Mrs. Badger. You're the healthiest person your age I ever laid eyes on. Everybody says so. Dyin'!

Why you'll live another ten years or more, I shouldn't wonder."

"Maybe. Hope so. But," with a contented shake of the head, "there's consider'ble comfort in knowin' that you can think about how old you are and not let it worry you. It's only real lately that I've been able to afford to think like that," said Aunt Lavinia Badger.

(¹)